SF Books

Visit VaughnHeppner.com for more information

The Lost Colony

(Lost Starship Series 4)

By Vaughn Heppner

ISBN-13: 978-1519636119
ISBN-10: 1519636113
BISAC: Fiction / Science Fiction / Military

COUNTER-ATTACK

-1-

Admiral Fletcher felt the blood drain from his features. He clutched the armrests of his chair and heaved himself to his feet.

"Excuse me," he muttered.

The admiral was a big man, and he was unsteady as he turned. His left leg brushed against the chair he'd been sitting on. As he fled the room, the chair went flying, skidding on its back to hit a glass case. Fortunately, nothing broke in the Lord High Admiral's office. Not that Fletcher would have noticed.

The admiral raced through the outer room. The secretary looked up, surprised and then confused, sputtering a few words.

Fletcher kept going, his gaze unfocused. His feet thudded down the hall. He was shaking his head, muttering, "No, not again. I've done my duty. I…"

"Sir," an aide said, shooting to his feet.

Fletcher never heard the man, crossing the lobby in seven swift strides. The admiral flexed his big fingers, wondering why he couldn't feel them. With a crash, he burst through a door, shouldering a commodore out of the way, causing the smaller man to thud against a wall.

Fletcher didn't notice, but the bloodless feeling departed at the physical contact. Anger began to wash across his features.

People who saw him stepped out of his way.

Fletcher wasn't sure about the actual path after that, he just kept moving. After pounding up several flights of stairs, he found himself on the roof of Star Watch's High Command Complex in Geneva.

The Marines on the icy roof muttered among themselves. The lieutenant made a call, explaining the situation to someone. The man listened, nodded and dispersed his men, putting them back at their respective posts. They would leave the admiral alone.

As Fletcher clutched the parapet, he gazed at the snow on the mountains. He wore only his uniform, beginning to feel the cold. He—

A man beside him cleared his throat.

Fletcher turned just enough to see that Lord High Admiral Cook stood beside him. The older man was bigger than he was, with a shock of white hair under his cap. Cook wore his dress uniform and a greatcoat over that, protecting him from the winter chill.

"Can't remember the last time someone just up and left in the middle of a meeting," Cook said in his deep voice.

Fletcher frowned, realizing he should apologize. Instead, he raised a hand, letting it make a small, useless circle in the air.

"You're my fire-breathing, fighting admiral," Cook said.

"I was," Fletcher muttered, "before…before losing half my command in Caria 323."

He referred to a space battle in "C" Quadrant. The New Men had tricked him at Caria 323, outmaneuvering his ships and nearly destroying the entire Fifth Fleet. He had fled with the survivors through the void to the Tannish System. Those had been a terrible six months, knowing the rest of his ships would perish at the enemy's hands. Then, Captain Maddox in Starship *Victory* had showed up, helping just enough so the remnants of Fifth Fleet had escaped back to Earth for refit and repairs.

"I'm not going to give you a speech," Cook said. "But I will say a few words. The Commonwealth needs time, several years, at least. A good battleship takes at least two and a half years to construct. Add another six months to shakedown a new crew. We can't let the New Men consolidate the planets of "C" Quadrant. We have to attack now that you bloodied them."

"Not me," Fletcher said, "but Maddox in that alien super-ship of his."

"*Victory* helped you," Cook said. "There's no doubting it. But you set the stage so we still had a fleet to fight with."

"Is *Victory* joining your Grand Fleet?" Fletcher asked abruptly.

"You know it won't. The scientists need more time to reverse engineer the vessel's neutron and disruptor cannons. If we had those systems—"

Fletcher faced the Lord High Admiral. "Listen to me. *Victory* is a fighting ship. We're never going to reverse engineer those alien systems. I've read the reports. The Adok science continues to baffle our best people."

"John," Cook said, putting a big hand on the admiral's forearm. "War is a gamble, you know that."

"The New Men—"

"Let me finish," Cook said, squeezing those big fingers.

The old man's strength surprised Fletcher. He nodded.

"We regular humans have taken hammer blows these past few years," Cook said. "The New Men have decimated Star Watch, smashing one battle group after another. What you did in Caria 323 was brilliant. What you did in the Tannish System with Captain Maddox's help was pure genius. You've hurt the enemy's invasion armada."

"The alien Destroyer—"

"Yes, the Wahhabi Caliphate is disintegrating now that its home systems are gone. But the Destroyer is also gone, melted in our Sun."

"Our paltry numbers mean we don't have—"

"John," Cook said. "You didn't let me finish in my office. You left too soon. The Grand Fleet will have more Star Watch vessels than any fleet we've ever put together."

"That will strip Earth of its protective warships."

"We'll be weaker for a time, until the Fifth Fleet finishes its repairs and new battleships join Star Watch. But we're talking with the Spacers. It's possible they'll add their ships to ours. You have to look at the positives here."

Fletcher turned away, studying the mountains. The idea of hell-burners raining down from the stratosphere made vomit rise, burning the back of his throat. Regular humanity had to stop the New Men. He understood that all too well. But he didn't know if he could accept such an awful responsibility again. The fate of billions resting on his choices... Once, he would have eagerly accepted the new command. The truth was he wasn't the same man after those six months in the void fleeing from the New Men. That dread time had stolen precious self-confidence from him.

"The Windsor League will add twenty-five hammerships to the Grand Fleet," Cook said. "Each of those is worth two Star Watch battleships. In addition, you'll have fifteen *Scimitar*-class Wahhabi laser-ships, all that's left of the caliphate's navy."

Fletcher felt the air go out of his lungs. This would be a coalition fleet in the truest sense of the word.

"It's getting worse out there for the average person," Cook said. "People are frightened. Many here don't know it yet, but the Commonwealth is starting to unravel at the edges. Some of the signatory planets are acting on their own again, just like in the old days. It took some hard negotiating, but the Social Syndicate and the Chin Confederation have agreed to send their fleets with you in the counter-attack. They're the two most powerful dissenters. We need those battle groups going with the Grand Fleet instead of sticking around and causing trouble for the Commonwealth."

"I understand all that," Fletcher said. "But why does it have to be me?"

"That should be clear to you. You have a magic name now. It's one of the prices of being a winner. Surely, you know what people say. 'Admiral Fletcher defeated the New Men in the Tannish System. He can do it again because he already has.'"

Fletcher squeezed his eyes shut. If that was true, why did he feel like a fraud ready to fold at the first sign of trouble?

"If we don't counter-attack soon," Cook said, "the fear will grow too powerful all across the Commonwealth. Everyone will think of themselves first. Star Watch itself might splinter."

Fletcher stared at the Lord High Admiral.

4

"Oh, yes," Cook said, with a slow but emphatic nod. "In some units, the morale is awful. The alien Destroyer seemed like the last straw to a few."

Fletcher made a helpless gesture.

"We have to show people that our successes mean we're back on our feet," Cook said in a ringing voice. "The Windsor League agreed to join the Grand Fleet because of your Tannish System victory and the destruction of the alien Destroyer."

Fletcher was shaking his head. "I've studied history. Coalition fleets quarrel all the time. The Battles of Salamis and Lepanto are prime examples."

"Correct me if I'm wrong, but those coalition navies defeated their respective enemies, enemies just as feared then as the New Men are now to us."

Fletcher stared at the mountains in silence. He felt his resolve crumbling. Did Cook truly think he could do this?

"You'll have the advantage of numbers," the Lord High Admiral said. "My strategists are certain of that. The New Men can't have our industrial capacity."

"They have superior technology with their fusion beams and better shields."

"The counter-attack won't be easy," Cook admitted. "They're good, damn good. Until the Tannish System, we thought the New Men were unbeatable. But we did defeat them. Now, we have to push back. Free the captured planets, John. Smash the invasion armada. And—"

Fletcher looked at the Lord High Admiral.

"Find the coordinates to the Throne World," Cook said. "We have to take the war to them if we're ever going to be safe."

"I don't know," Fletcher said, softly. "Who's the Windsor League commander going to be?"

Cook hesitated before saying, "Earl Bishop. He's the league's third highest-ranked commander. He's also a cousin to the king on both his mother's and his father's side."

Fletcher had heard of Bishop. "I know him," the admiral said with a frown. "Bishop will intrigue for the leadership of the Grand Fleet. It's in his blood. He'll try to take command from me."

"That's another reason I want you to lead," Cook said. "You're a bulldog, a fighter. At all costs, you must maintain command of the Grand Fleet."

Fletcher's frown deepened.

"You'll have to outmaneuver the earl politically," Cook said. "Play the long game with him. Just make sure you keep the Grand Fleet united. You must find the enemy and defeat him. Nothing else matters."

Fletcher ingested the advice.

"We have to counter-attack to keep the New Men off-balance long enough to rip the initiative from them for good," Cook said. "Otherwise, those geniuses will have enough time to find another Destroyer, or something like that ancient alien war-machine."

"I still don't think I'm the right man for this."

"There's no one else who can act as the glue," Cook said. The old man straightened to his full height, and his voice deepened. "You're duty-bound to accept the post, John. Humanity needs you." The Lord High Admiral paused, studying the admiral. He finally added, "Are you up to the challenge?"

Fletcher stared at the old man. A red flush had crept up his neck. "Damn you," he whispered.

Cook waited in silence.

Fletcher looked down at the ground far below. Thoughts swirled in his head both pro and con. Finally, he said, "Yes, I'll do it." *But Heaven help me if I fail. And if I don't.*

-2-

SEVEN MONTHS LATER
JUNCTION SYSTEM, "C" QUADRANT

Fletcher had been dreading this moment for a long time. He had seen the cracks growing but hadn't expected the earl to move this soon.

"You do realize this is exactly what the New Men want us to do, don't you?"

"Nonsense," Third Admiral Bishop replied.

The pale-skinned earl was the image of a quintessential British military man of old: tall, with a long face, a monocle over his left eye and a chest full of medals.

"The scoundrels are counting on our fear," Bishop added. "They need time, clearly. I expect that's what motivated their ruthlessness. The New Men did not anticipate our united and swift effort, especially after sending the horrible Destroyer at the Wahhabi homeworld."

Fletcher leaned back in his chair. They were in Flagship *Antietam's* conference chamber. "They" were the leaders of the coalition forces that made up the Grand Fleet.

Being in charge these past seven months had reinvigorated Fletcher. The Grand Fleet had already passed through the Caria 323 System. It was the same there as elsewhere: radioactive wastelands and smoking craters where cities once flourished. So far, they hadn't found any planetary survivors anywhere in "C" Quadrant. Instead of facing the Grand Fleet, the New Men had retreated without a trace of a sighting. As the enemy pulled back, they burned the inhabitable worlds, slaughtering the people in the process.

"The New Men are playing for time," Bishop was saying. "We simply cannot allow them the luxury any longer."

"I agree," Sub-commander Ko said, as if on cue, which it probably was.

"So we'll split our forces," Fletcher said, "making everything easier for them?"

"You fear a sudden ambush," Bishop said. "I'm afraid we're giving the New Men too much time to find another preposterous weapon. We must defeat their armada *before* they achieve whatever their next goal is. That means we must *thrust* at the enemy, not tiptoe like thieves in a dark house."

"Exactly," Sub-commander Ko said, slapping the table.

Fletcher felt heat rise in his neck, but he worked on maintaining a stoic face as he waited for Bishop to continue.

The earl plucked the monocle from his eye, polishing it on a sleeve and replacing it to squint at Fletcher.

"I'm not suggesting we face the New Men divided in battle," the earl said. "That would be operational folly. I am suggesting we find the extent of their destruction as quickly as possible. We must also discover how far they've pulled back and where they're willing to stand and fight. Our spreading out to scout the various star systems will considerably speed up the process. Naturally, we shall keep in constant communication through courier vessels. If the New Men show themselves somewhere in force, that group retreats as the rest of the Grand Fleet rushes to their aid. It should be obvious that my idea will bring about the battle we crave. Don't you agree?"

Fletcher did not agree, not in the slightest. But instead of answering verbally, he used silence to convey his reply.

The earl withdrew a handkerchief from a sleeve, coughing into it several times. "I hesitate to say this…"

"Please," Fletcher said, "don't stop now."

"We lead fighting men," Bishop said quietly, as if it pained him to talk about this. "Undue caution breeds hesitation among the officers, which trickles down to the men. Hesitation can turn into fear all too quickly. We're supposed to be advancing

8

against the enemy, not shivering at shadows. Each jump takes days to complete because we have to move such a vast force through a single Laumer-Point. The wormholes have become chokepoints instead of stellar pathways."

"We move slowly but forcefully," Fletcher said, "using our size to shield ourselves. That saves us from attritional losses."

Bishop tucked the handkerchief back into a sleeve, possibly giving himself time to think.

"We can defeat the enemy," Bishop said, "but only if we can catch him in time. That implies a modicum of speed on our part, not this…tepid advance. My men are becoming restless. They desire battle and wonder why we move so slowly against the foe. It is my duty to keep his Majesty's hammership crews fit for combat, which includes keeping their spirits high."

"I have a similar duty to the Social Syndicate crews," Sub-commander Ko added.

Bishop nodded, spreading his hands imploringly. "Let us keep the Grand Fleet intact in spirit but not necessarily in body. Order the dispersion as we spread out, scouting many star systems at a time. We must pressure the New Men with speed. Let them fear us for a change as they run away faster."

Fletcher had seen this coming for some time. He wondered if he should let Bishop have his way for a time in order to show everyone how foolish that would be. Doing so was a risk. But as Cook had said, "War was a gamble." The wise commander knew when to take the right risk.

"As you wish," Fletcher said quietly.

The answer seemed to surprise Bishop, as he allowed his monocle to drop out of his eye. The earl neatly caught the eyepiece, though. He glanced at the monocle before polishing it on his sleeve again.

As the earl replaced the eyepiece, he said, "That is an excellent decision, Admiral. I wish—"

"Just a moment," Fletcher said, interrupting the earl. He leaned near, putting a hand on the man's right arm the way a superior would act toward an inferior. "I'll agree to the dispersion if we operate it on my schedule."

"Eh?" Bishop asked, staring at the offensive hand.

Fletcher removed it by reaching into a pocket, pulling up a memory stick. He slid the stick into a computer slot. He'd dreaded this moment for some time but had expected it nonetheless. The trick today was to keep the Grand Fleet operative as a unit, not letting it fall apart into its component pieces. *That* would be a disaster in the making. Nor could he let command pass to the cunning third admiral.

"I like your idea of courier vessels," Fletcher said. "We will divide the fleet to move but be ready to unite in a day or so to meet the New Men with our combined forces."

The earl studied Fletcher. At last, he smiled. "You anticipated me, I see. That is a good thing, is it not?" he asked the sub-commander?

"I suppose," Ko growled.

"It is indeed," Bishop said, "for it implies a strategic mind of some scope. Please, show us our new marching orders, Admiral."

Fletcher picked up a clicker, switching on a holomap of "C" Quadrant. It would appear he still had nominal command of the Grand Fleet. One step back to take two forward, as the old saying went. The trick would be to prove to the others that he was right about remaining united without losing too many vessels in the coming object lesson. It was a mistake of the first order to split the Grand Fleet against the New Men. Fletcher knew that all too well. The New Men were going to make them pay for doing it. It was simply a matter of where and how.

Fletcher pushed the thought aside. He would give the riskiest assignments to the most troublesome commander. That was Third Admiral Bishop, of course. Sub-commander Ko merely followed the earl's lead. As he told them their new travel routes, Fletcher recalled the monitors he'd lost in the Battle of Caria 323. The Windsor League hammerships were critical to the Grand Fleet. Vessel for vessel, they were the toughest ships they had. He couldn't afford to lose too many of them.

How many star cruisers do the New Men have left? What is their plan?

Fletcher continued to show the others their new paths as he worried about the future encounter. The New Men were out here, waiting, plotting and preparing. The realization brought a cold knot of doubt to the admiral's gut, one that he worked hard to keep off his face.

Bishop was right about one thing. Fear was contagious. But so was courage.

Fletcher had to make sure the New Men's coming trick didn't steal the courage the Grand Fleet already possessed due to its exalted size. That's what Bishop and Ko didn't seem to understand. Humanity needed a giant fleet to give the soldiers enough courage to come out here in the shadows and face the impossible New Men.

-3-

Three weeks later, Fletcher scowled at a holoimage in his ready room. It showed the city of Caracas on New Venezuela III. Unlike anything else they'd seen in "C" Quadrant, the buildings were intact.

"This is from a strikefighter skirting the planetary atmosphere," the briefing officer explained.

Fletcher made a pass in the air, bringing the holoimage closer. He spread two fingers, zooming in on the ground.

"There aren't any bomb craters," he said.

"No, sir," the briefing officer said.

Fletcher continued to study the city. "I don't see any traffic."

"There wasn't any, sir."

"No?"

"According to the pilots—the *Excalibur's* commander ordered a second pass. According to them, nothing moves on the ground."

"Not even animals?" the admiral asked.

"Nothing, sir. It's a ghost town."

"I wonder why the New Men didn't drop any hell-burners here. What's different about New Venezuela III?"

The briefing officer shook her head, clearly not knowing.

Fletcher looked up. "What about the planet's other cities?"

"They're all like this, sir. Nothing stirs anywhere but there's no sign of destruction."

12

"Right," Fletcher said. "I'm sending down a landing party. I want them to scour Caracas. I want to know what happened. I want to speak to a survivor. As far as I know, no one has survived a New Men-conquered planet. We may have just had our first breakthrough."

***

The majority of the Star Watch warships in the Grand Fleet were presently in the New Venezuela System. There were three Laumer-Points here, all of them spread out. It meant days of normal space travel for the vessels to go from one wormhole entrance to another.

Only one carrier—the *Excalibur*—orbited New Venezuela III, along with several destroyers and two escorts. The rest of the fleet waited in the middle of the star system, ready to accelerate to a needed Laumer-Point in case a courier ship popped through and told them the enemy fleet had made its move against a different detachment.

The splitting of the Grand Fleet three weeks ago had begun in a high state of anxiety for the admiral. Every day, Fletcher had expected the enemy to pounce on the weakest element of the Grand Fleet. Instead, the combined fleets moved faster through "C" Quadrant, gathering information at five times the previous rate. Despite that, the admiral kept a tight reign over the movement schedules. It didn't take a genius to see the New Men were going to let them get overconfident and then sloppy. Fletcher was determined to prevent that.

Now, though, the holoimages he'd seen... Could Bishop have been right? By traveling faster, scouting more systems at an accelerated rate, could that have pressured the New Men into making a mistake?

Fletcher wanted more information before he made that decision. Where were the people of New Venezuela III? He had to know.

The admiral clicked on an intercom. "Any word yet from the landing party?"

"No, sir," *Antietam's* captain said.

The bulk of the warships were over one point five billion kilometers away from New Venezuela III. Messages took time to travel the distance. Launching shuttles from *Excalibur* took more time. So did actually traveling down to the planet and then walking around, recording whatever there was to see.

Fletcher forced himself to sit back. The data would arrive when it came and no faster. He wasn't going to hurry it like this. Instead, he was showing the captain and her bridge crew that the admiral was anxious. No, that wouldn't do.

"Thank you," he said.

"Yes, sir."

Fletcher put his hands over his stomach. He hated waiting. It was always the worst part. When would he know what had happened to the people of Caracas? This was driving him crazy.

***

Finally, the landing party sent its data packet to *Excalibur*. The carrier's intelligence officer beamed it via the laser lightguide link to *Antietam*. Soon, the flagship's briefing officer knocked on the ready room door.

"Enter," Fletcher said.

"I have the Caracas report, sir," she said.

The admiral waved her inside. Soon, he studied the holoimages of empty stores, empty houses and unmade beds. Everywhere the landing party went, it was the same. The people had obviously left in a hurry. The landing party had not found anyone to interrogate.

"What's this?" Fletcher said, spying movement in the holo-vid.

A second later, as the landing party person zoomed in, a red and white cat hissed. Then, it disappeared around a corner.

"Did you notice that?" Fletcher asked.

"I did, sir."

"Well? What do you think?"

"I-I don't know, sir," the briefing officer said, looking confused.

"I was referring to the cat's collar. You did see that, right?"

"Oh," she said, "the collar. Why, yes, of course." A moment passed. "Sir, I must admit that I didn't notice the collar."

"Hmmm," Fletcher said, thinking. "It was a house cat. I'm certain. I suspect it means the New Men did not gas the city."

"Sir?"

"That will be all," the admiral said.

The briefing officer nodded before saluting, turning sharply and leaving.

Fletcher waited another minute, collecting his thoughts. Then, he told the captain to send a message to the *Excalibur*. The landing party was to search for mass graves.

"May I ask a question, Admiral?" the captain said.

"The cat could have been away when the New Men gassed the others."

"Sir?" the captain asked, confused.

"Send the message. The sooner the landing parties start searching, the sooner I'll know the truth."

"Yes, sir," the captain said. "I will send the message."

***

Two days later, Fletcher ordered the fleet out of the New Venezuela System. He was behind his own maneuver schedule, having given the landing parties more time to hunt for mass graves. They had found nothing. As far as anyone knew, no people were on New Venezuela III. It was a ghost planet.

Fletcher was stretched on his cot in his quarters. He had his hands behind his head as he stared up at the ceiling bulkhead.

The landing parties had found no traces of gas. That theory seemed wrong. Could the New Men have forced everyone onto shuttles, carrying them into waiting cargo haulers? The implication was too…staggering. Moving several million people would take a vast logistical effort. Yes, New Venezuela had been under the enemy's control for almost two years. Yet, that would imply the New Men had been moving people from the beginning. Did that make sense?

"If I knew the reason it might," Fletcher told himself.

Why would the enemy drop hell-burners on one planet and take the people from another? Maybe New Venezuela III was an anomaly.

The Grand Fleet was halfway through "C" Quadrant already. More data would soon begin to flow in from the courier ships. He would simply have to bide his time for now.

A grim smile touched the admiral's lips. Finally, they had found something different, not just a radioactive planet. That would indicate…what exactly?

Fletcher shook his head. He didn't know. His gut told him it was time to recall all the ships and begin tiptoeing again as a giant group. He hated having the fleet spread out like this among several star systems. Was the enemy trying to lull them?

Yes. I know they are. We're just going to have to be smarter than that.

He would have to let the enemy strike one of the elements in order for the others to believe his caution was the best course.

Hannibal taught the Romans that, although the Carthaginian almost destroyed them before they learned their lesson. I'm going to have to play this just right.

Thinking about it kept the admiral awake for hours.

-4-

Two weeks after Admiral Fletcher left the New Venezuela System, a cloaked star cruiser observed a Windsor League detachment scouring the Ankara System.

Atmospheric league fighters swept over the skies of Ankara II. The pilots broadcast their findings to the nearest hammership. Shuttles soon left the large warship. They landed with scout teams, searching the planet's empty cities.

The commander of the cloaked star cruiser, a Methuselah Man by the name of Strand, chuckled upon hearing the landing parties' reports.

Soon, now, he would implement the third phase of his plan. He had already detected the travel pattern of the dispersed vessels. It indicated that Admiral Fletcher still had nominal command of the Grand Fleet.

Strand had expected no less, but it wasn't going to matter in the end. Yes, the old-style humans had proven more resilient than he would have believed. That came from several key sources: the hidebound Ludendorff, that infernal Captain Maddox with Starship *Victory* and the Adok AI, Driving Force Galyan.

None of those sources appeared to be with the Grand Fleet, however. That meant he could proceed with the fleet's destruction at his leisure. Not that it would be easy to accomplish. Strand could not perceive a quick fix this time. But if the old-style humans would react as predicted—which he had no doubt they would—then he could annihilate the juggernaut Grand Fleet and continue with his overall master plan for the human race.

-5-

In his wind-suit, Pa Kur hurried through the howling gale. The sky was dark red with dust and flashes of intense lightning as if gods dueled. Far away, rain fell onto sand and cracked rocks.

The water moon of Palain IV was the sole inhabitable body in the system. It orbited a gas giant, the source for the moon's deuterium-run factories.

In Commonwealth terminology, Pa Kur was a New Man, a golden-skinned dominant, Fifth Rank. He wore a protective wind-suit, which included a bubble helmet with fine scratches crisscrossing the tempered glass. He headed into the gale as his long strides ate up the distance to the interior landing field. He could barely make out the field's blinking lights.

Windsor League subhumans had entered the star system. One of their hammerships headed here while the other seven monster ships maneuvered toward a Laumer-Point six hundred thousand kilometers away.

Pa Kur did not smile, as it was not in his nature to do so. Yet, he was elated. Strand had been right so far. The Methuselah Man truly was a genius, maybe even a prophet concerning the sub-men.

The lower races now dared to send individual contingents to the various systems. Before, the entire Grand Fleet had moved en masse from one star system to another.

The Emperor's commander of the invasion armada had wished to attack a dispersed arm of the enemy fleet at once.

Strand had convinced the commander to wait. Since the Destroyer's annihilation in the Solar System, the Emperor and Strand had come to terms again. Necessity had predicated it.

The Methuselah Man had instructed the armada commander in his plan. Strand had said the subhumans needed time for boredom to mentally prepare them for the coming shock before the moment was right to psychologically pinprick them.

As Pa Kur crunched across sand, he squinted at a bullet-fast object coming toward him. He shifted leftward with a cat's quickness. A thick stalk of ras-grass flew past. If it had struck him, it could have easily breached the wind-suit. The storms here made breathing difficult without aid. He had no time for the theatrics of a torn suit.

Pa Kur had short silver hair and strange eyes even for a New Man. They were glassy like obsidian, showing no emotion. That took some doing on his part. He had never let anyone know that his Fifth Rank status rankled intensely. He desired greater rank with a seething passion. He also wanted to run a starship of his own. Those slots only went to Third Ranks and higher.

His yearning for starship command had been the prime ingredient for his taking so readily to Strand's plan. The Methuselah Man's idea was ingenious and subtle. It would also take perfect timing today. Pa Kur knew the others of his sept sneered at Strand's guarantee of total victory if they would only do as he said. Pa Kur wanted to teach them otherwise.

The obsidian eyes seemed to glitter for just a moment. Pa Kur had studied subhuman psychology, the key reason Strand had chosen him for this task. Pa Kur also had a theory. If one truly wanted to understand greatness—such as that of the New Men—one must first grasp the base stock from which they had come. It would be similar to sub-men studying chimpanzees to learn more about themselves. It was a radical idea, he knew. It also allowed him to understand the subhumans more deeply than his so-called superiors and peers. It never mattered what an inferior believed. Even the enlightened Pa Kur subscribed to that thought.

20

Despite his fifth rank status, Pa Kur believed he understood Strand's purpose better than anyone else on Palain IV's water moon. This pinprick attack would be the first step toward unsettling the subhumans, of teaching them to always doubt themselves.

Within the bubble helmet, a static sound from the implant in his left ear caused Pa Kur to tilt his head.

"Report," he said, in an emotionless voice.

"We've received the coded signal from *him*," the scratchy voice said. "The word is: go."

Pa Kur lowered his head and began to run. He sprinted extraordinarily fast like a humanoid cheetah. No regular human could have hoped to run a quarter of his speed.

The "him" meant Strand. The Methuselah Man must be in the system with his cloaked star cruiser. That was interesting.

It was time to ready the Palain sub-men. The coming foray would have to follow an exact procedure. If it worked—

No! Pa Kur refused to sanction the possibility of failure. He would strive and succeed or it would no longer matter because he would be dead. Success would surely elevate him to Fourth Rank. Even better, he would have a starship to command, even if only for a short time.

***

Pa Kur stood inside the interior hangar, watching through one-way glass. Eight subhuman-built shuttles waited on the other side.

He held a comm-unit, studying the approaching hammership. It was round and possessed three layers of shields like an onion. That was unique among the subhumans. The hammership also boasted thick hull armor with heavy ablating underneath.

The Windsor League people did not subscribe to beam weaponry. They trusted in railguns firing multiple types of rounds, the deadliest being thermonuclear warheads. Hammerships were most effective at close range. Their ultra-heavy shielding and hull armor theoretically allowed the vessel to survive distance assaults in order to get in close.

21

Today, Pa Kur wanted the hammership as close to the water moon as possible.

On his comm-unit, he watched the hammership's exhaust grow to absurd lengths as it braked hard. The enemy was coming in at combat speed, a wise precaution in most instances.

Pa Kur mentally calculated the braking rate versus the distance left to the water moon. He did not need a computer to make the calculations. Ah. It was time to start moving the Palain sub-men into position.

Raising the comm-unit, Pa Kur said, "Begin the procedure."

He hooked the comm to his belt afterward, peering through the one-way glass. The seconds ticked away, turning into minutes. Finally, a door into the hangar bay opened. A ragged-looking subhuman peered out. The creature held a stunner. Others behind the first one forced the man into the interior hangar bay. More poured out. They had just made a "successful" escape attempt, killing the hypnotized Palain guards. Likely, these subhumans couldn't believe their miraculous luck.

One of them pointed at the shuttles. Good. Their voices rose as they argued the possibilities. At last, in a group, they surged toward the shuttles. All the while, more subhumans poured out of the door.

Pa Kur had kept these creatures for years for just such an eventuality. Conditioning them to the correct pitch had been one of his chief assignments. It had been his task because of his keen understanding of subhuman psychology.

The former military colonists forced a shuttle door open.

Pa Kur unhooked the comm-unit, clicking a switch, timing them out of curiosity. He had a theory about their mental acuity. Ten minutes later, an upper hangar bay door began to open to the surface. Interesting. They had achieved the feat three minutes faster than he'd anticipated. It wouldn't make a difference, though, not to what Strand had in mind.

***

22

Pa Kur settled into position, lying on his stomach aboard a single-ship. It was a tiny, needle-shaped spacecraft with an ability to fold space for extremely short distances. As impossible as it was to believe, the Commonwealth sub-men had invented the tech. The superior New Men Intelligence Service had stolen the secret some time ago.

Pa Kur waited, clenching his stomach. Thirty seconds later, the booster rocket roared. The G forces pressed against Pa Kur as the rocket lofted into space at combat speeds.

The launch point was on the other side of the water moon from the approaching hammership. The few subhuman probes on this side had "malfunctioned" in such a way as to appear accidental. Thus, the enemy did not know about the booster rockets. The escaping Palain shuttles were already on the other side of the water moon, no doubt hailing the hammership, begging for rescue.

Each booster held a Seven. A Seven was the New Men equivalent of a sub-men's squad. In this instance, each pilot in a Seven had his own single-ship. Seven boosters roared for space, meaning Pa Kur had forty-nine New Men for the coming attack, his entire sept.

Soon enough, the boosters reached space. Pa Kur pressed a switch. With the clank of detaching hooks, his single-ship floated free.

One by one, the empty rockets began to drift aimlessly, the nearest one tumbling end over end. Each Seven maneuvered around its leader. Finally, they sent pulse messages to Pa Kur. Everyone was ready.

Pa Kur led the seven Sevens around the upper curvature of the red water moon. Storms swirled below in a vast panorama. Maybe it was beautiful. Pa Kur had a difficult time with the concept. He continued to lie on his stomach, holding onto handlebars, using a throttle to adjust his velocity. The gas giant appeared, rising out of the horizon like a massive moon. The Jovian planet was deep blue in color. Several deuterium-processing stations still existed in the upper clouds, although they were less than pinpricks and thus invisible to the naked eye.

"Go dark," Pa Kur said into the comm.

He released the throttle and tapped out a sequence on his board. His needlecraft no longer accelerated, but drifted with its momentum. He activated the mini cloaking device. It was his only defense against the mighty hammership.

The huge craft had reached the water moon's far orbit, although it still wasn't visible this far away.

The shuttles were visible as they burned brightly, their exhaust tails tiny streaks in the blackness.

Once more, Pa Kur tapped his comm. Excited, begging voices bubbled from it. The Palain subhumans pleaded with the captain of the Windsor League vessel. Several of them at once continued to explain how they had just escaped New Men captivity.

The commander of the hammership was cautious. The woman had an obvious right to be.

From on the water moon, a planetary cannon beamed. The ray struck perfectly, smashing a shuttle apart as metal melted and then exploded with air and water vapor, flesh and bones. A second cannon beamed. This one struck the outer shield of the hammership.

The two planetary cannons wreaked havoc among the shuttles, destroying one after another. Finally, the hammership's railguns targeted and fired, screaming shells through the atmosphere, silencing the planetary lasers. Hangar bay doors opened and fighters launched.

The last two Palain shuttles neared the hammership. The escapees pleaded anew, some of them crying in terror.

Pa Kur listened intently.

"Please," begged one of the escapees. "Board us and search the shuttles. We really are who we say we are."

"What about bombs?" the hammership captain asked.

"Don't you think we've already thought of that?" a shuttle speaker answered. "The New Men are cruel and inhuman. They'll do anything to win. We've searched everywhere through the shuttle. We're safe, I promise you. But you're going to have to see that for yourself. That's why we ask you to board and search us."

"Very well," the captain said. "Prepare for boarding."

It took ten minutes of maneuver for the two shuttles to stop fully and the fighters to circle them with their guns live.

More time passed as two shuttles left the hammership, accelerated and then decelerated. Finally, several spacemen left a Windsor League shuttle, using hydrogen exhaust to propel themselves to the nearest escapee shuttle.

"Thank you, thank you," wept one of the Palain escapees. "We owe you so much."

"No," Pa Kur said. "You owe no one anything as you are mere tools." He pressed a button.

Hypnotism was an interesting phenomenon. The sub-men were particularly susceptible to the practice. The people in the shuttles truly believed they had looked for thermonuclear bombs, when in fact they had not. How otherwise could they have sounded so convincing?

Pa Kur's radio pulse reached the two shuttles. Seconds later, each of them ignited, blowing apart. Powerful thermonuclear blasts also took out the hammership's two shuttles and many of the space-fighters. Even more important, gamma rays, X-rays and heat billowed at the hammership. Clearly, the blasts would fail to knock down the shields, but they would whiten the ship's sensors for a short time.

"We shall begin," Pa Kur told his Sevens, "in three seconds." The time passed. "Now," he said.

Pa Kur engaged the single-ship's thruster. As acceleration increased, he switched on a timer, watching it closely.

"Fold," he said.

His single-ship disappeared from its position and reappeared less than one quarter of a kilometer from the hammership. Just as Strand had predicted, rescue shuttles launched from the giant vessel. That meant a way through the shields for the attacking needlecraft.

"Ignore the shuttles," Pa Kur instructed the others. "Get onto the hammership at once."

None of his sept acknowledged his command, of course. None of them would understand why the sub-men practiced such a thing. They had heard; thus, they would obey.

Pa Kur noted the single-ships around him. That was good. On his tiny screen, he saw the opening in the three shields.

Once, Per Lomax had used single-ships against Starship *Victory*. The Emperor's people had studied the attack. Pa Kur used the new and improved tactics that came from the study. It was why he had forty-nine needle-ships and why they had appeared so near the hammership.

Surprise must have been total. The shuttles accelerated from the hammership, passing the tiny single-ships. The crews must not even realize forty-nine needle-shaped craft rushed at the open hangar bay entrances.

Pa Kur stared ahead. The large bay doors began to close. The sub-men on the hammership must finally recognize the threat. With his dark eyes filled with visions of glory, the Fifth-Ranked New Man knew it was too late for them to stop him now.

***

Pa Kur landed on a hangar bay deck with a jar. He released the handlebars and pressed a switch. His restraints exploded off him even as the canopy blew into the hangar bay.

As Pa Kur stood, he activated his stealth suit, engaged his enablers and drew a blaster. Around him, other New Men did likewise. Each disappeared from visual sight, although they could detect each other. The enablers would speed their reflexes and help their muscles move faster than was natural.

Hatches opened in the hangar bay and Royal Marines in battle armor clanked into view. Many of them raised heavy arms, letting their Gatling guns hose exploding bullets at the single-ships. Some of the craft began to shred into pieces. Other three-man Marine teams carried bigger machine guns.

Pa Kur sneered as he sailed through the air. He'd already vaulted from his craft. As more single-ships were hit, he landed on the deck. Dampers gave the hangar bay pseudo-gravity.

None of the subhumans had noticed him, of course. He wore the best in stealth suits. A glance around showed him forty-seven New Men. Only two of his sept had failed to enter the hammership.

"Open fire," Pa Kur radioed.

It was pathetically easy. As the Royal Marines destroyed single-ships, blasters opened up. Only a few of the sub-men survived the first withering volley. One or two looked around wildly, no doubt searching for the invisible killers. The next wave of blasters destroyed them too.

The boarding attack for the hammership had begun in earnest.

***

Pa Kur and his sept of soldiers from the Throne World, wearing stealth suits and enablers, captured the hammership in exactly fifty-three minutes.

During most of that time, confusion reigned on the Windsor League vessel. Lights shut down on deck after deck while ventilating systems worked sporadically. During the last ten minutes of the takeover, the subhumans attempted to self-destruct the warship three separate times.

Pa Kur thwarted each try.

Finally, with a Seven, he dropped from vents in the bridge ceiling bulkhead. The bridge crew heard the landing thuds and looked around wildly.

"Where are they, sir?" a woman shouted.

The hammership commander held a pistol, slowly rotating, searching for something. She raised her gun and fired, hitting a panel.

Pa Kur didn't want the woman accidently hitting an important board. He rushed the captain and hit her in the face. The force of the blow catapulted the captain over her command chair. She twitched on the floor with a broken neck and a crushed face.

The other woman screamed until one of the Seven hand-chopped her neck, breaking it as well.

Soon, Pa Kur controlled the bridge. But he did not attempt to control the ship, not just yet. First, he and his sept would sweep through the vessel, killing all but five of the crewmembers. He would need those five for later.

Strand's plan included Windsor League captives, but they had to be exactly the right kind. After the final killing was completed here, Pa Kur would escort the remaining New Men on the water moon to the nearest Laumer-Point.

Pa Kur sat in the command chair. He found it to be a good feeling. He did not even mind the dead sub-men littered on the bridge. His Seven would clean up the dead soon enough.

With an exhale and a glitter in his eyes, Pa Kur luxuriated in the moment. He had a starship command and Strand had a hammership, one of the ingredients to the master plan.

The other hammerships in the system would never catch this one in time. Those were six hundred thousand kilometers away and presently headed in the wrong direction.

Soon, word of this New Men attack and victory would spread to the rest of the Grand Fleet. It would continue the psychological process Strand needed to bring about the sub-men's abject and bitter defeat.

EARTH

-1-

Captain Maddox of Star Watch Intelligence frowned. What was wrong with him? Why did his head feel so woozy?

The last thing he remembered was playing poker with space smugglers. The room had been in Woo Tower, the fanciest casino in Shanghai.

By the breeze on his cheeks, he wasn't inside now, although a wall loomed to his left. Bottles clinked and women giggled somewhere.

He concentrated to the best of his ability, vaguely spying an open door in the wall. The sounds came from there, although it was dark inside. Should he call for someone to help him?

No. He needed more information first. He needed to think this through.

Why was he out here? Maddox realized he couldn't remember. What was wrong with his eyes? Everything was fuzzy or blotchy. He looked up. It seemed that stars twinkled in the heavens. It must be night.

Maddox closed his eyes, squeezing them tight. He tried to recall the causation of his predicament. He remembered that he had been nearing the end of a two-week leave. It had been quite some time since his crew had defeated the alien Destroyer. Little had gone to his liking since then, but that wasn't the issue here.

He sensed motion and started toward it one foot stumbling ahead of the other.

"No," a voice said, behind and to his immediate left.

Pain flared at Maddox's left elbow. He realized strong fingers dug into his joint and pushed him forward. Someone caused him to stagger out here, apparently directing his path.

Maddox opened his eyes. The fuzziness had departed although the blotchiness remained.

The one gripping his elbow made him turn, propelling him through a door and down a lit corridor. They passed closed doors, ones that lacked handles or latches.

That was interesting if ominous.

Fortunately for Maddox, he possessed a slightly higher core body temperature than regular humans. He was half New Man and half Earthling. He burned off alcohol faster than others did. Because of that—

Alcohol!

Maddox remembered lifting a shot glass and throwing the contents down his throat. He'd held onto his cards as he did so, sitting at a table in a smoky den. He'd been pretending intoxication in order to lull the other players: smugglers, captains of cargo haulers. One could argue his pretense had been unfair deception so they would drop their guard. Perhaps that had been so, but despite being on leave, Maddox had been engaged in a semi-official mission.

For the past three weeks, he'd felt someone trailing him. The sensation had intensified the last four days. He had come to believe Woo Tower was the locus for the spying. Surely, one of the hauler captains at the table had been a link to the person or persons interested in him.

Maddox had lifted the shot glass…right. The waitress had slipped the drink beside his hand, replacing the half-filled whiskey. She had done so in a fervent manner while pretending otherwise. Maddox had taken the drink, knowing it was a reckless gamble. He had been frustrated by the months of inactivity. He remembered the itch of it in his fingertips. In a rash moment—maybe wanting to throw himself into danger— he decided to trust his innate ability to shake off most ill effects. Besides, he'd wanted to know who was trying to drug

30

him by having them make a move afterward, which it appeared someone most certainly had.

It would also appear that the effects of the drink had been stronger than the captain had anticipated. One could argue he had…er, *miscalculated.*

Inwardly, Maddox shrugged. One could make that assertion, surely. He did not believe so himself, at least not yet. Clearly, someone had taken advantage of his dulled state. Likely, the one pushing him down the corridor had a connection with the hidden scrutiny. Now that the hidden person had finally emerged from the shadows, Maddox could react accordingly.

"Where are you taking me?" he asked, letting himself slur more than necessary. His lips weren't *that* numb.

The other said nothing.

"Are we still in Shanghai?" Maddox asked.

The other increased the pace, making the captain stumble faster.

Maddox could feel his body and mind shaking off the ill effects of the drink. He was tall and slender, with steely muscles and, normally, whipcord reflexes. Tonight, he wore his dress uniform complete with holster. By the lack of weight on his belt, he realized someone had taken his gun. That seemed like an obvious precaution on their part.

The blotchiness finally departed his vision and the corridor came into focus. The walls were metallic like a spaceship. The corridor slanted down, meaning they walked underground by now. The doors were really hatches. Yes. This might actually be a ship.

It was time to confront the other before it became too late.

Without seeming to, Maddox examined the hand on his elbow. The fingers were thick and stubby, and the fingernails gleamed as if lacquered. That seemed odd as tiny, individual hairs sprouted from the back of the hand. No…those weren't hairs, were they? It seemed…they might be tiny wires sprouting up as an approximation of hair.

Maddox was ready to make several assumptions. Either this was a modified man from a strange world or an android made to imitate a human. Either way, the being would likely think of

31

himself as strong. Thus, this move would come as a surprise maybe even as a shock to the other.

The captain planted his feet and twisted his arm. Instead of ripping his elbow free, greater pain flared. The stubby fingers had tightened their hold, surprising Maddox with their unusual strength.

"You must come with me," the man said, pushing harder, causing Maddox to stumble forward once more.

The captain glanced back. The squat man or android wore a stylish suit at odds with his girth. Maddox recognized it as a Woo Tower casino uniform. The pusher didn't seem fat but powerful. The face seemed wider than any norm Maddox knew about, although the man lacked any blemishes. That upped the chances he—it—was an android.

The man glanced up at him before looking away. "This isn't my preference, believe me," the man said. "I simply don't know how else to convince you."

"Try explaining it to me," Maddox said.

"I will explain, but not just yet."

"Do you have a reason for the delay?"

"Yes."

"Would you care to share it with me?"

"No, as that would invalidate the reason for waiting."

"Of course," Maddox said. "That's logical."

The man didn't reply to that.

"Still," Maddox said, "I'm afraid I insist we stop."

"You are not in a position to insist. Thus, your statement is illogical, likely driven by emotive needs."

Maddox twisted back to see if the other grinned or if a shine of delight twinkled in the eyes. The face was impassive, the eyes inert and the pace growing more relentless.

The eyes darted upward to look at him again. Maddox quickly faced forward before their gazes met. He'd just spied something most interesting and didn't want the other knowing that he—Maddox—knew. It would be the captain's hole card.

Maddox gauged his options given the new facts. His choices had grown fewer than he'd believed. Clearly, the man marched him to a place of restraint, one that would limit the captain's options even further.

Just as Maddox readied himself to make another attempt at escape, the man halted, jerking the captain to an abrupt stop.

Voices drifted up the corridor. Did the man not like that?

Maddox inhaled, getting ready to shout for help.

"No," the squat man said. With amazing arm-strength, he threw Maddox against the wall while keeping hold of the elbow.

The captain smashed against the hard surface, his face whipping against steel.

The man ran forward, pushing a stunned Maddox, who almost tripped as his feet shuffled faster. Then it became too much. The captain did trip, beginning to fall, but the man easily held him up. That indicated greater than normal mass as well as power.

There was a faint click behind the captain. A hatch slid up in front of him. The man pushed the captain into the chamber. It was a stainless steel kitchen with pots, pans and knives magnetized to the walls. With Maddox ahead of him, the man hurried down an aisle.

This isn't a spaceship. It's—

Maddox realized this must be a hotel or a casino's underground kitchen area. They must still be in Shanghai, maybe even close to Woo Tower.

The man headed for a pair of swinging doors. He was detouring around the voices. That seemed obvious.

Maddox did not inhale this time. The man seemed attentive, able to catalog the signs. The captain practiced deception, seemingly keeping himself in the exact stunned state as seconds ago.

Then, Maddox's right arm whipped out in a lighting move. He ripped a knife from the wall, twisted in the man's grip and stabbed with force. He expected the weapon to sink past the man's ribs. Instead, the tip of the blade sank two inches before snapping off in Maddox's hand. It left a small piece of steel lodged in the man's flesh.

The man did not cry out, although his eyes shined angrily. The fingers of his left hand tightened their grip.

At the pain, Maddox's air expelled from his lungs. It might have dropped him to his knees. With iron determination, as he attempted to ignore the agony, the captain slashed. Using the broken edge of the knife, he tried to blind his opponent.

The man was faster than humanly possible. He ducked his head so Maddox slashed at the skull. The blade cut through pseudo-flesh, sparking against a titanium plate underneath.

The creature was clearly an android.

Maddox realized the knife would not help him. The android was too strong, too fast and too well armored against a kitchen utensil. He let go of the handle even as he realized this.

The blade began to drop. The android's head rose and Maddox grabbed at his service pistol tucked in the android's belt—he'd seen the gun earlier, his hole card.

The android must have spied the move at the last second. It released the bruised elbow and leaped back. Perhaps its logic centers reasoned it could move away faster than Maddox could grab the gun. If so, the AI running the android had not calculated for the captain's phenomenal speed.

The android jumped back and Maddox raised his pistol, using his thumb to click off the safety.

"It's time we talked," Maddox said, finding it difficult to speak due to his throbbing left elbow.

The android froze. Maybe its logic centers had overloaded at this failure.

Maddox backed up several steps, increasing the distance between them. That would allow him fractionally more time to fire if the android unexpectedly attacked.

The android's face twitched with annoyance. That indicated an expensive AI processor. The user had bought the best, it would seem.

"You are making a mistake," the creature said.

"Apparently," the captain said.

"You must come with me at once."

"I might do that. First, you must tell me where we would go?"

"This is not germane at the moment."

"I most heartily disagree."

The android's face twitched again. "I do not represent personal harm to you, Captain Maddox. I assure you of this."

"That's a relief. You can't imagine my—"

"But I must insist that you lower the gun and continue with me," the android said, interrupting.

"And if I refuse?" Maddox asked.

"I will have to take the weapon from you."

"What's stopping you?"

"Is it not obvious?"

"I'm afraid not."

"In the ensuing struggle," the android said, "I could injure you. My protocols do not allow that."

Maddox studied the creature, the long gash on its head that didn't bleed. "You want me alive and unharmed, is that what you're saying?"

"I have already stated as such."

"Who would I see if I agreed to your proposal?"

"It is supposed to be a surprise. Please, lower the pistol and come with me. Time is pressing."

Maddox took several more steps away and raised the pistol so the barrel poked up against his own throat.

"What are you doing?" the android asked, sounding worried.

"I've decided to commit suicide."

The android blinked excessively as if the processors threatened to overload.

"Unless," Maddox said, cocking an eyebrow.

"Yes?"

"You tell me who sent you and where you plan to take me."

"Are you attempting to coerce me?"

"Maybe."

The android's features hardened. "I will not succumb to coercion."

"Yet you expect that I will?"

"Yes. You are…" The android paused.

"I am what?"

"Please, Captain, this is unseemly. I must return with you in my company. This is urgent, most urgent. You cannot conceive of the honor I am doing you."

Maddox decided he would receive no useful information from the android. He didn't know how he could capture it in his present state. He needed a communicator. He needed

Sergeant Riker. A neural net would surely do the trick. How to get his hands on one before the android left was the question.

"I'm leaving," Maddox said. "If you wait here, I'll return shortly."

"You are coming with me. We must go down to the…"

"Yes?"

The android cocked its head as if hearing an internal dialogue.

Abruptly, the android's mouth opened a trifle wider than seemed natural.

That made Maddox uneasy. He removed the pistol from his throat and moved even farther away.

A sonic blast erupted from the android's mouth. The horrible noise staggered Maddox, almost rendering him unconscious. The creature leaped, no doubt trying to catch him unawares.

Maddox was a pistol marksman and able to think faster than others in such a situation. The creature was made of pseudo-flesh with titanium sheathing underneath. Maddox had neither the time to pump enough bullets into the thing nor bullets with the penetrating power to smash the android into harmless smithereens. That meant he had only one option—the eyes. They were logically a weaker portal straight to the AI. But the leaps and bounds the thing made jiggled the eyes, making them a difficult target.

These thoughts flashed though Maddox's brain in less than a second of intuitive insight. Then, he pulled the trigger. A spark against the bridge of the nose told him he'd missed. Another shot ricocheted off the forehead, leaving a smear of what some might have mistaken for blood. The next bullet entered the eye, smashing its way into the delicate braincase. A second and a third shot followed, doing even more damage.

The android lost its coordination. The eyelids fluttered madly while the body sailed limply, propelled by momentum.

Maddox tried to dodge, but he was too late. The thing crashed against the captain, hurling him against a large refrigerator. The back of his skull slammed home with terrific force.

Together, broken android and unconscious man crumpled onto the kitchen floor, the gun clattering away into a small space under a cabinet.

-2-

Maddox groaned as his head throbbed painfully. For a moment, he had no idea where he was or what had happened to him. Then, he remembered the android and their strange conversation.

The captain unglued his eyes and found the construct on top of his chest. Maddox tried to push it off. That made his head throb even more painfully. For a second, his overloaded senses threatened to render him unconscious again.

Maddox quit pushing, letting himself relax. There were faint voices coming from somewhere. Did people hurry here because they'd heard shots? That seemed likely. That would mean he hadn't been unconscious long.

I have to get out of here.

Maddox grew more alert. He realized he felt something ominous approaching. The palms of his hands had become sweaty. The certainty that this android was only phase one of his attempted kidnapping came crashing down on Maddox.

He squirmed underneath the android. That threatened his head once more. This time, he didn't stop. Instead, his breathing grew labored as, bit by bit, he slithered free of the android's broken weight.

Instead of resting, Maddox searched for his gun. He looked around—

Heavy footsteps neared the outer door. Maddox raised himself by his arms, looking up. The hatch slid open and a second android entered the kitchen.

Maddox lowered himself out of sight.

This was a presumption, of course, of it being another android. Maddox didn't know it was just by looking. What made him think so was that the one standing by the door looked exactly like the one that had forced him into the kitchen, even down to the Woo Tower uniform it was wearing.

"Hello?" the new android said, sounding friendly. "Is anyone here?"

Maddox slithered across the floor as he searched for his gun. Several rows of stainless steel cabinets hid him from the new android. Once the creature entered farther, it would surely see him.

The captain reached his targeted cabinet and wriggled his arm under it. He strained to reach his gun in back.

"I hear something," the new android called out. "Please, show yourself. Time is limited."

Maddox strained harder so his fingertips brushed against the gun. If he did this wrong, he'd push the gun away from him.

Footsteps struck the floor. The android approached.

Gritting his teeth, Maddox used his fingertips to friction-move the gun close enough so he could pinch the barrel with his two longest fingers. Then, he pulled the weapon to him as he slid farther away from the cabinet.

"What is this?" the android asked. "Why are you stretched out on the floor? Are you injured?"

Maddox didn't look at the construct yet. Instead, he pulled the gun the rest of the way, sat up, swiveled where he sat and finally regarded the new android with its quizzical expression.

"Captain Maddox," the second android said. "Did you harm the construct lying on the floor?"

Maddox didn't believe this android would prove any easier to deal with than the first. Thus, from a sitting position, he aimed and fired, emptying the rest of the magazine into the second android's eyes. This one reacted in a similar manner to the first, crumpling where it stood, deactivating from the brain shots.

As Maddox stood, he realized he'd overreacted. He was out of bullets and he didn't have any more magazines on his person. If more androids showed up, he no longer had a method of dealing with them.

It was time to get out of here.

***

Soon, Maddox found himself wandering through dark hallways. He hadn't used the slanting metal corridor the first android had taken him through. That seemed unwise even if it was the most direct path back to the surface and street. He was sure something would be guarding that way. Instead, he crept through narrower passageways, trying to find a different, hopefully unguarded exit.

So far, the halls were empty and most of the doors locked. The open ones led into closets. The gun was back in its holster but useless for the moment without bullets. Maddox kept a short, sturdy cutting knife beside his right leg.

He wrestled with the problem of why someone would send an android after him. Did it have anything to do with the smugglers he'd been playing cards with in Woo Tower?

The captain suspected it might.

If so, what did that tell him? The most logical answer was that someone off-planet wished to speak with him. That implied the enemy. Before the last voyage aboard Starship *Victory,* the enemy had been monolithic. Everyone on Earth had known them as the New Men. Since the defeat of the alien Destroyer, the New Men had fractured into the Throne World New Men, those with sympathies toward humanity, and the New Men working closely with Strand. Strand was what Maddox had come to think of as a *greater* Methuselah Man. In the Commonwealth, the Methuselah People had taken longevity treatments, none of them older than several hundred years. Strand was something much older and more dangerous because the alien and unknown Builders were behind him.

The situation had become increasingly complex.

Professor Ludendorff was another of the greater Methuselah Men, lost in the Xerxes System with its mysterious silver pyramid.

Maddox halted, cocking his head. He heard …

40

There it was again. A man blew his nose. He doubted a woman would blow her nose that forcefully. Should he retreat or advance?

The captain stood in the gloom, debating with himself.

It had been some time since he and his crew had defeated the alien Destroyer. The vast ship had transported itself into the core of the Sun, where the terrific energies had obliterated the killing machine. Before that had happened, however, the deadly machine had annihilated the New Arabia System, the heart of the Wahhabi Caliphate, along with the majority of the caliphate's fleet.

That had slashed regular humanity's remaining space power by a quarter to a third. If nothing else, the Destroyer had done the Throne World's work for them. Star Watch had halted the New Men's invasion armada over two years ago now. The Commonwealth had taken staggering losses before that.

Maddox lurched in the direction of the nose-blower. The sound indicated regular people, not more androids. The captain moved like a stalking tiger, with energy coiled in his limbs and cool concentration shining in his eyes.

He wanted to be able to report to the Iron Lady more information than simply, "I evaded capture, Ma'am."

She would ask, "Yes, but what did you learn?"

"Not to gulp tainted drinks," would be a poor reply.

The truth was the captain prided himself on his Intelligence work, believing himself to be Star Watch's premier agent. He had considerable advantages—his dual heritage chief among them. That was the other reason he didn't want to report back empty-handed. Even if he didn't like to dwell on it, Maddox knew he was different. Despite everything he had done the past few years, too many people still distrusted his half-breed nature. One of his ways of compensating was by being better than anyone else.

Thus, Maddox peered around a corner into a dim hallway. A light shined sixty feet away, illuminating a door in the corridor. A guard in a suit waited there. The man stood with his feet planted and his hands held in front of his body as if he meant to hold the position for some time. He stared at nothing in particular, although he swiveled his head from time to time, glancing both ways.

Who was in the room that needed a guard? Was a meeting in progress or would one happen soon?

Maddox stood undecided. Finally, he tucked the sharp part of the blade through his belt behind his back so it wouldn't be visible to someone in front of him. He straightened his shoulders and rounded the corner in a long gait, swinging his arms like a man who had confidence in the situation.

The guard noticed him, naturally. The man stiffened, shifted his head to the side and spoke rapidly, no doubt using a microphone pinned to his collar. Afterward, the guard reached inside his suit but hesitated pulling out a gun.

That indication of uncertainty was interesting. Maddox hoped to get close enough to take the man's gun.

As the captain neared, the door opened. Three more men in suits stepped outside. Each was big, held himself with confidence and had the feel of being security. None of them had as of yet drawn a weapon.

"Gentlemen," Maddox said in a cheery voice. "I do hope I'm not late."

The guards glanced at each other. The one with a pinstripe suit stepped forward, clearing his throat.

"I know who you are, Captain Maddox," the man said in a deep voice. "You're not welcome here."

Maddox grinned, saying, "Nonsense. I want to speak to your boss."

The man drew a small pistol, aiming it at Maddox's belly. "Stop or I'll shoot."

Maddox heard the certainty in the guard's voice. He halted.

"Turn around, Captain. You have no business being here."

Acting on a hunch, Maddox said, "I played cards with your boss, earlier. I came to collect my winnings."

The guard opened his mouth to reply.

"You don't think I'd let him cheat me, do you?" Maddox added.

One of the other guards whispered to Mr. Pinstripe. He frowned, nodding, putting away his pistol.

"Just a minute," Pinstripe said. He reentered the room.

Maddox began to walk closer.

"Hey," the original guard said. "You're supposed to stay there."

Maddox spread his hands, shrugging as he did. "I just want my winnings. I'll leave right after that."

The three men glowered, but none reached inside his coat to draw a weapon.

Maddox neared the group as Pinstripe stepped back outside. The man's head swayed just a little. His hand darted into his coat.

"I told you to stop," Pinstripe growled.

Maddox only felt a little lightheaded from the head trauma earlier. He realized he was as close as he was going to get without a reaction. Therefore, Maddox exploded into action and charged the remaining distance.

Pinstripe was in the process of drawing the small pistol as the captain reached him. Maddox could have used the knife. This was the perfect situation for one: among a group of men trying to draw their guns. That meant, however, that Maddox would likely end up killing some of them. He did not feel the situation warranted the use of lethal force.

Instead, Maddox practiced dirty combat. Using knees, elbows and the meaty parts of his palms, and grabbing two of them, swinging them against the others, the captain incapacitated the four guards. Two of them got off a single shot each. The bullets gouged the wall. None punctured the captain, although the original guard managed a solid hand chop against the captain's neck. It hurt, but it also infuriated Maddox, goading him to hit harder. The guard who struck him thudded against a wall before collapsing into a groaning heap.

With swift economy of speed, the captain collected their guns, pitching the magazines in one direction and flinging all but one of the semiautomatics in the other.

Afterward, he plunged into the room, with his captured weapon held before him. He passed an empty bathroom and came to two large beds and a larger area with a sofa, several chairs, a table and desk. Behind the desk sat one of the space hauler captains from earlier in the evening. Maddox remembered the man's name, Taren Lucas the III. The man

43

was short, wore an English space navy uniform and had narrow features. Maddox remembered thinking earlier that Lucas was an oily conman who seldom told the truth when a lie would work just as well.

The man aimed a laser pistol at him. A stimstick smoldered in the ashtray while a communicator and tablet lay beside it. On the tablet was what looked like a business contract.

"I've summoned reinforcements," Lucas said. "If you kill me, you'll be held on murder charges."

"I doubt that will be the case," Maddox said. "All I have to say is that you fired your laser first."

"I'm recording everything."

"Of course you are. Still…" Maddox cocked an eyebrow.

"Are you saying Star Watch Intelligence will doctor the security data?" Lucas asked.

"Please," Maddox said. "I'm not ready to make a recorded statement. But I do suggest you lower your gun or I will be forced to fire."

"Are you arresting me? If so, I would like to know on what charge."

"As you wish," Maddox said, believing little of what Lucas was telling him. "By aiming your gun at me, you are knowingly threatening an officer of Star Watch Intelligence. To begin with, you will lose your hauler license."

Lucas scowled, setting the laser onto the desk. Picking up the stimstick, putting it between his lips, he inhaled, making the tip glow red as he leaned back in his chair. No doubt, he mentally flipped through various lies to tell, deciding on the most convincing.

"You should leave," Lucas said slowly. "This is none of your affair."

"What happened to me at the gambling table?" Maddox asked. "Surely, you saw everything."

Lucas shrugged.

"I can have you brought in for questioning if you insist"

Something sparkled in the man's eyes, the delight of having hidden knowledge, perhaps. "I don't think you can," Lucas said.

"You were part of a conspiracy to kidnap an officer of Star Watch. You'll lose more than your shipping license but also your freedom, and possibly spend the rest of your life on a prison planet."

"I pay my taxes," Lucas said as if that was something he should say.

"I very much doubt that," Maddox said. "You're a smuggler. We both know that. Now, I want to know, what happened to me at the gambling table tonight?"

Lucas stared at Maddox before looking away. He shrugged once more, almost as if deciding "What the heck, I'll tell the truth for once."

"You became limp and vacant-eyed during the game," Lucas said. "Esquire Noble asked if everything was all right. You didn't reply. He told us he would take you to the infirmary. You didn't resist as he helped you up. What were the rest of us supposed to do? The esquire was a reputable person. We thought nothing of it."

"As I recall," Maddox said, "I was winning at the time. What happened to my chips?"

"All I can tell you is that I don't have them."

"That wasn't the question," Maddox said. He sensed that time was running out. Something was wrong here. Lucas was too confident for a weasel confronted by an Intelligence officer.

The tip of the stimstick glowed once more. Lucas was thinking again. He said, "I don't know what happened to your chips. I lost too much money tonight and left early."

The smuggler fiddled with a tungsten ring on his middle finger as he said that. Maddox was sure Lucas was lying about the losing.

"Who is Esquire Noble?" Maddox asked.

"The man who escorted you from the table."

"Do you know him?"

Lucas twisted the ring again before shaking his head.

"Who are you meeting here?" Maddox asked, deciding to switch directions, hoping to throw the smuggler off balance.

To give himself more time, or so it seemed, Lucas laid the stimstick in the ashtray. "Stay and find out if you like. I'm sure you'll find it illuminating."

Had the man changed his mind? Whatever the case, it was time to accelerate this. Maddox slid his pistol through his belt, smiled, and stepped directly in front of the desk.

That must have made Lucas uneasy. The man grabbed for his laser.

Maddox proved faster, plucking it from the desk. With his other hand, he took the communicator. "Just what I need," he said.

Lucas swatted at Maddox's forearm. For just a second, the captain saw something glitter underneath the tungsten ring, a tiny spike aimed at his flesh. He snatched his forearm out of the way. The hand swept past. Abruptly, Lucas stood, trying to prick Maddox a second time by swinging once more. The captain was too fast for that. He flicked his arm out of the way, and backhanded the back of the smuggler's hand with his other hand.

The undoubtedly poisoned tip must have caused Maddox to hit too hard. Lucas's hand continued the swing in a parabolic arc, propelled by the blow. The smuggler ended up pricking the side of his own arm. Lucas jerked his hand away and stared at Maddox with an accusing glance.

The color drained from Lucas's face. He took a step back, then a second one. He opened his mouth to say something. Instead of completing his thought, his eyelids fluttered and he crumpled onto the carpet. His legs twitched. His entire body thrust up spasmodically. Then, he moaned and his body stilled as he quit breathing.

Maddox watched the display with fascination. That could have been him. Why had Lucas tried to murder an Intelligence officer?

Abruptly, Maddox punched an emergency code into the communicator. He put it to his ear, hearing a harsh buzz from the speaker. The communicator worked, but something or someone jammed the signal. This was getting complicated.

Maddox studied the dead smuggler. Could the man have a jamming device on his person?

46

Walking around the desk, Maddox knelt beside the corpse, feeling inside the jacket. As he did, people entered the room. Hadn't Lucas said he'd summoned others?

Maddox looked up, his eyes widening with surprise. Three Spacers regarded him.

The Spacers were short and slender with deep-space tans, wearing blue uniforms that were tight around the throat. Each wore dark goggles and skintight gloves. They were the last people Maddox would have expected here.

A Spacer woman stood in front of two men. She drew a projac—a stubby, hand-held weapon—aiming it at Maddox.

"Hands up," she said. "You are under arrest for assaulting and possibly murdering a Spacer national."

-3-

Maddox regarded the woman's impassive features. It was difficult to get a good read of her because the goggles hid her eyes. Why would Spacers be here?

A premonition of having made a terrible miscalculation struck the captain. He was in Shanghai. This couldn't be the...

"Is this the Lin Ru Hotel?" he asked.

"Yes," she said. "This is our Earth embassy."

The Spacers had odd conceptions of territory. What other people rented out rooms in their headquarters building? Still, if this was the embassy, this was technically Spacer territory, or more aptly said that legally this made it a Spacer vehicle governed under their...*unusual* code of conduct.

It meant the woman had a legal right to arrest him, and he lacked a legal right to resist.

If he could have placed his call, a Star Watch combat team would have been on its way already. That might have made even more legal complications, but it would have let headquarters know he was here. As it was, Maddox was still very much on his own and possibly in a sticky situation.

"You are not complying with my order," she said. "Are you resisting arrest?"

Spacers were intensely literal and known for their lack of humor or ability to understand shades of meaning. Maddox decided to mollify her so he dropped the laser.

"And the gun in your belt, please," she said. "Put it on the floor."

48

He stared at her, debating options.

"I will burn you down if I must," she said. "A Spacer national is prone and you were molesting his person."

"Taren Lucas the III is a Spacer?" Maddox asked.

The woman nodded curtly.

That didn't seem right. Maddox said, "Earth records indicate otherwise."

"I believe you are attempting to employ delaying tactics against me. Either you disarm immediately or I will fire. You have three seconds to comply."

Maddox plucked the pistol from his belt, dropping it beside the laser. Spacers did not make idle threats.

"Stand up," she said.

Maddox stood, assessing the situation as he did.

The woman must be a provost officer. By their circular pectoral patches, the two men were provost sentries, Marines in Star Watch terms.

Spacers were one of the major political entities in Human Space. Before the alien Destroyer, the key political forces had been the Commonwealth, the Windsor League, the Wahhabi Caliphate and the Spacers. A handful of other political conglomerates existed but none of any major significance.

As the name implied, the Spacers did not have a planetary abode, but lived in vast home ships. They did not claim any star systems as such, but traveled away from conflicts. The nature of their nomadic society had led to political conservatism rather than the radicalism practiced by the New Men. Spacers involved themselves in trade, exploration and mining, making their greatest technological strides in gas giant extraction. The most closely guarded secret among Spacers was the location of their giant industrial vessels.

The majority of Spacers were of Southeast Asian origin, particularly from Old Thailand, Cambodia and Vietnam. The Wahhabi Caliphate had gone to war against the Spacers thirty years ago, inflicting the most devastating losses against the Ninth Thai Fleet.

"Your uniform suggests you belong to Star Watch Intelligence," the woman declared.

Maddox nodded.

"This is an official spy mission then?" she asked.

"No. I was brought here under duress."

"I doubt that."

"I'm not suggesting a Spacer did it. In fact, an android brought me to the Lin Ru."

The woman looked as if she'd tasted a lemon. "We neither use nor condone the use of androids."

"I am aware of that."

The woman spoke with growing distaste. "Is the android presently in the embassy?"

"In one of the basement kitchens," Maddox said. "You'll find two of them, both dysfunctional."

Her head twitched in the negative. "I do not care for the direction of your allegations. In fact, by saying androids brought you to the Lin Ru you slur the embassy. That suggests this is a setup. I will have to inform the ambassador's secretary."

"As you wish," Maddox said.

"You are unnaturally calm. You must not be aware of the penalty for assaulting a Spacer in a ship. It is death by asphyxiation. But since we are not in space, death by any other means will suffice."

"I understand, but I did not assault Taren Lucas. He assaulted me and I defended myself. His own treachery killed...er, incapacitated him."

She sneered. "The evidence tells a different story."

"Examine the video."

She shook her head. "There is none to examine, as we do not allow recording equipment on our premises."

Maddox shook his head at Murphy's Law in action. The one thing he'd believed Lucas had told truthfully ended up being a lie. It figured.

"By the authority invested in me as the Provost Officer on the bridge, in this case, in the embassy," the woman said, "I declare you guilty."

"I appeal your verdict," Maddox said.

"And I reject your appeal." She raised the projac, putting pressure on the trigger.

Maddox realized she planned to kill him on the spot. The knowledge almost froze him. Instead, he shouted, trying to startle her.

She flinched. Then, her arm stiffened as she retargeted.

The delay allowed Maddox time to remember the knife tucked behind his back. He reached there, grabbed the handle and flung the kitchen utensil at her gun, hoping to knock it out of her hand. At the same time, he threw himself to the side, rolling.

The projac fired. A bolt of power sizzled, singeing the upper right shoulder of Maddox's uniform.

The spinning knife reached her, the tip entering the back of her hand in a nearly perfect throw. She cried out in pain, dropping the projac.

Maddox was already on his feet again.

"Restrain him!" she shouted, clutching her injured hand with the knife still sticking in the flesh.

The sentries came at Maddox. He towered over them and had to outweigh both combined.

Maddox shouted again, lashed with his left foot, sweeping the feet out from the first sentry. Maddox twirled martial-arts style, hopped onto his other foot and leg-lashed the second sentry. It catapulted the man so he crashed over a bed and disappeared from view onto the other side.

Seeing freedom, Maddox bolted for the door. The first sentry, who lay on the floor, hit one of Maddox's ankles in passing. That tripped the captain so he sprawled onto the rug. Like a spring, though, he bounced back up. That gave the sentry time to lunge at Maddox as he drew a shock rod. With a loud sizzle of power, the rod stroked the captain's left leg. It went numb, and Maddox fell back onto the rug.

The captain lacked the same speed the second time. He rose, balancing on one leg. The first sentry scrambled upright with his shock rod. The second was still unconscious behind the bed.

"Hold," the woman said.

The sentry glanced at her.

Maddox might have lashed out. He refrained, as the woman aimed the projac once more, using her left hand. She pressed her bleeding right hand against her torso.

"Fate has decreed you to die," she told Maddox. "There is nothing you can do to evade the penalty."

"Perhaps you're right," Maddox said. Gingerly, he put weight on his shocked leg. It had gone numb. Once he realized he wouldn't topple, he studied the woman.

Despite her insistence, she seemed hesitant to kill him outright. Had curiosity stung her? If so, he must cultivate her curiosity to prolong his existence.

"I'm surprised a provost officer isn't curious about androids invading her embassy," Maddox said.

"The answer is simple," she told him. "I didn't believe you about the androids. I'm curious concerning your combat technique, however. The knife-throw with a kitchen utensil—it was fantastically well executed."

Maddox nodded as if embarrassed by her praise. "Star Watch Intelligence teaches its operatives intuitive techniques. This allows us to use any item at hand, turning it into a deadly weapon."

That wasn't true. He had gotten extraordinarily lucky with the throw. But sometimes people were happier with outrageous answers. Besides, it was good for the Spacers to believe SW Intelligence had superlative agents.

"I'm impressed with your sentries," Maddox said. This seemed like a good moment for a compliment. "They fought much better than I had anticipated."

The woman gave a curt nod, saying flatly, "Our sentries are the best."

"I've heard that, of course." Maddox shook his head ruefully. "Until this moment, though, I hadn't believed it."

"Your Earth-centric prejudice blinded you," she said.

"No doubt true," he said.

There was a pause. She regarded him more closely. By her stiffening features, it seemed she had decided to continue with the execution.

"Do you know?" Maddox said, a second before she raised the projac higher. "Androids are notoriously difficult to stop. It's possible you, as a Spacer, don't realize this."

The woman seemed to consider the idea. Spacers had a well-known pathological hatred of androids. Maddox had forgotten the reason for this hatred. Sometimes, however, people who had an intense loathing of a thing also had a secret interest about the subject.

The woman delicately licked her lips, slightly bending her head forward, indicating curiosity. "Did...did the android possess a name?"

"Yes," Maddox said, "Esquire Noble."

The woman stiffened in outrage.

"You recognize the name?" Maddox asked.

"This is unwarranted," she hissed. "You mock us in our own embassy after slaying a Spacer national. You..."

Her cheek muscles bulged as she ground her teeth together.

"Who is Esquire Noble?" Maddox asked, astonished by her reaction.

"As if you don't know," she said. "That is the ambassador's name."

Maddox frowned. Hadn't the android worn the livery of a Woo Tower employee? Why would someone make an android to look like the Spacer ambassador?

"Lucas lied to me," Maddox said. "He's the one who told me the android was named Esquire Noble. I think he was playing a trick on me."

The Provost Officer said nothing and didn't twitch a muscle as the projac aimed at Maddox. Finally, she said, "Describe this so-called android."

Fearing the android might look like the Spacer ambassador, Maddox said, "It was tall with gray hair."

She relaxed her stiffness a fraction. "Esquire Noble is stocky by our standards. His strength is also legendary."

"Ah."

She motioned the conscious sentry to go and help the unconscious one. The man did so while keeping his distance from Maddox.

"Where did you say the androids were again?" the woman asked.

"I fought them in the lower levels but they managed to escape," Maddox lied. According to her description, the androids had looked like the ambassador. He didn't want her inspecting them while he was around. The woman was trigger-happy. He needed to escape the embassy and get back to Star Watch Headquarters.

"Tell me what happened with the men outside this room," she said. "You obviously assaulted them."

"I did," Maddox agreed.

"Since you freely admit your guilt—"

"Provost Officer," Maddox said, "I was kidnapped from Woo Tower earlier this evening. Soon thereafter, the android forced me into your embassy. I have been trying to escape ever since. The men outside this room hindered me. That is why I was forced to defend myself."

"That is a serious allegation," she said.

"Thank you," Maddox said.

The woman frowned. "I do not understand your reply."

"A kidnapped person has an obvious right to defend himself. This right I used."

"By attacking legitimate guards and assaulting a valued guest of the Lin Ru?" she asked.

"I thought you said Lucas was a Spacer national."

She became silent as her projac lowered some. "It's possible I spoke too hastily. Lucas was in the process of applying for Spacer status."

"Provost Officer—"

"Yes?" she said.

Maddox had almost accused her of bias. Spacers were extraordinarily proud of their rigorous thought. She seemed touchy, and a direct accusation might have a negative effect. That wouldn't do as long as she was the only one with a weapon.

"Taren Lucas was at a Woo Tower gaming table tonight," Maddox told her. "Someone slipped me a drugged drink earlier. I believed Lucas had a hand in that."

This seemed to finally get her attention. "Explain," she said.

Maddox told her about the card game, the slipped drink and his coming to while entering the Lin Ru.

The first sentry had helped the second to his feet by now. They stood behind the woman. While keeping the projac aimed at Maddox, she stepped beside the sentries. They conferred together in Spacer cant.

Try as he might, Maddox could not understand the quickly spoken lingo.

The woman stepped away from the sentries. "What is your name?"

"I'm Captain Maddox of Star Watch Intelligence," he said, bowing slightly.

The woman's lips thinned before she said, "That's preposterous."

"I have an ID if you'd like to examine it." As he said that, Maddox realized he'd lost his wallet.

The woman scoffed. "Are you suggesting you're the same individual who defeated the alien Destroyer?"

Maddox nodded, understanding her unease.

She remained motionless for a moment. Then, with a swift move, she holstered the projac as her demeanor changed.

"I beg your pardon," she said in a softer voice. "I did not realize—"

Maddox raised a hand. "It's no trouble, Provost Officer." He took out Lucas's communicator. "Someone is jamming the signal. I would like to report in."

She hesitated only a moment longer. Reaching into her jacket, she took out a unit and clicked a switch. "If you'll try it now," she said.

Maddox did so, calling headquarters. Major Stokes answered and agreed to send a flitter with Sergeant Riker. Maddox quietly explained one more item.

Afterward, he looked up. "The major would like a word with you, Provost Officer."

Reluctantly, the woman accepted the communicator, listening to Stokes. She handed the comm-unit back a moment later.

"I will escort you to the roof," she told Maddox.

He nodded. He wanted to examine Taren Lucas, the guards in the corridor and the androids in the sub-kitchens. However, he had a nasty suspicion that the androids looked exactly like the ambassador, and that could create trouble for him.

Thus, Maddox wanted out of the embassy at the soonest possible opportunity so the woman couldn't change her mind about letting him live.

"Yes," he told her. "Let's head for the roof."

-4-

Maddox stood on the roof of the Lin Ru, waiting for Riker to show up. Other Shanghai buildings surrounded the hotel, most of them taller. The stars glittered in the night sky, barely visible because of the city's bright lights. It made Maddox wonder how he'd seen the stars earlier.

The Provost Officer stood beside him. The sentries had remained inside.

Now that he was out here, with the threat of immediate death removed, the captain decided to attempt to 'rectify the android situation.

"Provost Officer," Maddox said.

She became more alert.

"Have you sent a team to inspect the androids yet?"

"You said they escaped," she told him.

"Are you sure that's what I said?"

"Yes. You..." She regarded him more closely. "You switched your story, didn't you? I should have noticed. My sentries..."

"Changing the story seemed convenient at the time," he said. "The androids were in a basement kitchen."

She spoke into a microphone, using Spacer cant so he didn't understand her. Looking up, she asked, "Could you be more specific regarding which kitchen?"

"It was off of a long slanting corridor." The captain described the entrance as best as he could remember, including the giggling women and clinking glasses just before that.

"You must have come through the service entrance," she said. "Yes, I think I know." Once more, she spoke into her microphone.

She waited expectantly, asking a question now and again into her microphone. Maddox kept watching the sky, wondering if he'd made a mistake regarding the androids.

Finally, a flitter appeared, flashing over Woo Tower. It was a small air-car with a bubble canopy, a two-seater with extra space in back for baggage. With only a little sound, the flitter floated onto the landing pad.

"Thank you for your help, Provost Officer," Maddox said, extending his hand.

She shook hands. Hers was narrow and fine-boned. "Just a moment, Captain," she said, keeping hold of his fingers. "The sentries are reporting in. There are no bodies in any of the sub-kitchens. Why do you think that is?"

"There must have been a third android," Maddox said.

She thought about that. "Yes. I suppose that's it."

Her grip tightened. "You are a great man, Captain Maddox. Your deed inside the World Destroyer has become legendary. I think it's a shame Star Watch hasn't released more information regarding your exploit."

"I didn't do it alone," he said. "Without my crew, I never could have achieved the miracle."

"We all need our crews," she said, releasing his hand.

Maddox agreed before heading for the flitter. Soon, he climbed in. Sergeant Riker sat in the driver's seat.

"Captain," Riker said, nodding.

The sergeant was an older man with leathery skin, a bionic eye and a fully bionic arm. The sergeant had lost the eye and arm in a blast many years ago on a desperate mission on Altair III. Some time ago in the Destroyer, Riker had lost the bionic arm. His latest model had a few advanced features compared to the previous arm. Riker was a salty operative, fiercely loyal but cranky at times. The Old Guard in Intelligence believed he acted as a foil for Maddox.

"Here you go, sir," Riker said, handing over several loaded magazines.

Maddox slid one into his service pistol.

Riker adjusted the controls, taking the flitter up.

"Head to Woo Tower," Maddox said, shoving the pistol into its holster.

"Begging your pardon, sir, but the Iron Lady would like a few words with you first."

"In time," Maddox said, "in time."

"Sir—" Riker said.

"You can tell the brigadier that I was in such a hurry that you forgot to relay the message."

"Sir—"

"Take us down, Sergeant. I want—"

"It's time you learned to take orders better, Captain," the brigadier said from the comm-unit in the dash.

Startled, Maddox quit peering outside and noticed Brigadier Mary O'Hara, the commander of Star Watch Intelligence, staring at him from the tiny dash screen. She had gray hair and a matronly image, and a reproving frown.

"Ma'am," Maddox said. "This is a surprise."

"So is your lack of judgment, Captain," O'Hara said.

Maddox pursed his lips, noticing out of the corner of his eye that Riker gave him an I-tried-to-tell-you look. The captain was surprised he hadn't noticed the screen being on as he'd entered. Could the drug still be having an effect on him?

"What happened tonight?" O'Hara asked him.

Maddox gave her a rundown of the situation, including his time in the Lin Ru.

"An android that looks like the Spacer ambassador," O'Hara said. "That's strange and ominous."

Maddox nodded absently.

"Surely you see the connection, Captain," O'Hara said.

"Connection?" he asked.

"With Professor Ludendorff," she said.

"Ah. Yes, of course," Maddox said. He should have seen it right away. The drug definitely still hindered his thinking.

During the Destroyer Incident, Starship *Victory* had been in the Xerxes System. The system contained a Builder pyramid. Fully functional Builder drones had appeared, as well as New Men star cruisers. The New Men used the silver pyramids sprinkled throughout Human Space and in the Beyond to make

59

one hundred light-year jumps. The pyramids contained Builder technology, as did the star cruisers. The point of the Iron Lady's comment was Professor Ludendorff in particular. When the professor had gone to an asteroid base in the Xerxes System, he or the Builders, someone in any case, had made a switch with Ludendorff. A nearly comatose android looking like the professor had returned to *Victory*. Was there a connection between the Ludendorff android with the Esquire Noble here in Shanghai?

"Have the Spacers been compromised?" O'Hara asked.

"That's a serious allegation," Maddox said, remembering with a grin that the Provost Officer had used the same term against him.

"You find that amusing, do you?" O'Hara asked.

"No, Ma'am," Maddox said. "It's dreadfully serious, if true."

"Whoever is using androids fooled us once already. Without the assassination at headquarters…we might never have learned the truth about Ludendorff."

An assassin among Lord High Admiral Cook's guards had shattered the Ludendorff android's head while he/it was in the custody of Star Watch. The act had saved the Commonwealth from giving high command to an android.

"This could be a much greater problem than I realized," Maddox said thoughtfully. "If an android is running the Spacer embassy…"

O'Hara waited.

"If the Builders, or whoever, have slipped an android into Spacer high command, why use that android to capture me? That's too small of a prize, considering the risk."

"I can think of plenty of reasons why," O'Hara said. "The most obvious is to make a switch. In fact…"

Maddox felt his heart rate accelerate. He couldn't believe what he was hearing. He already had trouble with many in Star Watch. Too many distrusted him because of his hybrid nature. One of his anchors through all this had been Mary O'Hara. In many ways, she had been like a mother to him. She defended him when everyone else was ready to burn him as an unnecessary risk. Now, the Spacers, or this Esquire Noble android had cast doubt on him in the Iron Lady's eyes.

"I suggest Star Watch give me a complete physical examination, Ma'am. If the Spacers have switched the real me with an android, I would like to know it."

Her features had become pinched. "I do not want to order this, Captain."

"I want you to, Ma'am. If our enemy can make us doubt each other, they'll be halfway to victory. Without trust…"

"You're right, Captain. I want you to head to Geneva on the double."

"Headquarters doesn't seem like the right place. If I'm comprised—"

"Captain, I am not in the habit of having my officers argue with me. You will proceed here at once. Do you understand?"

"Yes, Ma'am."

"I need my best people, now more than ever. We're finally on the offensive in 'C' Quadrant. That means we must be doubly on guard back here on Earth."

"I'm on my way," Maddox said. "Is there anything else?"

She hesitated before saying, "No. Until then, Captain."

"Ma'am," he said, clicking off the comm-unit afterward.

Riker glanced at him in a peculiar manner.

"You have something to say?" Maddox asked.

"Wouldn't you know if you were an android, sir?"

Maddox took his time answering. "I'm wondering if the Ludendorff android knew it was a fake. No. It's possible I wouldn't know."

"That isn't reassuring, sir."

Maddox shook his head. "No, it isn't." He positively hated the idea of being a fake. Also, if he was an android, where was the real Captain Maddox? Was that why he'd felt so fuzzy before, because he wasn't really himself?

"Can't you fly this thing any faster?" the captain demanded.

Riker glanced at him uneasily before accelerating, leaving the glittering lights of Shanghai far behind.

-5-

Captain Maddox sat stiffly on a hospital couch, stripped to his briefs. There wasn't an ounce of fat on him. In fact, he almost seemed *too* lean until he moved. Then his muscles showed to startling effect.

"Now I understand why the brigadier wonders if you're a living machine," the doctor said in a jocular tone. "I've never seen anyone in such a high state of physical conditioning."

Maddox refrained from responding. The more he dwelled on the subject, the less he liked it. Wasn't the ancient dictum, "I think therefore I am?" He thought. Yet, he could be a pseudo-person. He found that more discomforting than ever.

"This might hurt," the doctor told him. The older man in a white gown used a handheld device, holding it against the small of Maddox's back. The thing hummed and an area there became cold. A moment later, Maddox could no longer feel the spot.

The doctor picked up a longish needle.

Maddox tried to ignore it, but he kept looking at the needle sideways.

"Steady now," the doctor said. He put a warm hand on Maddox's back and pushed the needle in the numb area.

The captain clicked his teeth together, holding himself perfectly still.

"Interesting," the doctor muttered.

"What is it?" Maddox whispered.

"Just a minute," the older man said. He pulled out the needle.

Maddox looked back, seeing blood in the hypodermic. "Does that mean it's me?"

"I'll be right back," the doctor said, refusing to meet his gaze. The man hurried from the room, holding the hypodermic as if it were a prize.

For just a moment while the door was open, Maddox saw Marines outside, armed and stoic-faced. This was serious business.

The captain hopped off the crinkling white paper. He reached back, probing with his fingers. The spot was still numb. He withdrew his hand and saw a speck of blood on a fingertip. In his hurry to leave, the doctor hadn't swabbed or bandaged the area.

Maddox remedied that, although it proved awkward. Using a mirror to help him see, he pressed a bandage on the area. Then, he put on his uniform. Riker had brought him straight to the Navy hospital in Geneva at Star Watch Headquarters.

After closing the last button, Maddox began to pace. His mental unease surprised him. How could he doubt who he was? If he hadn't seen the Ludendorff android assassinated many months ago, he wouldn't be having such a hard time with this. The android had given every indication of being Ludendorff, even managing to infuriate just about everyone.

What had happened to the real professor? Maddox liked to think the man had survived his fate in the Xerxes System. Had the Builders scooped him up? Had Ludendorff fallen prey to the New Men stationed there? Had the professor slipped away into the Beyond, chuckling at his devilish cleverness?

The door opened.

Maddox spun around, relieved to see that it was the doctor. "Well?" he asked.

"You're human," the doctor said. "Uh, well…" the man hesitated awkwardly.

"I'm half human, you mean to say."

"No. You're fully human. But…"

"But part of me is mutated New Man."

The doctor nodded, still unwilling to meet his gaze. "You're free to go, Captain."

"Just like that, eh?" Maddox asked.

"I beg your pardon?"

"Do you know that I've—? Oh, never mind."

"Is something wrong, young man?"

Maddox shook his head, although inside he was nodding. There was something wrong, all right. He had doubted himself.

As he left the examining room and the Marine guards behind, Maddox thought about that. Causing a man to doubt his very identity could be a powerful weapon. Such a moment would be the perfect time for an enemy to strike.

Maddox stepped outside at street level. Riker had left with the flitter some time ago, leaving Maddox to his own resources.

The captain didn't feel like calling the brigadier yet. She must have gone home to bed. It was late in Geneva, well past midnight. The sergeant and he had traveled across a third of the world while staying ahead of the dawn.

Maddox felt groggy but decided against public transport. He could walk. It might help clear his mind. His internal time made it midmorning, what it would be in Shanghai about now.

He moved briskly along a sidewalk, replaying the latest events. Who stood behind the Shanghai androids? Was it the same people or beings that had given them the Ludendorff android? That seemed the most likely but it wasn't conclusive. The most logical answer was the mysterious Builders. They were aliens, having built the silver pyramids and having helped the Adoks six thousand years ago against the Swarm. Starship *Victory* was an Adok warship, which meant Galyan, the ship's AI, could have possible Builder connections.

Why would the Builders put androids in the Spacer embassy? Were the ancient aliens meddling with humanity again? Did the Builders really stand behind the New Men, or was it Strand and Ludendorff, as the facts seemed to indicate so far?

There were too many puzzles in play. Star Watch needed to know the truth in order to make the best decisions. Clearly, aliens had meddled with humanity in the past, meaning they could be doing the same thing now.

As his boots struck pavement, Maddox determined to answer the riddle. He loathed the idea of someone pushing humanity like ciphers for mysterious alien goals. Humanity had to be free. He wanted to be free, in control of his own destiny.

There were at least two wars happening at once. The open war was between humanity versus the New Men. The hidden war was between the android-makers and humanity. The ancient Methuselah Men, Strand and Ludendorff, also had their own agendas—if the professor was still alive, that is.

While lost in thought, Maddox reached his apartment building three-quarters of an hour later. He tapped in his ID code and entered the main lobby. He paused a moment, inspecting his surroundings. A feeling of unease caused him to stare at various shadows harder than normal.

After the drugged drink and the android incident, some caution might be in order.

Maddox clicked open his holster, putting a hand on the gun butt. He rode the elevator that way. Fortunately, it was late and no one else entered the lift. Soon, he sauntered down a corridor, pretending an easy manner but wary just the same. He could spy nothing amiss, finding nothing to validate the unease.

Reaching his door, he pulled his hand from the knob as if it was hot and stepped back. The unease had just intensified. With his fingertips, he brushed the door jam, running his fingers around the length of the frame. There hadn't been any forced entry that he could tell. Could someone have used a key?

He crouched, studying the lock. It didn't seem that anyone had tampered with it…

Maddox drew the gun, readied himself and tapped his thumb against the pressure lock. The door clicked open. With a foot, he pushed the door and hopped into the entryway. He stood listening, opening his person for greater feelings of wrongness.

The furniture was in the right spots. No items were misplaced, nor could he spy foreign objects. Quietly, he closed the door. His instincts told him something was wrong, but he couldn't see any evidence of that.

65

For two minutes, he stood waiting with his gun poised.

What do I sense?

Analyzing his senses, he realized it was just a feeling. No one had entered his apartment. If someone were hiding here, he would have detected it by now. Besides, he had countless security systems in place. Some sensors even watched outside despite his being many floors up.

Before leaving the first time to find *Victory*, gunmen in an air-van had attempted to ambush him in his apartment.

With his gun ready, Maddox tiptoed through the rooms. He moved like a great cat, straining his senses, traversing the entire complex, even checking the closets. He didn't find anything off.

Could he be overreacting? He didn't like to think so. He was Captain Maddox. If he were going to start jumping at less than shadows, how would he ever help to defeat the New Men and Strand?

Muttering under his breath, he reentered the living room, going to a small bar. He clunked the gun onto the countertop and poured himself a whiskey.

One thing was for certain, he would not drink from a tainted source again. That had been foolhardy. Messing with his mind—

Maddox dropped the shot glass. It hit the countertop, spilling amber-colored whiskey. Then the glass rolled until it fell onto the rug.

By that time, Maddox gripped the pistol again. He aimed it at a flickering image sitting on his sofa. The image was that of a man. It faded from view and then solidified once more.

For just a second, Maddox's hackles rose. If this was a ghost—

He almost fired a bullet through the now solidifying image. The medium-sized man wore a soft blue shirt with black slacks and shoes. The collar of the shirt was open and he wore a gold chain around his neck. The older man was bald, with deeply tanned skin and a prominent hooked nose.

The man looked up, seeing him. Maddox was sure of it. The intelligence in the eyes shined like twin diamonds with a hard and priceless quality.

The captain realized that he stared at a ghostly image of Professor Ludendorff.

-6-

Maddox blinked several times before rubbing the bridge of his nose. Carefully, he came around the bar, with his gun aimed at the apparition. The thing had all of Ludendorff's features that had become so familiar during their time aboard the starship. Maddox could see the garments and the gold chain. The captain could also see *through* the phantom to the sofa behind the image.

"I'm quite real," Ludendorff said in his smug voice. "You aren't imagining this."

Maddox had steely nerves, but the voice proved to be too much, particularly because he was alone. The captain's trigger finger twitched. The gun went off, and a bullet plowed through the ghostly professor, smashing through the sofa and gouging the rug and floor below. Bits of stuffing floated in the air, one particle traveling through the professor.

The image hadn't flinched at the gunshot, but it noted the event.

"Was that truly necessary, Captain?" Ludendorff asked.

Maddox licked his lips before clamping down on his emotions. He disliked the fact of the discharge and silently reproved himself for overreacting. He had never believed himself superstitious before this. He planned to pass any further tests of this nature from now on.

"You're too quiet," the image of the professor said.

Maddox cleared his throat, remembering more about Ludendorff.

The professor was supposed to be the smartest man alive. He had first met the man on Wolf Prime, where the professor had held his own against the invading New Men. Ludendorff had an inordinate curiosity about aliens, the ancient Adoks, the Swarm…and maybe the Builders too.

"We don't have much time," the professor said. "I can't maintain the holoimage for long."

"Holoimage," Maddox said. "You're a holoimage?"

"Of course," Ludendorff said. "What else could I be?"

Maddox took a step back, glancing around.

"I'm quite alone," the holoimage of Ludendorff said.

"How are you able to project yourself into my apartment?"

"It's a nifty trick, to be sure. But in the end, the technical aspect isn't as important as my message."

"I'm not sure I can agree," Maddox said.

"You're too contrary, young man. Just for once—"

"For instance," Maddox said, interrupting the professor. "How do I know you're Ludendorff? Well, that's not the right question. You're not Ludendorff."

"Oh, but I am, my boy, I most certainly am. That's the wonder of the technology."

"What happened to you at the Nexus?" Maddox asked.

"Perfect, my boy, just simply splendid," the professor said. "You have a way of jumping to the right conclusion at the first go. It's always impressed me."

"You're evading the question."

"I assure you, I'm not. Now, listen closely. Our time is limited."

"Professor—I mean the image of the professor. Anyone could be projecting a holoimage of you into my apartment." Maddox snapped his fingers. "Is this Adok technology? Did Dana find something aboard *Victory* to do this?"

"I'm surprised at your line of reasoning."

"Ah," Maddox said. "Maybe this is Builder technology."

The holoimage clapped its hands but failed to produce any sound. "Now, you're thinking again. Keep going on that track, my boy."

"What happened to you in the Xerxes System?"

"First, do you believe this is me speaking to you?"

69

"I don't see how," Maddox said.

"Nevertheless, how can I convince you this holoimage represents my true thoughts?"

"You want me to test you?" Maddox asked.

"It seems like the quickest way to gain your trust."

Maddox studied the smug holoimage. The thing had Ludendorff's manner down pat. Even so… "Who did you take with you from the Brahma System years ago?"

"You're referring to Dr. Dana Rich, of course," Ludendorff said. "Is she well?"

"No. She's devastated by your disappearance."

The holoimage frowned. "I've recently learned that someone put a Ludendorff android onto *Victory* in my place. Did the creature do anything…*vile* to poor Dana?"

"Your android tried to take over all of Star Watch," Maddox said.

The holoimage blinked several times. "Did it indeed? How did it… No, you won't tell me that. It would be restricted information. That means…" The holoimage looked away as if thinking. "Ah, it must have spoken about the Gilgamesh Covent to the Lord High Admiral. Am I right?"

The holoimage was spot on, but Maddox wasn't going to tell it that. Maybe this was the reason for its appearance, to pump him for top-secret information.

The captain did say, "A gunman assassinated you before you could complete your deception."

"Oh," the holoimage said. "Did you witness the event?"

Maddox nodded.

The holoimage rubbed its chin. "Captain, let us quit this game. It's proving too long and tedious. Do you believe me—?"

"Professor, I believe it's impossible for you to communicate like this…unless the real Ludendorff is somewhere nearby."

"No. I'm in the Xerxes System."

Maddox raised his eyebrows. "Then this becomes doubly impossible. Are you suggesting you are communicating with me across many light-years of distance?"

70

"No, no," the holoimage said. "That would be preposterous as you've suggested."

"Then what is this?"

"My engrams were imprinted—"

"Like Galyan?" Maddox asked.

"Yes. That's it. I think like the real professor. He sent me. He sent the androids earlier in Shanghai to guide you to him. You should have trusted the androids, Captain. Destroying them wasted time and it was foolish."

Abruptly, Maddox holstered his pistol. On unsteady legs, he staggered to a chair and sat down.

"*You* authored the androids?" Maddox asked.

"I have just said as much," the holoimage told him. "Captain, do you believe this is me?"

Maddox shrugged. Then, he straightened just as abruptly as he had sat down. "Yes! It's you, Professor. Only you would try such a harebrained scheme."

The captain had decided it was time to hear the holoimage's plan. This back and forth wasn't going to produce any worthwhile results.

"Good, good, you always were a fast read, my boy. I suspect you realize this isn't me exactly, but a nearly perfect duplicate. I sent it from the Xerxes System because I'm physically trapped by automated Builder machines of advanced complexity."

"Star Watch sent a flotilla to clear out the Xerxes System," Maddox said.

"Did they now? That's interesting. For their sakes, maybe even for mine—the real Ludendorff, I mean—I hope they're successful. Clearly, it has taken time for the androids and holoimage projector to travel to Earth. You have no idea of the process involved."

"Why don't you explain it to me?"

"Lack of time prohibits me, my boy. I need you to help me at once. I'm physically trapped and I doubt any Star Watch flotilla will know enough to free me from confinement. In fact, I doubt they will survive the surprises in store for them."

"You're obviously suggesting I take *Victory* to the Xerxes System to free you."

"Of course," the holoimage said. "What other vessel could succeed?"

"A Star Watch fleet—"

"Yes, yes, of course a fleet could annihilate every drone and pulverize each booby-trapped asteroid, but I doubt the Lord High Admiral would send such a fleet to the Xerxes System at this time. Strategy dictates his next move. He must send a massed fleet to "C" Quadrant. He must liberate captured Commonwealth planets. As he does so, he will of course be searching for the Throne World. To win the war, Star Watch has to take the fight to the enemy and occupy the New Men's homeworld."

"What are the Throne World's coordinates?" Maddox asked. "Surely, you know."

"Of course, I know—" The holoimage blinked repeatedly. "The professor must have anticipated your question, the sly devil. The real professor did not impart the Throne World's coordinates to me. I believe Ludendorff has the highest survivability quotient in the galaxy. I'm sure he will give you the coordinates once you free him from captivity. In a word, the knowledge you seek is a carrot to help goad you to action."

"It makes perfect sense that the engrams of the professor should boast about Ludendorff's greatness," Maddox said quietly. "Tell me something, Professor, why use coercive androids to drug me and take me to the Lin Ru?"

"Secrecy, for one thing," the holoimage said.

"The sting in Woo Tower had the feel of a kidnapping mission."

"You were quite safe, Captain, I assure you. Each android allowed you to destroy it rather than harm you. Surely, you realize each of them could have easily incapacitated you."

"I have a knot on the back of my head that says otherwise."

"Could you explain that?"

Maddox told the holoimage how the first android had slammed against him, propelling him hard against a refrigerator.

"Ah, that's perfectly understandable and explainable," the holoimage said. "The android miscalculated. It must have been trying to disarm you lest you hurt yourself."

"Of course," Maddox said drily.

The holoimage hunched forward. "I know you think you're very clever, Captain. And in many ways, your intellect matches mine, at least in the areas of security. But I am your mental superior in a host of avenues. You need me. Star Watch needs me. Do you know that Strand is a Methuselah Man, one of the originals just like me?"

"I've learned that, yes."

"You have? Oh, splendid, splendid, this is better than I realized. Strand will defeat Star Watch if you give him enough time."

"The Throne World seems to think otherwise."

"They're wrong, my boy. Star Watch needs me to help them find the Throne World, but more importantly, to capture Strand. I used to work with him, and then I let him go his own way when we disagreed. Now, I realize that was my greatest error. I have struggled these past months to make the supreme effort. Now, I need you to trust me enough to come and get me. Strand is free and I'm not. That could mean the end of regular humanity. I believe that would be one of the greatest catastrophes possible. It's much too soon to rely on human survival with a genetically narrowed, mutated species."

"You mean the New Men?"

"My boy, you have no idea of the real danger. I cannot tell you yet, but the New Men have a terrible Achilles heel. They need regular humanity; will need them for generations to come."

"I'm tired of these oblique hints," Maddox said. "What is their Achilles heel?"

"You must hurry to the Xerxes System with *Victory* and enter the Nexus. I'm inside at 12-3-BB. Can you remember that?"

"I already have," Maddox said, "but I don't know what your coordinates mean."

"You will at the right time. Hurry, Captain, I don't think I can remain lucid for many more months. I'm counting on you to reach me in time. If you fail, I doubt for humanity's future. I hope I've convinced you of the seriousness of the mission."

"No, I believe the opposite. I—"

The holoimage began to fade.

"Professor, you have to tell me more."

"I see I'm going to need emotive reasoning. Very well, do this one thing for me, Captain. Ask Dana, 'When will we see the New Hindu Kish again?' She'll understand the reference. Then, maybe, you'll know that I'm telling you the truth. Good-bye, Captain, and Godspeed. I look forward to your arrival."

A moment later, the holoimage was gone, the bullet hole in the sofa the only reminder that it had been there.

-7-

Sergeant Riker grumbled. He flew the flitter through the darkness, his eyes heavy with the need for sleep. Fifteen minutes ago, the captain had woken him from blessed slumber just after he'd finally nodded off after the long drive across Asia.

For insurance, and following his secret orders, Riker had called the brigadier's office before heading to the flitter. The Iron Lady hadn't been in. She was at home sleeping, as any normal person should be doing this time of night. Major Stokes had been on call.

"The captain is fit for duty, Sergeant," Stokes had assured him. "The doctor gave him a pass. Is there any particular reason you're calling me?"

Riker still didn't know if he'd done the right thing calling the brigadier's office. He plucked a tall cup of coffee from a holder and took a sip. It was still too hot, but it tasted mighty fine. He needed a caffeine hit if he was going to drive the flitter without crashing.

"I'm just checking in, sir," Riker had told the major. That hadn't been completely truthful.

"Couldn't you have waited until later this morning, Sergeant?"

"It is morning, sir."

"Are you getting cheeky?" Stokes had asked.

"No, sir. Thank you, sir. Couldn't sleep, you know. I-I was troubled for the captain."

"Ah," Stokes had said.

The point was that Riker had lied to a superior officer. That was a foolish thing for an enlisted man to do, especially a sergeant of his long standing. But there were conflicts of interest here. Any reasonable person could see that.

Riker took another sip. He liked his coffee hot with plenty of additives, sugar being his favorite. The captain had told him on more than one occasion the evil of continuous sugar consumption. It rotted the insides, aged a man, according to the captain.

As he drove the flitter into Geneva, the sergeant snorted to himself. It was funny, really. He liked sugar and it rotted his insides, and he was the one who was going to live long enough for it to be a problem. The captain, on the other hand, lived too dangerously. The man might be a genius when it came to combat and intrigue, but the truth was that Maddox was too rash by half. Riker knew he was supposed to temper the captain's worst excesses—

Why did I lie to the major?

Riker made a face. It wasn't hard to understand. Captain Maddox was family. The sergeant had his two nieces in the Tau Ceti System but he hadn't seen them for years. He expected they had kids by now. He should really go to Tau Ceti to see the young brats.

"Don't have the time," Riker muttered. He suspected that when he did have time, he'd be dead.

The nieces were his blood. He thought about them often, realizing why he did what he did in the service. It was old-fashioned duty, the need to protect. Old Sergeant Riker was a sheepdog, trying to protect his loved ones from the wolves out there.

Riker tapped the controls, taking the flitter down into Geneva. The captain was supposed to be waiting on the roof of his apartment dwelling. The man had barely gotten home and now he wanted to dash off on some fool mission he just thought of. It was inconsiderate of the captain to call so late— or rather, so early. It was hardly three A.M., Geneva time.

The sergeant exhaled through his nostrils before taking a long gulp of the sugary coffee. The jolt of caffeine would hit

76

soon. He yearned for it, wanting the sleep gone from his eyes and his sluggish mind.

Riker would be true to his blood, giving his life for his nieces if that's what duty called for. He didn't have to see them for that to tug at his heartstrings.

His Star Watch family, though, that was different. He believed in duty to country and unit. Even more, he believed in helping his military family.

The voyages in Starship *Victory* had forged an unbreakable bond between Captain Maddox, Lieutenant Valerie Noonan, Second Lieutenant Keith Maker, Dr. Dana Rich, Meta, Galyan the AI and himself, Sergeant Treggason Riker. They were family in the best sense of the word, struggling against the universe as a team.

Riker did not get teary-eyed over the concept. He was a military man who had fought with his family. He might present a dour face to most people. Others might think of him as a gruff old man, but the central focus of his ideals led him to view the crew of *Victory* as his family through thick and thin. If that was a cliché older than the hills of Earth, so be it. Riker never wanted to let the captain down, never wanted the man's death on his hands because he hadn't done his best.

But damn it, sometimes the captain made things difficult because he raced here and sprinted there as he tried to solve impossible puzzles. Sometimes, one had to lie down and go to sleep like a normal person.

Why did Maddox get into so many strange predicaments? It was enough to make a philosopher out of the sergeant.

He crumpled the empty cup and shoved it into the dispenser. Then, he adjusted the controls one more time, bringing the flitter onto the roof where Captain Maddox paced.

***

Riker peered at the captain in disbelief, having just heard his instructions.

Maddox appeared not to notice the scrutiny. Finally, the captain looked up. "Is there a problem, Sergeant?"

"The Mid-Atlantic, sir, in the flitter?"

"We've made the trip before."

"Yes…but Dr. Rich will be asleep when we reach there."

"No matter," Maddox said.

"Couldn't you just call her, sir?"

"I don't see how."

"The place is restricted, I realize that. Do you have permission to enter—?"

"Sergeant, you handle your end of the matter and I'll handle mine."

Riker hesitated just a moment longer. "Yes, sir," he said.

The dome slid shut, the engine purred and the flitter lifted from the roof of the apartment building.

"Wake me when we're a hundred kilometers from the landing site," the captain said.

"You're going to sleep, sir?"

"Are you tired?"

"I'm exhausted, sir. The trip from Shanghai took it out of me."

"I suggest you switch on the autopilot and take a catnap."

"I can't do that, sir. I drank an express cup of Java."

"That's a pity," Maddox said, crossing his arms and leaning against his side. Almost immediately, the man fell into a rhythmic breathing pattern.

He's asleep, Riker realized with frustration. The sergeant thought about putting the flitter onto autopilot, but he didn't trust the flight mechanism. Maybe in a bigger ship, it would be all right. For this little air-car, he preferred to keep at the controls.

For a couple of hundred kilometers, Riker stared out of the canopy. Far beneath them, Europe slid past.

As the air-car darted over the Atlantic, Riker yawned. Despite the shock of caffeine, he was dead tired. His eyelids had become heavy.

Maddox continued to sleep.

Riker put a comm-jack in his left ear and a sub-vocalizer onto his throat. Then, he turned on the comm, sending a signal to *Victory*. The ancient Adok starship was in Earth orbit. A tech crew was aboard the starship working under Lieutenant Noonan's direction. She guarded the scientists prowling through the vessel, keeping Galyan company and calming him when the AI became mulish over something.

"Hello," Riker said so softly he couldn't hear the words himself. He didn't want to wake the captain.

"Sergeant Riker," Galyan said in his robotic voice. "It is good to hear from you."

"Likewise, I'm sure," Riker said.

"You are with Captain Maddox, I see."

"We're heading to the Mid-Atlantic."

"I suspect you are going to visit the doctor. I should inform you that she is in a restricted area."

"That's why I'm calling," Riker said.

"I do not possess clearance powers," Galyan said.

"I know," Riker said. He also knew the alien AI had a fantastically powerful deductive probability analyzer. "I'm wondering why the captain plans to go there without preapproval."

"You should ask him."

"He might tell me to mind my own business," Riker said.

"Would that bother you?"

"Not at all," the sergeant muttered.

"One moment, please," Galyan said. "Ah. Is that a joke?"

Riker felt himself redden.

"One moment," Galyan said. "Oh. I believe you just lied to me, Sergeant."

"Now, see here, Galyan. You have no right—"

"It is possible that you just lied to yourself. Why does the captain's possible censure trouble you?"

"Galyan."

"Am I intruding into areas I should not?" the robotic voice asked.

Riker peered out of the canopy. He had a strange family, all right. Sometimes, he wondered if he would have been happier working with normal Intelligence people.

"I will work on the clearance for you," Galyan said.

"I don't want you to—"

"It is my way of apologizing to you for intruding where I should have left things alone."

79

"I just thought of something," Riker said. "You can track us, right?"

"Of course," Galyan said. "I have been doing so since I took your call."

"Were you tracking the captain during his time in Shanghai?"

"Lieutenant Noonan said I must respect people's privacy. Therefore, I was not."

"I agree with her," Riker said. "But…there's something odd going on. I want you to track the captain for the next few days."

"I am supposed to inform him of that first," Galyan said.

"Even if we're trying to throw a surprise party for him?" Riker asked.

"Valerie did not tell me of this party."

"Oh," Riker said. "That's right. I wasn't supposed to tell you."

"Why not? Have I done something to upset the captain?"

Riker shook his head. Why couldn't the AI make this easy? The Adok artificial intelligence asked too many questions.

"Galyan, would you just do this for me? I'll explain later."

"Yes, Sergeant, I will continue to track the captain. Would you like me to continue to track you, as well?"

"Yes," Riker said. He thought about the captain's androids and the brigadier's order to have Maddox examined to make sure he was still human. If the enemy had struck at the captain, might he strike at a lowly sergeant too? If an android took his place, it would be an easy matter to capture the captain—well, an easier matter, at least.

At that moment, the flitter's engine simply cut out. It must have affected the batteries, too. The comm-unit quit. The air-car lost its motive flight with the loss of power. It plowed ahead a short distance due to momentum. Then, the flitter began to plummet toward the ocean.

-8-

Riker didn't shout or frantically test switches. For a moment, he just stared at the dead board. There was no question, the flitter's electronics had stopped working.

The sergeant glanced outside. They were up a ways, so he had several seconds to get the machine working again. Methodically, he began the initiation procedure, which did nothing positive.

For another second, Riker sat still, debating if he should wake the captain or not. Maddox slept soundly so far. That would change soon, as the atmosphere outside began to whistle past the dome.

There was a soft jar, although nothing came on inside. The flitter's nose lifted as the air-car continued its flight path but without any internal power. The dash was as dark as ever.

The sergeant's brow furrowed. How could the flitter be flying—oh, right, Galyan must be using a tractor beam from orbit. The AI could do more than simply pull a craft closer, but used the tractor beam to guide the flitter.

Muttering under his breath, Riker pried open the panel. It took him fifteen minutes of sweaty, delicate work, but he found a strange little timer where one shouldn't be. Hmmm, if he—

"Don't touch that," Maddox said.

The sergeant grunted, lurching back, surprised at the captain's voice.

Maddox glanced outside, at the dark dash and then at the sergeant. "You managed to contact Galyan, I take it."

81

"Yes, sir," Riker muttered.

Maddox frowned. "You must have contacted him before the event."

"Right again, sir."

Maddox nodded. He took a small penlight from a pocket, clicked it on and shined it on the tiny timer in the electronics.

"Do you know what that is, sir?"

"Another complexity," the captain said. "Did you take the flitter to the shop after our Asia flight?"

"That's standard procedure, sir, especially after a cross-country jaunt from Shanghai to Geneva."

"Then we must presume someone hostile to Star Watch had access to the craft while in the garage. Meaning, this was an inside job. Ah, look at this."

Riker leaned forward, peering at the tiny device.

"Did you see the dot on top?" Maddox asked.

"I do, sir."

"That is the activation mechanism."

"It's unlit, sir."

"The timer must have absorbed energy from the flitter's electronics. It's a kill-switch. The lack of energy also deactivated the timer."

"I'd gathered as much, sir."

"Does Galyan know our destination?"

"He does, sir."

Maddox pursed his lips. "Give me the gist of what you told Galyan."

Riker did so.

Maddox studied him afterward, making the sergeant uneasy. "From now on, Sergeant, you will inform me if you put any spy systems onto me, including Galyan."

"I'll try my best, sir."

"That isn't a reassuring answer."

"I suspect not, sir," Riker said, who heartily disliked his secret orders. They explicitly said he could not reveal them to the captain.

"What is it?" Maddox asked. "What's wrong?"

"Nothing, sir," Riker said.

Maddox fixed those strange eyes on him and gave him a level stare.

The sergeant could feel the captain's mind spinning. The man had an uncanny ability to come up with answers.

A hint of a frown appeared on the captain's face. "I see," Maddox said.

Riker swallowed uneasily. The captain couldn't have logically figured out the secret orders, could he?

Maddox turned away, tapping a finger against a knee. "I'm still on the list, am I?"

"List, sir?" Riker asked.

"Hmmm, you've been sworn to secrecy, I presume. Yet…the secret command troubles you. That's small comfort. How am I supposed to…?"

"Sir?" Riker asked.

"Never mind," Maddox said. "You shall carry on as ordered and I will do my duty to Star Watch as my conscience dictates."

Riker knew the lad as well as anyone did. While the sergeant didn't have exalted brainpower like Ludendorff and Dana Rich, he was experienced in human nature. The secret order cut against Maddox, wounding him, although the captain would never admit it to anyone. He was a proud young officer. Maddox was also a loner by inclination and circumstance. His hybrid nature hadn't done him any favors in this regard.

"Are you with me, Sergeant?" Maddox asked softly.

Riker knew what the captain was asking. "One hundred percent, sir," he said.

"Even if…" Maddox left the question unasked.

"Yes, sir," Riker said, "even if."

Maddox nodded curtly. He couldn't show anyone how much the answer meant to him. "Then, let us proceed." He regarded the kill-switch timer with a penlight in one hand and a small caliper in another. Delicately, the captain reached in and plucked the sabotage device out of the interior dash system.

"Take this," Maddox said, handing Riker the penlight.

Riker shined the narrow beam on the spot.

Maddox reached in and twisted several loose wires together.

The flitter shuddered. The engine kicked on and lights reappeared on the dash.

The captain tapped the comm-unit and made an adjustment. It crackled into life.

"Galyan," Maddox said.

"I have analyzed the situation, Captain," the robotic voice said. "You are a victim of sabotage."

"Thank you,' Maddox said. "I have taken care of the situation. You may release us from your tractor beam."

"Yes, Captain."

"And Galyan," Maddox said.

"Sir?"

"Thank you for your quick action. It saved our lives. We're indebted to you."

"It was my pleasure," Galyan said. The AI paused before adding, "I am eager to renew our adventures. Earth orbit has become unbearably tedious. This episode tonight shows me I should be engaged in hot action, using my rarified abilities to defeat humanity's enemies."

"I'll keep that in mind," Maddox said.

"That is the best thanks of all then," Galyan said. "Do you wish me to begin analyzing possible suspects?"

"I do," Maddox said.

"Wonderful. Thank you, sir. It will help relieve the tedium of listening to the scientists rhapsodize about my past. It is not what I have done which interests me, but what I'm going to do in the future."

"Uh, Galyan," Riker asked. "Have you gained clearance for us yet?"

"I was just about to tell you. Dr. Rich has surfaced and left for Geneva. She is on a supersonic flight. I would suggest this means Dana has found evidence of past alien intrusion on Earth. I would love to ingest her data. Do you think I could listen in to her briefing?"

Riker sat back with a groan, massaging his eyes. He couldn't believe this. Dana had left for Geneva? He could have been home asleep the whole time.

"Turn us around, Sergeant," Maddox said.

"To Geneva, sir?" Riker asked.

"Exactly."

The sergeant hesitated, waiting for the captain to tell him he was sorry for having interrupting the sergeant's sleep time.

Maddox did no such thing. Instead, the captain leaned his head back against the bubble canopy and closed his eyes, falling almost instantly asleep.

Muttering to himself, Riker adjusted the flight path, heading back for Europe. He might even have turned on the autopilot and gone to sleep, but thinking about what Dana had uncovered kept him too edgy. Was Galyan right? Had the good doctor found real evidence of past aliens on humanity's home planet? Had the Builders been here in ancient times? Riker wanted to get to Geneva and find out the news.

-9-

Dr. Dana Rich stared out of the jet's window. It was bright morning in Western Europe, the sunlight bathing the beautiful Alps.

She had just woken up from a light slumber, having made the trip from the Mid-Atlantic in a little over an hour.

The doctor wore a red jacket and had let her dark hair cascade past her shoulders. It was presently tousled from her sleep.

Dana was in her late thirties and strikingly beautiful with brown skin and dark eyes. Born on Earth in Bombay, India, she had emigrated to the Indian Brahma System with her parents. A few years later, she had been the smartest student in the university system there, a girl in a world filled with boys. She had fled Brahma in the company of Professor Ludendorff, having lived with him on Brahma, creating a scandal for her family. The affair had ended in time and Dana had found herself back in the Brahma System. There, she had worked for the secret service against the Rigel Social Syndicate, a neighboring star system. Dana had been a clone thief, caught by Star Watch in the end and sent down to Loki Prime, the worst of the Commonwealth's prison planets. Captain Maddox had rescued her because he'd needed her services. For what she had done to help bring back *Victory* from the Beyond, Star Watch had pardoned her of crimes.

She had led the science team the first time in the Oort cloud studying *Victory*. After the professor, Dana knew more about the ancient starship than anyone else did. Because of her intellect and daring, she had uncovered old ship systems in *Victory* that had gone a long way to defeating the alien Destroyer in the Solar System.

Since then, she had spent many hours trying to uncover yet more deactivated Adok ship systems. Finally, having found nothing like her previous discovery, she had asked to work on the Alien Project in the Atlantic.

Star Watch had reluctantly agreed. They were much more concerned with finding solutions to present problems than reconstructing the past. But Dana had insisted on the work, and given her previous successes, Star Watch had agreed.

Dana had a different philosophy on the importance of the past than most others did. In her opinion, humanity knew too little about the Builders. Galyan had given some new data, but that had been sketchy. The mechanical people, as Galyan called the Builders, had aided the ancient Adoks against the Swarm, but they had remained mysterious to them, preferring to work in the shadows. In the end, Galyan had given them more Adok legends and myths than facts about the Builders.

The Builders were a mystery indeed. Surely, they could not have begun as cybernetic beings. They must have been fully biological at one time. So far, though, the evidence had proved otherwise.

From what Dana could tell, the Builders had been watchers, dabbling with the Adoks and humanity, constructing the silver pyramids but having no known planets. They had fought the ancient aliens who had made Destroyers and they seemed to have disliked the strange Swarm.

As Dana sat in the seat, she rubbed her hands in anticipation of the coming meeting. Yes, she was concerned about the greater war against the New Men. She also feared Strand, realizing he might be the greatest danger of all. Yet, like the professor, ancient aliens absorbed her intellect.

That was why she had gone to the bottom of the sea in the Mid-Atlantic to join the Atlantis Project, the new name for the Alien Project.

What they had found down there…it was amazing if one looked at it the right way. Could she help convince the Star

Watch oversight board that the scientists down in the Mid-Atlantic needed more funds and equipment?

***

Two hours later, Dana stood before a lectern, fingering a data chip. The oversight officers would appear soon. Over a comm, she had finally convinced them of the need for an emergency meeting.

Jotting notes on a piece of paper, she was in the process of deciding on the precise wording of her opening monologue. "Hit them between the eyes from the beginning." Dana liked to say, "Grab them by the nose and twist if you have to." That kept people awake no matter what they really believed.

The nose grab, in her opinion, was the Atlantis Project. Real buildings and artifacts existed down there, alien in nature. She suspected the Builders had constructed an Earth base in the distant past. If the scientists could dig deeper, Dana expected to extract ancient Builder technology. That was the nose twist. In the war against the New Men, each new tech could be the piece that turned the tide of the war fully in the Commonwealth's favor.

The similarities she'd seen down on the sea floor compared to other Builder tech she'd seen—they were very similar. Now it was true that most of the others in the Atlantis Project disagreed with her analysis, but that was because they were fools. They shied from the truth because the implications could upset their pet theories about human development.

What if humanity was a special project of the Builders? What if the world's religions all went back to shadowy remembrances of the alien cybernetic organisms? That would upset the main religions, but what did Dana care about that? She wanted to get to the truth, not continue to follow ancient myths.

Hmmm, what if she began her monologue like this? Dana began scribbling the idea on paper.

A door opened as she wrote. She looked up with a scowl. The meeting wasn't supposed to start for another half hour. She needed the time—

"Captain Maddox," Dana said, surprised.

"Hello, Doctor," the captain said a bit breathlessly. Had he been running?

"Sergeant Riker," Dana said with a smile. The older man panted, coming through the door behind Maddox. "It's good to see you two scoundrels. Have you come to hear my report?"

Maddox stared at her before saying, "When will we see the New Hindu Kish again?"

It took a second. Then, Dana's eyelids fluttered. She exhaled as if the captain had just punched her in the stomach. She took several steps back, rubbing her stomach, as her features stiffened. It felt as if all the air seeped out of her lungs. She grew faint and it seemed as if she was falling backward.

The next thing she realized, she was sitting on a chair with Maddox peering at her from another.

"What…?" Her mouth was dry. She frowned, looking up at the lectern. The last thing she remembered was standing behind it. How had she gotten here?

"Did I faint?" she asked.

"No," Maddox said, "but you were vacant-eyed for several seconds. I helped you sit down. Do you recall the saying?"

The words slammed home again, "When will we see the New Hindu Kish again?" How dare the captain speak such words to her? They were some of the most intimate words Ludendorff and she had ever shared. The last time Ludendorff had spoken them—

She straightened. "Where is he?" she asked, hope flaring in her heart.

"Excuse me?" Maddox asked.

"Don't play dumb with me, Captain. I know you know what I mean. It's clear you've spoken to Ludendorff. I demand to know what else he told you." Dana glared at him. "He gave you those words. No one else could possibly know them. He told you to tell me in order for there to be no doubt it was him. He wants me to go to him, is that it? Where is he? I demand you tell me this instant."

"I see," Maddox said quietly. "He spoke the truth. It really was Ludendorff. That changes the equation."

"Captain," she said in a warning tone.

Maddox studied her. She hated when he did that. "I spoke with a holoimage of Ludendorff." The captain proceeded to tell her of the holoimage claiming to be her ex-lover. At the end of the story, Maddox waited.

"What am I supposed to say to that?" she asked.

"Was the holoimage from the professor?"

"Yes, without a doubt," she said.

"Could...an enemy have subdued the professor, forced the engrams into an AI unit and then cataloged the needed secrets via machine?"

"You have a suspicious turn of mind," she said.

"I am an Intelligence officer when all is said and done."

"Are you implying Strand did this?" she asked.

"He seems like an obvious candidate or a Builder."

Dana looked away. "I don't think it was a Builder."

"Your evidence being...what?"

"According to my studies on the Atlantis Project, the Builders were exceptionally peaceful. They abhorred violence."

"Yet they developed weapons and fought wars," Maddox said.

"Your first assumption is correct. I do not agree with the second."

"They used proxies then," Maddox said. "Their minds still guided the conflict."

"I believe you are wrong again," Dana said.

Maddox grew thoughtful. Finally, he shook his head. "The evidence does not support you."

"The more I find out about the Builders," Dana said, "the more I believe that other species bewildered them with their bents toward violence."

Maddox continued to stare at her. Abruptly, he stood.

"Where are you going?" she asked.

"It's time I laid this before the brigadier. We need *Victory* and we need to hurry to the Xerxes System. I have to reach the professor before whoever set the timer in my flitter reaches Ludendorff first."

"What do you mean?" she asked.

Maddox disappeared through the door without answering.

Riker glanced at her and then at the door. The sergeant jumped to his feet, waved goodbye and ran after the captain.

-10-

"No!" Brigadier O'Hara said. "It's out of the question. Absolutely not."

Maddox sat in her office in front of a synthi-wood desk. He had just finished explaining his encounter with the holoimage, the reaction of Dana Rich to 'When will we see the New Hindu Kish again?' and had made his request to take *Victory* to the Xerxes System and rescue the professor.

"Excuse me, please," O'Hara said in a softer tone. "I did not mean to shout at you." She patted her gray hair and straightened her uniform. "You...you surprised me, Captain. Surely, you can see this is a trick to lure you and *Victory* to the Xerxes System."

"That was my initial response as well, Ma'am. Dana's reaction has changed my mind."

"Well, it hasn't changed mine."

"If you could have seen her—"

"That doesn't matter," O'Hara said. "Your first suspicion was the correct one. Frankly, I'm surprised at you. Isn't it obvious someone wishes to isolate *Victory* in a possibly hostile star system?"

"Star Watch sent a flotilla under Port Admiral Hayes. If anyone could have cleared out the ancient drones—"

"Yes, yes, old Admiral Hayes is as clever as they come," O'Hara said. "But this is the Xerxes System, a notorious star system that everyone has avoided for decades. It's legendary in its danger. Hayes has orders to proceed with extreme caution.

It's likely his flotilla is at the outer edge of the system, still collecting data on possible enemy star cruisers."

"*Victory* can help him," Maddox said.

"The Lord High Admiral doesn't want *Victory* anywhere near any conflict for the near future. We must discover ways to duplicate the starship's disrupter beam. So far, that has eluded our best people."

"This could be critical," Maddox said.

"In this, I can't agree with you. Critical is having an alien Destroyer readying its beam to annihilate Earth. Critical is a New Men armada about to obliterate the last mobile Star Watch fleet. Freeing Ludendorff does not fall into that category."

"I think you're wrong, Ma'am. Ludendorff knows more than anyone except for Strand."

"Exactly," the Iron Lady said. "Ludendorff may be too dangerous to rescue. He may have sent the Ludendorff android in his place. Why did he use androids to kidnap you in Shanghai?"

"He said for secrecy's sake."

O'Hara made an uncharacteristically rude noise. "Captain, I believe whoever used the holoimage is playing on your overactive curiosity. That means we must do exactly the opposite of what they're suggesting."

"That seems far too timid," Maddox said.

"Perhaps it does to the man who knowingly drinks drugged Mickeys."

Maddox sat back, surprised at her vehemence. "Maybe we should ask the Lord High Admiral his opinion."

"Oh, that is neatly done, sir," O'Hara said. "You are trying to jump over my head in my presence. I do not appreciate that in the slightest."

Maddox licked his lips. He had never seen O'Hara so worked up about an issue.

The Iron Lady stood, putting her fingertips on the desk, scrutinizing him coldly. Slowly, her shoulders deflated. She slumped back into her chair and swiveled around.

Maddox was more confused than ever.

A minute later, she turned back. Her eyes had become red-rimmed.

"Ma'am," Maddox said with concern. "Are you well?"

"You're a foolish young man, do you know that?"

Maddox did not know how to answer that.

"You run off on an outrageous quest, return with a magnificent starship, leave again and defeat an alien Destroyer against all reasonable odds. Some might say, 'Let Captain Maddox go and do another mythic feat.' I say, 'The odds have become too long. One of these times, events will overpower your good luck and you'll die.' Do you want to die, Captain Maddox?"

"I do not," he said.

"There's your answer," she said.

"But—"

"Someone has to shield you from your foolhardy desires to race off into danger. We will not go see the Lord High Admiral. This holoimage is a lethal trap meant to take you away forever. I know. I can…"

"You can what, Ma'am?"

"This may sound theatrical to you, Captain. But I can feel it in my heart that if you leave, you will never return. I…I do not wish that on my conscience."

Maddox sat stock still, finally understanding the nature of her refusal. She did not want to risk him again. For some unknown reason, that tightened his throat. Even so, he forced out words:

"If the Xerxes System is that dangerous," Maddox said, "Port Admiral Hayes needs reinforcements. Starship *Victory* is the perfect vessel for the strange system. You know that's true, Ma'am. I feel the Lord High Admiral would agree with me. I think you realize he would too, which is why you don't want to ask him."

"I realize no such thing," O'Hara said.

"We can't afford to have such a dangerous star system so near Earth," Maddox said. "It's eighty-three light-years in eleven jumps using the Laumer-Points."

"I'm well aware of the distance, Captain."

"Ma'am, I'm touched by your concern regarding me. I appreciate it."

"I don't believe that. Therefore, I ask you to prove me wrong by listening to me. What is the old saying? *Actions speak louder than words.*"

"I realize that. But Ludendorff has proved critical time and again. We desperately need the man's knowledge. I know you know that. He has the location of the Throne World. That in itself is worth the risk."

The brigadier sat quietly, ingesting the news, finally saying, "That is important. Very well, we can send someone else to fetch him."

"There is no one else who will succeed in this but me and Starship *Victory.*"

The Iron Lady put both hands on the desk. The redness in her eyes had departed. "You think this is strictly emotional on my part. I assure you that isn't so. I have studied the signs and listened carefully to your tale. I think a Builder lies behind this. You have sparked their interest in you."

"Ma'am, that's far too fanciful."

"No," O'Hara said. "I have read Dr. Rich's report, the one she is giving now. I agree with her that the signs down in the Mid-Atlantic show the Builders walked the Earth in our early history. The pyramids are the last example of their presence. Perhaps more interestingly, the lost city of Atlantis is their fallen abode."

"I'm unfamiliar with the topic."

O'Hara shook her head. "Captain, this is a dangerous moment in human history. It could be a fulcrum point. Pressure applied at the wrong spot could tip the balance the wrong way. These past few years we have survived amazing shocks. The New Men appeared out of the Beyond, smashing our fleets and conquering our planets. You found the great antidote—an ancient alien starship of unique technologies. This starship you used with utmost skill, allowing Admiral Fletcher to save half of Fifth Fleet while smashing the New Men's invasion armada. After that, Star Watch had a fighting chance against the demoralizing and frightening foe, superior to us in every way. But no, another shock appeared, the alien Destroyer. It burned to the bedrock every planet in the New Arabia System, destroying the heart of the Wahhabi Caliphate and annihilating the bulk of their war fleet. The Destroyer swept away an easy quarter of humanity's fighting ships—meaning we were going to have a much harder time attacking the New Men. Fortunately, the Windsor League and others have joined us in a grand crusade against the enemy. It's still possible we can defeat the mysterious supermen hiding in the Beyond. Knowing the location of the Throne World...I agree that is vital to our war effort, but other Intelligence operatives can hurry to the Xerxes System and inform Hayes."

"That's quite the speech, Ma'am."

"I'm not finished," she said. "There is one deadly ingredient in all this that frightens me terribly: Strand. The ancient Methuselah Man is deceptive beyond anything I've experienced. He is ultimately devious, and I believe you frighten him. Now, why is that, Captain?"

Maddox said nothing, not sure where she was taking this.

"You have thwarted Strand several times, a feat almost beyond measure. We have discovered that *he* created the Methuselah People and *he* created the New Men. Why has Strand done these things?"

"We know why, Ma'am."

"I don't agree. I think we *know* what he wants us to believe."

"No. I think we uncovered the truth. Strand did these things because he believes there are alien species out there—the Swarm in particular—that could annihilate humanity. The Methuselah People and the New Men were his way of improving the species so we could face the terrible enemy."

"Strand is evil, Captain. I know because he sent the alien Destroyer against Earth. That was a monstrous crime. He will do anything he can to win, not to save humanity."

"Why then?"

"*That* is the question we need to solve. We have a breathing space. The New Men, and Strand with them—whether in conjunction or not, I don't think anyone on our side knows. In any case, they used up their sleeper cells on Earth. For the first time, we are united, without Strand's agents working against us. Humanity must close its fist, as the saying goes, and strike hammer blows against the right target. We must no longer slap our enemies in the face with an open hand, merely stinging them to greater action."

"So far, I agree with your analysis."

"When we strike the decisive blow, we will need *Victory*. Even better, would be ten *Victorys* and even better than that would be one hundred."

"There's no question about that," Maddox said.

"The Commonwealth and Windsor League have superior industrial might compared to the New Men. We must use that, out-producing our genetic enemy. Yet would it not be even better to out-produce them with superior ships?"

"It would indeed."

"That is why we must keep *Victory* in Earth orbit as we laboriously attempt to reverse engineer the ancient weapon systems. If I had my way, we would tear the starship apart piece by piece. The survival of human existence might well depend on it."

"I can't agree to that, Ma'am."

"I know you can't. You're too invested in *Victory*, almost as if you think it's a living thing."

"It is a living thing," Maddox said.

"Driving Force Galyan is a machine, nothing more."

"I respectfully disagree. But that aside, if you know my thoughts, why say all this to me?"

O'Hara sighed. "I've begun to understand you better, young man. You yearn to race into danger with *Victory*. It's exciting, challenging, and it rewards your pride by having others heap accolades upon you for a job well done."

"That is not why I've done those things, Ma'am."

"It's possible you don't consciously realize it, but it's true nonetheless."

Instead of becoming angry, Maddox grew thoughtful. "Suppose you're right about me. What difference does that make to rescuing Ludendorff? Don't we owe it to the man to get him back?"

"Not necessarily," O'Hara said, "not if the cost is too high."

Maddox grew silent.

"This is bigger than emotive responses," the Iron Lady told him. "Until now, I have agreed with your desperate actions. Our plight was too awful for anything else. Now—"

Maddox sat forward sharply. "Do you watch football, Ma'am?"

"I do not. It is a deplorable sport, far too violent to no reasonable purpose."

"It engages the emotions, certainly, and it's filled with strategy."

"Violent strategies that force young men into far too violent of collisions," O'Hara said.

"That may well be," Maddox said. "However, it offers us a fitting example. Football games are intense contests that often rise and fall due to momentum. Consider the situation where a team is losing and becomes desperate. The coach sends in a few trick plays along with possible long bomb maneuvers. A few of the plays work, the team scores and the momentum of the game shifts their way. Soon, the formerly losing team is winning. Now, however, time is running out and the coach wishes to hang onto his lead. What does he do? He plays preventive defense and makes tepid offensive calls. The other team takes heart and attempts a few trick plays of their own. All of a sudden, the momentum shifts again, and the preventive coach causes his team to lose the game."

"Are you suggesting I'm saying we play preventive defense?" O'Hara asked.

"I'm afraid I am, Ma'am. We have gotten where we are by being bold, not by playing it safe."

"There is a time to protect our winnings, Captain."

"Undoubtedly," Maddox said. "This is not one of them, though. We have two enemies, at least. One of them is the New Men. We have sent Admiral Fletcher to liberate the captured planets of "C" Quadrant. At the same time, we have united regular humanity and begun massed production of warships. That is the correct strategy. You've pointed out a possibly more dangerous foe; Strand. What is the antidote to him? More knowledge. Professor Ludendorff can give us that knowledge. Therefore, we must rescue him at all costs. Strand knows this, and is likely doing everything in his power to stop us. That is why I must take *Victory* to the Xerxes System and free Ludendorff from the Builder traps."

O'Hara sat back. "You have presented a powerful argument, Captain."

Maddox knew when to keep quiet.

"In such a case, where we both feel so strongly, going to the Lord High Admiral seems logical."

Maddox still said nothing. He admired the Iron Lady. One of the things he loved about her was her ability to see the argument even when she didn't want to.

"Yes," she said, leaning forward, clicking on her intercom. "This is difficult for me to do. I hope you realize this."

"I do," Maddox said quietly.

"Major Stokes," O'Hara said.

"Yes, Ma'am," Stokes said out of the intercom.

"Could you send in the Marines, please?"

"At once, Ma'am," Stokes said.

O'Hara removed her finger from the switch. "I'm going to have to ask for your sidearm, Captain."

He nodded, taking out his pistol and setting it on the desk. "Is the Lord High Admiral in a restricted area?" he asked.

The door opened and three combat Marines in body-armor stepped through.

"You misunderstand the situation," O'Hara said. "You're not going to see the Lord High Admiral."

"But—"

"I hate to do this, but I know what you would likely do, which is to take *Victory* on your own initiative. Since Galyan listens to you, I'm going to have to put you into temporary confinement. The starship must stay in Earth orbit for the near future. I hope you can forgive me, Captain. In the end, this is for your own protection."

Maddox glanced at the Marines, their hard stares and readiness to act. He suspected there were more of them in the outer office. Even if he could overpower these three, the others would swamp him. He regarded the Iron Lady. There was a reason why she'd gained the nickname.

"You're making a mistake, Ma'am. We need the professor. If I don't leave now, we may never have another chance."

"I'll see you in several weeks. Goodbye, Captain. I dearly hope you don't take this too hard."

O'Hara opened a drawer and swept the service pistol into it, shutting the drawer with a snap.

One of the Marines put a gloved hand on Maddox's shoulder. "If you'll come with me, sir," the man said in a gruff voice.

Maddox glanced once more at the Iron Lady. She studiously scribbled a note, seemingly absorbed with the writing.

Suddenly angry, the captain shook his shoulder free of the Marine's grip.

The three combat men stiffened while the Iron Lady looked up.

With his gaze on the ceiling as he struggled to maintain his decorum, Maddox stood at attention and gave the stiffest salute of his life. Then, he spun around and marched out of the office.

Belatedly, the Marines hurried after him.

-11-

Seventeen days after capturing the Windsor League hammership, Pa Kur received a signal from Strand.

The Methuselah Man was in the Inferno System with him, but Pa Kur hadn't realized it until this moment.

The New Man ordered his sept into action. They began to maneuver the unwieldy vessel from behind Inferno III, a hot world of seething equatorial lava with jungle poles where empty settlements stood. Transports had vacated the planet's sub-men over a year ago already.

Pa Kur sat in the hammership's command chair. Over the past seventeen days he had made a detailed study of the vessel. The reports had left via shuttle, giving the rest of the invasion armada's commanders a better understanding of the Windsor League battlewagon's strengths and weaknesses. The hammership had plenty of both—not that either would come into play this time.

Strand's present plan was more subtle than that.

"Commander," the comm specialist, an Eleventh Ranked New Man, said. "The enemy is near."

Pa Kur did not say a word in reply.

Strand had ordered them behind Inferno III five days ago, at least behind in relation to the system's Laumer-Points. The Methuselah Man had used his cloaked vessel to invaluable ends, often studying the various enemy formations in different star systems without their knowledge. Strand's star cruiser had an extra propulsion system allowing it to make stellar jumps without the need of wormholes. He'd never shared this movement system with anyone else. It seemed to Pa Kur that the Emperor should demand the secret from Strand. If the rest of the armada possessed the ability to jump without using Laumer-Points...

Pa Kur's shoulders twitched. Obviously, the great Strand kept his secret for a reason. Together with the superior cloaking, it made the Methuselah Man invaluable. Without him, the armada would have a much harder time keeping watch over the Grand Fleet's careful maneuvers without being seen in return.

The Grand Fleet had bunched up for two weeks after losing the hammership. Now, they had begun to loosen their advance again, spreading out once more. The first time, Strand had given the enemy time to enjoy the privilege. This time, he would snap a trap shut.

"They're accelerating, Commander," the comm specialist said.

Pa Kur could see that for himself. He also knew his orders and the plan. Possibly, Strand expected him to have told his sept what the plan was. Pa Kur had not done so for a particular reason. Subhumans reacted favorably to a person with wizardly foreknowledge. He wanted to see how far that translated with those of the superior race.

"We will remain where we are," Pa Kur said.

The others on the bridge ingested the news in silence. They did not openly turn to each other, as sub-men would have done. Instead, they glanced slyly at each other, possibly attempting to assess each other's reactions before commenting.

"The enemy vessels are building momentum, Commander," the comm specialist said.

"You are perceptive," Pa Kur said, adding a subtle note of mockery to his tone.

The comm specialist stiffened his shoulders. Everyone on the bridge understood the rebuke.

The enemy vessels continued to accelerate. There were two Star Watch battleships, a carrier, six heavy cruisers and twelve destroyers. The ships were under the command of a woman named Commodore Garcia. Two years ago, she had faced them at Caria 323 and later in the Tannish System.

Strand regarded her as a clever tactician. The Methuselah Man said that would aid them here in the Inferno System.

"Commander," the warfare specialist said. "Enemy probes have passed Inferno III. The probes have begun transmitting images to the enemy flotilla. The commodore will know that we're the only ship in the system."

Pa Kur did not bother to acknowledge the statement.

The minutes passed, enough so Garcia would have received the intelligence data. Yes, her ships began to increase acceleration. No doubt, they believed they could capture the hammership or make him surrender.

"Commander," the warfare specialist said. "It is unwise to remain in orbit. We must maneuver to the inner system Laumer-Point and escape while we are able."

Pa Kur regarded the warfare specialist. The New Man wore a silver uniform with a close-combat badge on his left pectoral.

"Open channels with the flotilla's flagship," Pa Kur ordered. "I wish to warn them."

"Commander?" the warfare specialist said.

Pa Kur leaned toward the close-combat specialist. "Choose your next words with care," he warned.

The warfare specialist's lips peeled back as he stood.

Pa Kur likewise stood, staring at the other.

The warfare specialist was Ninth Ranked and would be dangerous in a hand-to-hand fight. Perhaps he recalled Pa Kur's higher status. The New Man touched his combat badge. Such symbols meant much among them, as they were hard won.

Pa Kur doubted he could outfight the other hand-to-hand. Therefore, he would not try. If it came to that, he would outmaneuver the other, sidestepping the issue.

"I am curious as to your plan," the warfare specialist said, sitting. "I await your orders, Commander."

Pa Kur turned to the comm specialist before the warfare officer saw his eyes glitter in triumph. This was a status victory, but he could not let the others see that he felt this way. That would diminish his superiority in the feat, as they would realize he saw it as a victory. A true superior would not feel that way. Thus, Pa Kur acted indifferently to the concession. The comm specialist would surely interpret the eye-glitter as the commander's eagerness to speak with the commodore.

"The channels are open," the comm specialist said.

Pa Kur sat stiffly in the command chair. He stared at the main screen. In moments, Commodore Garcia appeared.

She was a small, old woman with dark eyes and hunched shoulders. She also happened to be one of Star Watch's best strategists. It was another reason why this victory would diminish the enemy's courage another notch.

"Surrender or die," Pa Kur told her.

The transmission took several seconds to reach the enemy ships. Once she listened to his ultimatum, the commodore would have to mull over his statement, speak and wait for the transmission to reach him.

"I call on *you* to surrender, New Man," Garcia said in a sharp voice. "You have a single hammership. Thus, my vessels can easily destroy you. I know that you do not have any other ships behind Inferno III. Furthermore, I have detected no sign of life on the planet. Even if you have automated planetary cannons, they will not help you today. Decide, Invader, as I am about to launch missiles at your ship."

Pa Kur did not hesitate. "I am speaking to dead people. Remember, you had your chance. Now, your fate is upon you."

"Are there cloaked vessels with us, Commander?" the comm specialist asked.

Pa Kur kept the irritation off his features. "There is only one cloaked vessel that could remain hidden from Star Watch. Yes, it is with us."

The others on the bridge visibly relaxed.

"But Strand will do nothing to help us today," Pa Kur said.

The others looked at him with what appeared to be faint surprise. For New Men, that was like standing up and shouting their wonder.

Another transmission arrived: "I expected no less from you, New Man," Garcia said. "It is just as well. Humanity doesn't need your kind. Good-bye, Invader, your death is on your own head."

"They have launched five *Titan*-class missiles," the comm specialist said.

"That is too few," Pa Kur said.

"By the time the missiles reach us," said the warfare specialist, "our ship will be in range of the battleship's heavy lasers."

"True," Pa Kur said.

The two specialists traded glances with each other.

"I have a surprise for the sub-men," Pa Kur said. "It surprises me that neither of you has surmised that yet."

"I cannot fathom the surprise," the comm specialist admitted.

The warfare specialist thought about the problem with a furrowed brow.

On the main screen, five destroyer-sized missiles left the battleships and began to accelerate hard for the hammership.

"We must have mines," the warfare specialist said. "A new kind of mine," he added.

Pa Kur pointed at him. "That is well-reasoned."

The warfare specialist dipped his head at the compliment.

The comm specialist tapped his board furiously. "I do not detect any mines."

"I would be appalled if you had," Pa Kur said. "The mines were strewn by Strand some time ago. He analyzed the enemy commander and set the stage for her. These mines are part of the Methuselah Man's unique arsenal."

"But why plant them here, now?" the warfare specialist asked. "Such a superior tool should only be used at the maximum moment. We could have used the surprise in a larger battle where it would have given us bigger rewards."

"That, too, is well-reasoned," Pa Kur said. "However, the implication is clear. Strand only has a few of these special mines."

"All the more reason to save them for a more decisive encounter," the warfare specialist said.

"Wrong," Pa Kur said without emotion. In truth, he seethed with inner exaltation. To teach these two such a truth would gain him esteem in their eyes. They would pass this esteem to the others and cause his sept to trust him even more.

"The critical point today with these mines is not physical destruction but something more powerful," Pa Kur said. "Strand seeks to destroy their confidence by elevating our superiority to an incredible degree. They will stumble into a mine ambush and afterward believe we possess thousands of such mines. That will make them inordinately cautious everywhere."

"Ah," the warfare specialist said. "Yes, I see."

The comm specialist nodded with understanding.

Time passed. The *Titan*-class missiles reached fifty Gs acceleration.

"The commodore is hailing us again."

"Put her on," Pa Kur said.

Commodore Garcia appeared on the screen. She hunched forward to stare at him. "I will offer you one more chance to surrender."

He said nothing.

"Do not think your mines will save you," she said. "We have better sensors than you realize. We are beginning to maneuver around the hidden mines. Their blasts will brown our shields, nothing more."

The two specialists turned wordlessly to Pa Kur.

"Come," Garcia said, "why throw away your lives? Surrender to us and let us end the useless fighting."

Pa Kur motioned the comm specialist. He tapped his board. The commodore's image disappeared. In her place were the various flotilla vessels.

"Nine-Saturn-Elephant-Six-Three," Pa Kur said.

On the screen, hidden mines appeared. The Star Watch vessels indeed maneuvered around them. The mines moved through gradational forces, but they would not be able to move fast enough to put themselves anywhere near the accelerating vessels.

"Commander," the comm specialist said. "This…is a disaster."

Pa Kur nodded to himself. "Put the commodore back on the screen."

"Are we surrendering?" the comm specialist asked in a dull voice.

"Is that what you wish?" Pa Kur asked.

"No," the warfare specialist said. "We must dominate or perish. We have no other choice."

"Well?" Pa Kur asked the comm specialist.

"It has been an honor to fight for the Race," the comm specialist said.

"Well spoken," Pa Kur said. "Now, put the commodore back on the screen."

With a single tap, the comm specialist did so.

"You understand your hopelessness," Garcia said.

"Surrender or die," Pa Kur told her.

"Prides goes before the fall," Garcia said. "Have you heard that saying before?"

Pa Kur stared at her.

"A sage wrote that a long time ago," she added.

"The sage was a fool," Pa Kur said. "Good-bye, Commodore Garcia."

"Good-bye," she said, almost sounding sad.

That was strange, pity coming from a subhuman. It caused Pa Kur to shudder with revulsion. He despised pity directed at him. Only admiration would do.

"Philosopher-Eight-Star-Seven-Hippo," he said.

The images on the screen changed once more. Another set of mines appeared. These were already in the correct location.

"Commander?" the comm specialist asked.

"I have given our ship the code words that turn on the sensors we installed five days ago. Those sensors came from the Methuselah Man's star cruiser. What you see are the real and rare hidden mines. The others were there for the sub-men to find in order to make them maneuver into the correct position and to let them feel confident. Remember, it is their confidence in themselves that we are most attempting to destroy."

"Are those mines powerful enough to annihilate the flotilla?" the comm specialist asked.

"Strand believed so," Pa Kur said.

"Is the Methuselah Man always correct?"

Pa Kur paused before answering. "We know he is not always right."

Time passed. The warfare specialist targeted the approaching *Titan*-class missiles. Giant railguns fired round after round. It would take time for those rounds to reach the missiles. These were beam-firing missiles, though, and might attack before the railgun rounds destroyed them.

Pa Kur glanced at a timer. "Dampen the special sensors," he said.

The comm specialist complied. The hidden mines disappeared from the main screen, although everything else remained.

Soon, the invisible nova mines ignited. They overloaded the regular sensors, showing Pa Kur and his bridge crew expanding whiteness in space.

Titan missile beams reached them. The nova mines had been far behind the missiles. The first shield buckled, turning black. The middle shield absorbed what got through the first. More beams should have struck the shields, those from the battleships and heavy cruisers now in firing range.

"The nova mines must have worked," the warfare specialist said. The overload of the regular sensors meant they couldn't see yet what had happened to the flotilla.

"Commander," the comm specialist said. "I'm reenergizing the superior sensors.

Pa Kur nodded.

Soon, they viewed the mass debris where most of Commodore Garcia's flotilla had been. The carrier had survived along with two heavy cruisers and four destroyers. One destroyer showed severe damage, hard radiation leaking from its battered engines. All the surviving ships were in the process of changing their heading, still accelerating hard. They would sweep far past the hammership and Inferno III. No doubt, they would attempt to use Inferno I to pivot and head back to an outer Laumer-Point and eventual escape.

"Begin acceleration toward them," Pa Kur said.

"If they decelerate to fight us," the warfare specialist said, "we might be on equal footing. One Star Watch carrier, two heavy cruisers and three good destroyers should defeat a hammership."

"Even if Strand's hidden star cruiser helped us?" Pa Kur asked.

"No. We would have the advantage then. Is he going to help us?"

Pa Kur had already told them Strand would not help them. He said, "Strand's help is meaningless, as the sub-men will run away."

"I would not run if I commanded their vessels," the warfare specialist said.

"No," Pa Kur said, "but you are superior to the sheep."

It wasn't obvious at first, but the surviving ships did indeed run, and they accelerated as fast as they could. The one destroyer never made it, though, exploding seven hours after the initial mine explosion.

"Where is Strand?" the warfare specialist asked later.

"We are not attempting to destroy the last ships," Pa Kur said.

"We must whittle down the Grand Fleet ship by ship when the opportunities present themselves if we are going to win the final encounter," the warfare specialist said.

Pa Kur couldn't believe his ears. Didn't the other realize how powerful of a statement this was? The sub-men ran from a lone hammership. It showed an unwillingness to engage in battle even on superior terms. Another word for it was cowardice. The worst disease for a soldier had infected the survivors. The best option was to let the fear-carrier go to infect the rest of the ships of the Grand Fleet.

The Methuselah Man's master plan needed widespread fear in the Grand Fleet. Given enough time and enough enemy fear, Strand would give their side a miracle, one that would change the entire course of the war.

-12-

Several days later, Sergeant Riker worked in his yard. He had a small billet in the Swiss countryside, a cottage with a white picket fence.

Normally, when he was off on a mission, old Mrs. Tell kept his home clean, coming in three times a week to dust the place, cook a meal on his stove, watch a show, feed his dog and make sure the automated watering system had watered all his flowers, shrubs and trees.

One thing Riker detested was coming home to an unlived-in house, one that felt empty and devoid of life. He loved the feeling of normality in his house, that people consistently used the place. Since he so seldom was here, it had become even more of a fetish to him.

The sergeant wore work clothes and dug a hole for a new tree. He carefully piled the dirt to the side. Once the hole was the correct depth and width, he laid the store-bought tree onto its side and worked the dirt and root system out of the plastic pot. He crumpled the solid-packed dirt so the roots could breathe. Then, he set the tree in the hole, used his hands to shovel dirt beside it and finally reversed his shovel, using the handle to poke and tap the dirt tight. He shoved some growth-sticks into the soil afterward so the new tree would have plenty of nutrients.

Standing, feeling a crick in his back, Riker eased his torso straighter. While dusting his hands, he admired the new tree, a poplar. Once he put the new drip-line into place, everything would be set. Yes, the poplar would definitely add to the cottage's charm.

Riker turned to grab the spade, and stopped in shock.

An apparition flickered into appearance. It faded before solidifying, a perfect holoimage of Professor Ludendorff. He could see through the image to the back door fifteen feet away.

"Sergeant Riker," the holoimage said, using the professor's tone just as Riker remembered it.

"What do you want?" the sergeant asked.

"We need to talk."

Riker shook his head. "Go see the captain. I'm not interested in anything you have to say."

"Where is the captain?"

Riker shrugged. He had no idea. The young man had simply disappeared several days ago. It wasn't like Maddox most of the time. The captain could at least have given him a hint about what was going on.

"You don't know where he is, do you?" the holoimage asked.

"I suppose I don't," Riker said. "What is that to you?"

"Aren't you interested in what you don't know?"

Riker puzzled out the meaning before shaking his head.

The holoimage appeared annoyed at the answer.

Riker couldn't help it, but he grinned. The professor had grated on him. The man had been too smug by far. It seemed the holoimage was indeed a replica of the professor. Riker could see how it could have convinced the captain of its genuineness.

"I've come to you because I believe your captain has been taken into protective custody," the holoimage said.

Riker rolled that over in his mind. He hadn't thought of that. Could it be true?

"How do you keep track of the captain's comings and goings?" the sergeant asked.

"Does it matter?"

"Of course it matters," Riker said. "I'd also like to know how you knew where to find me."

"I astonish you by coming to your house to see if you're home?" the professor asked. "Why would that be surprising?"

111

Riker muttered under his breath before asking, "How can you appear like this? What's your operational range?"

"None of that concerns the issue at hand," the holoimage said. "If *Victory* doesn't start soon, I'm not going to be at the Nexus when you finally arrive. Time is critical."

"Even if that's true," Riker said, "what are you expecting me to do about it? I'm just an old man who knows a few tricks and to keep his gun ready and fire when it's most needed."

"That gun is definitely needed now, Sergeant."

Riker smiled. "Professor, you've come to the wrong man. I can't help you."

"You disappoint me, Sergeant. I thought you had greater imagination."

"No, sir, that's the captain."

The holoimage eyed him, finally shaking its head. "I shall have to seek out Meta, it seems. Where is she?"

"Don't know," Riker said.

"You're lying."

"Don't know about that either," Riker said.

"I fail to understand your unconcerned attitude."

"That's because you're a genius, seeing a hundred angles in a thing and wondering which one you'll try to solve. Me, I'm a sergeant. I know about pay grades and keeping my nose clean. See this place? It's me to a tee."

The holoimage glanced around before shaking its head again. "If—"

"You're wasting your time, Professor. I don't care about you enough to risk my career."

"They've imprisoned your captain."

"That's not my problem," Riker said. "Making sure I receive my pension when my stint is over—"

"Bah!" the holoimage said, throwing up its ghostly hands. Afterward, it disappeared.

Riker kept staring at the spot. His mind whirled at the implications of what the thing had told him. A second later, the sergeant sprinted for the back door. He burst through, tracking dirt onto his wood floor, something he usually never did. He grabbed a comm-unit on the kitchen counter, activating it.

A moment later, Galyan answered.

"Listen to me," Riker said in a rush. "I think this could be important."

***

Lieutenant Valerie Noonan sat at a station on *Victory's* bridge. It was a large circular area with the commander's chair in the center of the room, presently unoccupied.

Valerie peered at a screen on her panel. It showed Antarctica with heavy cloud cover as the starship passed below the Earth. To Valerie it seemed that the starship passed over the most beautiful planet in the galaxy.

The lieutenant wore her uniform. Most people considered her beautiful, with her long brunette hair. She'd been letting it grow since the Destroyer's destruction. She had also lost a few pounds since then, a result of more practice in the combat room rather than any conscious effort on her part. She wanted greater proficiency at hand-to-hand combat. Because of that, her uniform needed altering. It didn't fit quite as snugly as it used to, giving her a slightly rumpled look, in her opinion.

For months now, she had been in effective control of Star Watch's greatest combat vessel. The control had only been while in Earth orbit. Still, it was an honor to run the starship on a day-to-day basis. She had followed every routine with scrupulous precision.

While she had learned the art of command-while-in-danger from the best—Captain Maddox—in her heart, Valerie wanted perfect routine in these things. Yes, a good starship captain had to make fast decisions well. But she had a strong tendency to stick to regulations, as it felt better doing it that way.

Maybe the routine these past months had rubbed off on her. Or maybe the perfect routine had rubbed away the hard-won knowledge of space combat while in dire straits.

Valerie recognized all those things. She also knew that she felt much more comfortable running the starship like this. She had trained long and hard to win a posting to the Space Academy. She had earned everything she had ever gotten in her life, because she had not been born with any of the advantages or privileges of being in a taxpayer family. She had grown up in Detroit, a welfare city if there ever was one. And she had come up the hard way and was damn proud of her achievement.

A few days ago, Galyan had gotten antsy for reasons she didn't understand. Fortunately, the alien AI had settled down to the regular routine. Valerie appreciated that and hoped to keep it that way for the rest of her posting this time around.

The lieutenant swiveled around on her seat. Dr. Clifford was hunched over a weapons board. He was a tall man in a white lab coat and possessed wavy blond hair and the bluest eyes. The doctor looked like a surfer, and had to be the most handsome man she had ever seen.

Valerie was usually on the bridge when Dr. Clifford studied *Victory*. She tried to be as helpful as possible. After all, that was her chief duty. Star Watch needed *Victory's* weapons systems duplicated if they were going to beat the New Men.

The doctor happened to look up, catching Valerie staring at him.

She blushed, nodded and turned away.

"Do you know what bothers me the most?" Dr. Clifford asked in his rich voice.

Valerie faced him again.

"It's the Adok mindset," the doctor said. "It veers away when ours would keep going straight. They did not look at matters the same way we do. But it's difficult to know when they're going to do that. The Adoks had a very mathematical bent of mind."

"That's fascinating," Valerie heard herself say.

"I think so too," the doctor said. "I wonder if you could help me for a minute."

"I'd love to," Valerie said, surprising herself with her bubbling willingness. She had never acted like this before.

She rose from her position and stopped short.

A holoimage appeared before her. It had a humanoid shape, although it was much shorter than a regular man or woman. The Adok holoimage had ropy arms and extremely deep-set, dark eyes. It was Driving Force Galyan, the image of the living Adok who had commanded the starship six thousand years ago. His engrams had been imprinted into the ship's AI, forever changing it with its growing personality.

"Hello, Valerie," Galyan said. His voice was still slightly robotic although it had achieved a little more warmth than before.

"Hi, Galyan," Valerie said, stepping around him.

The holoimage shifted, standing before her again. "Could I have a word with you, Lieutenant?"

Galyan also had a sharper image than he used to. It showed his facial skin to greater effect than ever. The texture seemed like old saddle leather kept out in the sun too long. If one looked closely enough, she saw faint lines crisscrossing the Adok's "leathery" skin. The skin offset the deep eyes more, making it seem as if an owl peered from out of a hole in a tree.

"I'm busy right now," Valerie said. "Maybe we can talk a little later."

"I would like to speak to you now," Galyan insisted.

Valerie glanced past the holoimage at Dr. Clifford. He watched them. She smiled. The doctor smiled back, and it put goosebumps up and down Valerie's arms.

"I have work to do," Valerie said, and she did something she had never done before. She walked *through* the holoimage.

Galyan winced at that, spinning around, watching the lieutenant hurry to Dr. Clifford.

"Doctor," Galyan called. "I would like a private word with the lieutenant on the bridge."

Valerie stopped, turning in surprise. "Is something wrong?" she asked.

"Oh, no," Galyan said in a carefree manner. "It is routine maintenance. I wonder if you forgot about it, Lieutenant."

"Routine?" Valerie asked. She couldn't believe she would have forgotten a routine maintenance scheduling. She plotted all those into her tablet weeks ahead of time.

"Just a minute," she told the doctor. Giving Galyan a stiff glance, she returned to her station and picked up her tablet. Clicking it, she checked the schedule. She didn't see—

"Send him away," Galyan whispered in her ear.

Valerie looked up in exasperation. "What is this about?" she asked sharply.

"Please," Dr. Clifford said. "This is Driving Force Galyan you're addressing. Shouldn't we accord him the highest respect?"

Valerie seemed taken aback by this statement.

Clifford was more than just a weapons specialist. He also had a master's degree in X-Tee relations. X-Tee meant alien contact. Galyan was one of Earth's few aliens they had ever contacted.

"Would you like me to leave, Driving Force?" the doctor asked.

"If you do not mind," Galyan said.

"Of course not," the doctor said. "I'll see you in a while," he told Valerie.

"Yes," she said, trying not to sound crestfallen. The doctor had never asked for her help like this before. Would he remember to pick up where they had almost left off?

Taking his kit, the doctor left the bridge.

Something seemed to pass across Valerie's face at the man's departure. She turned to Galyan with disinterest.

"Well?" she asked.

The holoimage peered at the hatch and then at Valerie. "Do you desire to mate with the doctor?"

"What?" Valerie asked, outraged at such a personal question. "How dare you ask me something like that?"

"Yes. I disremembered. Some humans are quite private about reproductive procedures. I expect I interrupted a mating ritual. Is that correct?"

"Please, Galyan, don't be gross."

"In what manner was my observation 'gross'? I fail to understand."

"Never mind," Valerie said. "What's so important anyway? There isn't any scheduled maintenance."

"This I know."

"So you lied to me?"

"I practiced disinformation in order to lull Dr. Clifford. Do you think Captain Maddox would have approved of my maneuver?"

For the first time today, Valerie studied Galyan. The slightly bewildered look on her face faded away, replaced by sharp suspicion.

"What have you done now, Galyan?"

"I have been in communication with Sergeant Riker."

"And?" Valerie asked.

"He is worried about the captain."

"What has the sergeant up in arms?"

"The holoimage Ludendorff has contacted him."

"Holoimage? Ludendorff?"

"That is correct," Galyan said.

Valerie gave the Adok holoimage an even more suspicious stare. She hadn't gotten along with Captain Maddox in the beginning. She didn't approve of his methods and she hadn't altogether trusted him. The Lord High Admiral had once admitted to similar feelings. After all the small crew of Starship *Victory* had been through and all the times Maddox's unorthodox methods had saved them, Valerie had learned to trust the captain with her life and reputation. Now, it appeared, something was up again.

"Maybe you'd better start from the beginning," she told Galyan. "What's going on?"

The AI gave her a lengthy rundown, including the data concerning Shanghai, the kidnapping androids, the human test Maddox had undergone and now his disappearance.

"Back up just a minute," Valerie said. "You slipped something in during the story. You said Riker told you to keep watch over Maddox."

"This is true," Galyan said.

"You do remember I told you to tell the other person first."

"Yes, but because of the surprise party—"

"What surprise party?" Valerie asked.

"The one for Captain Maddox," Galyan said.

Valerie stared at the holoimage. "Don't you realize that Riker lied to you?"

"I had given that a thirty-nine percent probability. Since the probability of him telling the truth was at forty-seven percent, I chose to believe the sergeant."

"Well, your forty-seven percent proved wrong."

"I will add that to my humanity data."

"Okay, fine," Valerie said. "But let's not get sidetracked. Do you know where they took Maddox?"

"He is in an underwater maximum security area where Greenland used to be."

"That can't be right," Valerie said. "What's left of Greenland is still a radioactive mess. Everyone knows that."

The lieutenant referred to a planetary bombardment fifty years ago, the key event that caused the creation of the Commonwealth of Planets. Back then, the nations of Terra had fought a hot war, using colony world strength. One side had dropped hell-burners, pulverizing Greenland, making the former mass into a thousand radioactive islands. The outrage led to the first proposals concerning Star Watch as a protective organization.

"Tell me about the underwater facility," Valerie said.

Galyan waved a holoimage hand. Another holoimage appeared, showing an underwater security complex. The AI pointed out a column that went up into the stratosphere.

"What's that?" Valerie asked.

"The safe zone," Galyan said. "Transports going straight down avoid lethal dosages of radiation. The problem is that the zone is constantly watched by the best detection devices Star Watch possesses."

"Did the captain commit a crime?" Valerie asked.

"Negative," Galyan said. "Brigadier O'Hara does not want the captain leaving in me to rescue Professor Ludendorff in the Xerxes System."

"You'd better explain how you know that."

Galyan did so.

Valerie frowned. "I still don't understand how you listened in to the brigadier's conversation to Maddox."

"I am tracking the captain with my superior surveillance systems. How do you say? It proved to be child's play."

"No one likes a braggart, Galyan."

"Noted," the AI said. "In the future I will try to refrain from speaking about my greatness."

118

"That's a relief," Valerie said, rolling her eyes. She put her hands behind her back afterward, staring up at the main screen. Antarctica still showed below.

"We must rescue the captain," Galyan said.

"And go against a Star Watch directive," Valerie said. "I don't think so."

"We are a family. Is that not so?"

Valerie scowled. "This one is too big for me. I can't just—"

"Can we please forgo the platitudes to appease your conscience?" Galyan asked. "I know you will see the logic given time."

"You don't know anything of the kind," Valerie said hotly, beginning to get angry.

"I suggest you gather the others," Galyan said. "By the time you feel comfortable with the idea—"

"No!"

"Valerie—"

"Surely, you realize the brigadier is watching *Victory*. She may be monitoring your calls with Riker, too."

"You are correct on both points," Galyan said. "That is why I made certain those spy devices heard a different conversation than the actual speech."

"How did you manage that?"

"I can explain, but I am more interested in your change of mind. By your bearing, I see you mean to rescue the captain."

Valerie's chest rose and fell. Sometimes, Galyan could be too much. The Adok probability analyzer was spooky in its accuracy.

"I have a question," Galyan said. "You are the present commander. You now agree with my assessment. Therefore, knowing the brigadier is ready for us to act, how do you suggest we rescue the captain?"

The lieutenant's scowl intensified. She had been one of the few officers to live through the early encounters with the New Men. Through the years, she had read a hundred tactical manuals on space combat. She knew just about every procedure. She had also been watching Maddox these past years, beginning to appreciate his unorthodox style, how it often caught people by surprise, a valuable military virtue.

Maybe it was time to practice a Maddox maneuver.

"Valerie?" Galyan asked. "Are you well? The look on your face—"

"Let me think, Galyan. I may have an idea. It's going to be a sneaky one, too."

"Excellent. Then, you believe the captain is right regarding Ludendorff?"

She did believe that. But it was another thing entirely taking matters into her own hands the way Maddox did all the time. It could ruin her career if she did this. The idea of that left her breathless. Yet, one thing rang clear in her mind. Maddox believed the Ludendorff holoimage. The captain had been right too many times for her to believe he was wrong now. The football analogy had hit home—Galyan had told her of the Maddox-O'Hara conversation. Valerie had watched many football games on the holo-vid with her father before he'd passed away.

With Strand on the loose and Ludendorff locked away, it seemed like it might be time for one more long bomb mission, with *Victory* acting as the football.

-13-

Several days after Galyan and Valerie's talk on the bridge of the starship, Captain Maddox chafed at his confinement. He'd been finding it increasingly difficult to maintain a stoic indifference. Like a wild beast, cages grated on his psyche. His muscles twitched constantly with an intense desire to explode into action.

It was one thing to lie in wait as a predator. Then, he could show exemplary patience. To be trapped like this, not knowing how long it would last—

Maddox lay on a cot in his room, with his right ankle resting on his up-thrust left knee. He stared at nothing in particular. He'd grown bored watching movies and could no longer stomach reading an ebook. For several days in a row, he had exhausted himself in exercise. That too paled as he endured lock-up.

Star Watch Marines guarded the prison. By the clangs and strange groans, Maddox had guessed some time ago that the structure was underwater.

Did the Iron Lady believe—?

"Hsst, Captain," someone whispered from incredibly nearby.

Maddox had been tapping his right foot in the air. That stopped. He lay perfectly still on the cot, not even turning his head.

"Good, good, that's very good, Captain. Don't let them know you're talking to me."

Maddox forced his brow to smooth out. The whispering voice—it was Ludendorff. Was it possible the alien tech had breached Star Watch's best security? That made for grave concerns, particularly if the New Men had this technology as well.

"If you can hear me," the Ludendorff holoimage whispered, "continue to tap your foot in the air."

Maddox did so.

"Excellent, excellent," the holoimage said. "We shall continue to communicate like this. You will swing your foot up once for 'yes' and twice for 'no.' Do you understand?"

Maddox swung his foot up once.

"As always, you are a quick read, Captain. You may be interested to know that I have spoken to Sergeant Riker twice. He fooled me the first time, as impossible as that is to believe. The second, he told me your family's plan. Does that sound right to you?"

Maddox indicated yes with his foot.

"Do you know where you are?"

Tap, tap indicated no.

The holoimage Ludendorff explained about the underwater Greenland security complex.

Maddox continued to listen with his eyes unfocused. It had taken Galyan long enough to let the others know what had happened. That had been his hole card the entire time, the fact that the ancient alien vessel felt beholden to him for turning the AI back on when everyone else had been for leaving the Adok artificial intelligence off.

The question became this: did Maddox care to buck all of Star Watch? He had pretended to do that once at the brigadier's orders. This time, it would be the real thing.

As he listened to the invisible holoimage explain the plan, the captain silently debated its possibilities of success. He'd had a growing dread during his confinement. What if the Iron Lady planned to keep him down here indefinitely? Brigadier O'Hara had been his chief supporter among Star Watch. Now that she had done this to him, others might begin a whispering campaign against the hybrid. The brigadier's actions would show others that she secretly distrusted him—at least that's how many might take it. Despite everything he had done for Star Watch, those who disliked him would become comfortable again with the idea of placing him under guard at worst or under watch at best.

Maddox knew enough about himself to realize this was partly self-justification and partly hurt feelings on his part. He could not endure the confinement much longer. It was the one thing he truly dreaded: being locked away with nothing useful to do for a long time.

Yes. He would follow his family's lead. Maybe the brigadier had a point. He didn't fully trust the Ludendorff holoimage, either. This could be Strand pulling a fast one. Yet, he would rather risk that with a gun in his hand than lying on his back in confinement.

Besides, this was no way to reward his hard work. He had earned more trust than this. The brigadier had gone too far. Unless one actually committed a crime, no one had a right to lock up another, even if the primary reason was love.

There was one little stickler, though. Was he risking humanity by trusting his own judgment?

Maddox sighed. He was willing to take that risk and accept the consequences. To do otherwise was to do damage to his spirit—remaining locked away down here. There was an ancient saying concerning the matter. "It is neither wise nor prudent to go against conscience." Martin Luther had said that during his trial at Worms when he'd begun the Protestant Reformation.

Maddox's conscience told him to act, even if against the higher authority over him. Humanity needed Ludendorff and Maddox owed the arrogant Methuselah Man. The captain couldn't let the professor rot in the Nexus as a prisoner. He realized that now more than ever.

The captain closed his eyes, continuing to listen to the whispering, invisible holoimage.

***

Major Stokes strode down a corridor of the underwater facility. He had come at the brigadier's command to make sure the captain was doing well.

123

Her orders confining Maddox had been eating at the Iron Lady. She fretted constantly about the captain and had even developed a nervous tic.

"I shouldn't have done it," the brigadier had told Stokes more than once.

"He's too reckless," the major had told her.

"It's one of his charms."

"No. He's a rascal, Ma'am, an incorrigible idealist."

"The captain would not appreciate you saying such a thing."

"I realize Maddox thinks of himself as hardhearted, yet he's a romantic of the old school. He thinks of himself as a knight errant, a tarnished one, no doubt."

"Is that so wrong?" the brigadier had asked.

"In our line of work, most definitely it is," Stokes had said.

For a time, neither of them had spoken.

"No," the brigadier had finally said. "He won't understand. It will chip away at his morale. We're going to need the captain again."

"We've been lucky with him, Ma'am. One of these days, he's going to go too far. He'll pull down anyone associated with him. We've seen the type before."

There had been more along the same line. It hadn't helped the Iron Lady. She knew Maddox would hold this confinement against her. The captain tried to play the cool Intelligence operative. The hybrid even managed to fool some people. In reality, a fire burned in that one. He would blaze through existence, burning out far too soon.

The major showed his pass to the Marine on guard duty. The Marine nodded, speaking into an intercom. The door buzzed and Stokes entered the surveillance room.

Three individuals watched the various detainees on monitors, Maddox included.

Stokes spoke a few words to them. A woman pointed out Maddox stretched out on his cot.

"How long has he been like that?" Stokes asked.

The woman shrugged. "An hour, maybe," she said.

Crossing his arms, Stokes watched the captain. Every few seconds the right foot moved. The captain seemed a little too poised. The longer Stokes watched, the more he disliked what he was seeing.

"Has he become listless?" Stokes asked.

She shrugged, her harsh features showing incomprehension.

"Does he seem bored?" Stokes asked.

"No," she said, "more like stir crazy. He's not going to last long."

Stokes cocked his head. "Why do you say that?"

"I know the signs," she said. "That one doesn't like prison."

"Who does?"

"You'd be surprised," the woman said. "Most criminals have a lazy streak a kilometer long. Not that one, though. He's going to give us problems soon."

Stokes continued to watch Maddox. The foot moving began to get to him. He watched the foot more closely: one move, two, one, one, two.

"It's a code," Stokes said.

"What's that?" the woman asked.

"Scan the room," Stokes said.

"You're already seeing it," she told him.

Stokes studied the woman and then Maddox. "Give me sound," the major said.

"It's already on."

"Increase gain," he said.

The woman gave Stokes a look that suggested he was simple. She must have noticed he was a major, though, because that was all the complaint she made. With several taps, she brought a faint whispering voice to the speaker.

The other two monitors glanced at her. She became more alert. With a tap, she brought the sound to maximum audio.

"After that," a querulous voice said—a voice that definitely didn't belong to Maddox—"we'll use the submersible."

"Who's talking to the prisoner?" the woman asked.

"Initiate full lockdown," Stokes said. "Call security and alert Star Watch. Captain Maddox is about to attempt a prison break."

"Don't worry about him," the woman said. "Gas will do the trick."

"Gas?" asked Stokes.

"It will put him to sleep like a baby," the woman said, while tapping another control.

-14-

Meta adjusted her power gloves, wanting to get the rescue started already.

She sat beside Second Lieutenant Maker as he maneuvered a submersible under the radioactive ice of former Greenland.

The small Scotsman seemed right at home with the blue-shining ice above and the sluggish seawater all around. According to him, no one was a better space pilot or underwater operator than he.

Meta hated the aqua-environment. It felt alien with the hisses and groans and squealing metal all around them. Too much pressure pushed against their craft, which had never been designed to go quite this deep, she was sure.

"Soon now, lass," Keith told her. "Then the fun begins."

Meta nodded absently. She was a strong woman born on a two G planet. Her muscles and bones were denser than a regular human. She had learned that some of her differences were the result of New Men experimentation. Enemy agents had secretly run her mining colony world as a genetic laboratory.

Her body-armor hid a voluptuous figure, while her long blonde hair was tucked under a battle helmet.

Maddox and she were lovers. He had always come for her in the end. If she had to today, Meta was going to do the same thing for him.

"You're sure Maddox knows the plan?" Meta asked.

"Why are you asking me?" Keith said. "Ask the tin men."

Meta glanced sidelong at the two waiting androids. They looked human enough, but she knew the truth. Under the pseudo-flesh, they were composed of circuits, metal and cybertronic mesh. They also wore diving gear and carried weapons. They would be going into the tainted water to reach the prison complex and return with the captain.

"There," Keith said. "It's in sight. Do you see?"

Meta peered through the thick window at the underwater world. All she saw was gloomy murk. Not much sunlight made it through the ice.

"No," Keith said. "Don't look out there, but here." He tapped a radar screen with a green-glowing dot. The blue triangle on the screen was their mini-sub approaching the complex.

"Are you sure our friend-or-foe signal is working?" Meta asked. "If our signal doesn't match, the complex will launch torpedoes at us."

"Don't sweat it, love. Everything is under control."

One thing about Keith, he always had an optimistic outlook. Meta wondered sometimes if she should try for the same thing.

She smiled at the pilot, nodding. "This is going to work," she said.

"That's the spirit," Keith told her. "No more doom and gloom for you. Now—"

"We have a problem," the holoimage Ludendorff said.

Meta jerked around in surprise. The holoimage was supposed to be with Maddox. Why had it returned? She peered at the ghostly form with distrust. Maybe the others had faith in the fake professor, but she didn't.

"What's the situation?" Keith asked. "Why are you back?"

"The authorities have used gas on Captain Maddox," the holoimage said. "He's unconscious in his cell."

Meta swore under her breath. She'd known something was going to go wrong.

"Given these circumstances," the holoimage said, "we must abort. I dare not risk Star Watch capturing my engrams."

Meta glanced at a strange device in the back of the cabin. The androids had brought it with them. Apparently, the holoimage Ludendorff stored its AI engrams in there, projecting the holoimage of the snotty professor a certain distance and no more. She had figured that to be one hundred kilometers, which gave the holoimage quite a range.

Meta was sure the device was Builder tech of the first order. But it was signature Ludendorff to come up with something like that. He had been pulling stuff out of his rear since the day she'd met him. Why not a nifty little engram-holding box that could project a holoimage?

"We're not aborting the mission," Keith informed the holoimage. "They have our captain and we're going to set him free, as in right now."

"Negative," the holoimage said. "I demand you turn back."

Meta had been waiting for something screwy to occur. She powered up the gloves so they purred with exoskeleton strength.

"And since you are too emotionally invested in the rescue to calculate the odds correctly," the holoimage said, "I am enforcing my desire."

Keith turned around.

The two androids stood up, drawing small laser pistols, aiming them at the pilot.

Keith shook his head. "You're not seriously trying this."

"Reverse direction," the holoimage Ludendorff said. "We will attempt a recue at another date."

"Yeah, right," Keith said. "Once we've lost the element of surprise—"

Meta whirled around. She was closer to the androids than Keith was. They began to target her. She grabbed an android hand in each power glove and squeezed, crumpling each weapon and each android hand. They attempted to react. She heaved, tossing the androids onto the deck. With lethal precision, Meta attacked the first one, disabling it with her power-gloves.

"Stop at once," the holoimage said. "They are irreplaceable."

The second android sat up, glanced at its ruined hand and reached for a knife with its good one.

Meta didn't give the android time to complete the maneuver. With the gloves and swift hand-chops, she smashed the pseudo-man back onto the deck. Then, she destroyed the face, deactivating it forever in a shower of sparks.

"What have you done?" the holoimage cried. "They were the last ones."

Meta stood, her heart thudding with a rush of adrenaline. "If you don't shut up and do exactly as I say, I'm going to smash your little box next. That will deactivate *you*. Is that something you really want?"

The ghostly image studied her. "You are a bloodthirsty maiden, and you have ensured the mission's ultimate failure. We needed the androids as commandos."

"Keith and I can do that," Meta said.

"Count me out," the pilot said. "I'm not swimming in that radioactive soup."

"I'll do this myself then," Meta said. "And you're going to show me the way into the facility," she told the holoimage. "And if you're thinking of saying no, realize that I'll purge your box for good if you disagree."

"This is blackmail," the holoimage said.

"I'm glad you understand me," Meta said. "It will save time. Keith, how long until we're ready to launch?"

Keith grinned as he shook his head in admiration. "You do realize they know we're coming?"

Meta shrugged. She was still charged from the fight. Yet, there was a small part of her—the reasonable part—that told her this was suicide. If the others knew they were coming, couldn't they override the FOE signal and launch the complex's torpedoes at them?

"If you're game, so am I," Keith said. Then, he glanced meaningfully at the holoimage. "We're going to hit them one-two."

Meta nodded thoughtfully.

"What does that mean?" the holoimage asked, as it glanced at each of them in turn. "Did you just use a coded phrase to hide your real intention from me?"

Meta snorted as she opened and closed her power gloves. The AI in the box was almost as smart as the real Ludendorff.

130

It had guessed right about Keith's coded phrase just now. Galyan had suspected possible treachery on the holoimage's part. Thus, they had a Plan B, which was what they were about to implement now.

Still, would that stop the others from launching torpedoes?

***

Lieutenant Noonan's right hand hovered over the activation switch. She was on the starship's bridge in the commander's chair, with Galyan to her left.

The Adok AI watched her. Had his probability analyzer predicted each of her possible actions? Galyan had been right about several critical factors already. The AI had guessed the invisible holoimage would be caught talking to Maddox and that the prison authorities would gas the captain afterward. Galyan had also predicted the AI Ludendorff's reaction to all that.

"The AI has acted with self-preservation utmost in mind," Galyan had said.

Valerie tried to understand that. The AI computer with Ludendorff's engrams believed its primary motivation was self-preservation. Galyan had explained his reasoning, of course. The Ludendorff AI was Builder tech, which the hidden aliens absolutely did not want duplicated by primitive humans.

Did that mean the Builders were behind this, or did it mean the real Ludendorff had been unable to disconnect that part of the box's programming?

"You have already committed yourself to the rescue," Galyan told her.

Valerie turned toward him.

"You must know that I am correct," Galyan said.

"Do you remember what I told you about bragging?" Valerie asked in a dispirited tone.

"I do," Galyan said, "but that is not germane to your next decision. You must activate the emergency protocol. Anything else will lead to ugly problems we do not want on our consciences."

"You have a conscience?" Valerie asked.

131

The holoimage Adok appeared troubled. "That is an unkind dig, Valerie. Why do you attempt to cause me grief? For six thousand years—"

"I'm sorry, Galyan. I shouldn't have asked that. I'm…I'm nervous. I worked hard to get to this position. I hate the idea of throwing everything away by disobeying Star Watch."

"Delaying making a decision is still a decision. If you do not act promptly, Captain Maddox, Second Lieutenant Maker and Meta will all be imprisoned, possibly for the rest of their lives."

Valerie tapped the switch before sagging against the commander's chair, listening to a klaxon blare. "It's started," she whispered. "There's no going back now."

"Yes," Galyan said. "Is it not exciting?"

Valerie looked up at the main screen. The scattered islands of Greenland were directly below the starship. For the past few days, Valerie had delicately altered the vessel's course so the starship would be at this location as if by accident.

The klaxon continued to wail. The few remaining islands of Greenland disappeared from the screen. The handsome, worried face of Dr. Clifford appeared. He was in the main disruptor cannon chamber.

The doctor ran a hand through his wavy blond hair. "Lieutenant, what seems to be the problem? What's the emergency?"

Valerie found that she couldn't breathe. She didn't want to say this. Straightening, she said in a strained voice, "You and your team must evacuate the starship immediately."

Dr. Clifford frowned. "I thought there wasn't supposed to be any danger in Earth orbit."

"I know," Valerie said. "I-I thought so too. It's the reactors. A strange gas has begun to leak from their aft chambers."

"If you seal the bulkheads we should all be safe," Clifford told her.

"Under normal circumstances I would agree with you. But since none of us anticipated the danger, I keep wondering what else is going to go wrong that we aren't aware of."

"But—"

"Please, Dr. Clifford, you must hurry to the shuttle."

"No," he said, "I'm going to stay at my post and—"

Valerie took another breath. "This is an order, Doctor. I am ordering you and your team to evacuate at once."

Suspicion swam in his blue eyes. The doctor was as good-looking as they came, but it didn't mean he was stupid. He would need another nudge.

"The Home Fleet is already on high alert," Valerie lied. "Look if it helps you."

Galyan sent Dr. Clifford a carefully edited video of Star Watch battleships closing in on *Victory*. It was old footage from the Oort cloud a couple of years ago. When Dr. Clifford reappeared on the screen, the man had become pale.

"I'm on my way to the shuttle, Lieutenant. Will you be joining us?"

"I'll use the next shuttle," Valerie said. "There's one more procedure I want to attempt. I have to go now. Good-bye, Dr. Clifford, it's been a pleasure working with you."

"You say that as if we won't see each other again. I'll see you in an hour."

Valerie forced a pained smile. "Yes, an hour, two at most. Until then, Dr. Clifford."

She cut the connection, feeling more remote than before the call.

Galyan stared off into space. It meant he was looking through the starship's sensors. "I'm almost in position."

Valerie looked up. "Can you really do this?"

"Theoretically, it should be no problem."

"That wasn't the question."

"No," Galyan said. "It was not. I suppose we are going to find out soon enough if I can do this. In ten seconds, I shall begin the insertion code."

***

Meta settled a full-face mask over her features. The idea of swimming in irradiated seawater troubled her. It was going to be cold, too. The suit was supposed to protect her from the harsh cold, but reality often proved different from theory.

The craft lurched. She staggered, striking her shin against a bench.

"We're in position," Keith radioed into her ear.

"Roger," Meta said. She entered a tiny chamber, turning a wheel. A light flashed, and seawater began to gurgle around her ankles. She stared down at the liquid. It rose fast. She closed her eyes, telling herself this was no problem. It would not take long.

Don't think about the pressure, all the water over your head ready to squeeze you into pulp.

Meta opened her eyes and gave a small yelp.

"What's wrong?" Keith asked.

Meta couldn't speak. She stared at the water sloshing against her mask. This was just like spacewalking, right? So why was she freaking out about it already? This would be easy, easy…totally easy.

"Meta?" Keith asked.

"I'm here," she said, sounding angry.

"My board is showing that your chamber is flooded. It's time to go."

"Yeah," Meta whispered. She activated a switch. The outer hatch opened. Meta grabbed the edges and pulled herself through.

She was in Artic water. With a switch, she activated her pack. It surged with power, propelling her toward a massive structure. Lights glared around it, a prison for some of the worst offenders on the planet.

"Easy does it," Keith said into her ears.

Yeah, yeah, that's easy for you to say, snug in the sub.

Meta knew that was an unkind thought. Several years ago, Keith had come down with Maddox onto Loki Prime, the worst prison planet in the Commonwealth. They had rescued her from a much worse situation than this. It had been a long and interesting road since then, including time spent with Kane, an agent of the New Men who had kidnapped her and taken her into "C" Quadrant.

"Better slow down," Keith said over the comm. "You'll smash into the outer hatch if you're going too fast."

Meta shivered, realizing she'd been daydreaming. Wasn't that one of the dangers of deep diving? This was quite different from spacewalking. The water resisted her efforts.

134

She slowed down as a hatch loomed before her. Getting into the prison—

The hatch opened.

Meta grinned inside her diving mask. Maybe this was going to work after all. Galyan had opened the hatch, at least. The AI was supposed to have hacked into the complex's main computer. If it wasn't Galyan helping her—

Meta growled under her breath, kicking her feet, propelling herself into a chamber. The decisive moment was upon her.

***

Meta hurried through the silent corridors. No one moved in the underwater complex. On the upper left of her mask appeared a small schematic of the prison. She followed the route marked in red.

She had a laser pistol, which she most certainly would use. Maybe it would be wrong to kill the Star Watch Marines in here, but Meta didn't plan to go back to a prison planet ever. No one had better get in her way today. She wore body armor and—

"There's trouble," Keith said into her earphones.

"What are you picking up?" she asked.

"Someone is moving in there, either that or my motion detector is off."

"How far are they from me?" Meta asked.

"You're not going to meet them right away, but it looks as if the person is headed for the captain's cell. He must know why you're there."

"It's definitely a he?" Meta asked.

"Don't know about that. But you have to expect him to be armed."

"Roger," Meta said. She increased her pace. "Is he wearing a gas mask?"

"That seems like the best answer," Keith said. "That means you're dealing with a smart one. He must have seen the others dropping around him and realized we were gassing everyone— or that Galyan was, using their own security system against them."

"Great," Meta said. She had a nasty thought. What if this smart guy put a gun to the captain's head and threatened to shoot him. That was the one way to stop the rescue attempt cold.

Meta swore under her breath as she began to run.

-15-

Major Stokes stumbled through the corridors. He wore a gas mask as Meta had supposed. The brigadier had been right to suspect *Victory's* old crew. Given that, the Iron Lady should have locked every one of them away.

Sure, those people had done magnificently in the past, but that didn't mean they got a free ride whenever they felt like it. One had to obey orders. Without rules, a society turned into competing tribes and a military became a useless mob.

Star Watch would never defeat the New Men if Maddox and his people fell into an obvious trap. How could any of them be so softheaded as to fall for the Ludendorff holoimage? Clearly, Strand used the holoimage to lure the ancient starship to a place where he could board and capture it. The New Men had tried that at Wolf Prime. Gaining *Victory* would tip the military balance to the enemy. On no account could Stokes let that happen.

It's up to me to save the day. I can't let my humanitarianism throw away our greatest advantage. I'm sorry, Captain Maddox and whoever is trying to rescue you. I'm simply not going to let that happen.

Stokes wasn't a musclebound soldier. He was lean, smoked too much and was maybe a little too old for games like this. But he trusted his mind, which he believed was one of the sharpest in Intelligence. If that wasn't so, the brigadier wouldn't trust his judgment to the extent she did.

Maybe the others coming had the advantage in a purely tactical combat sense. He was trickier, though, and in the end, that was going to win down here.

The major drew a gun as a grim sense of rightness hardened his resolve. If he had to, he would shoot the captain in cold blood. It wouldn't be because he held any ill will toward the man. He rather admired the other's resourcefulness. No, he would kill Captain Maddox because humanity's fate might well rest on him doing so.

***

Meta raced around a corner, seeing an open cell door down the corridor. According to the schematic, it was the captain's cell. A hard knot squeezed within her stomach. The other had beaten her to the prize. What should she do?

"I know you're out there," a man shouted from within the cell. "I have a gun pressed against the captain's skull. If I see you appear in front of the door, I'll fire."

"I'm wearing body armor," Meta shouted.

"We both know I won't shoot at you but at him."

"If you do that, I'll kill you next."

"Yes, I suspected as much. That isn't my preference naturally, but so be it. I am an officer of Star Watch Intelligence and I will do my duty to ensure mankind's survival."

"And if Captain Maddox is correct in his assessment?" Meta asked.

"I'm willing to bet the brigadier is correct."

"Maddox hasn't been wrong yet," Meta said.

"He's clever, I'll grant you that. But I've told you my resolve. It isn't going to change."

"Who are you?"

"It doesn't matter. I'm guessing…you're Meta."

"It doesn't matter," she shouted back.

"I see. Well, make your choice, young lady. I've already made mine."

"Keith," Meta whispered.

"I heard him," the second lieutenant said into her earphones.

"Its checkmate," she whispered.

"Maybe," Keith said.

"You have another idea?"

"I'm sending over the holoimage," Keith said. "Maybe it can think of something."

Meta shook her head. She didn't trust the alien AI that pretended to have the engrams of Ludendorff. It—

The holoimage materialized before her. "The second lieutenant tells me we have a situation."

Meta stared at the ghostly apparition. Then, slowly, she explained the stalemate.

"The answer is obvious," the holoimage said. "I'm amazed you haven't already seen it."

"I haven't," Meta said, hating the thing more than ever.

"Now that you're committed, I'll give you the answer. Use the revitalizing gas. The captain's metabolism causes him to recover faster than ordinary. He will then overcome the major for you."

"I don't know," Meta said. "That means everyone else will wake up down here."

"None of that is going to work," Keith said in Meta's headphones. "I just called the starship. Galyan told me there is no revitalizing gas."

Meta squinted at the holoimage. She told it what Keith had just told her. "You deliberately tried to trick me."

"Nonsense," the Ludendorff holoimage said.

"What aren't you telling me?" Meta asked. "Is the captain coming to on his own?"

The holoimage hesitated before saying, "I'm surprised at you. You have reached the correct conclusion."

"Why not tell me in the first place?"

"Meta!" the major shouted from the cell.

"Yes?" she called.

"Either you leave or surrender to me," the major shouted. "If you don't do either, I'm going to shoot the captain and be done with it." Stokes was silent for a moment. "What's it going to be, Meta?"

Meta glanced at the Ludendorff holoimage.

139

"You must keep the major talking," the holoimage whispered. "The captain must hear that as he comes to. Otherwise, Maddox will give his awakening away to Stokes and the major will kill him."

Meta shook her head. This was an impossible situation. Just once, she would like everything to work easily.

***

In the cell, Captain Maddox was already coming to. His mind was groggy and his body felt weak and...

He recognized the feeling as similar to what had happened to him at the Lin Ru Hotel, the Spacer embassy. But that had...

He heard Meta, and he almost called out to her. At the last moment, he felt the cold barrel of a gun pressed against his left temple.

What was happening?

By slow degrees, all the while keeping himself motionless, Maddox realized he was in his cell underwater in the Greenland Archipelago. The gunman answered Meta, and Maddox realized Major Stokes held him captive.

"All right," Meta shouted. "I'm leaving. Just let the captain be. He has nothing to do with this."

Maddox could feel some of the tension ease from Stokes, but the major didn't take the gun from his head.

"I know you're awake," Stokes told him quietly.

Maddox opened his eyes, staring up at the major.

"I thought you would have tried something before this," the major said.

"Are you really going to kill me?" Maddox asked.

Stokes just stared at him.

"You don't like me, do you?" Maddox said.

"No. I never have. You're a hybrid. As far as I can tell, you're a sleeper agent for the New Men."

"That's why I've helped Star Watch time and again?" Maddox asked.

"It's a mystery, I admit." Stokes appeared thoughtful. "Maybe I should make this easy for both of us."

"Outright murder?" Maddox asked. "That doesn't seem like you."

Stokes gave him the tiniest of grins.

Maddox tried to interpret it. He realized Stokes wasn't speaking to him. Well, he was, but the words were for someone else. Yes, of course, he spoke for the benefit of the invisible holoimage. That must be how Meta had gained her intelligence of the situation in the cell.

"This time you're wrong, Captain," the major said. "Surely, you can see that."

"You say that because of the Xerxes System?"

"No, because of the Shanghai androids and the holoimage," Stokes said. "And—"

The holoimage solidified in the cell. "I have a message for you," the ghostly Ludendorff said.

Stokes swore and thumbed back the hammer of his pistol.

Maddox convulsed mightily, surging against the major. The gun went off. The ignition was deafening to Maddox. The bullet singed the side of his head in passing. He tried to grapple with the major. The gun lined up so it aimed between his eyes. Then, a spear of red laser light struck Stokes' firing hand. The major cried out in agony, releasing the gun.

Both Maddox and Stokes stood up at the same time.

Meta clanked into the cell in her body armor, the laser aimed at Stokes. The major cradled his smoking hand as blood dripped from it.

"You fired at him," Meta said, who still wore her mask.

"Sorry, old boy," Stokes told Maddox.

The captain barely heard the words. His ears were still ringing from the shot.

"It was nothing personal," the major added.

"It felt personal to me," Maddox said, too loudly because he wasn't hearing so well.

"I'd like to convince you to stay," Stokes said.

Maddox had an intense desire to slug the major. Instead, he shook his head. Taking the gun, he put it into his belt.

"You won't make it to the starship," Stokes said.

"Maybe not," Maddox told him.

"And even if you do, you'll never make it out of the Solar System. Star Watch can't afford *Victory* falling into enemy hands."

"Good-bye, Major," Maddox said. "Tell the brigadier I had to do this. I'll take every precaution concerning the starship."

"No you won't," Stokes said. "You're an adrenaline junkie. I think all the New Men are. And the lot of you are all too arrogant by far."

"Well, half of me is too arrogant anyway," Maddox said.

"I don't believe you're going to like what you find out there," Stokes said.

"I'm not sure I like what I've found here." Maddox turned to Meta. "Thanks for coming. Let's go."

"What about him?" she asked, pointing at Stokes.

Maddox stared at the major who had just tried to murder him. "We'll lock the cell. I think that will give us enough time."

Meta hesitated, looking as if she wanted to fire the laser one more time. Finally, she nodded, saying, "Okay. But we'd better hurry. The major is right about one thing, all of Star Watch will be gunning for us. We don't have much time to get upstairs to *Victory* and out of the Solar System."

-16-

Keith watched the two swimming through the radioactive water. Meta had succeeded. She was bringing Captain Maddox to the submersible. Once more, it was the team against everyone else.

The minutes ticked by. Would you look at this?—Keith studied the radar chart. There were attack submarines out here. That was fast work. Someone must have been anticipating them trying something at the Greenland complex.

Did the subs belong to Star Watch or had the Ludendorff box set up something for another play. Galyan had suggested they beware the Builder box. The Adok's probability analyzer suggested the person or people behind the box might be someone other than the real Ludendorff trapped in the Xerxes System. They would be foolish to trust the holoimage fully.

"Come on," Keith said, watching the two swimmers. "You've already taken too long."

***

Captain Maddox swam strongly, doing his best to keep up with Meta. Her jet-propelled pack was making that difficult.

Meta looked back. "Take my hand," she said, through the full-face mask comm. "I'm only going at half-speed and we have to go faster."

"Right," Maddox said. He kicker harder, grabbed her hand and felt her squeeze, the pressure from her power gloves nearly crushing his hand.

"Oh, sorry," she said, looking back at him a moment later. "My pressure indicator shows—is your hand okay?" She adjusted the gloves to release some of the pressure.

"Never mind about that," the captain said. He had been applying considerable squeeze to his hand to keep the bones from breaking.

A burst of thrust from her pack had them zooming through the murky water. Soon, they reached the submersible's hatch, entering an air-cycler, the water draining away from the chamber and a harsh spray decontaminating their suits.

"This could get rough," Keith said through the earphones.

The pilot immediately proved true to his word. The room tilted crazily as Maddox reached for the inner handle. He felt himself slipping and lunged, his fingers barely grabbing the metal in time. Meta wasn't so lucky. The room tilted and speed threw her so she crashed against one side and slammed against Maddox next. He grabbed her one-armed and opened the hatch. They tumbled into a larger chamber as the craft continued to jig wildly. There were no gravity dampeners in the submersible to dull the sudden moves.

Blood flowed from Meta's nose as she groaned. Maddox dragged her to a bench, hooking his feet and tightening his hold of Meta.

Now the cabin tilted the other way and half spun. Increasing speed threatened Maddox's grip.

"He's crazy," Meta muttered.

"Which means we might make it," Maddox told her.

The ride continued this way for a time. Finally, the chamber leveled out, which presumably meant so had the craft.

Keith confirmed the news by saying over an intercom, "Okay. It's safe. I hope you two are all right."

"Roger," Maddox said. "Do we have time to come forward?"

"Sure, mate," Keith said.

Maddox cleared his throat.

"I mean, Captain, sir."

"Let's go," Maddox told Meta, handing her a cloth.

She wiped the blood from her nose.

144

With Meta in tow, Maddox hurried into a short corridor and saw the holoimage waving them toward a particular hatch. Moments later, Maddox strapped himself to a chair beside Keith. Meta sat down at the weapons board.

"Glad to have you aboard, sir," Keith said, with his focus glued onto a battle screen.

"Trouble?" Maddox asked. He saw three fast-attack submarines giving chase on the screen.

"Just a mite, sir," Keith said, "but nothing a tactical wizard like me can't handle."

"What happened to all our decoys?" Meta said, as she checked her weapons board.

"I already used them up, don't you know," Keith said. "The boys behind us have been firing torpedoes like candy. I'm surprised you haven't felt the explosions."

"What does that even mean?" Meta asked.

"That Galyan had better know what he's doing," Keith said. "Hang on now. I'm about to give them a performance they'll never forget."

The submersible went sideways, and Keith increased speed yet again.

"They're launching torpedoes," Meta said.

"They're right on schedule then," Keith told her. "And that's why I'm headed for that underwater grotto below."

Maddox touched the powder burn on the side of his head. Major Stokes had actually tried to kill him. The brigadier must be serious about his incarceration. The attack submarines coming after them would kill them, too, if they could. The knowledge left a hollow feeling in the captain's stomach. After all that he had done, Star Watch still didn't trust him. If the brigadier could do this to him...who would stick up for him?

"No one," Maddox whispered.

"What's that, sir?" Keith asked, while focusing on a screen.

Maddox pondered his conclusion. He was a hybrid. He glanced at Keith, nodding. Here was one regular human who would go to the wall for him. Meta didn't count in that regard. She was a genetic experiment, meaning she was just as much in his camp as...as a New Man would be.

"This is pure genius on my part," Keith informed him. "Are you ready, sir?"

Maddox pursed his lips.

The submersible corkscrewed as Keith took them through a ring of rock. Something banged against the craft's side, though, causing a horrible metallic screeching that didn't seem to end.

The sound snapped Maddox out of his reverie. He stared at a bulkhead, waiting, waiting—finally, the terrible screech ended. They were alright, through the grotto.

Just as Maddox thought that, water burst through a seam in a bulkhead.

Meta shouted in surprise as water sprayed in forcefully.

Keith gave the breach a quick glance, muttered something and tapped his board. He did this several times. It didn't seem to help or change anything.

Water hosed into the cabin. The icy liquid swept up items, banging them against the other bulkhead. The green-colored water kept pouring in at a fantastic rate. Maddox kicked his feet, sloshing them through the rising water.

"That is bad," Meta said. "The water is radioactive. If it doesn't drown us first, we'll be irradiated to death."

"Hang on," Keith said. "We're not out of it yet."

Maddox glanced at the pilot's screen. A blossom indicated an exploding torpedo behind them against the rock of the grotto. Other bright dots showed even more explosions.

"I did that part perfectly," Keith said. "The torpedoes missed us."

While that was true, seconds later, the craft shuddered as the increased pressure from the explosions struck the submersible. A metallic tearing sound meant something burst apart. Then, twice the volume of water poured into the main cabin.

"We're going to drown!" Meta shouted.

Maddox was already on his feet. He surged through the swirling water, wading to an emergency repair unit on the wall.

"We have no choice now," Keith said. "It's time to go up. Hang on, Captain, sir. I'm changing course."

Maddox barely did so in time, grabbing the wall unit.

The submersible tilted violently upward as water continued to gush into the cabin. In a wave, the mass washed against Meta as the water flowed to the back of the sub, adding more weight by the second.

"Come on, you bastard," Keith told the sub. "Give me more thrust." He tapped his board.

From the bulkhead, Maddox stared at the water still pouring in. They had a bare few minutes before they were flooded and drowned.

"Level the craft," Maddox said in a commanding voice. "I have to patch the hole."

Keith glanced at him before shaking his head. "I'm sorry, sir, but that's a buggering bad idea."

"Second lieutenant," Maddox barked. "You will—"

"Hang on, sir. Give me twenty more seconds."

Maddox hung on, silently fuming. Still, in these kinds of situations, no one was better than Keith Maker, so Maddox waited to see what the ace had up his sleeve.

Twenty-five seconds later, the submersible lurched onto the surface like a flopping whale. It banged hard against the waves, shaking Maddox loose from his hold. He toppled into the water.

"Now, sir," Keith said. "If we don't repair the breach fast, we're going to run out of air."

That didn't sound right, but it confirmed to Maddox that Keith had an idea he wasn't tracking yet. The captain surged to his feet, grabbing the emergency repair kit.

"We'd better move from our location," Meta said, barely able to peer at her board. It was only an inch above the waterline. "There's another spread of torpedoes coming our way."

"Galyan, come in, Galyan," Keith said into the comm-unit. "You have to start us upstairs, mate. You have to do it now or we're dead."

Maddox only listened with half an ear. He wrestled the kit to the breach. As he pressed it against the bulkhead, the submersible lurched once more. The room tilted back and forth.

The captain glanced out the forward window and blinked in amazement. The submersible was in the air and rising.

"That's *Victory's* tractor beam, sir," Keith explained. "We came in down under to fool Star Watch and we're escaping through the atmosphere. The unexpectedness of our moves might give us the edge we need to make it onto the starship."

Maddox nodded thoughtfully. Then, he finished his hasty repair, sloshing through the water, replacing the empty repair kit. Finally, soaking wet, he returned to his spot near the pilot, buckling in.

Keith had auto-opened some hatches, causing the water to drain away faster than it had come in. He tapped his board. The hatches closed with loud *clangs*.

"Yes," Maddox said. "I like the plan. It was well thought-out and executed, Second Lieutenant."

"Boom," Meta said.

Maddox glanced back at her.

"The torpedoes have exploded on the surface," she said, staring at her board. "Let's hope the attack subs don't have any missiles."

"I wouldn't worry about the subs or their missiles," Keith said. "The air interceptors heading our way are going to be the real problem."

-17-

Far away in Geneva, Brigadier O'Hara stood beside the Lord High Admiral. Cook was a big man, red-faced with thick white hair and a white uniform.

They both studied a large screen, with various personnel around the room at monitoring stations. On the screen, a damaged submersible increased speed as it floated upward toward space.

"Clever," Cook said. "But it won't be any match for the interceptors."

"I'm beginning to wonder if that's wise, sir," O'Hara said.

The large admiral glanced at her. "You'd better speak quickly, Brigadier. In half a minute, the pilots will launch their ordnance."

"*Victory* is in play now," O'Hara said. "We tried to stop that from happening and failed. I believe the difference changes the equation. If the Adok AI sees us kill Captain Maddox…"

"Yes," Cook said, "I see your drift. We cannot afford its displeasure and possible anger." With his thick fingers, he motioned to an alert colonel nearby.

She spoke rapidly to the interceptor pilots, forbidding them to launch.

"Should we call the captain?" Cook said. "Maybe he would be open to reason."

149

"We're far past reason," the brigadier said. "I spoke to Major Stokes a minute ago. He admits to attempting to kill the captain."

"You're fond of the captain, I believe," Cook said after a moment.

The brigadier nodded.

"This Major Stokes—"

"Acted on his own in this," O'Hara said. "I wish he wouldn't have fired, but I understand his reasoning. Loyalty to Star Watch motivated him."

"Still," Cook said. "This is Captain Maddox we're talking about. He has many detractors, for sound reasons, I believe. At times, you're the only one who has backed him."

"I still back him."

"Then why let him go like this?" Cook asked. "Won't he be disillusioned with us?"

The brigadier took her time answering. She watched the submersible reach the stratosphere, continuing for space and *Victory* in orbit.

"I'm afraid for our side," she said. "The Builders and Ludendorff, and Strand..." She shook her head. "Ever since the Destroyer almost annihilated Earth I've been wondering about the wider universe. I don't know if we're going to get the chance to build up enough to withstand the challenges out there."

"You're thinking too far ahead," Cook said in a chiding voice. "First, we must defend humanity against the runaway New Men. We're well on our way to doing that."

"I agree. But what if there are worse things out there? How would we defend ourselves against several Destroyers for instance?"

"That's a legitimate question," Cook said. "The answer is that I don't know right now."

"Neither do I," the brigadier said.

"So your point is...?"

"Maybe Captain Maddox has the right idea. We have the new wave harmonics shields, antimatter missiles and ground-based fusion cannons. Those are pluses. We have greater industrial capacity; meaning if we have the time, we can build masses more ships and those new cannons. But will that prove enough against whatever surprises the New Men have in store for us?"

"Do they have any more surprises?" Cook asked.

"You're making my point for me, sir. We lack knowledge. I suggest that means we need Professor Ludendorff and we need his understanding *now*. It's true that I don't want to risk my boy—er, risk Captain Maddox in yet another hazardous mission. I'm afraid I'll never see him again. I'm afraid we might lose Starship *Victory*. I intensely dislike rolling the dice against fate. For a long time, I have believed we should do this the old-fashioned way by outbuilding our enemy. Now I've begun to doubt myself. If only we knew more about the New Men and their full capabilities. That is the knowledge Captain Maddox is seeking, and it may be the edge we need. There is one other critical point. We can't afford to alienate the Adok AI."

"I understand your thinking," Cook said. "Your captain is forcing our hand, I admit. What I don't fathom is why you aren't willing to say good-bye and wish him luck."

The brigadier forced herself to remain stoic and dry-eyed. She wasn't going to let the Lord High Admiral see her eyes turn red.

"I have a gut feeling about this, sir," O'Hara whispered.

"Go on," he said. "Tell me about this feeling."

"I think this time..." O'Hara had to pause, biting her lower lip so it wouldn't tremble. Once the danger had passed, she said, "I think this time the captain is going to need *bitter* determination in order to succeed. I can't say why I feel this. It's...it's just there, sir," She broke off weakly.

"Do you think it is a mother's feeling?"

"Please, Admiral," O'Hara whispered.

Cook waited for her to add a true denial. Finally, the large old man put his hands behind his back, staring at the screen. The submersible had left the blue-tinted atmosphere behind as it headed for a double-oval-shaped warship higher up in space.

"We should be able to stop *Victory* from leaving, but it might cost us half our battleships. We can't afford any losses, not after sending so many ships to the Grand Fleet." The old man sighed. "I dearly hope you're right about this, Brigadier."

"Yes, sir," O'Hara whispered. "So do I."

-18-

Sometime later, Captain Maddox settled into the commander's chair on *Victory's* bridge. He had run from the hangar bay where the submersible now rested. The sprint had left him breathing slightly harder than normal.

"Welcome back, sir," Valerie said.

"It's good to be back," Maddox told her.

The lieutenant sat at weapons, a panting Keith slid into the pilot's chair and Galyan stood watching.

"I take it Dana and Riker are aboard," Maddox said.

"Yes, sir," Valerie said. "We're all aboard, and this time, it's just the six of us."

"I'm surprised a security team isn't on *Victory*."

"There used to be," Valerie said. "I, ah, used a Maddox maneuver to clear the starship a little over an hour ago."

The captain raised an eyebrow. "I see."

Upon the submersible's landing in the hangar bay, the starship had immediately begun to accelerate, breaking out of Earth orbit. *Victory* did so with Luna Base on the other side of the planet, keeping the Earth between them and the huge rail-guns on the Moon.

"Where are the nearest battleships?" Maddox asked.

"I don't understand this," Valerie said as she studied her board. "None of the battleships, no Star Watch vessels, have begun acceleration toward us. I don't even see any sign of planetary defenses attempting to gain lock-on against us. High

Command can't be under any illusion about what we plan to do."

Maddox put an elbow on an armrest and his chin on his fist. He thought about that.

"Any ideas, Galyan?" the captain asked.

"I lack sufficient data for a reasonable analysis," the Adok AI said.

"It fits with what we've seen since leaving the Greenland Archipelago," Maddox said. "In the atmosphere, the interceptors could have engaged. I doubt they held back for our sakes." The powder burn on the side of his head still stung too much for him to forget it. Stokes' shot hadn't been fake. No it had been all too real. "That leaves only one possibility." He turned to Galyan. "The difference is you."

"Me?" the AI asked.

"Yes," Maddox said. "Would you take it badly if you saw Star Watch obliterate my vessel with me in it?"

Galyan didn't hesitate. "Most certainly I would, Captain."

"That must be the answer," Maddox said. "I'm guessing the Lord High Admiral decided to let us go. I'm sure they don't like it, but they're not going to risk openly upsetting Star Watch's best answer to defeating the New Men."

"Sounds plausible to me," Keith said.

"That puts a heavy responsibility on us," Valerie said. "We can't let anyone else gain control of *Victory*." The lieutenant became thoughtful. "But if you're right, sir, why aren't they talking to us?"

Maddox had been wondering the same thing. He now said, "If they talk to us, they'll either have to order us back or give us permission to go. They don't agree with our agenda... So they're going to go with the fiction that we're renegades."

"What fiction?" Valerie asked. "We *are* renegades. We...we fought against our own people. I can't say I'm happy with that, sir."

Maddox stared at the main screen.

"There is another possibility," Galyan said. "They could be trying to lull you, Captain, while attempting an unforeseen maneuver."

"Right," Maddox said. He thought a moment and then clapped his hands, startling Valerie. "We're leaving under combat conditions. We will not assume anything. That means we'll use the star drive to jump out of the system. We're going to use our greater speed to get us to the Xerxes System before Star Watch can send a message to Port Admiral Hayes. That way, we can use the port admiral's help in the Xerxes System instead of having him fight against us."

"What are we going to do once we have Professor Ludendorff?" Valerie asked.

"Return with him to Earth," Maddox said.

"Surrendering ourselves to the authorities?" Valerie asked.

Maddox looked away as he said, "That's my plan, Lieutenant. Each of you will have to decide for yourself whether you'll join me in my surrender."

"So this may be our last mission together," Valerie said.

Maddox hadn't thought that far ahead. He nodded. "Yes, that's a good possibility."

"I do not agree," Galyan said. "If your first theory is correct, that my agreeability is desirable to Star Watch, then you may have many more voyages left."

"I call that a splendid point," Keith said, grinning. "We didn't know it the first time going out, but we know it now. We've become the indispensable team."

Maddox found that hard to believe in light of the throbbing powder burn. Stokes had tried to kill him, and the major had been acting under the brigadier's orders. Despite their success in reaching *Victory*, a pang of loneliness touched him. He wondered if that feeling would ever go away.

The more he thought about that... "Lieutenant," Maddox said. "I want you to open channels with Star Watch Headquarters."

Valerie gave him a quizzical stare but finally nodded slowly. "I've opened channels," she said, tapping her board, "but no one is responding, sir."

Maddox cleared his throat. "Lord High Admiral," he began, "this is Captain Maddox speaking. I'm taking Starship *Victory* to the Xerxes System. I will aid Port Admiral Hayes if I am able. My primary objective is to free Professor Ludendorff and return with him to Earth. At that point, I will surrender to your authority. If you feel it is necessary to put me back in the Greenland prison…"

Maddox could not force out the next words. What did he owe Star Watch? What did he owe the Commonwealth? Did his loyalty to them mean he would accept any indignity they put on him? He had served Star Watch and the Commonwealth loyally for years. He had risked his life for both. Didn't Star Watch and the Commonwealth owe him something? Was it a soldier's lot to obey any command no matter what it was?

No. Captain Maddox did not believe that. A man had a higher duty to perform that ruled out following immoral orders. If Star Watch wronged him, he had an obligation to himself and to the truth to right that wrong. In this case, the ultimate objective was to protect humanity from oblivion, from extinction. If Star Watch acted in such a way as to ensure humanity's end, he owed the future of man to do the right thing. Normally, a lowly captain obeyed the higher authority because without order chaos ruled. Realistically, the higher authority should have greater knowledge. In this instance, he could make a case that he had greater knowledge than Star Watch. Was he being presumptuous thinking this?

Not if he was right. Thus, to surrender to Star Watch for making the correct decision—that sounded foolish.

I do not plan to play the fool with anyone.

"Let me amend my last point," Maddox said. "My plan is to return with Professor Ludendorff so Star Watch can make the best decision regarding human survival. I realize you would like me to apologize for taking such a high-handed approach in this. However, I found *Victory* for you, coaxed the starship to aid humanity and helped to defeat the first New Men invasion of 'C' Quadrant. I also defeated the alien Destroyer. I believe I have earned the right to attempt this mission. I believe Star Watch made a critical mistake putting me in the Greenland complex. Frankly, Lord High Admiral, Star Watch acted in an ungrateful manner toward me and I resent that."

Keith laughed as he pumped a fist. "I've never heard anyone tweak High Command's nose better than you are now, mate—I mean Captain, sir."

"Furthermore," Maddox said, while ignoring the ace.

Valerie clicked a switch. "Captain," she said. "I think you've said enough."

Maddox drew a breath. Before he could speak his mind to her, a red light flashed on Valerie's board. He pointed at it.

Hesitantly, Valerie tapped her panel. "Ah, it's the Lord High Admiral, Captain."

"Good," Maddox said. "Put him through."

Valerie gave him a meaningful glance before tapping her board.

The main screen shimmered. Then, old Admiral Cook appeared, starring at Maddox with flashing eyes.

"I hope your gall serves you well, young man," Cook said. "This is a reckless mission, and you're absconding with Earth's best chance to defeat the New Men. We need those ancient Adok technologies in the coming conflict."

"Sir," Maddox said. "If our scientists haven't cracked them yet, I don't think they're going to in the foreseeable future."

"Do not seek to lecture me, Captain," the Lord High Admiral said, locking stares with Maddox.

The captain saw genuine anger there, and for once, it daunted him. Who was he to take on the entirety of Star Watch? At that moment, Maddox knew something about himself. He did this for more than the truth. He had a duty to his mother, to the woman who had risked everything to save a small boy from the New Men. Behind everything, he sensed her courage, the fire in her heart to do the right thing for her unborn son. He was going to honor that.

"I don't mean to lecture you, sir," Maddox said. "You gave me a task several years ago. I'm simply trying to finish the job, sir."

"If you mean to return to Earth with *Victory*—"

"That's exactly right, sir, returning with victory against the New Men. This time, I don't mean the starship, but winning the war. I've been with Professor Ludendorff. That causes me to worry about Strand. The New Men have deep knowledge, sir. We need that knowledge if we're going to defeat them. Maybe my hybrid nature lets me see that truth a little more clearly than others."

157

"Now see here, Captain."

"The New Men are better than us, sir. We have an edge, but I don't think it will be enough to beat off their next attempt, not with Strand helping them."

"Are you not aware," Cook said, "that Strand and the New Men appear to be at odds with each other?"

"I am, sir. But given their situation, I suspect they will reunite and work together until regular humanity is defeated. That's the New Man side of me speaking, sir. As I said, I have a greater insight into the enemy's mindset because I share some of it. You trusted me before, sir, with the highest stakes. I'm asking you to trust me again."

The Lord High Admiral's features hardened into a flinty look. "Your exploits have unhinged your thinking, Captain. You are not as smart or as important as you seem to think."

The powder burn still stung. That kept Maddox from backing down.

"I am ordering you—"

Valerie cut the connection with a click. The image of the Lord High Admiral vanished from the main screen, replaced by a dot of Mars in the far distance.

"Shouldn't we be jumping soon, sir?" Valerie asked, paled-faced and with shaking hands. Maybe she couldn't believe what she had just done.

Maddox studied her, surprised by her daring. This Valerie was different from the one he remembered. She appeared to have absorbed some of the lessons of their last voyage.

He nodded. The extent of his words and actions just now began to settle in. This time, more than ever before, he was going for broke. If he was wrong—

I'll cross that bridge when the time comes.

***

A day later, as the starship skirted the Tau Ceti System, Captain Maddox jogged around the vast area of the hangar bay, burning off excess energy. He had been doing some deep thinking regarding the Builder AI box.

A moment later, Galyan appeared beside him. That startled Maddox, but he hid it, nodding a greeting.

"May I speak with you, Captain?" Galyan asked.

"Of course," Maddox said, as he ran. He noticed the holoimage floating even with him. "Ah, I would prefer if you ran beside me. The floating is a bit disconcerting."

"Oh," Galyan said. The small Adok moved its legs as if running. "Is that better, sir?"

"Much," Maddox said. "You said you wished to talk with me?"

"I have been processing old memories for quite some time. The extra computing power Dana found has given me these memories and the ability to sort and accept them. However, I am having trouble with one particular set."

Galyan glanced at the captain. "Perhaps I should not bother you with my personal problems."

"It's no problem," Maddox said. "We're always coming to you for your help. I would be honored if you let me help you."

"Quid pro quo?" asked Galyan.

"That isn't how I meant it to sound. We're…"

"Family, sir?"

"Yes," Maddox said.

"Can an Adok be part of a human family?"

Maddox ran for a time without answering. "We're a strange group, a half-breed, a welfare kid, a former drunk—"

"You should not disparage yourself, sir."

"What I'm saying is that you are one of us."

"I'm not sure I welcome the comparison, sir."

"Oh," Maddox said, glancing at the holoimage. It surprised him to see a brooding Galyan, his owl-like eyes more intense than usual. "Maybe the better way is to say that we are each unique and you are the most unique among us."

The two beings ran in silence after that, circling the hangar bay once.

"I am not sure where to begin, sir," Galyan said.

"I have time."

"That is kind of you."

"What's wrong?" Maddox asked.

A wistful note entered Galyan's robotic voice. "When I was flesh and blood in the days my homeworld existed, I had a wonderful mate. She loved me and I loved her. We united our

159

flesh, hoping for a large family. After several years, we learned that she could not bear children. Oh, she wanted offspring so badly. She began working in the crèches, teaching the youngest their first lessons. I tried to persuade her otherwise. Seeing the young every day tormented her but they also gave her joy."

"That is sad," Maddox said after Galyan had fallen silent.

"You must understand," Galyan said, as if Maddox hadn't commented, "that I came from one of the oldest lines of honor on the planet. I did not have any siblings. I was the last of a glorious line. But I would never pass on my genes to the future. It used to trouble me. Perhaps that is why I strove so hard. I believed that I would be the last of my line. Thus, I tried to be the noblest and the grandest."

Galyan glanced at Maddox.

"Is it not strange, sir? I now am the last, but not in the manner that I envisioned it. I am the sole representative of an ancient and glorious race. I did not have to trouble myself about offspring, because no Adok would have them."

Maddox did not know what to say.

"I miss my mate," Galyan said, quietly.

"Yes," Maddox said.

"I am having trouble equalizing these ideas. It helps to be part of a new family, sir. I am alone in the universe, and yet, I am part of a group. We aid each other, is that not so, sir?"

"It is," Maddox said. "If it helps, I am glad to call you my friend and my brother."

"We are brothers?"

Maddox glanced at the small Adok with his faint lines crisscrossing his "leathery" skin. Was it possible to feel loyalty to a computer-generated personality? The captain decided it was.

"Yes, Galyan, you and I are no longer alone. We are brothers who help each other. We have each other's back."

"That is an idiom, sir?"

"A human can't watch his own back. He needs a friend to watch it for him."

"I perceive the idiom. It is a good one. We have each other's back. Thank you, Captain."

"While I thank you, Driving Force Galyan."

They ran in silence for a time.

"Sir, I believe you have something else on your mind."

"Your probability analyzer has told you that?"

"Yes, sir," Galyan said.

"You're right. Tell me. Is the Ludendorff holoimage listening to us?"

"No, sir," Galyan said.

"Has the Ludendorff holoimage practiced its invisibility trick while aboard the starship?"

"Constantly," Galyan said. "I would have already informed you, but I thought you wanted to give the holoimage license to explore so I could catalog where it went, giving us that much more information about the Ludendorff image and engrams."

"I take it you have cataloged its various investigations."

"I have, sir. It has invisibly visited three hundred and nineteen locations to date. It is presently exploring the disruptor cannon chamber."

"I see."

"Do you wish me to inhibit its exploration?"

"You can do that?" Maddox asked.

"If we put the AI device in a sealed max chamber with an electromagnetic screen, yes."

"Can we do that easily?"

"No, sir," Galyan said. "I expect it would take Dana and me several days to set up such a place."

Maddox ran faster as he considered that. A lap later, he asked, "Do you think the holoimage will be aware of what you're doing while building this chamber?"

"I give that a ninety-nine percent probability," Galyan said.

"Do you think the AI has a virus insertion ability as you practiced on the Greenland complex computer?"

"The AI box is shielded from me," Galyan said. "I am unable to say regarding its ability to do this to me."

"Where is the box now?" Maddox asked.

"It has remained in the submersible."

Maddox glanced at the craft in the hangar bay. If the AI box had the computing ability to insert a virus into Galyan, would it have already done so? Maybe it wanted to lull the crew and lull Galyan first. The Ludendorff identity had acted secretly the entire time it had been on Earth. The captain reminded himself that the secretive behavior didn't necessarily mean it had an ulterior motive.

"Galyan, you will jettison the submersible from the hangar bay as soon as I leave. Then, go into protective mode and shut down."

"Sir?" Galyan asked.

"I think I may have inadvertently allowed a Trojan horse onto the starship. I will immediately turn you back on once we're out of the AI box's range. We must act with haste to forestall a takeover."

"You will allow the device freedom at the edge of the Tau Ceti System?" Galyan asked.

"No, I have an idea concerning that. First, I want to make sure nothing can harm your AI core. This is an emergency, Galyan. We dare not let anything corrupt you, my brother."

"Yes," Galyan said, a moment later. "I trust you, and my probability analyzer gives me a ninety-four percent chance that you will turn me back on. Those are high odds."

"I'd say so." Maddox veered for an exit. "Are you ready?"

"I am."

"Right," Maddox said. "So am I." He sprinted for an exit hatch.

-19-

"I should be the one to do this," Dana said, two hours later.

The crew met in the briefing room around a large table.

A distant Tau Ceti escort had sent a query some time ago regarding their identity. So far, the captain had maintained comm silence.

"Why should you be the one to do this, love?" Keith asked the doctor.

"It should be obvious why," Dana said. "Ludendorff and I had a deep relationship once. His fond memories of the time will help to protect me."

Keith laughed. "I don't think so. This is a computer, an advanced AI. It doesn't have emotions."

"Is that true, Galyan?" Dana asked. "Is it impossible for an AI to have emotions?"

"I have emotions," Galyan said.

Dana gave Keith a studied I-told-you-so look.

"Galyan is different," Keith said. "For one thing, he has a living creature's engrams."

"So does the Ludendorff AI," Dana said.

"It claims to, you mean."

"I fail to see the difference."

Keith looked around the table. "It should be obvious. Galyan is huge. There's space for advanced technology. And his engrams came from a dying Adok commander. Ludendorff's engrams are just a copy."

"How can you or a computer tell the difference?" Dana asked. "Engrams are engrams."

Keith seemed ready to speak, but hesitated.

"I hope you're not suggesting that Galyan's *spirit* or *soul* entered the AI with his death," Dana said in a mocking tone.

"Maybe I am," Keith said, sounding defensive.

"That's ridiculous," Dana said. "Captain, I am the logical choice to speak to the Ludendorff...holoimage."

Maddox wondered if that was true.

Two hours before, Galyan had used a tractor beam to shove the submersible and the Builder AI box out of the hangar bay into space. The Ludendorff holoimage had pleaded with him for a short while to return the box to the starship. Finally, the device had separated from them by ten thousand kilometers, which seemed to be out of its holographic projection range in space, which was different from its planetary-bound range. The holoimage had simply faded away. Could it still send comm signals, though?

Galyan had not sensed any, no hostile computer takeover attempts, either. Now, the crew discussed who should go in a shuttle to speak to the Ludendorff AI.

"Why would any of us go?" Valerie asked. "Establish a simple radio link. The Ludendorff AI can speak to us through that. If we're worried about its ability to take over computers, why wouldn't we be worried it could take over a shuttle? It could threaten to kill the occupant by opening all the hatches."

"Ludendorff would never do that," Dana said.

The others regarded the doctor.

"Nor would a Builder do such a thing," the doctor said. "From my discoveries in the Mid-Atlantic, I believe they were entirely peaceful."

"We'll establish a link," Maddox said. "How long will it take to set up?" he asked Valerie.

"Several hours, at most," the lieutenant said.

"Speed is warranted," Galyan said. "Several Star Watch vessels are headed in our direction, including the Patrol escort which first hailed us."

"How long until they're in firing range?" Maddox asked.

"Three days minimum," Galyan said.

"I'd say that gives us a good safety margin," the captain said. "Now, let's get started."

***

Nearly four hours later, the captain sat in his chair on the bridge. A flare of light on the main screen, a little larger than a star, showed the link maneuvering into position. It was halfway to the submersible.

Valerie touched her right ear implant. "Everything's ready, sir," she said.

"Open channels with the AI," Maddox said.

Valerie made the needed adjustments before nodding to the captain.

"Hello, Professor Ludendorff," Maddox said. "Can you hear me?"

"I do indeed," the AI said. "These precautions are quite unnecessary and wasteful of our most precious commodity, time. The real professor could be dying as we sit on the edge of the Tau Ceti System bickering at a distance from each other."

Valerie tapped her board, muting the comm. "Sir," she said. "My readings indicate the submersible is online."

"The AI switched on the sub's interior systems?" Maddox asked.

"That's the likeliest explanation," the lieutenant said. "It proves the AI can infiltrate and override computer systems."

"Not necessarily," Maddox said. "The androids were onboard. Perhaps the AI reactivated them in some manner. They could have manually turned on certain interior systems." He motioned to her board.

Valerie unmuted the comm.

"Therefore," the Ludendorff AI was saying, "we should be traveling at maximum speed to the Xerxes System."

Maddox waited several beats before he said, "There's more at stake than just Professor Ludendorff. For instance, suppose you are a subtle attempt by Strand to lure the starship into a position where he can board and take us over?"

"Such is not the case, I assure you," the AI said.

Maddox remembered the flitter ride from Shanghai to Geneva. He'd spent much of it wondering if he was an android.

If Strand had sent the AI box, why would the Methuselah Man let the AI know it?

"I fail to understand your certainty," Maddox said. "If you truly had Ludendorff's engrams, you would see the possibility of enemy trickery through you."

"Now, see here, my boy, such an idea offends me. I have the engrams of Ludendorff indeed. I know very well how I should react because that is exactly how I do. Now, I've had enough of this tomfoolery. I demand that you send out a shuttle and bring me back to *Victory*."

"We will, Professor, after we've rigged a special chamber for you."

Several seconds went by in silence.

"Professor, are you still listening?" Maddox asked.

"Is Dana there?" the AI asked.

Maddox motioned to Valerie. The lieutenant tapped her panel, waiting a moment and nodding to the captain.

"She's online now, Professor," Maddox said.

"Dana?" the AI asked.

"I'm here, Professor," Dana said.

"I have always hated good-byes, but I'm afraid we're going to be parted again, my dear."

"What do you mean?" Dana asked in alarm.

"I cannot tolerate confinement."

"You're already in a Builder cube," Maddox said. "How much more confined can you become?"

"You do not understand," the AI said. "I have strict parameters. Do not forget what I have told you, my boy. The professor is holding on as best he can in the Nexus. This...excessive caution on your part is going to cost him his life. I cannot allow that and I cannot allow you to confine my..." The AI's voice faded away.

Maddox turned to Valerie. "What happened? Did we lose the connection?"

Valerie tapped her board. "No. There's nothing wrong with the link. He's just pausing."

"No," Galyan said. "It is over. Observe."

166

Maddox looked up at the main screen. A flash appeared. It was a point of brilliance. A moment later, it died down and was gone.

"What was that?" Maddox asked. "What did I just witness?"

Valerie initiated a scan.

"The submersible self-destructed," Galyan announced. "Now we understand why the AI box had turned it on."

"Lieutenant," Maddox asked, "is that what your scan tells you?"

"I have just told you they are gone," Galyan said. "But if you wish a living being to check on my accuracy, go ahead. I do not mind."

"This has no bearing on our feeling toward you," Maddox told the Adok holoimage.

"I have already said I do not mind," Galyan said. "I do not. Go ahead. Scan the area, Valerie. Commit a redundant act and waste more time."

Valerie gave Maddox a meaningful look.

"Do as I ordered, Lieutenant," Maddox said. "I am not going to be held emotionally hostage by a computer system."

"That is an unkind statement," Galyan said. "I suggest that indicates you are under a great deal of stress."

"I've completed the scan, sir," Valerie said, looking up. "The submersible is gone. In its place is expanding debris and gas. I can no longer pinpoint the Builder AI box. It appears we've lost it, sir."

"And we've lost the androids with it," Maddox said. "Galyan, why did the AI self-destruct?"

"Now you desire my help? I find that interesting."

Maddox glanced up at the ceiling. "Yes, I desire your help, as that will help to lower my stress levels."

The holoimage regarded Maddox more closely. "I accept your regret, Captain. I realize you are not capable of giving a full-throated apology. Thus, you use self-deprecation, which is a thing you find repugnant, all in order to attempt a mollification with me. This I indeed accept, as it is the extent that you can give me."

"You don't forget a slight easily, do you, Galyan?" Keith asked from the piloting board.

"I remember longer than anyone I have met to date," Galyan said.

"I would still like an analysis on the Ludendorff AI's self-destruction," Maddox said, drily.

"The reason appears elementary to me," Galyan said. "I suspect it was enforced by a Builder code. The code abhorred capture and possible study for technical duplication. Therefore, the code forced the Ludendorff AI to commit self-destruction."

"Yes, but why now?" asked Maddox. "That doesn't make sense. The box wasn't in any danger of confinement yet. It could have argued longer. That's what the real Ludendorff would have done."

"I have to agree," Dana said from a comm-unit. "If it truly thought as Ludendorff, he would have waited until the last minute before destroying himself."

"What does that suggest to you?" Maddox asked the doctor.

"One of two possibilities," Dana said. "Either, the AI didn't really have Ludendorff's engrams…"

"Yes? Or?"

"Or it sensed an immediate danger," Dana said, "one that involved capture."

Maddox whirled around in his chair. "Valerie, do a hard scan. Galyan, I want you to do the same—"

"Captain," the holoimage said. "I sense a missile heading toward us."

"Where?" Maddox asked.

"It is three hundred thousand kilometers and closing at high speed," Galyan said. "It is cloaked, using a cloaking device superior to what Strand's star cruiser used many months ago in the Solar System."

"Why didn't the Ludendorff AI warn us about it?" Valerie asked. "That can't be the reason it self-destructed. There must be another danger."

"It doesn't matter," Maddox said. "Lieutenant, get ready to use the star drive. We're leaving the star system."

"Yes, sir," Valerie said, tapping her board. After a moment, she tapped harder.

"Is there a problem?" Maddox asked.

Valerie paled as she looked up. "Yes, sir," she said. "The star drive is malfunctioning."

"Galyan," Maddox snapped, "how much longer until the cloaked missile is in explosion range?"

"It is too late," the holoimage said. "The missile is detonating."

"Give me full power to the shield!" Maddox shouted. As the captain spoke, a purple line appeared as if from nowhere. The line speared at light speed, reaching the starship's shield, turning a small area a bright red that went to brown and then black. At that point, the remaining beam achieved a burn-through and stabbed the collapsium-armored hull.

-20-

"We've been hit," Valerie declared.

"What's the damage?" Maddox asked.

"One minute, sir," Valerie said, as her fingers roved over her panel, tapping fast.

"Galyan," Maddox said. "Are any more missiles incoming?"

"Affirmative, sir," the holoimage said. "I count seven more approaching. The nearest is…five hundred thousand kilometers and closing fast. The next is seven hundred thousand kilometers."

"Why didn't you detect them earlier?" Maddox asked.

"I can run a self-diagnostic to find out."

"Will that harm your present efficiency?" Maddox asked.

"Possibly."

"We'll wait. Is the disrupter cannon ready?"

"No, sir," Galyan said. "That will take time. But I can warm up my neutron cannon in seven seconds."

"Do it," Maddox said. "Lieutenant, I'm waiting on the damage report."

"The collapsium armor held, sir," Valerie said.

"Why did it take you so long to find out?"

"There's an anomaly on the outer hull, sir."

Maddox frowned. "What is it?"

Valerie shook her head. "I don't know…"

"Should I go outside and check?" Galyan asked.

"Negative," Maddox said, who appeared thoughtful. "Ready the neutron cannon. Target the third missile."

"What about the second one, sir?" Galyan asked.

"We're going to absorb its shot," Maddox said. "Lieutenant, are the shields at full strength?"

"Yes, sir," Valerie said. "There won't be a burn-through this time."

"There it goes!" Keith shouted. "I can see it."

Maddox looked up at the main screen. Once more, a bright explosion appeared. From it, a purple neutron beam—what he thought must be a neutron beam—flashed the distance at the speed of light. It struck *Victory's* screen, turning it red but no deeper color.

"Our neutron cannon is ready, sir," Galyan said.

"Are you targeting the third missile?"

"Affirmative," Galyan said.

"Fire at will," Maddox said.

The ancient engines purred with power. A moment later, a purple beam lashed into the darkness. Galyan's fantastic computing power targeted where the missile would be at the precise instant the speed-of-light ray reached the spot.

The missile exploded without energizing a beam.

"Good work, Galyan," the captain said. "Keep knocking them down."

Before Galyan could respond, a missile self-exploded from much farther away. It took the enemy beam longer to travel the greater distance and it stuck the shield with less power, but now all the missiles ignited, adding their beams to the same area of the shield.

The shield went from red to brown and started turning black.

"That can't be a pure neutron beam," Maddox said. "Otherwise, our shield would have stopped them already."

"I agree with your analysis," Galyan said. "This is a mystery. According to my sensors, those were indeed neutron beams."

Maddox pondered that. "Have you found their launch point yet?"

"Negative," Galyan said. "I—" The holoimage wavered, becoming fainter as its words faded away.

"Galyan," Maddox said. "Don't cut out on me now."

Valerie hissed from her board, "That's what it is. Sir," she said, looking up, "the enemy landed some sort of computer damper on our hull with the first shot."

"How is that possible with a beam?" Maddox asked. "A beam isn't a material thing."

Valerie shook her head helplessly.

"Second Lieutenant," Maddox said. "You will initiate a star jump at the first possibility."

"Manually, eh, mate?" Keith said, as he rubbed his fingers before his controls. "I've always wondered if I could do it. Yes, sir. Right away, sir. Still, you'll have to give me several minutes."

"Sir," Valerie said. "I'm not sure we should—"

"Belay your verbal doubts," Maddox said. "Give me an estimate on the cloaked missiles' launch point. Who's firing at us? Is this a New Men infiltration attack? If so, how did they know to be at the edge of the Tau Ceti System to ambush *Victory*?"

For the next few minutes, each crewmember worked at their task. A faint Galyan stood there the entire time, silently talking.

"Dana," Maddox said into an armrest comm, "you're our Adok expert. What's wrong with Galyan?"

"I'm headed to the AI core to check," Dana said through the intercom.

Maddox stared at the main screen. It showed the various planets of the Tau Ceti System as superimposed dots. Dotted lines showed the orbital paths. Far in the distance shined the system's star. A secret enemy was attacking the starship. It would seem the enemy had made the assault in order to get to Galyan. That made sense. If one couldn't knock out the starship directly, the second best thing would be to knock out the ancient artificial intelligence running the ship's systems.

"Is Strand behind this?" the captain asked.

172

"The Methuselah Man faced us in a cloaked star cruiser before, sir," Valerie said. "Strand had the gall to enter the Solar System while you faced the Destroyer."

Maddox nodded. He had gone over the videos of the event many times. Strand and Ludendorff were two of a kind, the oldest Methuselah Men, far older than the young Methuselah People like the Lord High Admiral or even Octavian Nerva, who had died in the nuclear blast in Monte Carlo many months ago.

Over one hundred and sixty years ago, Strand had sent Thomas Moore Society colonists into the Beyond to set up a secret colony. There, they had genetically created the New Men. Strand had wanted to fashion Defenders of regular humanity, used only in a stellar emergency. He hadn't wanted humanity to rely on the Defenders and become dependents. Unfortunately, the idea had backfired, with the New Men deciding they should rule instead of serving.

Many months ago in Star Watch Headquarters, the Ludendorff android had said that Strand had also given humanity longevity treatments. That had been the genesis of the Methuselah People.

Maddox pondered the idea of longevity. Long, long ago— nobody knew how long—Builders had done something to Strand and Ludendorff, making them nearly immortal and perhaps increasing their intelligence.

The point was that Strand had deep motives and fantastic abilities to do things nobody else could do except perhaps for Ludendorff. Was the key to understanding Strand the Builders? Star Watch knew so little about the ancient aliens.

Maddox made a mental note to talk to Dana about her discoveries in the Mid-Atlantic. At this point, he needed to concentrate on the main issue. Why had the cloaked missiles gone after Galyan?

"I wonder if our enemy realizes how small of a crew we have," Maddox said.

Valerie looked up, stricken. "Are you suggesting the attack was planned in advance of our having arrived here?"

"Most definitely," Maddox said. "Consider. Eliminating Galyan would cripple us. That would allow an enemy a much easier time boarding and controlling the starship. Reason suggests this was a preplanned maneuver."

"If that's true," Valerie said, "then the Builder box double-crossed us."

"At first blush I'd agree," Maddox said. "But then why would the AI box have destroyed itself? If it was in league with our hidden attackers, it would have waited for pickup by them, would it not?"

A *beep* alerted Valerie. She turned to her panel, becoming absorbed with it. Soon, the lieutenant tapped furiously, her head swiveling as if reading various sources at once.

"Sir," she said. "I've found the launch point."

"Put it on the screen."

A moment later, the stars vanished as she zoomed in on a particular area of space. There was a wavy zone like heat off a hot road. It seemed to expand a moment like a hole in space, suddenly snapping shut. The heat-like waves reappeared. Soon, they faded away and it was just normal space again.

"What am I seeing?" Maddox asked. "Is that some kind of Laumer-Point?"

"I don't see how, sir," Valerie said. "We can't detect Laumer-Points without a Laumer Drive, and then we have to be much closer to the anomaly in order to detect it."

"Yet, the missiles came from somewhere," Maddox said, "somewhere *not* in the Tau Ceti System."

"I think that's right, sir."

Maddox contemplated the implications.

Faster than light travel normally involved the Laumer Drive, with Laumer-Points and tramlines. Most stars possessed wormholes that connected various systems. Delicate ship instrumentation found the precise entrance location. The special drive then allowed a ship to jump almost instantaneously between the two points, moving many light years along the tramline in the blink of an eye. Coming out of a Laumer-Point often strained the passengers, causing physical symptoms that ranged from mild, flu-like symptoms that passed quickly to more severe ones like vomiting, fainting and even death. Most computer systems—electrical, bio or phase—often shut down after a jump and took precious time to reboot.

It meant that most warships coming out of a Laumer-Point were vulnerable to a swift enemy attack—if the enemy vessels were close enough. The cloaked missiles should have been visible when they came out of the anomaly, as the cloaking system should have malfunctioned for a few minutes, at least.

"If the anomaly isn't a wormhole exit," Maddox said, "could it have been what the Destroyer used to transfer from one spot to another?"

Valerie snapped her fingers. "No wonder it seemed familiar. Yes, that's exactly right, sir. I think it was like the Destroyer's drive."

Maddox rubbed his chin. "Does that mean we're facing someone with Destroyer technology?"

"We annihilated the missiles too easily for that to be true," Valerie said.

"Yes," Maddox said. "Still, it appears we have an enemy who can open a path between distant points, possibly from one star system to another. Maybe even more incredible is that the transfer does not induce Jump Lag, or they've found a way to thwart it. If that's true, we've just witnessed a revolutionary tactic."

"Star Watch sends nuclear missiles through Laumer-Points all the time," Valerie said.

The lieutenant was right; it was standard military procedure. Since crews and spaceships experienced Jump Lag coming out of a wormhole, the answer was to send through huge thermonuclear warheads with simple timers. The warheads exploded, annihilating any nearby enemies waiting for them.

"The beam-firing missiles were different from our jump-procedure thermonuclears," Maddox said. "These selectively targeted our starship. Perhaps as interesting, they aimed at us from the other star system. Otherwise, we would have seen their exhaust plumes as they accelerated and targeted while in the Tau Ceti System."

"How can the enemy track us from another star system?" Valerie asked. "That should be impossible."

"Unless they could open a different window first and target us through it."

175

"I've never heard of such technology," Valerie said.

"Neither have I," Maddox said.

"Are the New Men doing this?"

"We have no idea who attacked us," Maddox said. "All we know is that they possess advanced cloaking, with neutron-beams and an unexplained transportation portal."

"The implications of this, sir…" Valerie said. "It would be impossible for us to hit back at an enemy that can shoot from a different star system."

"Get ready," Keith chimed in. "I've manually set up the conditions. We're going to use the star drive in: three, two, one—"

Maddox sat down.

"Now," Keith said, activating the drive.

A moment later, Starship *Victory* transferred three light years away.

***

Maddox was the first to recover from Jump Lag. He didn't wait for the others, but headed for an exit, hurrying down the corridor.

The Adok starship was huge and could have held thousands. Instead, there were merely six humans aboard. The nearly empty ship made for a lonely place.

The sensation caused Maddox to think of his mother. She'd fled from a genetic laboratory somewhere in the Beyond, carrying him in her womb. His father had been a New Man. Had he raped her? Had the haughty enemy scientists used artificial insemination?

I know so little about my origins. The New Men stole that from me.

Maddox frowned. Why did these questions about his parents keep bothering him? He had to push them aside. They didn't matter. He had to find and free Ludendorff. This time, though, he wasn't going to let the professor get the upper hand.

Maddox thought about the last voyage. Ludendorff had corrupted Galyan, taking control of the starship. Did that have any bearing on this latest attempt to fiddle with the AI?

Don't accept coincidences. Rather, use them as signposts.

As Maddox considered the idea, he came to the AI core chamber.

The hatch was open and he heard sounds from within. Before he reached the hatch, Dana stepped outside. There were smudges on her face and scratches on her hands. Last voyage, the doctor had found a hidden computing chamber on the ship. Once they brought it online, it had given Galyan more of his original Driving Force personality and more tech abilities. Dana knew the alien starship and AI better than anyone in Star Watch.

"Well?" the captain asked.

"It was a clever attack," Dana said, sounding tired. "By asking a mathematically impossible question, structuring it in such a way that Galyan had to answer, it put the AI into a thought-loop. In other words, the enemy directive kept Galyan thinking like a hamster on a wheel. That allowed the AI's basic functions to continue, but dimmed him, you could say."

"Is Galyan fixed?" Maddox asked.

"I am, Captain," Galyan said, appearing outside the AI core. "Thank you for your quick work, Doctor. Now that I have observed and analyzed the question, I know how to defend against it and similar ruses. Unfortunately, by initiating the defense, adding a redundancy sequence, I will compute seven percent slower than before."

Dana nodded as if all that seemed sensible.

"The structuring of the question was a highly advanced technique," Galyan added.

Maddox's eyes brightened. "By the technique, can you tell who made the assault?"

"That is an interesting angle of investigation," Galyan said. "Let me ponder it." The holoimage stood still, with only its eyelids fluttering.

"Why does he do that?" Maddox asked.

"I suspect it is an Adok adaptation," Dana said, "allowing regular crewmembers to see that the AI is busy."

"That's interesting. It shows we had some similarities with the Adoks."

"More than some," Dana said. "In most ways, Adoks thought and acted similarly to humans. If that were not so,

177

Galyan would not be able to communicate with us as effectively as he does."

"But...I've seen reports concerning the AI. Its different modes of thought have made it difficult for our scientists to understand most of the ship's secrets."

"It's a matter of degree," Dana said. "I'll give you an example. Great apes and human DNA have a ninety-eight point five percent similarity. Yet even that small variation—the one point five percent—makes for huge differences between apes and men. The same is true for the Adoks and us. As I said before, if we weren't so similar, communication would be impossible between us, as we would have no common reference points."

Before Maddox could ask more, the wall-comm buzzed. "Captain," Valerie said. "Is Galyan back?"

"He is."

"Then I suggest we hold a meeting, sir," Valerie said. "Our new discovery could have changed the parameters of the mission."

Maddox pursed his lips. He didn't want a meeting, but it might be better to go ahead and use it to gauge the crew's reactions to the latest event.

"Finish your diagnostic and recheck the damage to the collapsium armor. We'll meet in an hour."

***

They met in the briefing room around a large table. As Maddox had expected, Valerie wanted to abort the mission to race home to tell High Command about the portal missile attack.

"Negative," he said.

"But if the New Men are doing this—"

"The New Men did not make the attack," Maddox said.

Dana looked up. "How can you be certain?"

"We've seen how New Men attempt a takeover. They use commandos to board and storm."

"They could have tried a different tactic this time," Dana said.

Was he the only one who could see this?

178

"If the New Men had attacked," Maddox said, "commandos would have appeared after the Galyan-dampening missiles struck. No. This was someone else with a different agenda. The exotic technology proves my hypothesis. I agree with the lieutenant that High Command must learn of this. Therefore, Lieutenant, you will make a data packet and beam the missile attack information to the approaching Star Watch vessels."

"We're no longer in the Tau Ceti System," Valerie said quietly.

"We'll jump back in order to relay the news," Maddox said. "Afterward—Second Lieutenant, you will plot the fastest course to the Xerxes System."

"Including regular Laumer-Points?" Keith asked.

Maddox nodded. "Doctor, I would like you to ready a briefing about what you found in the Mid-Atlantic. The professor's holoimage told us he—it—operated from a Builder AI box. The Nexus in the Xerxes System is a Builder construct. I believe it's time we understood the ancient aliens a little better."

"You think the missiles could have been a Builder attack?" Valerie asked.

"No!" Dana said before Maddox could respond. "That's impossible. The Builders were peaceful and would not initiate such a thing."

Maddox studied the doctor. What made her so certain? He hoped to find out during her briefing about the Atlantis Project. Thus he adjourned the meeting without further comment.

-21-

Two jumps after delivering the data packet, Maddox sat in a darkened room with everyone else except for Keith. The ace remained on the bridge. Galyan presently worked in conjunction with Dana as a holoimage began to take shape before the seated crew.

"Behold," Dana said through speakers, "we are descending deep into the Mid-Atlantic Ocean."

The holographic display was clear and realistic, almost like being in a deep-diving sub. The squat vessel descended down, down, down into the heavy-pressure depths. Sunlight no longer reached this region of the ocean, making everything dark except for the sub's lights. To add to the effect, metallic groans sounded around them.

In the gloom, Maddox noticed Meta shiver. Perhaps she recalled the submersible in the Greenland Sea. He put a hand on her shoulder. She looked up at him and smiled.

"This is something we don't understand yet," Dana said. "There is no indication this part of the Mid-Atlantic ever possessed land above sea-level. It's one of the many mysteries concerning the alien base and its Atlantis connection."

"Aren't there underwater mountains here?" Valerie asked.

"Certainly," Dana said. "But they are far too low to have ever reached the surface. This is not a volcanic region like the Hawaiian Islands."

"What does that mean?" Valerie asked.

"Hot spots that push lava to the surface, forming islands," Dana answered. "In time, the lava mass shifts off the hot spot. That spot then builds another mountain, which in turn becomes an island. That's how the Hawaiian chain formed. We have no geologic evidence this ever happened in this area of the Atlantic."

"Then how could Atlantis have been here?" Valerie asked.

"Precisely," Dana said. "That's what many of the Atlantis Project scientists asked."

The doctor fell silent as the holoimage sub kept descending into the black depths.

Maddox squinted. He could make out a dot of light seemingly far below them.

"That is our destination," Dana said.

The bottom light grew and the sub slowed its advance. Finally, the light became a dome. It was a kilometer from the surface.

"There are much deeper canyons in the area," Dana explained. "But this is—was—the area with the most concentrated metal under the ocean floor."

"Who discovered the concentration of metal?" Maddox asked.

"His name is Dr. Orrin," Dana said. "He was the world's leading aqua-archeologist, having studied every underwater structure found on Earth, from Japan to the Persian Gulf to Malta. He commissioned a deep-sea scan three years ago."

"Why did he do that?" Maddox asked.

"I don't know. No one does."

"Dr. Orrin isn't part of the Atlantis Project?" the captain asked.

"I imagine he would be if he was alive," Dana said. "Dr. Orrin died a year ago. It was a foolish and wasteful death. Food poisoning," she said.

"That doesn't strike you as suspicious?" Maddox asked.

"It didn't before this," Dana admitted. "Now, though…that is odd, isn't it?"

Once more, the doctor fell silent.

The holographic dome grew so they could see the octagonal cells making up the skin of the dome, like a beehive.

The squat sub soon shuddered, parking beside the dome. A short tube moved, connecting with the sub's main hatch.

"We went through the tunnel into the dome," Dana said. "It was quite unpleasant."

The holoimage changed. They passed through the short tube, listening to deep groaning all around them. Soon, they entered the dome. It was much like a starship, with small chambers, hatches and thick bulkheads.

"I've shown you this part," Dana said, "to give you an idea of how daunting the environment was down there. The cost to construct the dome proved staggering."

"Did Star Watch fund the construction?" Valerie asked.

"Let me check my notes," Dana said.

Maddox twisted in his seat, looking at the doctor seated on a tall stool. Her face glowed with an eerie green color from her tablet.

"Oh," Dana said. "This is interesting. Octavian Nerva put up half the money for the dome's construction."

"Where did the other half come from?" Maddox asked.

Dana clicked her tablet, finally shaking her head. "I'm afraid I don't have that information."

"Could the funds have come from Strand?" Meta asked. "I mean the Strand clone that used to work in Nerva Tower."

"I'm not sure I like the direction of your thought," Dana said. "I'd like it even less if it proved true." She sighed. "In any case, the dome lies over the densest area of underground metal."

The holoimage changed once more. It felt as if they were in an elevator going down. It stopped with a clang, and the room's temperature got colder.

"It was always cold in this area," Dana said. "We wore pressurized suits and worked with extreme caution. The first discoveries mandated this."

On a holographic table appeared a black cube. A force saw cut through it, splitting the cube in half. Blue sizzling lines bubbled in the two halves.

"That's what happened the first and only time we cut a cube," Dana said. "All the circuitry in it fused, destroying the connections and whatever information the cube held."

"Was it a Builder device?" Valerie asked.

"We believe so, particularly because we couldn't scan into it"

"Why did it fuse?" the lieutenant asked.

"There are as many theories as scientists on the project," Dana said. "My belief is that the Builders did not wish to infect our culture. The aliens seemed to desire a civilization to produce its own technology at its own pace. If we could technologically leap ahead…centuries possibly, that would corrupt our culture with advanced technology that we wouldn't be culturally ready to use."

"What causes you to project such benevolent behavior on their part?" Maddox asked. "Why couldn't they have done it out of fear? Maybe they did not want to create a species too powerful to handle?"

"Some of the others believed that," Dana said with a hint of reproof. "I think the evidence points otherwise."

"Do you have an example of this evidence?" Maddox asked.

"We're getting to that," Dana said. "First, I'd like you to see this."

The holoimage changed around them. Bulky, suited workers moved through a slanted shaft. They used power drills on rock, chipping deeper. Shafts of light from their helmets crisscrossed through particles of dust. Then, after what seemed like speeded time, the workers broke into a chamber through the ceiling. The shafts of light speared down on cubes of various sizes. Beside them were tubes. Inside the tubes were frozen people.

A shock at the base of Maddox's skull caused him to frown and rub the spot.

"Were those captives?" Riker asked.

"We don't think so," Dana said. "We opened three tubes and took tissue samples from the frozen individuals. Each person was six thousand years old."

"The same as *Victory*," Maddox said.

"Yes," Dana said.

"What time period would that have put the people?"

"Pre-dynastic Egypt," Dana said.

183

"What does that mean exactly?" Maddox asked. "I'm not that familiar with ancient Earth history."

"That would be before anyone built pyramids or the sphinx. I think the sphinx might be the most important structure of ancient Egypt."

"Why is that?" Valerie asked.

"Because of this," Dana said. As part of the holographic display, they entered another chamber. This one contained five metal sphinxes, each of them larger than a big African lion.

"Are these statues of Builders?" Maddox asked.

"Some of the scientists think so," Dana said. "I'm inclined to think not."

"They don't appear to be mechanical people or cybernetic organisms," Maddox said critically. "Galyan."

"Yes, Captain."

"Do the sphinxes seem familiar to you?"

"No, Captain," Galyan said. "But I never saw the mechanical people who helped the Adoks, or spoke to anyone who had."

"Doctor," the captain said. "Did you look at the sphinxes' paws?"

"Oh, we did," Dana said. "They were not like a cat's paws, but more like a baboon's, which would seemingly give them the benefit of human-like hands."

"So..." the captain said, "the Builders left statues of sphinxes and held humans in tubes. I don't see why you think they were strictly peaceful. Furthermore, I don't know how you conclusively call this a Builder structure."

"You haven't seen the most interesting thing yet," Dana said. "You've looked at a few chambers. You haven't seen what the outer structure looks like. I'll give you a cutaway of the entire building."

The holoimage shrank until it was clear that the structure under the seafloor was a giant metal pyramid.

That caused a second slight shock at the base of the captain's skull.

"Was it a Nexus?" Valerie asked.

"I've wondered that," Dana said. "We planned to go deeper, but our digging units always cut out after this point."

"In what way did they 'cut out'?" the captain asked.

"We're not sure," Dana said. "It seems something deeper inside the pyramid sucked out the energy."

"Lasers positioned higher up might have beamed deeper," Maddox said.

"You can't be serious," the doctor said. "You would use lasers against such a fantastic archeological discovery?"

"Yes. I would laser down into an alien base on Earth, one that kept humans in tubes like butterflies. I would not hesitate to do so."

"Which shows that you're a soldier at heart," Dana said, "not a scientist with a yearning to know why."

"You may be right," Maddox said. "Is there more?"

"Isn't this enough?"

Maddox found that an odd comment coming from the doctor. Her curiosity was usually insatiable.

"How did you conclude this was a Builder structure and that they were peaceful?" Maddox asked. "The last aspect, in particular, has eluded me."

"I'll answer the last question first," Dana said. "Think of what you're seeing. The Builders were on Earth six thousand years ago. They did not subjugate humanity. Instead, they held a few people in tubes. There is reason to believe the tubes were some type of advanced medical equipment. That would mean they were not holding those people against their will, but trying to save them. In answer to your first question, the pyramidal shape implies Builders, as does the age of the humans in the tubes."

"I agree that the Builders did not appear to be aggressive," Maddox said. "They seemed to have left humanity alone, at least the vast majority of people. Yet, I fail to see the evidence of utter peacefulness. Could it be this is what you wish to see, Doctor?"

"Nonsense," Dana said in a brittle tone. "I am well known for my objectivity. I do not appreciate your slander."

Maddox pursed his lips, nodding after a moment.

As the briefing ended, the captain rubbed his neck, recalling the two shocks. Something was off here. He needed to

185

think, to ponder the last few days and find the connection to his growing unease.

-22-

Two jumps later, Maddox stood in a vast, nearly empty room, speed drawing his pistol, firing at a distant object. The kicks against his hand aided his thinking. He continued like an automaton, drawing faster and faster, his aim becoming uncanny.

"Maddox!" someone said, sharply.

The captain halted his descending hand a centimeter before it would have grasped the gun butt. He turned in a languid manner, although the narrowness of his eyes belied his seemingly easy way.

Meta eyed him with concern. She wore a formfitting one-piece accentuating her voluptuous figure. Normally, this might have caused one corner of Maddox's mouth to quirk upward. Instead, he regarded her dispassionately.

"I shouted your name three times before you finally acknowledged me," she complained.

Maddox said nothing.

Her concern visibly grew. "Are you well?"

He nodded.

"What's wrong?"

"Yes," he said. "That's what I'm trying to deduce."

Meta blinked several times before she appeared to understand him. "Oh. Is it Dana?"

"Do you care to elaborate on that?"

Meta glanced at her hands. She clasped them, kneading her intertwined fingers. "It's small things, well, maybe not that small. So far, she hasn't talked to me about old times. We usually do that after being apart."

Dana and Meta had spent hard years together on Loki Prime, surviving against some of the worst people in the Commonwealth. It had forged a bond between them.

"She's barely given me a nod, in fact," Meta added. "I tried talking to her yesterday in the cafeteria. She smiled absently and listened to what I had to say. Once she finished her coffee, though, she excused herself, saying she had work to do."

"What kind of work?"

"That's what I asked. She became secretive. I've seen her that way with others, but never with me. I don't know. I'd like to say she's worried about Ludendorff. But…"

"Her interest in the professor seems staged?" Maddox asked.

"Yes!" Meta said. "You've noticed too?"

Maddox took his time answering. "It dawned on me during the briefing, certain items that refused to mesh. And the enemy beam attack on Galyan—" The captain shook his head.

"What does the beam attack have to do with Dana?"

"After the attack, Dana came out of the AI core," Maddox said. "There were scratches on her hands. What caused the scratches?"

"You think Dana had something to do with the missile attack?"

"That strikes you as wrong?" Maddox asked.

"Dead wrong," Meta said, with heat. "You make it sound as if she's working against us. The first voyage that was true. I'm surprised you can doubt her now. Hasn't she proved herself many times over?"

"She has," Maddox admitted.

"Then…how can you suspect her?"

Maddox smiled faintly.

"Did I say something stupid?"

"No," he said, coming closer, pulling her hands apart, intertwining his fingers with hers.

Meta searched his eyes. He embraced her, kissing her softly. After a time, she pulled away.

"What was that for?" she asked. "Not that I don't like it. But you were so remote just a moment ago."

"I decided to take a moment and remember my humanity. Your…garment helped in that regard."

"Do you like it?" she asked, posing for him.

"Very much," he said.

"Good," she said, pressing against him, kissing him again. "That's for noticing. Sometimes, you're too busy thinking to notice what you should."

"Hmmm," he said.

"Let me ask you again, how can you suspect Dana?"

Maddox released Meta, taking several steps toward the target. He paused, and it seemed he might draw and fire again. Instead, his shoulders relaxed and he faced his Rouen Colony woman.

"Do you remember how Dana hypnotized you last voyage?"

"Of course," Meta said. "She helped me remember what happened on the star cruiser in Wolf Prime orbit. Strand used a machine on my mind. He…" Meta's eyes widened. "Do you think someone has tampered with Dana's mind?"

"That would be the easiest explanation to the missile assault. In particular, how they knew where we were."

"You're suggesting Dana is a traitor?"

"Not intentionally," Maddox said. "Still, I've come to believe it would be extremely difficult to target *Victory* with weapons-firing portals. And this beam that asks a question in order to thought-loop Galyan—I cannot accept it. Instead, I think we have a similar situation as last voyage, except that this time it is the doctor who may have altered the AI. I also find no concrete evidence to conclude the Builders are entirely peaceful. If there are any thought-loops, they appear to be in the doctor's mind."

"If you're right," Meta said, "that would explain why she hasn't acted normally to me."

Maddox nodded.

"What do we do?"

"Precisely nothing," Dana said. The doctor stepped into the chamber with a laser pistol aimed at Maddox.

Meta whirled around. "Dana, don't! Don't shoot the captain."

"I have no intention of shooting him, provided he cooperates," Dana said, her gaze locked onto Maddox. "Move with extreme slowness, Captain, and unbuckle your gun-belt. Meta's life depends on it."

"What?" Meta asked. "You'd shoot me?"

"Only as a last resort," Dana said.

"But we-we're friends," Meta said. "Don't you remember Loki Prime?"

"Shut-up," Dana said.

A third shock at the base of Maddox's skull must have struck a thought loose. The captain believed he understood what was going on. It was simple, direct and oh-so obvious now. Yes, and it meant he must act at once.

"I am ice," Maddox said.

Meta stared at him in surprise and then with understanding. "No, Maddox!" she shouted. "No! Don't do it."

Dana glanced at Meta.

Maddox drew his pistol with lightning speed. He fired three times, each slug shattering Dana's face. That proved it was not actually Dana but an android. The thing had amazing reflexes of its own. The laser pistol beamed, shooting an intense ray that burned between the captain's left pectoral and shoulder.

Horrible agony struck Maddox. His gun clattered onto the deck. He staggered backward as waves of pain slammed home, threating to make him vomit and fall unconscious.

He hung on, though, having to know if he'd put it down.

The Dana-android's ruined face showered blue sparks. Bits of metal and bloody pseudo-flesh rained onto the floor as the creature staggered backward. This must be a different kind of android than the ones in the Lin Ru Hotel, which hadn't bled when shot. This time, Maddox had loaded his gun with special, high-powered bullets. He hadn't wanted to continue aiming for an android's eyes to stop it as had happened in Shanghai.

The android's laser-pistol hand had lowered. Now, it jerked up and swayed leftward. A second beam burned through the room. It came uncomfortably near the captain.

The agony grew in his body with waves of pain. His eyelids fluttered.

I refuse to fall unconscious. But he couldn't bend down for his gun no matter how hard he willed it. His body simply wouldn't obey those signals from his brain.

In time-stop frames of sight, Maddox watched Meta. His Rouen Colony woman tackled the android so they slid across the floor. As they slowed, the thing attempted to club Meta with the butt of its laser-pistol. Maddox recalled the strength of the Shanghai androids. Meta grappled with the hand, trying to hold it. The creature wrenched its captured arm, almost ripping it free. With a martial arts shout, Meta bent the android's gun-hand back so sharply that something broke in it.

"Meta," the android said, as the laser clattered across the floor.

With a second shout, Meta slammed an elbow against the android's ruined face. The back of the head struck the deck.

At that point, Maddox sank to his knees. The shock of laser burn was overcoming his will. It would seem there was only so much a man—even a hybrid—could do against such shock.

"You must—" the android said.

Meta struck again so more pieces flew off the face.

"Wait," the android said. "Allow me to—"

The creature never finished its words. Meta grabbed its broken head and twisted savagely, snapping a connection, no doubt, causing metal to screech.

At that point, a new voice devoid of humanity spoke out of the android. "Detonation in five seconds," it said.

That's all Maddox heard. Then he slumped forward, unconscious before he fell.

-23-

At first, Maddox heard voices. They were indistinct, droning voices, as annoying as flies. He didn't try to understand them. It was enough...

What was enough?

He faded out and came back sometime later. Memories began to return in bits and pieces. He recalled a shattered face, sparks, pain—oh, yes, terrible pain that, that...

Everything faded once more as he fell asleep again.

Later, the droning voices returned. They sounded far away. Each had its own note, though. That was different from last time. He attempted to concentrate, but that made his brain throb.

"Let him rest."

Maddox heard that. A woman spoke it. She seemed familiar, and it haunted him because he thought she was, was...dead?

"Meta?" he croaked.

"I'm here," said a voice very near his ear.

He could feel soft hands stroking his arm. He liked that.

"Is...?"

That's all he heard before fading away yet again,

The next time Maddox came to, he opened his eyes. It took him several seconds before he realized he lay in the infirmary on a cot. Bandages swathed the left side of his torso and shoulder. He felt so weak, so helpless. It was a terrible sensation.

I have to get up.

The thought burned in him. If he was weak, the others might find him like this. They would not hesitate to kill him, ending his quest to find…

Maddox took a shuddering breath, knowing it would likely be painful. Yes, he felt a twinge in his shoulder. He realized he was under the influence of powerful drugs.

The captain turned his head, which remained on the pillow the entire time. A person slept in the chair beside his cot. She was beautiful beyond conception. She—

"Meta," he said, although it came out a whisper.

Nonetheless, her eyes opened. Their gazes met and a lazy smile spread across her gorgeous features. He liked that.

A second later, Meta bolted upright. "Maddox!" she shouted.

His smile grew until it felt as if it would tear off his face.

She stood beside him, stroking his good arm. "You had us worried, love," she said.

"What…?" He wet his lips with a numb tongue. "What happened? I thought I heard something about a detonation."

"You did," Meta said. "But don't worry about that now."

"How can you be alive? How can I be alive?" Maddox frowned. He wondered if Galyan had remained under Dana's control—under the control of the android posing as Dana. If so, this might be another android, but posing as Meta.

"Don't worry, love," Meta said. "You're going to be all right now. Galyan had an advanced—"

"Are you real?" he asked, interrupting her.

Meta frowned with worry.

"Are you an android?" he demanded.

"No. It's me. Meta. Don't you recognize me?"

"The drugs are altering his thoughts," Galyan said as he appeared beside Meta.

That's when Maddox realized this was a conspiracy. They had drugged him. Meta was dead. The android had detonated, and Galyan must no doubt be performing according to the android's codes. How had he ever been so foolish as to let an android into Galyan's AI core? After all this time, an android had bested him.

193

"He must sleep," Galyan said. "It's not good for him to be this anxious."

"Rest, darling," Meta said, stroking his arm again. "You'll feel better in a day or two."

"More like three," Galyan said, "barely in time, too."

"Why?" Maddox whispered. "Why is it barely in time?"

Meta gave the holoimage a questioning glance.

"He's recovering," Galyan said. "The danger of laser shock is over. Rest is the best medicine now."

Maddox tried to resist. It was as if the AI had power over his eyelids. He fought it, but he had no strength. Increment by increment, his eyelids closed until he was asleep once more.

***

Maddox shuddered, and his eyes flew open. This time, Riker sat in the chair. The sergeant played a video game on a tablet.

Was that really Riker, though? Maybe it was another android.

With care, Maddox drew up his knees. Maybe the android heard the fabric move. Riker looked up.

"Captain," Riker said. The sergeant set aside the tablet, standing. He put his hands on the bed's rail. "How are you feeling, sir?"

Maddox inspected the Riker android.

"Galyan said you shouldn't be feeling any more pain," Riker said.

Maddox sneered.

Riker stepped back. The sergeant appeared thoughtful. "You went into laser shock, sir."

"Did I?" Maddox asked.

"Galyan prescribed medicine."

"Ah," Maddox said.

"The AI said he's been studying human bodily systems. We had to do something, sir."

"I know," Maddox said. "So let us forgo the pretense."

"Know what, sir?" Riker asked, appearing confused. The creature did it well.

"You're an android, of course," Maddox said.

194

"Do you mean my arm, sir?"

"You know exactly what I mean."

Riker frowned until understanding lit his eyes. "The Dana android—the detonation, right, you must think she controlled Galyan."

"It's obvious she had to," Maddox said. "She was alone in the AI core chamber."

"I don't dispute that, sir. And you're partly correct. The doctor, well, her android double, did attempt to suborn the AI. None of us counted on Driving Force Galyan's cunning, sir. The AI has been busy these past months in Earth orbit. Galyan explained it to us."

Maddox watched the lying android. He had to kill them all and regain control of the starship.

At that point, the holoimage appeared. Galyan approached the bed, peering into the captain's eyes.

"You are finally lucid," Galyan said.

"He thinks you're a pawn of the android-makers," Riker told the holoimage. "He believes I'm an android."

Galyan froze as his eyelids fluttered. That lasted two seconds. "I see," the AI said. "It makes sense from a hypersensitive mind, a possible conclusion given his limited evidence. Captain Maddox, I tricked the Dana android."

"How?" Maddox demanded.

"Do you remember I spoke about a redundancy limiting my core power by seven percent?"

Maddox managed to nod yes.

"Before that," Galyan said, "I added an earlier redundancy. It worked on the problem while the majority of my computing systems aided the android. That's why we were in the right— the wrong spot—in the Tau Ceti System for the missile attack."

"That doesn't make sense," Maddox said.

"It would to an Adok," Galyan said. "My true identity remained hidden in the redundancy. It observed the android's actions—along with the missile assault—and waited for the proper moment to resurface."

"Who made the portal missile attack?" Maddox asked.

"The exact personages remain hidden," Galyan said. "However, they are directly linked to the Builder AI box and the androids. By using the plural, I am referring to the Dana android and those dispatched to the submersible to help you escape the Greenland complex."

"That means the Ludendorff holoimage was in league with the android-makers," Maddox said.

"I rate that the highest probability," Galyan said.

"It means we're likely heading into a trap."

"I concur with your reasoning."

Maddox frowned. It caused a thumping rhythm to beat in his forehead directly over his eyes. It hadn't become all-encompassing yet, but it might get there soon.

"Was there really a mathematical question in the enemy beam?" Maddox asked.

"Affirmative," Galyan said.

"When I came running to the AI core, the Dana android was tampering with you."

"Correct," Galyan said. "Without my hidden redundancy, it would have gained control of me and likely the starship."

"What was its directive to you?"

"To follow her instructions and remain silent concerning the takeover."

The thumping in Maddox's mind had gotten worse. It made the edges of his vision black.

"What happened to me?" Maddox asked. "Why am I so weak?"

"Laser shock," Galyan said. "Surely, you have heard of it."

Maddox had. Sometimes, those beamed with a laser went into shock, showing all the symptoms he had.

"Fortunately," Galyan said, "you have a robust physique. In another day, you will be up. In a week, you should be as good as ever."

"How far are we from the Xerxes System?"

"Half a day from the final jump point," Galyan said.

Maddox had been striving to sit up. He now relaxed, letting himself sink into the pillow and mattress. If they were near the Xerxes System, he must have been out for almost two weeks or more.

"You don't mean laser shock," the captain said, "but laser poisoning."

"You took it hard, sir," Riker said, with worry in his voice.

"So it would seem," Maddox said. He stared up at the ceiling. If he'd been out that long, anything could have happened aboard the starship. Why would Galyan pretend to be okay if he wasn't? What would they hope to achieve by fooling just him? Or could Galyan have done exactly what he'd suggested. This redundancy…it sounded crazy enough to be an Adok thing. It didn't strike Maddox as something plausible an android would make up to fool the hybrid.

"I'd like to speak to Lieutenant Noonan," Maddox said.

"I shall summon her," Galyan said.

"I want to speak to her alone," Maddox added.

"Sir," Galyan said. "Time is critical."

"You will do as I order, Galyan," Maddox said.

The AI turned to Riker. The sergeant nodded. "Very well," Galyan said.

***

"You wanted to see me, sir?" Valerie asked, as she entered the chamber.

Maddox was sitting up, reading a tablet. He hadn't heard the lieutenant enter. That troubled him. The laser poisoning seemed to have dulled his senses. He hoped that wasn't a permanent situation.

The lieutenant stood at attention before him.

"Please, sit," Maddox said.

Dutifully, Valerie sat down.

Maddox laid the tablet on his blanket-covered lap. "It would appear that we and Star Watch have no idea what really goes on down at the dome in the Mid-Atlantic."

"I've argued for turning around and going home, sir. We have to warn High Command about this. Who knows how many people—how many androids have taken the place of real people."

Maddox had reached the same conclusion. "I believe the Builder AI box and the Esquire Noble androids all came from the Mid-Atlantic dome."

"Given the elaborate security around Earth, that makes better sense than the box or androids having arrived by

197

spaceship." Valerie said. "There's just one thing. That implies the pyramid down there is another Nexus. Do you think that's possible?"

Maddox shook his head ruefully. "We have no idea what's really down there. Maybe the Dana android kept as close to the truth as possible, unaware how much any of us already knew. In fact, I suspect that's the most likely conclusion."

"Do you think Dana is still alive somewhere?"

It surprised Maddox that he hadn't thought about Doctor Rich yet. If she was still alive—

"Dana must be down in the dome," he said.

Valerie shivered. "Do you think the New Men are behind this, sir?"

"That's an interesting question. When did this pyramid become operational? We don't really know. One clue may be Dr. Orrin's death a year ago. That's likely when the pyramid became operational. The man must have been legitimate."

"If what the android told us is the truth," Valerie said.

"It will be our working assumption."

Valerie nodded, and she seemed to hesitate, finally saying, "Can I ask you a question, sir?"

"By all means," Maddox said.

"Why did you ask to talk to me alone?"

Maddox smiled. "You are my foil, Lieutenant. You have a tendency to speak your mind." He didn't add that he believed Valerie would be the hardest among the crew for the androids to duplicate in such a way that he wouldn't notice. What did that say about Meta and him that he knew Valerie better?

"And?" she asked.

"I want truth in hard doses," Maddox said. "I've been floundering too much lately. I have the feeling someone is trying to maneuver me, and I have no idea who or why. I mean to find out."

"Yes, sir," Valerie said, with enthusiasm.

Maddox nodded inwardly. He finally believed the others. This was the real Valerie Noonan, and she wanted to help him defeat Star Watch's enemies.

The captain was surprised how good he felt knowing he was still among friends. It made him determined to rescue the doctor if she was still alive.

"I'd be surprised if the New Men were behind this one," Maddox said. "They sent the Destroyer against Earth. Why would they do that if they had this Trojan horse in our midst? It could be Strand, though."

"Or?" Valerie asked.

"Or it could be Ludendorff," Maddox said.

Valerie lurched out of the chair. "Why do you suspect the professor?"

"One reason is because of the Ludendorff and Dana androids," Maddox said.

"But...I don't understand why Ludendorff would act against Star Watch."

"He's old, Lieutenant. How old we don't know, except he's likely as old as Strand is. Does such great age change one's thinking process? I would expect so. What does Ludendorff really desire? He's been as tricky as Strand. Given the professor's cunning, I continue to wonder why he went into the drone base when we were chasing the Destroyer. Did he do so in order to pull a switch on us, or did something surprise him down there and force the switch?"

Valerie sat down, maybe considering the idea. She began to fidget in the growing silence. Finally, she said, "I have the horrible feeling we're missing something right before us. What if the greatest danger to Star Watch is the pyramid on Earth? Maybe whoever is behind the androids wants *Victory* far away from the Solar System."

"So they can do what?"

"Exactly what we've seen: replace important people with androids. You said before that capturing the governing AI would be just as good as capturing *Victory*. Wouldn't the same hold true with Star Watch High Command?"

"That's a profound insight," Maddox said. For the first time, he truly considered turning around and rushing back to Earth. If they hadn't been just one jump from the Xerxes System, he might have ordered it.

199

"No," he said. "Let's see if Ludendorff is really locked in the Nexus. It shouldn't take more than a day or two. Afterward…we'll race back to Earth faster than we came."

"Yes, sir," Valerie said.

Maddox sighed. He felt tired. It was galling. "I'm going to sleep a bit. Then, I'll get up." He nodded. "And then we'll make the last jump. It's time we figured out what's really going on."

-24-

Through a long and circuitous stellar route, guided by messages from Strand indicating when it was safe to use a Laumer-Point and when it was not, Pa Kur and his hammership had finally swung behind the entire Grand Fleet.

They entered the New Venezuela System, exiting the Laumer-Point linked by several jumps to Caria 323.

Pa Kur stirred first on the bridge, the least affected by Jump Lag. He sat to the side at a sensor console. It was several minutes before the sensors started working. He scanned the star system, particularly near New Venezuela III.

Ah, he was in luck. Three Star Watch destroyers orbited the Earthlike planet along with a Chin super-junk and a Windsor League hammership. That was interesting. It looked as if Admiral Fletcher was attempting to integrate the Grand Fleet. Strand had predicted that would happen after the incident in the Inferno System and Commodore Garcia's death.

The sub-men were becoming scared. They listened more intently now to the one sub-man who had bested a New Men fleet. He'd done so in the Tannish System two years ago with Starship *Victory's* help. Did Fletcher think his integration would save the Grand Fleet from annihilation?

According to Strand, the Grand Fleet had bunched-up once again, and this time it would stay bunched-up possibly until its end. That had allowed Strand to guide Pa Kur around to New Venezuela. The enemy still had several brave Patrol officers willing to scout on their own. The rest of the ships moved with the Grand Fleet, hoping their size would save them from the clever New Men.

It actually might do so...except that Strand had a surprise for them once the Grand Fleet entered the wrong star system. First, in order to frighten them even more and cause their herd-like instincts to harden, they needed this last example.

Pa Kur turned in his chair, hearing the others begin to stir. Soon, messages would reach the hammership, as the sub-men in orbit around New Venezuela III would detect them and send queries.

"Captain," a sub-woman said, wearing the uniform of his Majesty's Windsor League service. She was one of the five surviving crewmembers from Palain's water moon, saved for this very reason.

Pa Kur had spent countless hours hypnotizing the Windsor League officers. All five were on the bridge at their normal stations. Only Pa Kur and the warfare specialist were with them.

Their hammership, renamed as the *Resolute*, accelerated toward the sub-men in orbit around New Venezuela III.

The sub-man playing captain for Pa Kur raised his head. The man had glazed eyes and slack features.

"Captain," a woman said. "I'm receiving signals from the *Golden Hind*." It was a hammership. "They want us to identify ourselves."

The pretend captain peered at Pa Kur.

The New Man nodded slightly.

The slack skin tightened on the captain's face. His eyes shined and he spoke confidently. "Put them on the main screen," he said.

Soon, an enemy sub-man appeared on the screen. He wore a Windsor League uniform, the symbols showing him to be a commander. He asked the usual questions.

The shiny-eyed captain said this was the *Resolute*. "His Majesty has decided on sending early reinforcements," the hypnotized sub-man said. "There are four more hammerships on their way. How goes the counteroffensive, Commander?"

Time passed as the questions and answers traveled back and forth. The time lag made it a painful, drawn-out process.

Finally—almost an hour later—the sub-man commander in orbit around New Venezuela III welcomed them to the Grand Fleet.

The hours grew as the *Resolute* headed in-system. New questions came and were answered more quickly, as the time lag between ships was constantly shortened. After half a day of this, the hypnotized captain began to show signs of strain.

Pa Kur realized the sub-man's former personality was trying to reassert itself. It was time for some comm problems. He signaled the comm officer, the woman.

She leaned toward the comm. "Come in, *Golden Hind*. I say again, come in, please." She glanced at Pa Kur.

He chopped his hand through the air.

The comm officer promptly clicked off the comm.

"Why did you do that?" the sub-man captain asked her.

"Attend me," Pa Kur said, sharply.

The five subhumans stopped their various activities, looking up, turning toward him robotically.

"Captain," Pa Kur said.

The sub-man sitting in the command chair did not respond properly. Instead, he hunched his head.

"Captain."

The sub-man hunched more.

Pa Kur hesitated trying again. Three failures in a row might begin a new conditioning. The captain's hindbrain might be able to lever free using that.

"Look into my eyes, Captain," Pa Kur said.

The sub-man fought the compulsion. He scowled and squirmed in his chair. Finally, he gripped the armrests until his fingertips turned white. Ever so slowly, however, his neck muscles forced his head upward. His eyes jerked up and down like the frisky colts the New Men kept on the Throne World. Against the man's will, his gaze locked on Pa Kur's black eyes.

The New Man began to speak to him quietly, gently.

"No!" the sub-man screamed. "No! You're devils! You're using me." He twisted around on the chair. "Wake up, people. Can't you see—?"

The sub-man gurgled, his eyes widening in shock and in pain. Deftly, Pa Kur removed the force blade from the man's back and stepped to one side. The man gasped once more as the smell of charred flesh wafted through the bridge.

"Emergency!" Pa Kur shouted. "Flee the bridge. We're having an electrical fire."

The four remaining subhumans glanced at each other.

"Hurry," Pa Kur told them. "The captain died trying to save you. Run to safety before it's too late or he'll have died in vain."

They got up, hurrying to the exit. The chief engineer turned around, staring at the dead sub-man on the floor.

Pa Kur marked that sub-man for death. He did not want another problem like the imitation captain.

After the Windsor League captives had departed the bridge, Pa Kur turned to the warfare specialist. "Clean him up. Wipe away the blood. I'll have to modify the others."

The specialist nodded.

Pa Kur closed his eyes a moment. He had a few difficult hours ahead. The comm officer should prove the most malleable. They had to get in close for this attack, and it had to be a complete surprise. He opened his eyes and headed for the exit.

***

The *Resolute* began to brake. The former comm officer now sat in the captain's chair. The engineer was missing from his station. Like the former captain, he was dead, already processed through the ship's incinerator.

One of the Star Watch destroyers left through a Laumer-Point. It was going to bring the good news to the main concentration of warships that reinforcements were already here.

The *Golden Hind* was beginning to slow its orbital path around New Venezuela III. It was going to match velocities with the approaching *Resolute*. All the while, new messages from his Majesty's hammership became more insistent.

"You may proceed," Pa Kur said.

The new captain pressed a button on her armrest. The planet, hammership and super-junk coming into view around New Venezuela III disappeared from the main screen. The

Golden Hind's commander appeared there now, a small, bearded man.

"You fixed your comm problem?" the Windsor League commander asked.

"Yes," the sub-woman comm officer said, smiling.

"Where's the captain?"

The comm officer hesitated, opening her mouth but saying nothing.

"Is something wrong?" the *Golden Hind's* commander asked.

The comm officer glanced at Pa Kur.

"The captain is sick," he said softly.

The sub-woman licked her lips, facing the main screen. "The, ah, captain fell sick," she said. "We had…had trouble on the bridge."

Pa Kur stiffened. What was wrong with the sub-woman? She wasn't supposed to say those things.

"What kind of trouble?" the Windsor League commander asked.

"Electrical," she said. "It was a power outage. The captain ran to repair it and was electrocuted."

"What?" the commander asked.

"It fried him," the sub-woman said in a robotic voice, with her eyes wide and staring. "It was horrible."

The *Golden Hind's* commander stared at her in shock and disbelief.

Pa Kur made a swift calculation and decision. He turned to his board and tapped fast. The *Resolute* quit braking and began accelerating instead. He motioned the warfare specialist, who immediately brought the shields online and warmed up the railguns.

New Venezuela III was still too far out for effective fire under normal circumstances, but with their special rounds, it was time to attack.

"I'm not sure I understand this," the *Golden Hind's* commander said. "You've raised your shields. Is there a reason for this?"

"Fire," Pa Kur told the warfare specialist. "Aim the first volley at the *Golden Hind*. Aim the next at the super-junk."

The comm officer stared at the screen.

"Tell him we're having mechanical trouble," Pa Kur ordered the sub-woman.

The comm officer turned to stare at him.

"Captain," the *Golden Hind's* commander said. "What is the meaning of this? Who is giving you orders?"

Pa Kur cut the connection and concentrated on his board.

"What is wrong with me?" the sub-woman asked, rubbing between her eyes.

Pa Kur took time from his tapping to draw his blaster. He set it on needle-fire and beamed the remaining subhumans. They each toppled onto the deck, dead. They were no longer useful, and he didn't have time to escort them to the brig. He had a battle to fight, and he'd lost the all-important element of surprise.

***

The hammership, super-junk and destroyers were accelerating out of orbit from New Venezuela III. They were still deep in the gravity well. They'd had two choices and they'd made them fast. Each had decided to come up out of the gravity well to fight instead of trying to race around the other side of the planet to hide.

The *Resolute* bored in, heading into the gravity well. Pa Kur had already played his chief card, the initial shots launched from the hammership's railguns some time ago. They were nova bombs although without any cloaking. Otherwise, they were the same weapons that had annihilated the majority of Commodore Garcia's flotilla.

The *Golden Hind's* railguns chugged auto-fire, sending solid rounds at the approaching nova bombs. It was next to impossible to hit those until the bombs were only five thousand kilometers away or so. By then, because of the bombs' massive damage radius, it would hardly matter. The sub-men couldn't possibly possess targeting computers good enough to hit farther out.

Then, a nova bomb ignited fifteen thousand kilometers from the *Golden Hind*. An enemy auto-round must have been on-target, setting off the nova bomb's proximity switch.

The nova blast must have damaged the enemy, but Pa Kur had no way of knowing yet. Although the *Resolute* was much farther away, the blast overloaded his hammership's sensors, whitening the main screen.

"I need sensors," Pa Kur said.

The warfare specialist took the sensors offline, saving them from another nova blast. They had lost the use of the superior sensors, as Strand had taken them back after the incident in the Inferno System. The minutes passed. The other nova bombs should have already ignited. The specialist brought the sensors back online, removing their outer combat coverings.

Some of the former whiteness had dissipated.

The bridge door opened and the comm specialist ran into the chamber, sliding into his spot at the comm. His fingers blurred across his board.

"The *Golden Hind's* triple shields are down," the comm specialist said. "The hull armor is breached. They're losing water and oxygen. Fifth Rank," he said. "They're firing railguns."

Pa Kur listened to the data in silence. How had the sub-woman broken through her conditioning? She had ruined a perfect surprise.

"I'm retargeting the *Golden Hind*," the warfare specialist said.

Pa Kur focused on the main screen.

With New Venezuela III behind it, the *Golden Hind* trained its railguns on the nearing *Resolute*, firing thermonuclear rounds. Air and water boiled out of gaping wounds in the crippled hammership's hull. The giant craft shuddered. A piece of hull armor ripped loose, spinning away.

The super-junk was nearer. Its shield was dark and it held onto its fighters. Maybe its commander realized the strikefighters would never survive the coming nuclear holocaust.

"Can Strand help us?" the warfare specialist asked.

Pa Kur's shoulders twitched. The Methuselah Man would help them only if that helped himself. For all he knew, Strand had already left the star system.

"Send another salvo at each," Pa Kur said. "Then, shut down the sensors."

The two New Men tapped their consoles.

Pa Kur's stomach clenched. Thermonuclear rounds approached. He had to save their now brittle sensors. If they were blind, the enemy could annihilate them at their leisure. Pa Kur would then cease to exist. He did not like how that made him feel.

After several minutes passed, he said, "Turn on the sensors."

The came online again but only partially worked.

"Enemy nuclear blasts have breached our two outer shields," the warfare specialist announced. "The third shield is dark. We must finish this, Commander."

Pa Kur signaled with his hand.

The hammership's mighty railguns chugged one round after another at the reeling *Golden Hind*. Meanwhile, the super-junk began to launch fighters.

"Impressive," the warfare specialist said. "They're launching into a radioactive mess. None of those pilots are going to survive the fight."

"The strikefighters are suiciding against us," Pa Kur said. "They could prove dangerous."

The normal procedure for a carrier or a super-junk was to stay back and launch fighters and bombers. The mothership was precious. This time, the super-junk continued to accelerate at *Resolute* as it launched craft the entire time.

"Commander," the warfare specialist said. "We have a situation. All the sub-men in their various craft are boring in against us."

Pa Kur could see that for himself. He had an elbow on an armrest and rested his chin on a fist. What did this mean? Strand's actions were to have demoralized the sub-men. Those attacking did not seem demoralized in the least.

"They have reckless courage," Pa Kur said.

"I'm targeting the super-junk," the warfare specialist said.

Pa Kur nodded absently.

"The destroyers are coming up behind the junk," the warfare specialist said. "It's as if they're using the bigger ship as a shield."

"Is desperate courage a symptom that occurs before cowardice strikes deep?" Pa Kur asked.

"Commander," the warfare specialist said. "What are your orders?"

Pa Kur frowned. "Destroy them, of course. Destroy them all." No matter what happened, he must survive.

The hammership continued to send railgun rounds at the super-junk. The *Resolute's* auto-defense cannons chugged away at the closing strikefighters.

The junk had defensive lasers, beaming as many nuclear warheads as they could before they ignited. The *Resolute* sent too many rounds, however, swamping the junk's defenses. Thermonuclear blasts hammered the junk's shield. It went from red to brown to total collapse. The next nuclear blast tore away armor plating. Then, the huge carrier shuddered for a long moment and exploded. The monstrous blast blew heat and debris in a growing circumference.

One of the destroyers zoomed through the destruction. The other never appeared. The blasts from the super-junk must have annihilated it.

Three of the *Golden Hind's* last thermonuclear rounds blew down *Resolute's* last shield. That allowed a cloud of strikefighters to fire their guns and launch missiles and space-marine pods directly at the hull armor.

The Star Watch destroyer added its laser beams. They were not heavy battleship beams or even cruiser beams. But they did help. Without a shield to breach, the lasers began to burn into the hammership's armor.

"Sir," the comm specialist said. "I have discovered a problem."

"The junk and hammership are gone," Pa Kur said. "We're out of danger."

"No, Commander, there is a danger. The—"

The bulkheads shuddered around them on the bridge as a massive blast shook the hammership.

"What was that?" Pa Kur asked.

"Antimatter warheads, Commander," the comm specialist said. "It is a new weapon."

"Marine pods are landing on the outer skin," the warfare specialist said.

"How many marines?" Pa Kur asked.

"The first wave—almost one hundred," the warfare specialist said. "Another five hundred are on the way."

"We can defeat six hundred space marines boarding us in waves," Pa Kur said.

"True," the warfare specialist said. "But we cannot defeat them and fight the strikefighters at the same time."

Another destroyer appeared, adding its lasers and firing more antimatter missiles at them.

"This should not be happening," Pa Kur said.

"What are your orders, Commander?" the warfare specialist said.

"We fight," Pa Kur said.

And fight they did, trading shots with the destroyers and clouds of strikefighters. The *Resolute* took out eighty percent of the enemy. While the hammership did so, hundreds of sub-men space marines entered the captured Windsor League vessel.

The marines did not attempt to take control. Instead, as they fought their way deeper into the ship, battling New Men, they planted demolition devices. Those began to explode, crippling the mighty warship further.

"Sir," the warfare specialist said. "The sub-men have behaved in a suicidal fashion throughout. It appears they are willing to die as long as they can kill some of us."

"I have concluded the same thing," Pa Kur said.

"While we have annihilated almost all of their ships, enough strikefighters remain to finish our hammership. What, now, sir?"

Pa Kur stared the warfare specialist in the eyes. "It is wasteful to throw away our lives."

"That is so."

"Come," Pa Kur told the other two. "We will abandon ship."

"What shall I tell my brothers battling the space marines?" the warfare specialist asked.

"Tell them nothing," Pa Kur said, "as they are doing their duty. We must escape in order to inform Strand of this new enemy tactic."

"Escape how, Commander?" the warfare specialist asked.

"By using our single-ships," Pa Kur said, heading for the exit.

"Where will you go, sir? The planet is no refuge."

"Where will *we* go," Pa Kur corrected.

The warfare specialist shook his head. "I will remain at my post, Commander, fighting until death claims me. I will not let the sub-men outperform me in battle."

Pa Kur glanced at the comm specialist.

"I, too, shall remain at my post," the New Man said. "I will kill the enemy. Long live the Throne World."

Pa Kur gave the formal salute. Then, he hurried out the exit. He couldn't understand what was wrong with those two. They had a chance to live. Maybe it was his prolonged study of the sub-men that allowed him his greater perception. Glorious death in battle was one thing. Living to fight again and winning in the end was another. He had to take his information to Strand.

First, he had to survive and reach the single-ships.

-25-

Easing near an open hatch to the hangar bay, Pa Kur peered through the opening. He wore a spacesuit because he hadn't been able to reach a stealth suit. Chin space marines had been in his way to the armory. He'd been forced to detour around them.

The way seemed clear into the hangar bay.

Pa Kur propelled himself into the vast chamber. The dampeners no longer worked here. Thus, he floated toward the remaining single-ships. The outer bay door had been blown open. The stars shined outside along with a corner of New Venezuela III.

Pa Kur forced down thoughts of radiation poisoning. He would deal with that later when the time came. He could not believe how the situation had so dramatically changed against him. It was the sub-woman's fault. Her mind had been too dull to properly hold onto its conditioning. That wouldn't have happened if she'd had more wit. Instead of sneaking through his own ship, he would now be reporting to Strand about a job completed.

Thinking about the sub-woman's failure almost enraged Pa Kur. He was too superior, though, to let such an emotion grip him at an important moment like this. He must survive. It was imperative to the war effort. He served the Throne World best by surviving, not by throwing away his life in a futile gesture as the others of his sept did. Perhaps that was why he was Fifth

Rank and they so much lower. A superior being saw his utility to the universe and worked hard to preserve it for future use.

A space marine pod shot through the bay door. Pa Kur's lips drew back in a snarl. He raised his blaster, aiming for a fuel tank, and fired an intense beam.

Grabbing a stanchion, he yanked himself down behind a shuttle. An instant later, the pod crashed against the rear bulkhead. An explosion rained metal, heat and tumbling space marines. The shuttle Pa Kur hid behind moved, knocking him backward. He tumbled across the floor, holding himself limply to prevent self-injury.

Pa Kur hit an object and caromed upward. He blinked, trying to keep conscious.

Several space marines moved where they had landed. He clicked the blaster's setting, narrowing the aperture. Then, he aimed at each struggling marine, breaching helmet after helmet. At the last moment, he looked back to see where he sailed. Terror squeezed his stomach. He released the blaster and reached as far as he could. Barely, he grabbed the edge of the outer hangar bay door, catching himself before tumbling out of the hammership and into space and oblivion.

Pa Kur yanked himself as hard as he could, hurling himself toward a single-ship. He caught his spinning blaster just in time. A space marine saw him, firing gyroc rounds.

Pa Kur beamed the three accelerating cones before they could hit him. Then, he beamed the marine in the faceplate, killing the sub-man.

By that time, still moving rapidly, he neared the single-ship. First holstering the blaster, he grabbed the stern of the single-ship. The momentum hurt his fingers and almost tore the gloves free of the metal. But he was a New Man, possessing superior strength.

By degrees, he worked his way to the front of the single-ship. This one lacked a canopy. Maybe they all did. That wasn't going to matter now.

In less than a minute, Pa Kur strapped himself in. He pressed a switch, charging the engine so it thrummed with power. A last check showed him that none of the space marines lived. He manipulated the controls, lifting from the deck, turning the craft and heading toward the open bay door.

He was going to have a fighting chance at survival. For the first time in his life, Pa Kur almost smiled.

***

Pa Kur built up velocity, fleeing from the stricken hammership. He didn't have much time left. The warfare specialist was getting ready to self-destruct, taking the space marines, the decelerating destroyer and the landing strikefighters with him.

Within his bubble-helmet, Pa Kur stared intently at his controls. A warning bleep alerted him.

He looked up from where he lay. Through the windshield, he saw a strikefighter's exhaust. The craft headed straight at him.

The unit beeped again and then blinked red. The strikefighter had radar lock-on. Another bright streak showed outside. It was the first launching missile. A second one meant the pilot wanted a certain kill.

Pa Kur's gloved fingers typed madly over the single-ship's controls. He had seconds left. The missiles streaked straight at him.

The strikefighter pilot began firing exploding bullets at his craft.

"No," Pa Kur said. The procedure wasn't quite complete, but he stabbed the fold switch. The engine knocked, the missile ignited and then everything disappeared from his sight.

***

Pa Kur woke to another warning beep. Groggily, he opened his eyes. He still lay in his single-ship. Red lights flashed everywhere on it, indicating many problems.

The warning beeps in his helmet were the most important. He was almost out of air.

How long had he been unconscious? No. The better question was: did he have more oxygen containers? His present one was almost out of air. He unbuckled and twisted around. The helmet beeps made it difficult to search. So, he turned off the warning.

214

There were no new air containers in the single-ship. He was doomed. Pa Kur looked around. He saw New Venezuela III but none of the warships or strikefighters. He had no idea if they survived or had all blown up.

A small part of him sneered at his dilemma. He had been the hammership's commander. He should have gone down with it fighting to the end. But wasn't his data more important than such a futile gesture?

Did it matter now?

As Pa Kur thought of these things, the last of his air dissipated. At the very end, he believed he saw a star cruiser appear nearby. Death must be certain, as he had already begun to hallucinate.

***

By slow degrees, Pa Kur came to in a white room. He didn't understand it at first.

Am I alive or dead?

He shuddered at a horrifying idea.

Maybe the sub-men were right about an afterlife. No New Man subscribed to the ancient cult. He'd discovered the concept through studying subhuman psychology. Heaven and Hell were primitive beliefs, thus, they could not possibly be true. What if it turned out they *were* true? Did that mean he was destined for Hell?

A frown touched his features. He inhaled through his nostrils. The sterile environment caused Pa Kur to change his assessment. This was a hospital chamber. That would logically mean he had survived running out of oxygen. That in turn meant the star cruiser had really been there.

Of course. This was the Methuselah Man's ship.

It would seem natural that Pa Kur would have been elated with this revelation. Instead, he knew despair. He had failed to annihilate the enemy vessels while retaining his own. Strand had planned further uses for the *Resolute*. Now, the captured hammership was gone.

With a groan, Pa Kur sat up. He wore a silver suit without any insignia. Something felt wrong, but he couldn't place it.

He studied the white environment. It was seamless. The wrongness didn't come from there. No, it was...a cool sensation. It came from his scalp.

Pa Kur felt his head. He was bald. Someone had shaven his hair. A sinking feeling hit him then. There were hairline scars across his scalp. Who had cut him and why?

Gingerly, Pa Kur slid off the cot, standing unsteadily on his feet.

A hatch slid up. A New Man walked into the chamber, setting a chair on the floor.

"Excuse me," Pa Kur said.

The New Man ignored him, exiting the chamber. The hatch slid shut at his heel.

Pa Kur blinked at the chair. Was that for him? He pushed off the cot and began to stagger for it.

The hatch slid up again. Pa Kur halted, looking up as he swayed where he stood.

An old man wearing an Earth suit walked into the chamber. He had wrinkled hands and his large head seemed too heavy for his frame. The facial skin looked waxy as if it belonged to a mannequin. The blue eyes...the blue eyes burned with power.

"Get away from my chair," the old man said.

It surprised Pa Kur, so that he lurched backward, almost falling, as he hurried to comply with the order.

The old man moved briskly, coming to the chair, plopping into it.

Pa Kur realized he knew the man. It was Strand. He wanted to ask what the Methuselah Man had done to him. Instead, he waited quietly, respectfully.

Strand settled himself, stretching his lips in an ugly smile. "How do you feel?"

Pa Kur blinked several times. "I'm tired."

"That's to be expected."

"And I'm concerned."

"Indeed," Strand said. "What concerns you?"

Pa Kur touched his head. "These scars indicate a surgical procedure."

"Correct," Strand said. "The doctor used a scalpel and then a saw."

"Are you suggesting the doctor removed part of my skull?"

"Exactly," Strand said. "I do not allow anyone on my ship without first going under the knife. It makes everything much simpler that way, preserving my sense of ease."

Pa Kur rubbed his skull again. The Methuselah Man's words implied the doctor had done something to his brain to…to modify him.

"It's beginning to sink in, I see," Strand said.

"Did you implant a control unit in me?"

"I call it an obedience chip," Strand said. "Don't you think that's more accurate?"

Pa Kur shuddered. This was inconceivable. His horror loosened his lips. "Do you distrust us to such a degree?"

"You're right, of course," Strand said. "Distrust lies at the root of my longevity. It's why the others perished. They let their guard down one too many times. I never let my guard down. Thus, I will be the last one to die."

Pa Kur thought about that. "May I ask why you saved me?"

"Oh, it's because I like you," Strand said. "And because you're different, quite different from the others. It must be why you fled your hammership and they remained at their posts."

Pa Kur kept his features emotionless, blank. "I did not flee."

"No?" Strand asked, with humor in his voice.

"I came bearing data I believed you needed."

"Oh, well, a noble New Man," Strand said. "One who thinks about others before his own precious hide. That is a vast improvement."

"You are mocking me."

"Quite right," Strand said. "I detest liars and fools. Those who lie to themselves are the biggest fools of all. Don't you realize why you fled the hammership?"

"To bring you valuable data," Pa Kur said.

"I already told you that's a lie."

"No," Pa Kur said.

Strand laughed in an ugly manner. "Is it so wrong to desire to live?"

"You desire to live," Pa Kur said.

"That's it. Throw it back in my teeth. See how well that does aboard my star cruiser with an obedience chip in your brain. I could make you strangle yourself. That's always a hoot to watch."

"Do you seek to lie to yourself?" Pa Kur said, refusing to truckle in fear.

The old man seemed to freeze in his chair. Only the eyes moved, and they burned with menace. "Well, well, well, the coward has teeth, does he? Maybe I can use you after all. A proud man who loves his skin above all else is one I can trust to the fullest. It lets me know your motivation."

"You are attempting to demoralize me."

"No. I'm teaching you the true nature of yourself. You're a New Man. Thus, you think you're the prize of life. You think there's nothing better under the sun than one of your kind. Well, you're wrong. I'm the best. What do you think of that?"

"You're too old and slow to be the best."

Strand laughed, nodding.

"I do not think you would have escaped the hammership as I did," Pa Kur said.

"Yes, you're a prize, Pa Kur, a genuine rarity among New Men. Even better, you can blend in with the others as long as the situation isn't too perilous. You're going to be a positive addition to my crew."

Pa Kur felt a wave of weakness come over him. He rubbed the scars on his head and leaned against the cot. He frowned, thinking, and finally studied Strand.

"I have a drug in my system," Pa Kur announced.

"Quite true," Strand said.

"It has made me talkative."

"That's right."

"I have spoken my mind too freely."

"Not too freely," Strand said, "but honestly. It lets me know that you still think you're special. You are, but not in the manner that you believe. Don't fret over it. You have a lot to learn. Now, quickly, what data did you wish to give me?"

Pa Kur tried to keep silent.

"Speak," Strand said, as if talking to a parrot.

Pa Kur told him about the sub-men's suicidal fury, explaining how it was wrong at this point in their demoralization process.

Strand pinched his lower lip. "That is interesting. I think you do have a handle on…" The Methuselah Man smiled. "On the *sub-men's* psychology."

"They should not have attacked with such fury."

"You're right," Strand said. "This will take some thought. I'd hoped to use the hammership again, but no matter, it's gone. Hmm, I suppose this means I'll have to drop a few hell-burners onto New Venezuela III."

Pa Kur cocked his head. "I do not think any sub-men were on the planet."

"You're wrong. There's around a thousand, but that isn't the only reason I'll use the hell-burners."

"Why else then?" Pa Kur studied Strand. He did not care for the Methuselah Man's vile smirk.

"I'll do it because it will make Fletcher wonder why I did it," Strand said. "That will drive him crazy, as he won't be able to come up with a reason."

"I can't think of a reason, either."

"And that is the reason," Strand said. "It's called sowing confusion. I'm better at it than anyone, well, anyone other than that damned Ludendorff."

"Your alter ego," Pa Kur mumbled.

Strand's head snapped up.

Pa Kur almost shrank back in fear. Such a maneuver would have sullied him, however. He straightened, awaiting the worst.

"Go back to sleep," Strand said. "I need to think about you a little longer. You're a strange combination for a New Man. I wonder what happened to make you that way."

Pa Kur would have like to think about the last statement. Instead, without conscious thought, he climbed back onto the cot, laid his head on the pillow, closed his eyes and fell asleep.

-26-

Maddox settled gingerly into the command chair on the bridge. The journey from the infirmary had tired him out. It was awful being so weak. He despised it.

Seeing that Valerie and Keith watched their panels, the captain pulled out a cloth and wiped sweat off his face.

He shifted on the chair so the wound didn't rest against fabric. He had stopped taking pain inhibitors some time ago. It surprised him how well they had worked. Now, his joints ached and he had a flu-like sensation. Thinking about it caused him to wipe his face again.

He tucked away the rag. It wouldn't do for the others to see him so incapacitated.

"We're approaching the Jovian planet," Keith said.

Maddox studied the main screen. A huge gas giant with seething storms raging across its surface showed the nearness of the final Laumer-Point.

Some time ago, Meta had written a journal about her period with Kane, an agent for the New Men, who had kidnapped her from New York City. Kane had brought her here the first time, racing to Wolf Prime afterward.

"The gas giant is massive," Keith said while studying his board. "Its tug on us is greater than I'd anticipated."

"We'll almost have to skim its surface to reach the Laumer-Point," Valerie added.

Maddox might have nodded, but it felt as if that would have taken too much energy.

"Are you sure it's wise for you to be on the bridge, sir?" Valerie asked.

Maddox didn't bother answering such a question. He was better already. A few aches, some chills, it didn't mean anything.

Valerie and Keith traded glances. Maddox noticed, but he refrained from commenting.

"I'm switching on the Laumer Drive," Keith said, tapping his board.

What he meant was that the ship's special Laumer sensors began hunting for the often-elusive wormhole entrance. According to Meta's notes, this Laumer-Point was small. Was it too small for *Victory* to use? They would have to catalog its size before trying.

The Xerxes System had a bad reputation, much like that of the Bermuda Triangle on Earth back before the Space Age. Like in the triangle, ships had disappeared under unusual circumstances. The worst story had occurred over thirty years ago. The Boron Company had set up a mining colony on a metal-heavy moon of the third planet. The colony had vanished, leaving no traces of the colonists or buildings or landing zones. Until *Victory* had passed through a year ago, no military or commercial routes had gone through the Xerxes System Laumer-Points.

Last voyage, *Victory* had fought silver drones in the strange system. The drones had used the same fusion beams New Men star cruisers employed. The conclusion had been obvious: the New Men had stolen or acquired the Builder weapons by plundering such a place with Strand's help. The drones could well have been the reason for the system's terrible reputation.

"There it is," Valerie said. "I've found the Laumer-Point."

Maddox straightened. On the main screen, the wormhole opening appeared near the gas giant's stratosphere.

"This is going to be a tight fit, sir," Valerie said.

"Is the message beacon ready?" Maddox asked.

"Aye-aye, sir," Keith said.

"Launch it."

Valerie cleared her throat.

"Is something the matter, Lieutenant?" Maddox asked.

221

"Shouldn't we wait to launch the packet, sir?" she asked. "We're still too far to activate the Laumer-Point."

"Of course," Maddox said.

Once again, Valerie and Keith traded glances.

Maddox wanted to pull the cloth back out and wipe the sweat off his forehead. Their actions had begun to irritate him.

Valerie appeared as if she wanted to add something. Finally, she turned back to her panel.

Ten minutes later, Keith spoke up, "I'm in range, sir. Should I launch the packet?"

"Do it," Maddox said.

Keith tapped his board. A few seconds later, a small missile left the starship.

"The gas giant is affecting its trajectory," Valerie said. "Its—"

"I have it under control," Galyan said, who chose this moment to appear.

The missile had begun to veer off course. Now, it continued straight for the wormhole, zipping into it and disappearing from the main screen.

"The packet is on its way," Keith said. "Thanks for the tractor beam, Galyan."

"You are welcome," the holoimage said.

Maddox swiveled his chair toward the bridge exit so the others couldn't see him. He pulled out his cloth again, wiping his face. As he completed the turn, he tucked the handkerchief away.

"How long should we wait, sir?" Keith asked.

"Two hours will be good," Maddox said.

Valerie waited, finally saying, "Should we wait a little farther from the gas giant?"

"See that it's done," Maddox told Keith.

The message missile would enter the Xerxes System and broadcast to Port Admiral Hayes that *Victory* was coming through. They didn't want to surprise the admiral and have him accidently order the flotilla to open fire on the ancient vessel if the flotilla was near the wormhole exit.

Time passed slowly for Maddox. He felt wretched. Why didn't his body heal faster as it usually did? He wasn't used to such prolonged weakness.

Once again, he shifted his position on the chair, searching for a way to relax without his wound touching the backrest. A little later, his eyelids grew heavy. He fought it for a time. Then—

"Sir!" Keith said, loudly.

Maddox's head snapped up as he opened his eyes. He was disoriented for just a moment. His mouth tasted awful and—

The captain's lips firmed. He realized that he'd fallen asleep in the command chair. He felt foolish, like an old man. That bothered him more than he cared to admit.

Both Valerie and Keith seemed absorbed with their boards. Hadn't the ace just shouted?

"You should return to sickbay," Galyan said.

"No," Maddox said.

"You snored, sir," the holoimage said.

Valerie looked up, shaking her head at Galyan.

Maddox drew a deep breath and realized his joints didn't ache as much as before. In fact, the flu-like feeling had lessened.

"The nap refreshed me," Maddox said in a crisp voice. "Are we ready to jump?"

"Yes, sir," Keith said.

"Let's do this."

"Are you sure, sir?" Valerie asked.

An angry retort almost left the captain's mouth. He settled back in the chair and nearly lurched out of it as his wound touched the fabric. A tremor washed through him, and the renewed flu-like feeling almost made him gag.

Maddox forced himself to sit up slowly and then stand, locking his knees. He was going to force himself to act normally even though he felt off.

"What are you waiting for, Second Lieutenant?" he asked.

"Ah, shouldn't you sit down, sir?" Keith asked.

Maddox reached into his jacket, putting his hand on the cloth. He squeezed it so a knuckle popped. Then, he removed

223

the hand without extracting the handkerchief. Only then did he sit down.

"Maneuvering for the Xerxes System entry," Keith said.

On the main screen, the wormhole expanded. So did the massive, atmospheric-swirling gas giant.

"Planetary gravity has begun to affect our flight path," Valerie said. "The gravity dampeners are at thirty percent. Thirty-three. Thirty-five. We're skimming the outer surface."

"No problem, love," Keith said.

The wormhole entrance grew larger yet.

Maddox gripped the armrests. He wasn't looking forward to this.

"Three, two, one..." Keith said. "We're entering the Laumer-Point."

Starship *Victory* fell into the wormhole, zipping a little over three light-years in less than two seconds, popping out on the other side in the Xerxes System.

***

Maddox raised his head. The others were still in the grip of Jump Lag. Galyan did nothing. The AI was always the worst affected.

To the captain's surprise, he no longer sweated. In fact, the ache in his joints had abated and he felt...good.

Maddox flexed his right hand and moved the shoulder near the wound. That tugged at the wounded flesh and sent a spike of pain there. He winced. It throbbed for a moment but it was more bearable now.

The others began to revive. Ten minutes later, Galyan solidified.

"The sensors are rebooting," Valerie said.

"Initiate scan," Maddox said. "Any messages yet?"

"No, sir," Valerie said.

"Do you see the packet?"

"I do, sir. It's right where it should be."

"Are there any messages in its files?" Maddox asked.

Valerie tapped her board. "No, sir, nothing."

"Galyan?" Maddox asked.

The holoimage shook his head. "I haven't received any signals, sir."

Keith adjusted his controls.

Maddox studied the main screen. The Xerxes System had several planets and a tight, manufactured asteroid belt. Deep within that collection of rocks, asteroids and hidden drone bases was the Nexus, a silver pyramid with an incredible power to send a starship over one hundred light-years in a single super-jump.

"No message buoys?" Maddox asked.

"Nothing," Keith said. The ace turned around. "Could the system be empty of ships, sir?"

"Galyan, take us toward the asteroid belt while remaining at full alert. Scan for anything unusual. Port Admiral Hayes went from Earth directly to the Xerxes System. He should be here. Maybe he's on the other side of the star."

"Maybe," Keith said, "unless Builder drones took him out."

"I doubt that," Valerie said. "Admiral Hayes was to proceed with utmost caution. I studied his record when I used to work for the Lord High Admiral. Hayes would be the last person to let others take him by surprise."

"Any sign of a space battle?" Maddox asked.

"Negative," Galyan said.

"His flotilla can't just have disappeared," Valerie said.

"We have yet another mystery," the ace said.

"Keep scanning," Maddox said. "Galyan, I want the disruptor cannon ready."

"Affirmative," the AI said.

The starship headed for the asteroid belt, the shields at full power and the main armaments primed for firing.

Four hours later, Valerie shook her head. "Sir, there's no sign of silver drones, no sign of New Men star cruisers and absolutely no sign of Port Admiral Hayes. This star system is empty."

"I'm open to suggestions," Maddox said.

Valerie swiveled around to face him. "Sir, we must approach the Nexus. But I urge extreme caution. This doesn't make sense but the silver pyramid strikes me as the most likely reason for whatever has gone wrong."

"Unless weapons-portals appeared and sent missiles at the Port Admiral's flotilla," Keith said.

"Show me the debris," Valerie said. "Show me the radiation signatures. There hasn't been a battle here since we fought the drones."

"Did Hayes leave the system?" Keith asked.

"That seems like the only explanation," Maddox said.

"Why would he leave?" the ace asked.

"Maybe someone forced him to," Valerie said.

Maddox regarded the holoimage. "You haven't suggested anything, Galyan. Do you have an opinion?"

"I do," Galyan said. "The port admiral's disappearance would suggest someone has readied the Xerxes System for us. The Ludendorff AI desired you here, as did the Shanghai androids."

"Maybe Ludendorff is really stuck in the Nexus," Maddox said.

"I give that a thirty-five percent probability."

"What is the greatest probability?" Maddox asked.

"That our hidden enemy wishes to capture you," Galyan said.

"Why?" Maddox asked.

"I have insufficient data to say."

"How will they make the attempt?" Maddox asked.

"That seems clear," Galyan said. "They will attempt it as you personally enter the Nexus to rescue Professor Ludendorff."

"I agree," Maddox said. "Well, then, let's get started."

"Sir?" Valerie asked.

"Let's head to the Nexus as you suggested," Maddox said. "We need to see their next move if we're going to use it to help us solve the mystery."

-27-

Starship *Victory* spent the next day accelerating toward the Nexus' known location. As the asteroids neared, the ancient vessel decelerated.

On the bridge, Valerie threw her hands into the air. "This doesn't make any sense. Wouldn't the port admiral have left a message buoy or sent one of his ships back home? He knows how important knowledge is to Star Watch."

"You worry too much," Keith said.

They were alone on the bridge, the captain having told them several hours ago he was going to exercise.

"And you don't worry enough," Valerie shot back. "I've never understood your carefree attitude. You know how harsh the universe is. Your brother's strikefighter death—"

"Leave my brother out of it, thank you."

Valerie turned from Keith, fiddling with her controls. She hated it when she shot her mouth off. Why couldn't she learn to think before speaking? Her dad used to tell her to use her noggin before yapping, tapping a finger against her head while he said it.

"Look," she said. "I'm sorry. I didn't mean—"

"It's nothing," Keith said.

"No. It's something. You—"

"Lieutenant," Keith said, sharply.

Her teeth clicked together, and she held herself rigidly.

227

The small ace frowned as he studied his board. He began shaking his head. "I...I don't like talking about my brother. I miss him, you know."

Valerie nodded. She missed her dad.

"He was the good one," Keith said. "I've always been the troublemaker. It runs in my blood. I like to have fun. I like to race along the edge so I feel alive. He didn't have to do it that way. He could read books, be normal..."

"You must love working for the captain then," Valerie said.

"That I do," Keith said, grinning. "The man has style."

"I bet he's sleeping, not exercising."

"Are you kidding," Keith said. "Don't you know you and me would be howling like mad dogs if we took a shot like that? I've seen laser poisoning before during the Tau Ceti Conflict. It's ugly. The captain—I can't believe he's even on his feet. He's a superman."

Valerie snorted. "That makes two people who think so, you and the captain."

"Aye, me and the captain, two lonely people—"

"Lonely!" Valerie exclaimed. "You think the captain is lonely?"

"Oh, I do, love, I most certainly do. The man believes he's an island, maybe because he's had to be. He's hard. I admit that. But he's good, none better, if you ask me. Yes, I love serving on *Victory*. Let the good times roll, I say."

"What do you think happened to the port admiral?"

Keith stared at the main screen. "This is a haunted star system. We know that, right?"

"No."

Keith grinned. "Oh, aye, you know, but you want a steely world without ghosts. You want everything in its place because Detroit showed you what happens when civilization takes a vacation."

Valerie stared at Keith, surprised at his sudden insightfulness. "I think you're right. I want order because of all the disorder I faced while growing up."

She checked her board. At the very edge of the asteroid field floated a medium-sized rock. Beyond it by several hundred kilometers was another, and another, and tens of thousands more just like it.

"Better call the captain," she said. "*Victory* is about to enter the minefield."

***

Maddox had indeed gone to his quarters to sleep. He lay in bed, having slept for several hours. Now, he debated taking a pain pill. The wound was healing, but much slower than it should, in his opinion.

"Captain," the intercom said.

He swept back the covers and sat up gingerly.

"Captain."

"I'm coming, I'm coming," he said. Finally, he reached the intercom, clicking it. "Yes?"

"We're entering the asteroid belt, sir. We should be near the Nexus in three hours."

"Thank you," he said. "I'll be there shortly."

He pulled back the bandage, studying the angry-red skin around the burn. He swung his arm, testing the wound.

"Ah…" he said, pressing the bandage back into place. He dressed, drank some water and strode through the corridors.

Was Ludendorff waiting in the Nexus for him? The idea of leaving the ship and heading to the silver pyramid with Meta appealed to him on one level. He wondered how wise it would be, though.

Soon, he found himself by Meta's hatch. He knocked and she shouted for him to enter.

Meta combed her hair before a mirror.

"We're entering the asteroid belt," he said.

"You're wondering just how well I remember my time with Kane, aren't you?" she said finally

He nodded.

"Too bad Dana isn't here to help me replay the memories," she said.

"We'll find her once we get back to Earth," Maddox said.

"What's in the dome down in the Mid-Atlantic? I can't stop thinking about it."

"I'm more concerned about what's in the Nexus. The professor said he's at 12-3-BB, whatever that means."

"Maybe once we're inside it will make sense."

Maddox looked away. He was tired of this cat and mouse game. It struck him as Strand's play. Would Strand trap him in the Nexus, or...?

"If star cruisers appear, Galyan will destroy them piecemeal," the captain said.

"You still think this is about capturing *Victory*?"

"What else could it be?" he asked.

Meta shrugged.

"Let's go."

She rose, coming to him, beginning to hug him until he groaned painfully. She jerked back.

"I'm sorry," she said. "I forgot about your wound. Are you—?"

"I'm fine," Maddox said, turning to go.

"It's okay to be injured," she said. "You don't have to be perfect all the time."

He nodded without turning back to her.

"What is it, Maddox? Something more is troubling you."

She was right. But the problem was that it hovered just out of sight in his mind. It was as if all the pieces were there, spinning and rolling, and he couldn't put them together. If he could jam them in the right sequence, he was certain he would know the game.

The captain flexed his gun hand. He wanted to grapple against the hidden foe. This padding around in the dark was starting to get to him.

It must be the laser burn. It will heal. I just have to give it time.

"Wait," she said.

Maddox waited by the hatch.

"Okay," she said, slipping a compact weapon into her pocket.

They left her room and hurried down the corridor.

"Captain," Galyan said, appearing beside them.

Maddox nodded.

"I've detected an anomaly near the Nexus."

"Yes," Maddox said under his breath. Then, he broke into a sprint for the bridge.

***

On the bridge, Maddox stood before the main screen. Meta had hurried to engineering. "What am I seeing?" he asked.

The holoimage of Driving Force Galyan stood beside the captain. The image turned to look up at Maddox.

The vast asteroid field surrounded the ancient structure of the Nexus. The Builder pyramid was massive, much bigger than *Victory* and larger even than the hugest containership used by the transport corporations.

Beside the pyramid by three hundred kilometers was swirling space, a stellar whirlpool of silvery complexion.

"Meta never said anything about this from her journey with Kane," Maddox muttered.

"We never saw anything like this last voyage, either," Keith added. "It just appeared several minutes ago."

"What is it?" Maddox asked.

"Unknown," Galyan said.

"What's causing it?"

"I am picking up strange signals from the Nexus," Galyan said. "It is possible the pyramid is causing the...anomaly."

"Is there matter in it?" Maddox asked.

"Negative," Galyan said.

"What causes the silvery color?"

"Unknown."

"Is matter drawn to the whirlpool?"

"None that I can sense," Galyan replied.

"Do we back up, sir?" Valerie asked.

Maddox didn't answer. He watched the swirling location. The starship was twenty thousand kilometers from it, almost next door in system terms.

"Could that be a frozen exit for the one hundred light-year jump?" Maddox asked.

"Nothing indicates that to be so," Galyan said.

"But it seems as if that might be the likeliest possibility," the captain said. "That implies star cruisers might be coming through soon."

"Or something much worse," Valerie said.

Maddox glanced at her.

"Maybe another Destroyer is trying to transfer here," the lieutenant said.

"Aren't you the cheerful one," Keith told her.

"The disruptor cannon is ready to fire, sir," Galyan said.

"The disruptor doesn't mean anything to a Destroyer," Valerie said. "We'd better be ready to jump out of the system if one appears."

Maddox nodded absently, raising an arm and signaling Keith.

"Aye-aye, sir," Keith said, "initiating star drive procedures. If you want to jump, sir, give me the word and we'll be gone."

For the next fifteen minutes, *Victory* waited, unmoving.

"Too bad we can't communicate with the professor inside the pyramid," Keith said. "He could tell us what that is."

Maddox snapped his fingers. "Lieutenant, try to hail the pyramid."

"Is that a good idea, sir?" Valerie asked. "I have a terrible feeling about this. The anomaly didn't appear until we closed. I think its waiting for us to approach closer."

"You truly believe the swirling non-substance has the ability to reason?" Galyan asked.

"Bad choice of words," Valerie told the AI. "Whoever caused the whirlpool to appear is waiting for us to do something."

"Thank you for the clarification, Valerie."

"Raise the pyramid," Maddox said. "See if we can communicate with Ludendorff."

"Yes, sir," Valerie said, as she tapped her board. "Professor Ludendorff, can you hear me? Come in, please, Professor."

"Look!" Keith shouted. "The anomaly is moving! It's heading for us."

Maddox had noted the sudden movement as well. The silvery swirling non-substance lurched directly at the starship as soon as Valerie opened communications with the Nexus.

"Anything?" Maddox asked the lieutenant.

"What?" Valerie asked, tearing her gaze from the main screen.

"Did you receive a reply from Ludendorff?" Maddox asked.

Woodenly, Valerie studied her panel. "No, sir, no reply."

"Try again."

"Sir—"

"Please do as ordered, Lieutenant."

"Yes, sir," she said, trying to reach Ludendorff a second time. Soon, she looked up at the captain and shook her head.

"Shut off the comm, please," Maddox said, as he watched the swirling anomaly advance toward them. "Second Lieutenant, back up with increasing speed. I do not want the anomaly reaching us."

"Aye-aye, sir," Keith said, his nimble fingers roving over the flight panel.

Everyone on the bridge watched the main screen. The anomaly kept advancing, closing the distance between them.

"It's still tracking us," Valerie said. "Turning off the comm hasn't changed anything."

"Do you sense tracking signals coming from the anomaly?" Maddox asked the AI.

"Negative," Galyan said.

"It's gaining on us even faster, sir," Keith said.

"Increase speed."

"I am, sir. I suggest—"

Maddox turned to stare at the pilot.

"I'm waiting for further orders, sir," Keith said.

"Galyan," Maddox said, "fire on the anomaly with the disruptor cannon."

Immediately, the starship's antimatter engines began to build up. The bulkheads thrummed at the power. Then, a beam lanced from *Victory*, striking the anomaly and passing through into the void behind.

"Do you detect any difference in the anomaly?" Maddox asked.

"Negative," Galyan said. "The disruptor beam had zero effect on it."

"Sir," Keith said. "It has increased speed yet again. It's closing with us."

"I can see that for myself," Maddox said in a calm voice. "Steady as she goes."

"This one feels bad, sir," Keith said. "For once, I'm with the lieutenant."

"Thank you for your statement," Maddox said absently. His focus zeroed-in on the fast approaching, swirling whirlpool.

The captain was thinking, trying to put the pieces together. The Shanghai android had kidnapped him. The Ludendorff holoimage had begged him to come here. Port Admiral Hayes was gone, with utterly no sign of the flotilla. Surely, in time, Hayes would have inspected the Nexus. The anomaly must be—

"Lieutenant," Maddox said, crisply. "Turn on the Laumer Drive."

"Sir?" Valerie asked.

"Please act with alacrity," Maddox said. "Every second may count."

"I'm turning on the Laumer Drive," she said, tapping her board.

Immediately, the silvery whirlpool changed complexion. The silver color vanished. In its place was darkness that seemed to vanish into infinity like a tunnel.

"A portal," Valerie whispered.

"Good thinking, sir," Keith said.

"But I don't understand this," Valerie said. "If it's like a Laumer-Point, how can it be moving? That doesn't make sense."

"A new type of physics perhaps," Maddox said.

"I suggest we jump out of danger," Galyan said. "Let us evaluate this at our leisure."

"Your advice is noted," Maddox said. "But I will decline it today. Second Lieutenant, stop retreating. I've changed my mind. We will advance into the anomaly."

"Captain," Valerie said, growing pale. "That seems unnecessarily rash."

"Shut down the disruptor cannon," Maddox said. "We don't want it on while we go through and Jump Lag distorts critical systems. Second Lieutenant, do we have any Baxter-Locke shots?"

"That we do, sir."

"Listen to me," Maddox told the others. "We're going in ready to fight. Our enemy expects us to run. It will take too long to use the star drive. That means it's unlikely we can outrun the anomaly. Thus, we will commit the least expected action—we will charge it. "

"This is extremely rash, sir," Valerie warned.

"The anomaly strikes me as the answer to what happened to Port Admiral Hayes," the captain said. "I plan to rescue him and the flotilla if I can."

"I know we saved the Fifth Fleet before, sir," Valerie said, "But this time—"

"Hurry with those shots," Maddox told Keith.

The small Scotsman leaped up with a fistful of hypos in his hand.

Maddox retreated to the command chair. Soon, Keith came to him, giving him one of the injections. The shots helped against Jump Lag, although it could cripple, too. The injection made the captain feel itchy and sticky, which was good. That meant the drug was working.

The swirling blackness raced nearer. It had grown to an immense size, easily able to swallow the starship.

"The disruptor cannon is offline, sir," Galyan said.

"Be ready to warm it up as soon as we exit the wormhole," Maddox said.

-28-

Victory had halted its run while the anomaly's speed increased. The Adok vessel had almost reached a complete stop by the time the strange entrance engulfed the starship.

"Dear God," Valerie prayed, "please help me. Help all of us."

"Aye," Keith muttered, crossing himself.

Then, the ancient starship was in the transfer point. Maddox forced his eyes wide open. One second, *Victory* entered the blackness. The next, a sensation of incredible speed took hold. Everything became dark and everything seemed to flash past the starship. The bulkheads around them shook.

Maddox called out, but the sound came out distorted, as if time had twisted out of sorts. Colors changed. The captain felt the gorge rise in him. He snapped his mouth closed, refusing to give in to pain or weakness. The shaking around him increased. The sense of speed and vast distance grew disproportionately. A warbled scream floated across the bridge. At that point, the bridge seemed to flow together as if in a nightmare. The captain felt as if he *smelled* the weird colors and *saw* sounds like waves in a sea. His gripping fingertips *tasted* the ends of the armrests.

Abruptly, the weirdness reversed itself. The bridge quit melting into odd forms and hardened back into its regular shapes. The blackness around the ship remained the same—

No! He spied an exit that rushed toward them. Everything slowed and the mighty starship popped out of the transfer tube—if that's what it was—and drifted once again in normal space.

The screen and most of the ship's systems shut down at that point due to Jump Lag.

Maddox stood. The Baxter-Locke shot had done its trick. He hardly felt the ill effects of the journey, just a dryness of the tongue.

"Is anyone else okay yet?" the captain asked.

"I am, sir," Valerie said.

"Good. Did you experience anything bizarre during the journey?"

"Yes," she said in a small voice. "It was…frightening."

"Right," Maddox said. "Let's get our ship working. We don't know what kind of committee is waiting for us."

Valerie turned to her panel, tapping away. "It's dead, sir. It's going to take—"

At that moment, the starship's systems began to come back online.

"That was quick," Valerie said. "Much quicker than usual."

"Oooo," Keith said, raising his head off the flight panel. "It feels as if I have a hangover."

"You're fine, Second Lieutenant," Maddox said. Just like Jump Lag, the Baxter-Locke shots worked differently on different people. "Get the ship ready for battle."

"Aye-aye, sir," Keith muttered, as he tried to rub something off his tongue.

After several minutes, the main screen finally flickered on, but Galyan was still motionless.

Maddox slid to the edge of his chair, studying space. Something felt off, but he couldn't place it. He kept searching. The system star was muted, more than any other he'd seen in his travels.

"Is that a white dwarf?" the captain asked.

"Sir," Valerie said, with dread in her voice. "I can't believe what my sensors are showing me." She fell silent, staring at her instruments.

"Spit it out, Lieutenant. Every second may count."

"Sir…" she said, waving her hand in a vague manner.

"There's an enemy ship directly behind our stern!" Keith shouted. "It's firing."

"Give me a visual," Maddox said

Keith tapped his board.

The image on the main screen shifted. A huge, saucer-shaped vessel possible three times *Victory's* size fired a beam. It struck the collapsium hull armor, as the shield hadn't come back online yet.

"Give me propulsion," Maddox said. "Don't let them keep hitting the same spot. Lieutenant, hail the vessel. Tell them we're friendly. Galyan—Galyan are you awake yet?"

There was no answer from the frozen holoimage.

Once again, a beam struck the starship, but it was at a different location.

"It's a heavy laser, sir," Valerie said. She seemed hyper-focused on it, as if she didn't want to look at other sensor readings. "At least they don't have better weaponry than us. That suggests the enemy ship doesn't belong to the New Men."

Maddox clicked the comm on his armrest. "I am requesting that you stop firing. We are friendly. I repeat—"

"There's an incoming message, sir," Valerie said. "I'm putting it on the main screen."

The main screen wavered. Then a metal construct, vaguely humanoid, appeared. The head was box-shaped. It opened its orifice and high-speed words came out.

"Can the computer analyze that?" Maddox asked.

"Maybe," Valerie said, sounding dubious.

The metal creature tilted its head. Lights flashed in its eyes. The orifice—or mouth—closed and opened again.

"You use a variation of Anglic two point three," the robot said. "That is interesting. Now, we will work on specifics. I demand your immediate surrender."

"Of course," Maddox said. "We do surrender. Who do I have the privilege of addressing?"

"That is not germane to your surrender," the robot said. "I am sending a launch to your ship. Your crew will board the launch and head to the habitable sphere."

"Can you point out the sphere?" Maddox asked. "We haven't spotted it yet."

"Your curiosity suggests you are planning a deception. A moment while I coordinate."

The main screen went blank.

"Galyan," Maddox hissed.

"Yes, Captain. I am awake."

"Good. Get the disruptor cannon ready. Lieutenant—"

"The shield is energizing, sir," Valerie said.

The main screen flickered and the robot reappeared. "You must lower your shield immediately, as that is part of the surrender process."

"Yes, of course," Maddox said smoothly. All appearances of concern had vanished from his face. "Thank you for your—"

"Do you understand what lower means?" the robot asked, interrupting. "De-energize your shield this instant."

"I do indeed understand the term 'lower,'" Maddox said in a friendly tone. "And I appreciate your query."

"That you understand means you have affirmed my command."

"That is correct," Maddox said. "May I add that communicating with you is a delight?"

"Your courtesy is noted and appreciated. However, your shield is still up. I demand an immediate lowering to prove you are surrendering to me. I have strict protocols. Your delay, whether manufactured or by accident, will soon result in the destruction of your vessel."

"I have ordered the shield lowered," Maddox said. "At times, my crew acts in a slovenly manner. I will have the slack crewmembers punished for this unconscionable delay."

"A slovenly crew," the robot said. "I had not anticipated such a thing. A moment while I check—warning! My instruments reveal that your ship is readying a disruptor cannon."

"That can't be," Maddox said. "I have not ordered such a dastardly action. We are guests in your star system and wish to comply in every way."

"Lower your shield and shut down your offensive weaponry."

"I hesitate to suggest such a thing," Maddox said. "And please believe me when I tell you that absolutely no slight is intended. But could your instruments be at fault?"

"They cannot possibly be faulty, as I have perfect instrumentation."

"How fortunate for you," Maddox said, sounding envious. "I wish I could say the same for my ship's instruments. Ah. I have good news. My crew has informed me that they are shutting down the shield and cannon. We await your launch with—"

"One moment," the robot said. It eyes flashed with blinking lights. When they returned to normal luminosity, the creature asked, "Are you Captain Maddox?"

"Who is he?" the captain asked.

The eye-lights dimmed and then brightened once more. "You fit the suggested form of Captain Maddox. I also detect a deception in progress. I will fire in three seconds unless you lower the shield and turn off your weaponry."

"May I ask you a question first?"

"Yes."

"Have you heard of Professor Ludendorff?"

"I have. He is the one who instructed me in your appearance and placed my protocols."

Keith cursed at his station.

"This changes matters considerably," Maddox said. "I will only surrender to Professor Ludendorff. Please put him on the screen."

"Negative," the robot said.

"They've started firing again," Valerie said.

The main screen wavered, showing a heavy laser striking the shield. Another laser beam lanced out from the giant saucer-ship, and another and a fourth. They concentrated on one tiny spot, turning the shield there a cherry red and then a deeper brown color.

"They will achieve a burn-through sooner than we like," Valerie said.

"Shall I employ the neutron beam?" Galyan asked.

"No," Maddox said. "We're going to hit them hard with the disruptor."

"That will be cutting it close, sir," Valerie said. "These are incredibly heavy lasers. Their wattage is equal to seven SW battleships combined."

Maddox nodded, waiting, wondering if the real Professor Ludendorff had told the robot these things or if that Ludendorff had been an android.

"Second Lieutenant," Maddox said. "Do you have any idea of our location compared to our last known spot in the Xerxes System?"

"Not yet," Keith said. "I've been too busy to check."

"I know our stellar position, sir," Valerie said, as she worked her board. "I figured it out almost right away. It's what had me speechless. You're not going to believe this, sir, but we're one thousand light-years from our last location."

Maddox stared at the lieutenant.

"I wish I could enjoy the moment," Valerie said. "I don't think I've ever seen you startled before, sir."

Maddox shifted on his chair, closing his mouth. "Galyan, how much longer until the disruptor cannon is ready?"

"Three minutes, sir."

The area of shield was changing color from brown to black.

"I can still use the neutron beam, sir," Galyan said.

Maddox shook his head. He wanted to put as much of the ship's power as possible into the disruptor beam at the first strike. He wanted to obliterate the enemy vessel if he could as fast as possible.

One thousand light-years—that was incredible. He didn't doubt the lieutenant. The technology for such a leap…these must be Builders. Maybe the creature speaking to him was a Builder. But then why did its ship only have heavy lasers?

There was something else. Had the thousand light-year transfer tube swept up Port Admiral Hayes and his people? That seemed like the most obvious answer.

"Does the enemy vessel possess a shield?" Maddox asked.

"The same kind as a star cruiser, sir," Valerie said.

"The same strength, too?" the captain asked.

"Maybe fifty percent stronger," Valerie said. "Oh-oh," she said, "they have burn-through."

241

The enemy beams punched through *Victory's* shield to strike the collapsium hull armor. Collapsium was the best armor anywhere, made of collapsed molecules. That made the hull armor incredibly dense.

The beams where they hit turned the collapsium red. They continued to strike in one area. A slug of collapsium wobbled off the hull, floating away. The lasers were digging deeper.

"Our cannon is online, sir," Galyan said.

"Excellent," Maddox said. "Fire at will until the enemy ship is destroyed."

The antimatter engines built up power. Then, the disruptor beam shot from *Victory*, reaching across the fifteen thousand kilometers to strike the enemy vessel.

The disruptor cannon was much more powerful than a mere laser, even a laser seven times stronger than one on a SW battleship. The disruptor beam turned the enemy shield to brown almost right away.

"Sir," Valerie said.

Maddox waved her to silence. He didn't want any warnings about this. Either their beam chewed into the enemy's innards first or the enemy did it to *Victory*. It was a simple equation with only one winner and possibly two losers.

"If these are Builders," Galyan said, "why is our weaponry superior to theirs?"

"You think they're Builders?" Maddox asked.

"It is the most logical answer, but it isn't conclusive."

Maddox watched the disruptor beam strike the blackening shield. The enemy ship dwarfed theirs, but it wasn't anything like the alien Destroyer. He did not sense vast age, either. There wasn't a feeling of evil to the spacecraft. Of course, he wasn't as close to it as he'd been to the Destroyer.

"Look," Valerie said, her voice quivering. "There's a fifth laser. Sir, we're in danger of a burn-through to the hull. Maybe…maybe surrender is better than destruction. If Professor Ludendorff is here, we can still bargain, can't we?"

Maddox shook his head. He wasn't surrendering his ship one thousand light-years from the Commonwealth. He would either win through or die. He did not believe—

"Yes!" Keith shouted, slapping the piloting board. "We're through. Now you've had it, you bastards."

The powerful disruptor beam swept past the enemy's blackened shield and struck hull armor. It was some metallic alloy, definitely not collapsium. In seconds, the beam smashed into the interior saucer. The beam ignited breathable air, causing interior explosions.

Valerie shouted the news as she used her sensors to probe for further data.

Vast batteries blew aboard the enemy vessel, causing more explosions. Reactors melted. Others burst into nova flares. Sections of enemy hull armor shuddered. Explosions erupted on its outer skin like volcanos. They spewed shredded metal, air, radioactive material and clouds of water vapor into space. All the while, the disruptor beam continued to slice into the giant saucer. Entire sections of hull armor now burst away. Then, for a moment, the vast spaceship vibrated wildly.

"It's finished, sir," Valerie said.

Seconds later, a titanic explosion blew the vessel apart. An intense white light consumed much of the substance. Heat, blast, gamma and X-rays traveled outward in an ever-expanding circumference.

"A-ha, mate!" Keith shouted, banging the piloting board with a fist. "You suckered us down your hole and that's what you get. That's what you get. Bugger off, you bastard, Ludendorff."

"Here it comes," Valerie said.

The gamma and X-rays struck the shield, making it buckle and turn a dark brown. Auto-defense cannons blasted at the largest chunks of following debris. Galyan used the neutron beam to take down the biggest dangers.

"Let's move," Maddox said.

Keith's fingers flew across the board. He made the sluggish starship twist out of the path of masses of debris, but he couldn't dodge everything. Like a wave, the expanding junk struck the shield. The engines whined as they pumped extra power to the electromagnetic defenses.

"The shield is holding, sir," Valerie said.

Maddox watched, absorbed at the extent of the destruction and the possible deathblow the enemy ship was attempting to deal them after the fact.

Galyan had been analyzing the matter. "Captain," the holoimage said. "I suggest this is a more serious danger than we could have reasonably expected."

"Continue," Maddox said.

"I believe the enemy…intelligence knew it was defeated. It added munitions of hell-burner strength to its destruction, attempting to defeat our shield after its demise."

"It would appear you're correct," Maddox said.

"I can understand the maneuver," Keith said. "But it's dirty just the same. We beat them after they tricked us down their tube. The least they could have done was die with dignity."

"There is no dignity in dying," Maddox said.

"Sir?" Keith asked.

Maddox turned to Galyan. "Are there any more saucers nearby?"

"Negative, Captain."

"Lieutenant, turn on the Laumer Drive. I want to get out of here while we can. Let's find the transfer tube."

"Yes, *sir*," Valerie said.

The aftershock of the destroyed saucer had passed on. They'd survived the deadly gamma rays and debris. The heat from the blast dissipated the quickest, posing the least danger.

"Nothing so far, sir," Valerie said.

"Let's move to the region of the destroyed ship," the captain said. "I suspect the entrance is there. Galyan, keep scanning for approaching vessels. We don't want another surprise like that."

"Affirmative," the AI said.

Keith worked quickly, moving the starship, turning them back toward the late enemy vessel.

"Is the Laumer Drive still on?" Maddox asked.

"Of course," Valerie said. "I'm still not picking up anything, though." A half minute later, she added, "What if it's a one-way tube?"

Maddox shook his head. "I don't accept that. Continue to scan."

Ten minutes later, it was clear. The Laumer Drive had failed to discover the entrance back into the one thousand light-year tube.

"Sir," Galyan said. "My analyzer has computed the odds. The highest probability by many factors tells me we are stuck here. It will be years, if ever, until we return to the Commonwealth. Given such a situation, what are your orders, sir?"

-29-

Maddox carefully leaned his back against the command chair. His features were impassive. He could feel the gravity dampeners' pull against his flesh. Despite his vaunted vigor, he felt tired. Maybe everyone did.

"Turn off the Laumer Drive, Lieutenant," he said, calmly.

"Begging your pardon, sir," Valerie said. "But I suggest we try a little longer."

"We will use our reason and regular sensors to find the answer," the captain said. "For the moment, however, we are stuck one thousand light-years from the Xerxes System."

"Sir," Valerie said, giving him a stricken look. "We can't give up looking. If it's years before we return home—"

"We will not remain out here *years*," Maddox said, confidently. "I assure you of that."

Valerie blinked at him. "But if there's no opening—"

"Lieutenant," Maddox chided. "I expect my officers to use their reason. We cannot find a tube, or whatever the jump technology was that transported us across the vast distance. That might seem disheartening. But we also haven't seen the silvery swirl that indicated the entrance the first time."

Valerie tilted her head. It took a few seconds before a smile twitched into place. "You're right, sir. The silvery swirl had indicated something must have turned on the…the tube for us to use."

"Such is my own belief. According to Galyan, the Nexus had beamed certain signals into the area of the whirlpool. Our

Laumer Drive simply showed us a little more clearly what the Nexus had already opened. The conclusion seems obvious enough. We must find another Nexus in order to create another thousand light-year tube."

"I have been running an analysis," Galyan said. "I believe we traveled through hyperspace, for want of a better term. But we moved through a tunnel or tube. That would have made it a hyper-spatial tube. That is how we traveled such an extreme distance in a short amount of time."

"Hyper-spatial tube," Maddox said. "Good. Now we have a name for it."

Valerie exhaled. "We must find another Nexus. Yes. That means we're not marooned."

"I never thought we were," Keith said.

"That's because you're a lunatic," Valerie told him.

Maddox cracked his knuckles. "We destroyed the enemy waiting for us, one enlightened about our coming by Ludendorff. That would indicate the professor is in this star system. I suggest we find him."

"And twist his scrawny neck," Valerie said. "Why do you think he turned on us, sir?"

"An excellent question," Maddox said. "One I plan to discover. Lieutenant, begin scanning the dim star. Galyan, I expect you to search for evidence of life. I want to know everything about the system. We're going to make whoever is responsible for our predicament rue the day he tampered with a Star Watch vessel."

***

The information began to gather. *Victory* had entered the system along the outer edge in a Neptune-like range compared to the star, meaning they would have to travel billions of kilometers to reach the inner system. There were no planets, no asteroids, no comets, apparently no Kuiper belt or Oort cloud or any debris of any kind—except for the expanding matter of the destroyed vessel.

"The lack of comets, of any stellar dust seems odd," Valerie said. "Our Sun acts like a giant vacuum cleaner, using its intense gravity to pull every comet and particle of dust to itself. But the process takes an incredibly long time, which is why the Solar System still has plenty of comets and space debris. The lack of comets and dust here suggests one of two things. This is either an incredibly old star system—the dim star might point to that—or it's like the asteroids of the Xerxes System."

"Groomed," Maddox said, nodding thoughtfully.

"Yet, to groom an entire star system so there are no dust particles left would entail an incredible amount of work."

"It would also indicate high technology," Maddox said, softly.

"That's just it," Valerie said. "The vessel we defeated shows a *lack* of such high technology."

"The saucer-vessel is not conclusive evidence," Galyan said, "although it is certainly an indicator."

"Right," Maddox said. "Mr. Maker, you will increase our velocity toward the star. Since there's nothing else here, I suspect that's where we'll find our answers."

Keith tapped his board.

"I will increase the intensity of my scan for cloaked vessels and hidden habitats," Galyan said. He froze afterward, his eyelids fluttering.

The captain's excitement faded as time passed. He was tired and the laser wound still bothered him. Finally, he closed his eyes.

"If I snore," Maddox said, "don't bother waking me. We'll begin to work in shifts. We'll also remain on the bridge, each taking catnaps in turn. We don't know how long it will be until the next emergency."

"Do you expect something bad to happen, sir?" Valerie asked.

"With Ludendorff in the mix, I do."

Neither Valerie nor Keith replied. The tiredness seemed to leap up and yank Maddox down to slumber.

"Captain!" Valerie said. "Keith! I've found something incredible."

Maddox lurched awake, leaning forward. It felt like seconds since he had closed his eyes. His focus went to the main screen. Everything looked the same.

"How long have I been out?" he asked.

"An hour and a half, sir," Valerie said, as she studied her board.

Keith snorted, lifting his head off the piloting panel.

Maddox glanced at Galyan. The holoimage was still frozen, although his eyes fluttered faster than ever.

"I know why the star is dim," Valerie said. "It also explains why there aren't any planets, comets, anything in the system." She pointed at the faint star. "There's a Dyson sphere around it."

"Never heard of a Dyson sphere," Keith said. "What is it?"

"Exactly what it sounds like," Valerie said. "A giant sphere built around a star. The sphere captures the star's entire energy output. Given that the Builders manufactured an atmosphere inside the sphere and that it's one AU out from the star, it has 550 million times the square footage as Earth."

"Come again," Keith said.

"Think about it," Valerie said. "It's a giant, hollow ball built around the star. The surface is the same distance from the star as the Earth is from the Sun. That means all the area in a circumference is habitable. That's a lot of land. In fact, it is 550 million times the amount of land on Earth, and that's including the oceans."

"Give me a second," Keith said. "You're saying that isn't the star. That's the glow we're seeing of what shines *through* of the material surrounding the star?"

"Correct," Valerie said. "And that's why there aren't any planets here."

Keith shook his head. "Why?"

"Think of it as a construction project," Valerie said. "The Builders needed material to put around the star. But 550 million square kilometers more than the Earth's surface is…vast. Where did they get all the stuff? Easy. They tore down the system's planets, comets, everything, using that matter to build with."

Keith whistled. "That would take fantastic technology."

"Or a lot of time," Valerie said.

Keith scratched his head. "One thing bothers me. Where would they get enough people to fill up the sphere?"

Valerie thought about it, soon shrugging.

"Was the saucer's robot going to send us there?" Keith asked.

"I believe so," Maddox said. "Recall. It said we were going to board a launch and head to the habitable sphere. Now we know where it meant."

"Something that vast..." Keith said. "We have our proof, eh? The Builders must have made the sphere."

"The logical deduction," Maddox said.

"And it's one thousand light-years from the Commonwealth," Keith added. He turned to Maddox. "Sir, Ludendorff knows about the Builder sphere."

"This changes everything, doesn't it?" Valerie asked. "The magnitude of what we're seeing. It makes the New Men a flyspeck of a problem."

"I disagree," Maddox said. "The robot demanding our surrender said Ludendorff had given it the protocols."

"So?"

"How was Ludendorff able to do that?" Maddox asked. "It would suggest he was in charge, not the Builders."

Valerie shook her head.

"Consider the Destroyer," Maddox said. "It was ancient, with an ancient Builder creature trying to control it. Yet, everything seemed rundown, as if the makers hadn't been around for quite some time."

"So...?"

"The Builders have left vast monuments of their time," Maddox said. "We haven't seen a Builder, just the things they left lying around. Maybe the Dyson sphere is on the same order. Once, the Builders ran it. Now, who knows if it's just a relic of past glories?"

Valerie thought about that. "Okay. I see what you're saying. But something's going on in the pyramid on Earth, right?"

"It is," Maddox said. "But who's running the something; Builders, Ludendorff, Strand or New Men? From what I've seen these past years, I've begun to suspect that humanity is late to star voyaging. Others have gone before us. Maybe the galaxy used to swarm with intelligent life. They're all gone now, or mostly gone. We're the slow ones who finally showed up after everyone else quit playing."

Valerie peered at the main screen. "I don't like your hypotheses, sir. It's eerie."

"That may be," Maddox said. "But is it correct?"

Keith had become thoughtful. "Are you saying Ludendorff is in the Dyson sphere?"

"It seems quite possible," Maddox said.

"Then I say let's go get him and make the bastard pay for all our troubles," Keith said. "I'm sick of his games."

"Going after him is one possibility," Maddox said. "Maybe it's even the wisest course."

"It's why we went to the Xerxes System," Valerie said.

"Yes," Maddox said. "But I've begun to wonder. Maybe we can find something useful here in our war against the New Men."

Valerie stared intently at the captain. "Hearing you say that…you really think we can get home again."

"I've never doubted it for a minute," Maddox said.

An uneasy smile appeared on the lieutenant's face. It dropped away a second later. "This is all theory."

"A theory that seems to fit the evidence," Maddox said.

The three of them fell silent, studying the dim star, the incredible Dyson sphere.

"I have an announcement to make," Galyan said. "I have been deep scanning for some time. Now, I have conclusive proof. Port Admiral Hayes' flotilla is orbiting the Dyson sphere by a few thousand kilometers."

Valerie clapped her hands. "Have you contacted them yet?"

"That is the only negative to my report," Galyan said. "I have been hailing them for some time, and have received no replies. It would indicate the crews are unconscious, their equipment is wrecked or that the vessels are devoid of people."

-30-

Maddox drew his pistol and fired, hitting the target at the end of the vast chamber. The kick this time proved greater than ever. He fired three more shots in quick succession, producing bullet holes around the edge of the first shot.

A wisp of smoke trickled from the barrel.

"Good shooting, sir," Riker said.

Maddox nodded, flicking the safety on and shoving the gun into its holster.

"Your wound doesn't bother you anymore?" Riker asked.

"I feel a twinge now and again. The last two days have made the difference."

They'd been traveling from the outer edge of the system for over forty-eight hours. Soon, they would begin deceleration at a Mar's-like distance from the Dyson sphere.

"What do you think about the new ammunition?" Riker asked.

"I've adjusted to it," Maddox said.

"It kicks like a mule, and I imagine a man's hand will go numb after too many shots. But the slugs will knock down an android."

"More importantly, they will shred the creature."

"That they will, sir," Riker said, grinning.

Maddox whirled around, drew the gun and emptied the magazine into the target.

"One thing has been bothering me, sir. You don't expect to go into the monstrous sphere, do you?"

Maddox took his time answering. "It's crossed my mind."

"Searching for Ludendorff, I take it?"

"I mean to take him home, Sergeant."

"I find that a dubious proposition, sir. It doesn't strike me as logical. One thousand light-years—"

"We will return home," Maddox said, "and we will do it within the year."

The sergeant studied him.

Maddox noted the cloaked anxiety in the older man's eyes. He'd been observing his crew, his family and responsibility. The others had shown similar fear, although it appeared in different ways. Truthfully, he also felt anxious. Being one thousand light-years from anything he knew was a daunting sensation.

The Patrol arm of Star Watch routinely sent ships into the Beyond on exploring missions. The Patrol Board searched for the right type of people to crew the vessels, using an exacting and specific standard. The board did so for a sound reason. Most military people possessed physical courage. They could risk their lives in battle, and function as necessary during high stress combat situations. Heading into uncharted territory took a different kind of personality and courage. The farther one traveled from known space, the more jittery most people became. The Patrol Board believed they had lost more than one crew due to fear. Dread could lead to mutinies, to nervous breakdowns and other mental maladies.

Maddox doubted any Patrol ship had ever found itself one thousand light-years from Human Space. The feeling of isolation was powerful out here, battering at their psyches. Fortunately, the captain believed his makeup and life experiences had better prepared him for this. He was used to isolation.

I must feed them my strength.

Maddox realized he could not do this forever. There was a limit to his mental endurance. Action and hope would be more help to the others. The best chance, as far as he could determine, was finding Ludendorff. The professor was a scoundrel and a cunning manipulator. The Methuselah Man also knew more about space, the Builders and strange phenomena than anyone except possibly for Strand.

"How are we going to get home, sir?" Riker asked. "There's no Nexus out here."

"That's a mere trifle, Sergeant. It's clear how we'll do it. That's why I'm readying myself for the sphere."

"Do you really think you can defeat Ludendorff? The man always had a hundred tricks up his sleeve."

"Of course I can best him. I'm surprised you doubt it."

The beginning of a wry smile touched the sergeant's lips. "I have to admit one thing, sir. If I was going to be stranded a thousand light-years from home, trying to get back, I can't think of anyone better than you to do it with."

"Your vote of confidence has propelled to me to rarified heights of delight. Now, you look tired. If I'm going down to the sphere, I plan to have my left hand with me. That means you need to catch up on your sleep so you'll be ready to fight and think."

Riker absorbed the news calmly enough. "Don't you mean your right hand, sir?"

"No. That will be Meta." Maddox nodded before heading to the hatch. "I suggest you hurry to your quarters while you can. The more sleep you can log now, the better for all of us later."

***

Lieutenant Noonan paced back and forth in the briefing chamber. She wanted to sleep. Her eyes had taken on a slightly sunken quality. Every time she put her head on her pillow, though, she stared at the ceiling, her thoughts churning.

This was madness. The incredible voyage down the hyper-spatial tube, the Dyson sphere, the drifting warships of Port Admiral Hayes' flotilla…it was mindboggling. She wanted to go home. She wanted regular, sensible duties. Yes, she wanted a line command even if it was of an escort. She would have dearly liked to join Admiral Fletcher, facing the New Men in "C" Quadrant.

That's the real fight. We have to drive the New Men out of the Commonwealth. This place…is so alien, so frightening and unreal.

Her world kept turning upside-down, changing direction and speeding faster than light toward madness. She just wanted normal routine, a hard battle decision now and again. This, though—

She waved a hand in the air. This was too much. It felt as if she floated outside her body, watching herself. She hadn't joined the Space Academy for this. Spinning silver pyramids in space was bad enough. Underwater pyramids at the bottom of the Atlantic Ocean—

Valerie moaned softly. Android doubles, alien Destroyers—

The door slid open. Valerie whirled around. Captain Maddox stood in the doorway, watching her. He wore a gun at his hip and stood as calm as you please. He waited with his gaze boring into her.

Something seemed to pass from him to her. Her heart rate decelerated. She seemed to breathe just a little easier. Maybe…maybe they could find a way home again. Maybe they could find something here to help in the war effort. They had Starship *Victory*, didn't they? They'd defeated every obstacle so far. Why couldn't they do it again? Impossible odds were the captain's M.O.

The lieutenant yawned and her eyes felt heavy. For the first time since entering the pristine star system, Valerie felt as if she could actually catch a few winks.

The captain entered the chamber. The door slid shut behind him.

"Sir," she said.

"Lieutenant, would you do me a favor?"

"Of course, sir," she said.

"I have to do some thinking. But I find I prefer company while I am at it. However, I want it quiet."

"Didn't you want to talk to me, sir?"

"That can wait. Why don't you lie down on the couch over there?"

"I couldn't do that, sir."

Maddox shrugged as if it didn't matter. Afterward, he pulled out a chair and sat down. He stared at the table's surface, apparently deep in thought.

Valerie sat down too. Her eyes got heavier and heavier. She glanced at the captain. Whatever he was thinking, the man was absorbed with it. Could she lie down for just a bit?

The minutes ticked by in silence. Finally, Valerie rose, went to the couch and lay on it. Ah, it felt so good to relax. She shut her eyes and that felt even better. Shortly, she fell asleep with her ankles crossed on the armrest.

Captain Maddox looked up, staring at the lieutenant. He had seen the fear on her face. He'd also seen it drain away as she stared at him. With the peacefulness, her exhaustion had leapt up and grabbed her. He'd wanted to speak to her, but he'd divined that her need to sleep while she was able was more important.

Maddox watched her, and his lips stretched into a rare smile. He lay back against his chair, stretching his legs under the table. It felt good to relax. It felt good to know that his presence helped put Valerie at ease.

The others fed off his confidence. He could feel it draining him. But that was okay.

The smile slipped away and a scowl touched his youthful features.

What are we going to do? Is it possible to find Ludendorff among 550 million times Earth's area? In truth, a man could spend the rest of his life down there trying to do just that.

Maddox held his pose, thinking deeply, realizing *Victory* and its crew might be in the most impossible situation of their rather short career.

-31-

Admiral Fletcher sat in his ready room looking at holoimage after holoimage of Hades IV, an Earthlike planet in the Hades System.

After atmospheric recon units had determined that nothing moved on the planet, the landing parties had gone down. They had swept through various communities, recording everything. As Fletcher tapped holographic controls, he viewed empty homes with beds, tables, counters, tablets all covered with dust. It was the same in the business establishments. It was clear the cities had been empty for some time.

Fletcher stood. With a wave of his hand, he turned off the holoimages. First cracking his knuckles, he strode to a display case of old-fashioned airplanes. Building them was a hobby of his. He had a Brazilian Zipper from World War III, a Russian MIG 29, a British Spitfire and the Red Baron's Fokker Dr. I triplane from World War I. He'd won an award with the Dr. I in high school, having to recite Baron von Richthofen's history before a panel of judges.

That would have been something, flying by sight and stick with the wind whipping in your hair. Men must have been tougher back then. Having to line up the machine guns with your naked eye, watching red tracers zip through the sky. That would have been the era to be alive. It was so different these days, flying through space in perfectly comfortable starships.

The admiral swiped a protein bar sitting on the display case. He unwrapped it and ate methodically, staring at the fighters from bygone times.

Wiping his hands on his uniform—something that would have driven his mother wild—he turned back to his desk.

"Give me 'C' Quadrant, Section Two," he said.

A star-map with the Laumer-Points glowing appeared in the air. The bulk of the Star Watch's ships were with him in the Hades System. Third Admiral Bishop was a jump away in the Hermes System with the Windsor League vessels. The rest of the fleet was a jump from Bishop in the Diana System.

They had come a long way, apparently driving the New Men before them, while the New Men kept their main fleet out of sight. All the while, though, the enemy had whittled away at them.

Once, a handful of New Men using traitorous humans as a lure had captured a hammership. Later, the hammership had lured Commodore Garcia to her death, losing precious battleships in the process. Those hidden mines were a frightening new development. Did the enemy have a limited supply of them? Why had they only used them there?

After the mines, the most amazing development had been the hammership showing up in the New Venezuela System. How had it slipped all the way around, past the various patrols, without anyone sighting it? It showed the enemy could dance around them at will.

Fletcher scratched his left cheek.

The enemy had tried to trick them, at New Venezuela, into believing the hammership was reinforcements. Luckily, the traitorous humans helping the New Men had regrown a conscience at the last minute. Even so, it had been a bitter fight. The Star Watch commander had destroyed the hammership, but at heavy cost.

Clearly, the New Men practiced deceit wherever they could. Each of their moves had begun with a trick. The deceit gave them an incredible force multiplier each time. Yes... The fakes before each attack seemed to be their signature style. In fact, it fit with their maneuvers against him in Caria 323 two years ago.

258

During the present campaign, the enemy had made two mistakes, one of them more an accident than an error. The first mistake had been the space bombardment against the empty cities on New Venezuela III. It seemed like a nonsensical move. Once word of the planetary bombardment had spread to the Grand Fleet, it had hardened everyone's resolve. It had been the senselessness of the act, showing the enemy destroyed for no appreciable reason. It showed this was a fight to the death.

The second error had been in the Remus System. Several star cruisers had struck like lightning there. They had pounced upon Sub-commander Ko's forces, which had been stiffened with hammerships. The hammerships had lagged behind, though. At the end of the engagement, they'd accelerated and driven off the star cruisers, although at a cost. The New Men had fought savagely before cunningly slipping away through an unstable Laumer-Point.

The error had been an accident of battle, but it had changed so much for Fletcher, so very much.

The admiral almost smiled thinking about it, but he refused to permit himself such a luxury. Good men and women had died in the ambush, Windsor League and Social Syndicate people. The battle had cost them two hammerships and four Social Syndicate cruisers. Even more importantly, Sub-commander Ko had died. In his place had risen Sub-commander Sos, a woman of dignity and reason.

For reasons Fletcher still hadn't fathomed, Sub-commander Sos had switched Social Syndicate policy, siding with him at the next meeting instead of Third Admiral Bishop as Ko had done.

That had been a decisive moment in the campaign. From that time on, he'd gained popularity instead of seeing it dwindle. These days, Bishop plotted in secret instead of aloud at the meetings.

Fletcher studied Section Two of "C" Quadrant. They were nearing a critical star system named Thebes. If the New Men let Thebes III fall to the Grand Fleet...

Fletcher shook his head in a silent quandary. Could the New Men have fewer star cruisers left than anyone suspected?

He had begun to believe in the possibility. The other side of him realized the possibility could be a gigantic lure. Maybe the New Men *wanted* him to believe that, hoping to cause him to become reckless.

The admiral's nostrils flared.

He'd studied military history as a cadet. Fletcher saw the New Men as Hannibal of Carthage, a magician of battle, able to perform combat miracles. The Romans had waged bloody war year after year against the Punic magician, slowly wearing down the genius. In the end, the Romans had produced a genius of their own, taking the fight to the city of Carthage, beating Hannibal on the field of Zama.

Fletcher dared to desire to emulate Scipio Africanus, the battlefield master of Hannibal Barca. The idea of people regarding *him* as the conqueror of the New Men filled Fletcher with the resolve to try.

I must use the enemy's maneuvers against him. Yes, he had to fight the New Men on *his* terms, not theirs.

Could the Lord High Admiral have known he would feel this way? Fletcher couldn't see how. Still, he appreciated Cook's confidence in him those many months ago. Somehow, somewhere, Fletcher wanted to repay the Lord High Admiral for that confidence, for giving him his life back.

The comm unit beeped on his desk.

"Admiral Fletcher here," he said, voice activating it.

"Sir," the comm officer said. "A landing party has found a survivor."

With immediate excitement, Fletcher activated the holoimage display, putting the comm officer up. "What did you say?" he asked.

"Lieutenant Bergstrom from *Excalibur's* 'A' Force found a delirious man asleep in a bunker. He didn't make much sense, groaning more than talking. The lieutenant put him on a shuttle and routed it to *Excalibur*. The psychologists are preparing for him."

"I want an hourly update," Fletcher said. "Remind the psychologists I want to know what happened. Where did everyone go?"

"Yes, sir."

"And this Lieutenant Bergstrom, tell my coordinator she's up for an Admiral's recommendation."

"Will do, sir."

"Did Bergstrom find anything else?"

"That was it, sir."

"Fletcher out," he said, as he closed down the comm. "Yes!" he said afterward. It looked like they were finally going to get some answers to this mystery.

**

Several hours later *Excalibur's* doctors still couldn't tell Fletcher anything. The man was badly malnourished and raving, almost out of his mind. Once, he had grabbed a doctor's arm, telling the man to run for the forest.

The admiral shook his head as if shaking away those thoughts. He would have his answers soon enough, he hoped. Ever since Bergstrom found the survivor, Fletcher had begun to feel uneasy. Was the survivor another lure to a trap?

The admiral drummed his fingers on his desk in the ready room. Was he becoming too paranoid? How could the New Men have set that one up?

He glanced at the tablet-papers spread before him. The Grand Fleet possessed an impressive number of vessels, more than any human fleet in history. There were also many different *kinds* of spaceships, each better at one form of fighting than another.

There were the twenty Windsor League hammerships left. Each was worth two Star Watch battleships *at close range*. Together with their supply ships, that gave the Windsor League the greatest tonnage of vessels along with considerable political influence at the conference table.

The Wahhabi sheik-superior had brought fifteen *Scimitar*-class warships, a type of craft between a Star Watch battleship and a heavy cruiser. Those ships had the best heavy-mount lasers in the Grand Fleet. They were also the best at long-ranged beam combat. Fletcher wished he had more of those.

The Respectable Kim Sung commanded twelve super-junks, each the equivalent of a large Star Watch carrier. The Respectable Kim also had twenty strike cruisers and a host of

261

destroyers. The Chin Confederation had put up many warships fast. They must have been preparing for something like this for some time.

Sub-commander Sos of the Social Syndicate had seven cruisers left and eleven destroyers. She had the largest number of vessels from a single system political entity. Adding in others from semi-independent systems gave another three battleships, ten heavy cruisers, twelve strike cruisers and forty-three destroyer-sized vessels.

The final component of the Grand Fleet belonged to Star Watch. Fletcher commanded the mightiest gathering of ships to date, many of them having come from the Home Fleet. By scraping together the remaining Star Watch forces into one giant mass, Fletcher commanded eighteen battleships, fifteen carriers and thirty-five cruisers of various classes. It had been bigger at the beginning, but losses here and there had continued to mount.

In all, the Grand Fleet boasted 167 capital ships with masses of lesser vessels so he had almost 400 combat ships, a vast force. Perhaps as important, the majority of the Star Watch ships had advanced harmonics shielding, while plenty of vessels carried the new antimatter missiles. And there were the experimental jumpfighters in three of the carriers.

At the beginning of the Battle of Caria 323, the New Men had faced him with forty-eight star cruisers. If they had forty-eight now, which he doubted, would they dare face the combined might of the Grand Fleet?

Have we misjudged the New Men's strength? That would be a galling thing. Yet, that didn't seem right. The New Men could have waited longer before launching their initial invasion. No one had known about them until they suddenly appeared out of the Beyond.

If all the enemy ships had cloaking like Strand's star cruiser…that would be a different story. But as far as Fletcher knew, the other star cruisers could not cloak like that.

A blare of noise startled Fletcher. He whirled around. It was a red alert.

The big man strode to the hatch, entering Flagship *Antietam's* bridge. There was a flurry of activity as aides crisscrossed the bridge and executive officers ran scans and analyses.

"Admiral on the bridge," a Marine said, loudly.

Fletcher went to his command chair, sitting erectly, watching his people. They moved smoothly and efficiently. They had purpose and—

"Admiral," the sensor officer said. "We have incoming data."

"Give it to me on the holoimage, please," Fletcher said.

The sensor officer nodded, manipulating her board.

The Laumer-Point at a three times Jupiter-mass gas giant glowed with energy. Another star cruiser came through. There were already three in the Hades System. The tramline the New Men were using meant the enemy had come in *behind* the Grand Fleet.

This was like the New Venezuela hammership-attack in that regard. Fletcher had been expecting something tricky like this.

"Let's start counting," he said, softly.

The sensor officer did just that, along with probably everyone else. The New Men hadn't shown themselves so openly yet. This was a new development.

"They're pouring out," the weapons officer said. "This could be their main fleet."

"Maybe," Fletcher said.

The officer raised his eyebrows in astonishment at the admiral's comment.

"The New Men have used decoy forces before," Fletcher said. "I wouldn't be surprised if they were using them again here."

It seemed as if a half-hour passed in a blink. Sensors had counted twenty-three star cruisers so far.

The main Star Watch fleet in the Hades System was halfway between the Earthlike planet and the massive Jovian giant out there. Five hundred thousand kilometers separated them from the enemy-held wormhole.

Soon, sensors counted an amazing *fifty-four* star cruisers.

Along with everyone else, Fletcher watched the enemy vessels gather. A growing certainty had taken hold in him.

263

Every New Men assault this campaign had begun with a trick. He knew that. Now, he had to muster the courage to act upon his knowledge. But it was so hard. If he was wrong about this…the stakes meant his defeat could bring total victory to the remorseless New Men.

Fletcher warred with his heart. He wavered, almost decided and then flinched from committing himself. Sweat beaded under his collar. His palms felt moist and his breaths became harder to take.

Suddenly, as he suppressed a groan, Fletcher pounded the arm of his command chair. "We're heading for them," he said. "Pass the message to the other ships."

The captain of *Antietam* turned around. "Begging your pardon, Admiral," she said.

"I don't want to hear it," Fletcher snapped. He took a long breath, the first one like this for a while. "Get that order out *now*," he told communications. "I also want a courier ship leaving for Bishop. Tell the third admiral to hurry here. We finally have our fight. I want to hit the New Men while I have a chance."

The bridge crew stared at him.

"Now!" Fletcher said, pounding the arm of his chair again.

In a subdued manner, the flagship's bridge crew went about their tasks.

Soon, Star Watch's battleships, carriers, cruisers and masses of destroyers and escort vessels began accelerating toward the half-a-billion kilometer distant Laumer-Point and the largest enemy fleet to date.

"I'm counting sixty-two star cruisers," the sensor officer said. "And I think more are still coming through."

"Good," Fletcher said.

The captain of *Antietam* had become pale. "Admiral, sixty-two star cruisers? We didn't think they had that many. Now, we're going to face them all by ourselves?"

Fletcher stared at her. Why was this so difficult to say? He knew the truth. With an effort of will, he forced out the words: "Those aren't real star cruisers, Captain. You're viewing decoy ships."

Several of the crew glanced at each other.

"Uh...how do you know that, sir?" the captain asked.

"Because I know the New Men's methods," Fletcher said. "So do you. We've discussed it often enough."

"But sir, isn't that the point? No one can outwit them. The New Men are always three steps ahead of us."

"Not this time," Fletcher said.

"How can you be so certain, sir?"

Fletcher eyed the captain, a good commander, willing to take reasonable risks. But this didn't seem reasonable to her. Star Watch had a few more capital ships in the Hades System than the number of star cruisers. By the calculations of battle as previously fought, they didn't stand a chance against sixty-two star cruisers.

"I want maximum acceleration," Fletcher said.

"Admiral," the captain said. "I don't mean any disrespect by this, but I think you should call a commander's meeting. The others are going to balk at this."

"The sixty-two star cruisers have begun accelerating away from the Laumer-Point," sensors said.

"What is their direction?" Fletcher asked.

Sensors found it difficult to speak. "They're...they're on an intercept course for us, sir, heading straight for our fleet."

-32-

Fletcher had the meeting, as there'd likely be a mutiny if he didn't. After the fleet had accelerated at the star cruisers for a time, they paused as shuttles ferried the many commanders to the *Antietam*. Soon, Fletcher stood outside the hatch. He thrust his shoulders back and strode into the conference chamber.

It was crammed with commanders and their chief executives. For many it was standing room only as they stood shoulder to shoulder against the walls. Ventilation worked overtime as a sour smell of sweat hung in the air.

Fletcher knew the smell. People were scared, afraid that tomorrow they would die under a hail of fusion beams. He didn't blame them. A knot of fear twisted in his own belly. He simply chose to ignore it, as he knew he could not trust it.

Fletcher walked to the front of the long table. Anxious faces peered up at him. A few looked angry. Clearly, no one understood why the fleet raced at an incredible number of star cruisers, the most dangerous warships in the galaxy. They all believed they should wait for Bishop and the Chin Confederation warships.

"Good day gentlemen, gentlewomen," Fletcher said with a nod. "I'm glad you could join me for this historic occasion."

He scanned the throng. They were his men and women. The Lord High Admiral had trusted him to lead them in order to save the Commonwealth, to save regular humanity when one came right down to it. Today, he had to win them to his plan. He had already decided on the best means for doing that.

"This is a historic occasion," Fletcher said, "as the New Men have finally made a mistake."

Officers blinked at him, some of their fear turning into confusion.

"You're the best Star Watch has," Fletcher said. "I know, because the Lord High Admiral handpicked you for the assignment. We're to drive the golden-skinned invaders out of 'C' Quadrant. Until this moment, the enemy has retreated from us out of fear, burning some planets and no doubt taking the people off others. Well, we're going to find out why in the next day or so."

"Admiral," said Commodore Harold, commander of a task force of the newest battleships. "I don't understand your thinking, sir. We're accelerating toward sixty-two star cruisers. We'll be fighting the New Men at a numerical parity. Since they have vastly superior equipment, they will decimate us."

"That's just it," Fletcher said. "They aren't sixty-two star cruisers. They're using decoys today, trying to bluff us."

"That isn't what the sensor readings are saying, sir."

"You're exactly right, Commodore," Fletcher said. "I..." The admiral smiled. He scanned those in the room. Could he trust these people?

If I can't, I'd better step down from command.

"I'll let you in on a secret," Fletcher said. "I do not *know* one hundred percent if these are decoy ships or not. But everything I've seen and studied about the New Men leads me to this conclusion."

"Do you care to tell us your reasoning, sir?" Harold asked.

"I would be delighted," Fletcher said. "The truth is I can't do this unless you're all on board with me. We're a band of brothers facing the worst enemy the universe has thrown at us."

Fletcher inhaled, nodding. "I faced the New Men at Caria 323. There, the enemy suckered me. I lost many good ships because of it. I learned then that New Men are masters of deception. They used decoy forces to draw me out of a fortified position. Today, I believe they are attempting to get us to use the Laumer-Point, to flee there."

"But—"

267

"I've asked myself a question," Fletcher said. "If the New Men appear in strength like this, isn't my only logical choice to cut and run?"

"That's exactly what I think," Harold said.

"And I did, too, at first. Then I realized the New Men would know that about us. That meant the enemy was trying to herd us in a particular direction. They would do so in order to spring a trap on the fleet. To escape the trap, I should do the exact opposite of what they're trying to get me to do. Realizing that, it dawned on me that the sixty-two star cruisers are decoys, or most of them must be."

Many present appeared thoughtful.

"I think I understand, sir," Harold said. "But what if the New Men have accounted for it? Maybe they believe you'll think they're bluffing. In that way, they can cause us to race toward our destruction."

Fletcher shook his head. "Every move of theirs this campaign has begun with a ruse."

"You said they miscalculated."

"I did," Fletcher said. "I suspect that a few real star cruisers are hidden among the decoys. They need a few to fire some fusion beams to make everything seem legitimate. I wish to annihilate those vessels. The New Men can't afford any losses, and that's what we're going to give them. This time, we're going to whittle their numbers down."

"This is a gamble, sir."

"I've told you my reasoning," Fletcher said. "Remember, the New Men aren't gods. They're just good. We can outmaneuver them sometimes. But if we're going to head against sixty-two decoys or so, I need my people understanding why we're doing it."

The admiral nodded at them before saying, "Now. Let me hear what you think."

No one spoke in the sudden silence.

Finally, Commodore Harold cleared his throat. "I like your reasoning, sir. They're trying to frighten us. They want us to run. That means we should do the opposite. Yes. Let's attack."

"Right," a woman said. "I agree."

Others said likewise.

"Does anyone disagree?" Fletcher said.

No one did verbally.

"Excellent," Fletcher said, beaming at his people. Now he knew he could trust them. "Then, let's get back to our ships and continue to accelerate."

***

Thirty-six hours brought many changes to the equation.

The majority of the sixty-two star cruisers continued to bear down on the Star Watch fleet. Two star cruisers had veered away at a sharp angle, accelerating hard for a different Laumer-Point.

The admiral had ordered a change of heading for the entire fleet. They chased the two star cruisers, trying to bring them in range of the battleships' heaviest and longest-ranged beams.

Meanwhile, reports from the Hermes-Hades tramline brought bad news. Three hammerships had sustained grave damage from invisible mines near their wormhole entrance. Fortunately, Third Admiral Bishop had let his hammerships accelerate in a staggered formation. Thus, instead of many of the Windsor League warships taking damage, it was a mere three.

Fletcher sent a communiqué among his ships, telling his officers that those hidden mines had been for the Star Watch ships that would have been in the grip of Jump Lag. They might have lost half the Star Watch fleet if they had fled from the supposed sixty-two star cruisers.

The hours grinded away as the fleet chased the two star cruisers. Ever so slowly, the fastest cruisers gained on the enemy.

"Sir," the sensor officer said.

Fletcher sat in his command chair. "Go ahead, Major," he said.

"Look at the ghost fleet, sir."

Fletcher smiled grimly as the images betrayed themselves. He had been right about decoy forces. Not until this moment, however, did the knot in his gut go away.

Ninety minutes later, the running battle entered its most interesting phase.

Fletcher ordered a massive salvo of missiles. He did not use antimatter missiles, as he wanted to hold onto those for the big one. Instead, several flocks of conventional missiles accelerated at fifty gravities, targeting the two star cruisers. The missiles gained velocity hand-over-fist against the New Men.

"The heavy cruisers are in beam range, sir," the sensor officer said.

"I'm going to talk to the enemy," Fletcher told comm.

Soon, Admiral Fletcher called on the New Men to surrender. They did not answer. He kept trying and they kept ignoring him.

"We gave them a chance," Fletcher said. "Now—we finish them."

The battle was anticlimactic, as Star Watch vastly outgunned the two lone star cruisers. The missiles zoomed in, and the New Men used auto-defense fire and their famed fusion beams.

It was a steady progression of missile destruction. Finally, though, one of the missiles got close enough to detonate. The thermonuclear pulse must have hurt the enemy's sensors. Soon, a second and third missile ignited even closer than the first one.

"Hit, sir," sensors said. "One of the star cruiser's engines is running too hot."

Fletcher felt as if he was part of a pack running down rabid wolves. He liked the feeling, and was sure everyone else did as well.

Heavy cruisers pounded the New Men vessels with beams. The enemy shields absorbed that for a time. The shields went through the regular hues, finally reaching black.

"Open channels again," Fletcher said.

He offered the New Men a last chance to surrender. They did not say a word in reply.

Finally, the first star cruiser went critical, exploding in a nova blast.

Antietam's bridge erupted into cheers. Fletcher smiled indulgently. He could actually do it. He could outthink the enemy. It was a wonderful feeling. He would gladly trade three hammerships for two star cruisers. The enemy could not afford such attrition. The Grand Fleet could.

The last star cruiser ejected a pod.

Fletcher noticed that and had the pod marked. "We'll pick up the occupant later. First, finish the last star cruiser."

It took eight more minutes. Then, that vessel went nova as well.

Fletcher sat back. He'd done it. He'd destroyed two star cruisers. The New Men would have two fewer when the fleets finally engaged.

He turned to sensors. "What are the readings concerning the life-pod?"

"There's a single survivor, sir," sensors said. "The readings indicate a New Man."

"Open channels with the pod," Fletcher said.

"They're open, sir," comm said.

"This is Admiral Fletcher hailing the escape pod."

The main screen wavered and a battered New Man stared at them. He had haughty golden features and a buzz cut of hair.

"Do you surrender?" Fletcher asked.

"I am Fifth Rank Pa Kur," the New Man said, "and I request asylum with Star Watch."

"Say again," Fletcher said, not sure he'd heard right.

"I am a political refugee," the New Man said, "and I request political asylum with the Commonwealth."

"That's a new one," Fletcher muttered. "Very well," he told Pa Kur. "We accept your surrender. I will send a shuttle to pick you up."

"I am not surrendering," the New Man said. "I repeat, I request asylum."

"Right," Fletcher. "We're picking you up." He motioned to comm, and she cut the connection.

"What do you make of that, sir?" *Antietam's* captain asked.

"I'm not sure," Fletcher said. "I suppose I'll find out during interrogation."

-33-

Before Fletcher had the pleasure of watching the interrogation of this Fifth Ranked Pa Kur, *Excalibur's* Intelligence chief wished to speak with him.

It would be via a laser lightguide link. The carrier was still in orbit around Hades IV.

Antietam headed toward the Laumer-Point linking this system to the Hermes System. The majority of the fleet did likewise.

Fletcher sat in the conference chamber with several other officers. This was concerning the lone survivor in the bunker on Hades IV. It seemed the man had finally begun to talk coherently.

"Open channels," Fletcher said.

A holoimage appeared in the center of the room. It showed Commander Rainy Fells, a sixty-year old woman in Star Watch Intelligence. She had eagle-like features and a manner of staring as if watching a tasty mouse cross a field.

"Good day, Admiral," she said.

Fletcher returned her greeting and made the introductions, finding it was a good link with minimal delay.

"We're all very interested," Fletcher told her. "What has the survivor said?"

The Intelligence officer cleared her throat. "His station is Service Tech Three. His name is Monsieur George Dunbar, age: 38. He worked on a dam, on the turbines specifically. He happened to be on vacation at the time, in the wilds. His chief hobby is botany, which makes little sense given his occupation. He had hiked to a lonely valley thick with vegetation. Monsieur Dunbar believes that's why the New Men's scanners missed him. He was good at living in the wild, a bit of a survivalist, I believe."

Fletcher nodded, absorbed with the information.

"He was coherent while explaining all that," Commander Fells said. "But once we spoke to him about the New Men, he began to stammer and then rave. I'm not sure how much faith I would place in his explanation. The doctors assure me this could all be a hallucination. The truth could be many times worse."

"What did he say?" Fletcher asked.

The Intelligence officer checked her tablet. "Monsieur Dunbar spoke about a construction project. The New Men built... He called them chambers. Each one sucked up tremendous levels of energy. He snuck back to his dam once, watching the power drain when they turned them on."

"Turned what on?" Fletcher asked.

"The chambers, sir," the Intelligence officer said. "Monsieur Dunbar claimed the New Men stuffed each one to capacity. He was quite emphatic about one particular. They only put women in or men in, never a mixture."

"Go on," Fletcher said, his stomach beginning to churn with uneasiness.

"People went in, according to Monsieur Dunbar, but they never came out."

"They were annihilation chambers?" Fletcher asked in horror.

"That's my assessment, sir," the Intelligence officer said, briskly. "The New Men have practiced genocide elsewhere. Why not here on Hades IV as well?"

"Monsieur Dunbar agrees with your assessment?" Fletcher asked.

"Most emphatically not, sir," the officer said. "He said a ghostly beam appeared from the chamber reaching up into space. He suggests...well...a teleportation device."

"What?"

"I know that's preposterous," the officer said. "Dunbar claimed that's why the New Men packed women into one and men into another."

"Why?"

"Because the New Men sent the women to one place and the men to somewhere different," Commander Fells said.

"Where does Dunbar think the New Men teleported these people?"

"He has several theories, the sanest being into waiting cargo haulers in orbit."

"And the most insane theory?" Fletcher asked.

"To another planet in another star system," she said.

"If that's true, why haven't the New Men used the teleporting device as a military weapon?"

"Precisely," Fells said.

Fletcher glanced at his people. "Any questions?" he asked them.

They had none.

"Do you have anything else to report?" Fletcher asked Fells.

"Not yet," she said. "We're still trying various treatments. He's raving now, completely incoherent. We're hoping to restore his sanity as quickly as possible."

"Thank you for your report," Fletcher said.

After the holoimage winked out, the admiral's Intelligence chief spoke up:

"If the New Men have teleportation capabilities…"

Fletcher shook his head. "They would have used such a power by now."

"What if it's a new technology?" the man asked.

"It was used at least a year ago," Fletcher said, "possibly longer. That means the enemy has possessed it for some time— if Monsieur Dunbar is telling the truth."

"Do you doubt him?" the psychologist asked.

Fletcher pursed his lips. "No. He saw something. I'm willing to bet it seared his thinking."

"I agree," the psychologist said. "This is likely the source of his psychosis. The New Men set up chambers where women went in and a ghostly column appeared that reached into space.

I doubt it was a death chamber. They could have as easily dropped hell-burners from orbit if they wanted to kill everyone."

"Are they searching for something among the people?"

"Possibly," the doctor said. "Or maybe they're using the people for a project."

"What kind of project?" Fletcher asked.

The doctor examined his fingernails before saying, "I've been wondering about that for some time, Admiral. I imagine when the New Men stand and fight, and if we win, we'll finally discover our answer."

On that note, Fletcher dismissed them.

Here was another piece of the puzzle. Maybe the New Man who was asking for asylum had some answers.

-34-

Pa Kur endured the questions, the medical probing and the X-rays to his head. He even let the sub-men touch him, without going into a berserk fury and slaughtering them with his bare hands.

He had asked for asylum but they believed he had surrendered. It was a galling state of affairs. They had no idea he had escaped from the star cruiser. He had escaped the service of the hateful Strand.

Strand had put him under a machine. The Methuselah Man had used him, programmed his mind. That was a frightful injustice. Strand had acted upon a superior as he would act upon weak sub-men.

Pa Kur knew that Strand secretly laughed at him.

As he waited in this cell, Pa Kur shivered with suppressed rage. The Emperor had been right after all. The New Men must not trust Strand. They must make their own way in the universe, achieving more and climbing higher than their genetic predecessors, Homo sapien man.

It was a mistake invading Human Space. We should have traveled in the other direction, launching even deeper into the Beyond. Homo sapiens always marred whatever they touched.

Pa Kur wondered if that meant they had already marred him.

The hatch abruptly slid up. Pa Kur tensed internally, although he hadn't let a single muscle twitch.

"Stand, you," a Marine captain growled. "We're taking you to another chamber."

Pa Kur turned his head on the pillow. The Marine wore space armor, aiming a heavy caliber gun at him. Behind the human were other Marines in combat armor.

The sub-men were not taking any chances with him. He did not blame them, although he hated these subhuman creatures.

"Do you want us to manhandle you?" the captain asked.

Without a word, Pa Kur, stood and headed for the hatch. He walked erectly, proudly, knowing that he was superior to everyone in the sub-men fleet. What he did not understand was how the lower order had found the courage to attack an apparent sixty-two star cruisers.

Pa Kur had toyed with the idea that one of the commanding sub-men had figured out the deception ahead of time. Yet, try as he might, he found the hypothesis impossible to accept.

The Marines marched him through ship corridors, bringing him to a new chamber. It had armored bulkheads. Even without weapons, they feared him. How truly weak these sub-men were.

There was a table in the middle of the room. A man already sat in one of the chairs.

Pa Kur entered with the armored Marines. He sat on the other chair while they lined the walls, five armored killers with weapons.

As he placed his golden-colored hands on the table, Pa Kur noticed one-way glass. Important people would be watching today. He wondered who stood behind the one-way glass.

"Fifth Rank Pa Kur," the man at the table began.

Pa Kur focused on the specimen. He was short and stocky but possessed a large braincase. This one might have a modicum of intelligence.

"You claim a desire for asylum," the stocky man said.

"Yes," Pa Kur answered.

"Are you repudiating your citizenship to the Throne World?"

Pa Kur hesitated before saying, "Yes."

"You wish to join the Commonwealth of Planets?"

"I do."

"That requires an exchange on your part. We can give you asylum, but it will cost you information about the Throne World and the star cruisers."

Pa Kur stared at the stocky fool.

The sub-man tried to stare back into his eyes, but failed, looking down.

"We desire the Throne World's coordinates," the man said.

Pa Kur said nothing.

"If we do not grant you asylum, you will be considered a prisoner of war."

Pa Kur continued to remain silent.

"Do you comprehend my words?" the man said.

"Yes."

"Then, why don't you answer?"

"I cannot give you the Throne World's coordinates, as I do not know them."

"That's a lie."

Pa Kur stiffened. The desire to reach out and rip out the man's throat almost caused him to twitch. He must not do that, and yet, he did not know why.

"You don't like me calling you a liar, do you?" the sub-man asked.

"I do not lie."

"Why did your two star cruisers flee?"

Pa Kur said nothing.

"Do you know the reason?" the man asked.

"I do not."

"That is another lie," the man said.

Pa Kur's obsidian-colored eyes glinted with rage.

"If you attempt to harm me," the stocky man said, "these Marines will subdue you."

Pa Kur said nothing.

"For a man who wants asylum, you are strangely reluctant to speak."

"You have not asked me a question I can answer."

"Why did the New Men build chambers on Hades IV?"

"Chambers?" asked Pa Kur.

"Teleporting chambers?" the man asked.

278

Pa Kur bent his head, staring at the table. A throb beat in his forebrain. It opened something in him. He looked up at the quizzical sub-man.

"Who desires this knowledge?" Pa Kur heard himself ask.

"I do."

"Who watches us?"

The stocky man glanced at the one-way glass.

At that moment, it happened. It felt to Pa Kur as if tumblers moved in his mind. He put his hands under the table and heaved as hard and as fast as he could. The table flipped against the stocky man, hurling him and his chair toward the Marines.

Pa Kur was up and moving as the table flew through the air. He had entered overdrive, realizing vaguely that Strand must have meant for the sub-men to capture him all along. Strand had out-guessed the enemy commander.

Pa Kur had been the only New Man on his star cruiser. Both vessels had run on automated systems. He realized these things as he reached the first Marine.

The stocky man thudded against the bulkhead and the table splintered into many pieces due to the violence of its trajectory.

Pa Kur knew that his body would burn out, the muscles and tendons would tear under the intense strain. That did not matter today. He had a final purpose. Strand had seen to that. The Methuselah Man had an opponent in the enemy fleet.

Ripping the raised gun out of the Marine captain's armored grip, Pa Kur turned the weapon on the sub-man, blowing out the faceplate.

He dodged other bullets. The secret enablers wired into him allowed him to do so. In a matter of seconds, he destroyed all the Marines in the cell. Afterward, Pa Kur raised the gun and fired at the one-way glass, shredding it.

Star Watch officers shouted in horror, several of them ducking. One of them went down hard, with a shard of one-way glass sprouting from his eye.

Pa Kur's lips twitched into a smile. He raised his gun, aimed at a harsh-faced officer with admiral tabs on his shoulders and squeezed the trigger.

It clicked empty. Pa Kur had used the final bullets to shatter the glass. No matter, the New Man hurled the gun at an officer aiming one at him. The thud dropped the officer.

At that point, Pa Kur launched himself through the broken frame.

The admiral did not flee, but snarled like an animal. They were all animals. Pa Kur sailed at the admiral, crashing against him, his iron strong fingers clutching the throat.

A hard impact blew the air out of Pa Kur's lungs. He knew without looking down that a force blade had entered him. The admiral jerked the blade, twisting and sawing.

Pa Kur clutched harder. He must kill Admiral Fletcher. He must destroy the brains of the Grand Fleet.

Pa Kur eyelids fluttered as life drained from his glorious body. As he slipped away, he wondered if he had killed the admiral. He hoped…he hoped…

Pa Kur frowned. Had he attacked at Strand's will?

I hope I failed, Pa Kur thought. Then, he died, hating Strand with his final breath.

-35-

Victory neared the Dyson sphere. The starship had been braking for some time. It was presently at a Luna-like distance from the monstrous spheroid's surface.

Captain Maddox sat at the command chair. He studied the main screen where Valerie had zoomed in on the port admiral's flotilla.

The flagship was a *Bismarck*-class battleship, the *Leipzig*. Its sister battleship, the *Vienna,* was also part of the flotilla, which included three strike cruisers armed with antimatter missiles, five destroyers, two escorts and three supply ships. High Command had believed the antimatter missiles gave Hayes the needed destructive power necessary to defeat any silver drones the port admiral might have found in the Xerxes System.

"Still no sign of damage to the ships?" Maddox asked.

"Negative," Galyan said, standing beside the command chair.

"Not a scratch on any of the hull armor?"

"Checking," the AI said. "Oh. Please excuse my error. Yes, I detect more than scratches. There are strange buff marks. I have seen similar—ah. It should have been obvious. Captain, I detect the aftereffect of neutron beam-shots."

"Neutron?" Maddox said. "Did they cut through the hulls?"

"Negative."

"Then—"

"Captain, please allow me to complete my report."

Maddox nodded.

"I have seen one similarity to this, the neutron shots against *Victory* that induced a thought-loop in my AI core."

"So there's one mystery solved," Valerie said.

Maddox turned to her. "Explain your reasoning, Lieutenant."

"It seems simple enough, sir. The flotilla's computers went cold after the special neutron beam thought-looped all of them. With the computers offline, maybe the life-support systems shut down. Maybe everybody over there is dead." The last words came out higher-pitched than the first.

"That's one possibility," Maddox said in calm voice. "Until we know, though, let us not jump to conclusions. I hope to find the port admiral and his people quite alive. Until I have reason to know otherwise, that is our operating assumption."

It took a second before Valerie said, "Yes, sir. I think that's the better assumption too."

There was a moment of silence as that sank in.

"What's next, sir?" Keith asked.

Maddox slapped an armrest. "Galyan, have you spotted any life anywhere?"

"Negative," the holoimage said.

"Have you spotted any sensor devices attempting to scan us?"

"I would have immediately informed you of such an event, sir."

Maddox used the knuckles of his right hand to brush his cheek. "I'm going to use a shuttle—"

"Sir," Valerie said, as if she'd been waiting for him to say those words. "I don't think you should use a shuttle to go anywhere. Frankly, sir, we don't want to lose you."

Maddox studied the lieutenant.

"What if Ludendorff is waiting for exactly that?" Valerie asked. "What if he uses a tractor beam on the shuttle and yanks you onto the Dyson sphere?"

"We must inspect the battleships," Maddox said. "We must determine the crews' fates. That is our first priority."

"Send a probe, sir," Valerie suggested. "You're too valuable to risk."

Maddox considered that. "While that is a noble sentiment—"

"I think everyone aboard *Victory* will agree with me," Valerie added, interrupting the captain.

Maddox noted the anxiety in her bearing. He glanced at the Second Lieutenant. The pilot's fingers drummed against his board too fast—nervously, it would appear.

"I see," Maddox said to himself. "Mr. Maker, maneuver closer to the flotilla, please. We will come within several kilometers. Then, I shall send a probe as the lieutenant suggests."

Out of the corner of his eye, Maddox saw that Valerie almost said thank you. Instead, she nodded to him and went back to her board.

Maddox studied the main screen. What would the probe find once it reached the *Leipzig*? Were Hayes and his people dead, or was there a different explanation to the mute vessels?

***

Tension mounted on the bridge as *Victory* eased toward *Leipzig*, with only a few kilometers separating them. Beyond the flotilla's flagship loomed what now seemed like a wall of Dyson sphere, although the outer surface of the sphere was several thousand kilometers away.

"All stop," Maddox said.

Keith tapped his board.

"Send the probe," Maddox said.

Valerie manipulated her panel. On the main screen, a small object left the starship, with hydrogen exhaust propelling it toward the battleship. The distance was minuscule and the probe's speed almost nonexistent compared to normal starship velocities.

The minutes ticked away.

"Shall I increase magnification, sir?" Valerie asked.

"Please," the captain said.

Instead of the battleship and Dyson sphere background, the *Leipzig* magnified into sight with big laser cannons showing their orifices.

"The hull armor looks clean," Keith said.

Maddox nodded in silent agreement.

"I'm maneuvering the probe to a hangar entryway," Valerie said.

Several minutes later, as the lieutenant tapped quickly, the main battleship hatch began to open.

"We know one thing," Valerie said. "The *Leipzig* is still responding to code. That would indicate the main computer still works."

Maddox watched the probe maneuver into the lit hangar bay. It was smaller than *Victory's* bay, but full of strikefighters.

"Are any missing?" Maddox asked.

"They appear to all be there, sir," the lieutenant said, checking a manifest.

Soon, the probe landed on the deck.

"Detaching a crawler," Valerie said.

A vehicle much like the ancient Mars explorer dropped off the probe's hull and began to rove across the battleship's hangar bay. The lieutenant controlled it through radio signals, although it could make limited command decisions with its onboard computer.

During the next half-hour, Maddox, Keith, Valerie and Galyan watched the probe crawl through the empty battleship. No one was aboard. However, the lieutenant was unable to find any evidence of combat or a struggle.

"It appears as if they simply left the ship, sir," Valerie said later.

"Let's get the ship's log," Maddox said.

In time, the crawler reached the battleship's bridge. It used a link-tube, connecting with the computer system.

"Ready to transfer," the lieutenant said.

"I just had a thought," Galyan said. "Transfer the data into a separate computer file here."

"What are you thinking?" Valerie asked.

"Maybe a Builder virus infected the battleship's computers. We do not want the virus to infect my systems."

"Good thinking, Galyan," the lieutenant said. "Give me a few minutes to set this up."

Time passed slowly as the others waited.

"Okay," Valerie said. "I'll begin the transfer." She tapped her board, but nothing happened. She tried again with the same results.

"Trouble?" the captain asked.

"Either the crawler isn't responding or something in the battleship's computer is not responding."

The main screen suddenly wavered, shivered with fuzziness, and then Professor Ludendorff regarded them. At least, the humanoid shape appeared to be the Methuselah Man they had come to know.

"Greetings," the professor said. "I see you made it to the Dyson sphere."

"How did he cut into our comm stream?" Maddox demanded.

Valerie manipulated her board, soon shaking her head. "This is from the battleship's main computer, sir. We're not in a direct comm-link with him."

"By now," the professor said, "you must surely have begun to wonder about my intent. I can assure you that it is completely benign. Given Captain Maddox's temperament, though, I doubt you will believe me. I suspect you destroyed the guardian ship. It was set to defeat any vessel except for yours. I urge you not to worry about the port admiral and his people. They are fine. Captain, I would like you to join me inside the Dyson sphere. There is something I must show you and you alone. Please come down at once. Time is fast running out for all of us. Until then," the professor said. He bowed, smiled and disappeared from the screen.

"This is interesting indeed," Galyan said. "It appears the professor has been expecting us."

"Lieutenant," Maddox said. "I want more information. Bring up the rest of the data in the *Leipzig's* computer."

Valerie manipulated her board, trying harder and soon shaking her head. "I'm sorry, sir. I can't download anything else. There's a firewall in place I can't breach."

"Galyan," Maddox said. "Break down the firewall."

"At once, Captain," the AI said.

After several minutes, the holoimage stirred. "I cannot break the firewall, Captain. This is most disturbing. I will—"

"Just a moment," Maddox said, who had been thinking. "Maybe that's the game. The professor *wants* Galyan to dig deeper. In some manner, Ludendorff will spring a computer trap, attempting a takeover. Galyan, exit the probe."

"It is done," the holoimage said.

"What do we do now?" Valerie asked. "It seems we're stymied."

"Sir," Keith said. "It's the Dyson sphere. A door is opening on its surface. What do you think that means?"

"Battle stations," Maddox said. "Galyan, ready the disruptor cannon. Lieutenant, make sure the shield is fully charged. Mr. Maker, begin backing away. I want you to warn the others in the ship we might have to make some violent maneuvers."

"Aye-aye, sir," Keith said.

As the others went about their tasks, Maddox watched the giant hatch. It had to be ten times the size of *Victory*. Soon, a vast metal object with a huge orifice eased out of the opening. Was that like the Destroyer's main weapon?

"What is that?" Keith asked. "I don't think it's aiming at us."

"I do not detect any tracking systems fixed upon us," Galyan said. "That would not preclude optical sighting, however. Will it launch missiles?"

"Sir," Valerie said. "There are more of those metal objects. They've appeared all over the surface of the sphere."

A bad feeling swept over Maddox. He leaned forward, rubbing the fingers of his right hand.

The orifice near them glowed orange.

"The shield is at full strength," Valerie said.

"I'm maneuvering behind the *Leipzig*, sir," Keith said.

As the orifice grew hotter orange, a blue line appeared. The blueness grew larger and brighter. The same happened elsewhere with the other squat cannons.

"Exhaust," Valerie said. "Those are exhaust tails."

"You're kidding," Keith said.

Valerie tapped her board, studying the readings. "That's an ion exhaust. The sphere isn't firing at us. It's...it's moving." She turned to look questioningly at Maddox.

"Is the sphere a spaceship?" Keith asked.

"That is entirely the wrong conclusion," Galyan said. "I have been running calculations. The Dyson sphere's physics suggests the answer."

"What's that mean in English?" Keith asked.

Galyan stared at the Scotsman.

"Elaborate on your answer," Maddox told the AI.

"It is elementary and fundamental," Galyan said. "Adok scientists had long projected such a construct as we're now seeing. I have listened to the lieutenant suggest an inhabitable area 550 million times that of Earth. She has not taken into account some of the major problems concerning the sphere."

"If you're so smart," Valerie said, "why don't you enlighten us?"

"Gladly," Galyan said. "The propulsion we are witnessing addresses one of the problems. The sphere or shell lacks a net gravitational interaction with its englobed star. Therefore, the shell drifts in relation to the interior object. Given enough time, the sphere will collide into the massive energy unit. These propulsion systems must be engaged in a corrective endeavor."

"That makes sense," Valerie said. "I'm surprised I missed it."

"Notice the rotation of the sphere," Galyan continued. "If it lacked rotation the inside of the shell would have zero artificial gravity. Everything in the interior surface would thus fall into the star. Given the rotation—the artificial gravity—the contents of the interior surface will pool around the equator. In your parlance, the sphere is acting like a Niven ring for habitation purposes."

"Why go to all that trouble to build a global shell then?" Keith asked.

"Once more the answer is elementary," Galyan said. "It is to collect the star's energy output. I have made a simple calculation. Given a Sol-like star, that is 384.6 yottawatts of power."

"What?" Keith asked.

"It is 33 trillion times more power than 12 terawatts," Galyan said.

"Oh, sure," Keith said, rolling his eyes. "Now, I understand perfectly."

"Twelve terawatts was humanity's power consumption in the year 1998," Galyan said.

"The sphere is amazing," Maddox said, dryly. "But we'll consider its grandeur later. I'm more interested in the professor's prerecorded message and the whereabouts of Hayes and his people."

"Yes," Valerie said. "I don't trust Ludendorff, sir. I think that message was meant to lure us here so he could lure you yet again down onto the sphere."

"Either that," Keith said, "or he gave the message under duress."

"I very much doubt that," Valerie said.

"I don't doubt the *possibility* of duress," Maddox said. "But I find no evidence for it. The professor is cunning. He could have slipped hidden references into the recording for us if someone had forced him to make it. I did not hear any hidden warnings."

"If you're right," Keith said, "I'd like to know why the professor went to such extreme lengths to lure us out here."

"Agreed," Maddox said. "Let us consider this. The request began on Earth with the Shanghai androids and then the holoimage. It would appear the professor desperately desires my presence in the Dyson sphere. The extent of his efforts seems proportionally exaggerated."

"What?" Keith asked.

"Galyan," Maddox said, crisply, ignoring the ace. "You will begin to search the outer spheroid surface. Concentrate on the equatorial region. If the professor desires me down there, he must have a particular entrance in mind."

"You're not really going to give yourself into his hands, are you?" Valerie asked.

"Not as of yet," Maddox said. "I appreciate my freedom too much. There is another consideration, however. If he has been this persistent, I doubt he will stop now. The more he tries, the more he reveals. I still need a few more revelations before I make my move."

"You're matching wits against him," Keith said. The ace grinned. "I like our chances, sir. This time, we're going to beat him and take him back to Earth as a proper prisoner."

Maddox nodded absently, continuing to study the Star Watch ships floating nearby.

"We'll use the probe to explore each vessel," Maddox said. "There is always the possibility the professor made a mistake somewhere. If so we must find it."

"He said it was in our interest that you go to the sphere," Galyan said.

"Ludendorff did indeed *say* that."

"You are in agreement with the lieutenant?" Galyan asked. "You do not trust the professor?"

"No," Maddox said, "not in the slightest."

-36-

During the next few hours, Valerie guided the probe to each Star Watch vessel. She didn't find any more clues. It would seem that Professor Ludendorff hadn't made any mistakes.

By the time she was done, the sphere's engines had stopped glowing and had retreated so the giant hatches closed.

Shortly thereafter, Captain Maddox reentered the bridge. He had taken a catnap.

"Nothing new to report," Valerie said.

A comm beep sounded from her board just then. She glanced at Maddox before turning to it. A second later, she regarded the captain. "Sir, someone from the sphere is hailing us."

"Put him or her on the main screen," Maddox said.

"Yes, sir," Valerie said, hesitantly tapping her board.

Maddox, Valerie, Keith and Galyan all turned toward the main screen. A smiling Ludendorff appeared. He sat in a room with windows. Behind him were giant ferns. Far beyond the ferns shined the system's englobed star.

"Captain Maddox," Ludendorff said, "how good to see you again."

"Yes," Maddox said. "Galyan," he said under his breath. "Is that the real Ludendorff?"

"Analyzing," the AI said.

"I'm sure you're wondering about all the cloak and dagger," Ludendorff said. "I can assure it is for a good reason, a splendid reason, in fact."

"Excellent," Maddox said. "If you would please enlighten us then…"

"Oh, my boy, not by transmission," Ludendorff said. "You'll need to come onto the Dyson sphere first as my recording suggested. It's also best if you come alone."

"Ah," Maddox said.

"Don't you find the sphere amazing?" Ludendorff asked.

"I do," Maddox said. "Before we speak further, I should let you know that I'm not entering the sphere."

Ludendorff blinked several times as the smile slipped. Then, the smile appeared again in full force. "That's a poor joke, Captain. Of course, you're coming. You must. It…"

"Yes?" Maddox asked.

"It is required," Ludendorff added.

"You are addressing an android," Galyan said quietly. "It is a very good replica of the professor, but I finally concentrated on the pupils. From time to time, I can see through to the circuitry working back there."

"Suppose I decline your offer?" Maddox asked the android.

"Surely, you're curious about the sphere," the Ludendorff android said.

"Quite curious," Maddox said, "but not so much that I wish for my nonexistence."

"I do not understand the relation."

"It is elementary," Maddox said. "By entering the sphere I could lose my life."

"No, Captain, I can assure you that is not the case, at least not immediately." The android's grin widened. "I know that didn't sound right. It was not a threat. I merely mean that all organisms die in time."

"On the Dyson sphere," Maddox said, "is that what you're saying?"

The android blinked repeatedly. "I must insist you come. But since you have declined to come alone, now I ask that your entire crew join me. You will all love it in the Dyson sphere."

"Quite possibly true," Maddox said, diplomatically. "By the way, where are Port Admiral Hayes and his crews?"

"Oh," the android said, "do not worry about them."

"I am a Star Watch officer," Maddox said. "It is my duty to worry about them. In fact, I am quite willing to take military action to free them. Perhaps it is time I turned *Victory's* disruptor beam on the sphere."

"Captain, are you seriously threatening me?"

"Who are you?" Maddox asked.

"Why, I am Ludendorff. That was a strange question."

"That is a lie," Maddox said. "You are not Ludendorff. You are an android made in his image."

The construct blinked more than before.

"Worse," Maddox said, "you're an inferior android. Why is that?"

"Captain, please, this is such a glorious moment. I have long anticipated it. You must come down and let me see you in the flesh. I have read such wonderful reports about you. But I cannot fathom the reason for your continued successes against your superior enemies. Those successes are quite marvelous and unusual. I wish to know the reasons behind them."

"I'm afraid—"

"Captain," Galyan said. "Powerful tractor beams have locked onto the starship. We are being pulled toward a vast opening."

"Magnify," Maddox said.

The Ludendorff android disappeared from the screen. In its place appeared a huge hatch ponderously opening on the outer surface of the sphere.

"Can *Victory* fit through that hatch?" Maddox asked.

"Affirmative," Galyan said.

"At the rate we're being pulled, how long until we reach the…" Maddox waved a hand. "The Dyson hangar bay?"

Before Galyan could answer, Keith asked, "Do you want me to try to break free of the tractor beam, sir?"

"That will not work," Galyan said. "The force of the contest will destroy the ship."

"Let's jump free then," Keith said.

Maddox considered the idea.

"I'm afraid the decision has just been taken out of our hands," Galyan said. "My special jump mechanisms have just gone offline. Something from the Dyson sphere is interfering with my systems."

"Is it a Builder virus?" Maddox asked.

"Captain," Galyan said. "I have detected an alien presence. It is attempting to take over my personality. The only way I can protect myself is to shut down completely. Do you swear to turn me back on when you're able?"

"You know I do, Galyan," Maddox said.

The holoimage glanced at each of them in turn. Then it appeared beside each of them, doing so in the blink of an eye. A ropy holo-arm reached out, attempting to touch each of them. Afterward, the holoimage wavered and disappeared.

The screen came back on, with the Ludendorff android smiling benignly.

"What just happened, Captain?" the android asked. "Why did the comm link separate?"

Maddox moved to the command chair, sitting down. "You're bringing my starship into a hangar bay. That means you have what you want. Why continue with this charade then? Show us who you really are and tell us what you want with us."

"I don't want anything from your crew," the android said. "It's you alone who interests me, Captain."

"Why?"

"You will find out soon enough once you reach my main chamber. I'm sure it will interest you. Even more, you will enlighten me. I am looking forward to the encounter."

"Star Watch needs me," Maddox said, "and it needs *Victory*."

"Yes, both statements are true."

"Therefore, it is a crime to do this to us."

"No," the android said, as if speaking to a child. "Star Watch cannot win in the end. They are overmatched. Thus, I am showing you a kindness. Perhaps it is kind to let them perish faster. I hate to see creatures suffer unnecessarily. With *Victory* helping Star Watch, it will only prolong the agony."

Maddox's thoughts moved at lightning speed. They had been for some time. "Are you a Builder?" he asked.

293

The android smiled cryptically. "Come to my chamber, Captain. I will explain everything there. Until then, you will have to wait for your answers."

"Where is Professor Ludendorff?" Maddox asked.

"I am he."

"Ludendorff has always been an android?"

The android blinked, blinked some more and finally stared in a frozen manner.

"You broke him, sir," Keith said. "You asked him one too many questions."

"No…" Maddox said, studying the unmoving android. "This is a deception, although I can't fathom a reason for it."

For a time, no one spoke.

Valerie kept working her controls. She spun around with anxiety in her eyes. "What are we going to do, sir? We can't— we can't go down there. We have to do something to break free."

"Yes," Maddox said. "Something is exactly what I plan to do."

-37-

"Sir," Valerie said. "You have to let us come."

"No," Maddox said. "That's what the thing wants. Meta, Riker and I will move fast."

"Keith and I can't keep up with the sergeant?" Valerie asked.

"I want you to guard the ship," Maddox said. "That is an order. I plan to find a way to free *Victory* from this insane confinement. Once we do, I want the ship ready to race away."

"Galyan couldn't find a way, sir," Valerie said. "And he's ten times smarter than any of us. How are you, on foot, going to do better?"

Maddox recognized her fear. Separating was difficult and waiting was always hard. As captain, he had to bolster his crew's morale.

"Lieutenant, perhaps you don't remember the story about a young woman caught in a dire situation. She grew up with nothing in the worst Welfare Island on the North American continent. Instead of admitting defeat, she fought every day of her life, scratching her way to a coveted spot in the Space Academy. I doubt she knew the answer at the beginning of her struggle, but she tried just the same."

Valerie looked away, soon saying, "I hate when you do that, sir."

"Noted," he said.

She nodded. "Do you have any idea how long you'll be away?"

"No idea," Maddox said, "although I plan to return within three days."

The lieutenant regarded him, nodding once more. "Supposing you don't show up in three days, how long do you want us to stay aboard the ship?"

"A month," Maddox said.

"You could all be dead by that time."

"We are Star Watch officers," Maddox said. "We each have our duties. You are primarily a ship officer. Meta and Riker are hand-to-hand specialists. According to what we saw in the last transmission, there is plant life here. This could be like Loki Prime."

"Okay," Valerie said. "But after a month, Keith and I are going to rescue you, sir."

"That's good to know."

"Good luck, sir."

"Thank you."

Impulsively, Valerie stepped forward and hugged him. Maddox stiffened, finally patting her on the back. She hugged Meta and Riker afterward. Keith stepped forward, shaking the captain's hand.

"Good luck, sir," Keith said.

"To you as well," Maddox told him, refusing to believe this might be the last time he saw either officer. Somehow, he was going to free his ship and his people.

After Keith hugged Meta and shook Riker's hand, Maddox led the way toward the hangar bay's outer hatch.

Valerie and Keith retreated into the ship proper.

"I hope you know what you're doing, sir," Riker said.

Maddox did too, having prepared the best he could. He, like Meta and Riker, wore an EVA suit with a breather and recyclers. The sphere had air. The recyclers purified it for their use. He also shouldered a Khislack .370 rifle, kept a gun with a suppressor in a holster and carried food, water, survival equipment and extra ammo in a backpack. The helmets used short speakers, so they wouldn't give anything away to eavesdroppers when they communicated with each other.

Meta and Riker were equally weighed down with suit, supplies and weapons.

The outer bay hatch began to rise, stopping after it was several meters off the deck. Outside was a vast, cavernous hall big enough so *Victory* could have sailed down it. Almost as surprising, lights shined down from the ceiling.

"This place is crazy," Meta said.

"You stole my words," the sergeant said.

"The starship was never built to rest in a one G environment," Meta added.

Maddox kept his thoughts to himself. The tractor beams had guided the starship into the vast bay. Afterward, gigantic doors had closed. Later, cyclers had pumped an Earthlike atmosphere around the ancient Adok vessel. According to the sensors, one G pulled at the ship's structure. They were in the Dyson sphere by several hundred meters. Did that mean they were trapped here forever? Why hadn't the intelligence that ran the sphere pulled in the port admiral's warships as well?

It was a mystery, one Maddox planned to solve.

Meta attached magnetic clamps to the deck and uncoiled a long rope ladder. She swung her legs over the edge and began to climb down.

"Do you even have a plan?" Riker asked the captain.

"I do," Maddox said.

"Care to let the rest of us in on it, sir?"

"Certainly," the captain said. "I plan to defeat the intelligence holding us prisoner."

"Oh, is that all?"

"No. I envision it giving us reasons for its actions. I will also search for super-weapons to help us in the war against the New Men once we return to Human Space."

Riker stared at the captain. "Oh, well," he said weakly, "then by all means, let us begin. I can hardly wait. This is an adventure, is it, sir?"

"No, Sergeant, it is an Intelligence mission, one I aim to win." With that, Maddox went to the ladder, beginning his descent from the starship onto the Dyson sphere.

***

From the floor, Maddox looked up at *Victory*, impressed as ever by the ship's size. The only trouble here was that the sphere made it seem like a flea-carrying vessel.

"Do you notice that?" Meta asked, pointing at the nearest oval section of the ship.

Maddox did indeed. Most of the ancient vessel rested on magnetic holders. Two things impressed him about the holders: that they could carry the starship's weight and that they seemed to have been designed for this very craft.

"What do the stanchions suggest to you?" Meta asked.

Maddox thought about it. "That whoever pulled us in knows our ship's specifications."

The three of them studied the starship and the giant clamps holding the underside of the vessel. The hum of the magnetics was audible from their spot on the hangar's deck.

"I can't get a grip on the size of this place," Meta said. "It's baffling to me. I don't understand how anyone could build a sphere around a star, particularly one an AU in radius."

"It is daunting," Maddox admitted.

"How long do you think it took them to build it?"

Maddox finally detected the strain in her voice. It was one thing to talk about exploring the sphere, another to be out here at the beginning of the quest in this…vast structure.

He stepped closer, putting an arm around Meta's shoulder. He squeezed her against him until she turned her helmet to look in his eyes.

"I hope to discover the answer soon," Maddox said.

Riker cleared his throat. "Am I the only one, or did the rest of you think someone was going to be here to show us the way to Professor Ludendorff?"

"That did seem implied," Maddox said, as he released Meta.

"How long are we going to wait for them to show up?" Riker asked.

Maddox shook his head. He wasn't sure.

"Where would you propose we go if we just went on our own?" Meta asked the sergeant.

Riker pointed into the mammoth hall. "That way seems wisest. It's toward the inner surface. I'd like to see what a Dyson sphere looks like on the inside."

"This...failure of an escort fits with the rest of the star system, at least what we've seen so far," Maddox said. "A lone saucer-ship attacked us after we exited the hyper-spatial tube. Port Admiral Hayes' flotilla drifted aimlessly near the outer sphere. There is no space traffic here, nothing to suggest a lively community. Instead, the system feels...maybe not deserted, but certainly empty."

"And old," Meta said, "as if this was built a long time ago."

"That's why no one is here to greet us?" Riker asked.

Maddox pursed his lips, scanning the cavernous chamber. They were less than mice in a house, more like fleas traveling through a giant's castle. The sheer volume of this hall weighed against his spirit.

It would be better to do something than wilt here at the edge of the Dyson sphere. Action was the cure. So thinking, Maddox slid the Khislack's carrying strap over his EVA-suited shoulder. "Let's get started then, shall we. I've decided I like your idea, Sergeant. It's time to see the sphere's interior surface."

***

They walked for an hour with lights shining down on them the entire time. The vast hall was empty, devoid of machines or any living beings. They moved along the center in case something, anything, should use an unnoticed hatch to charge them. The longer they traveled, the more it felt as if unknown space gods had built the giant edifice.

Maddox stopped, looking back the way they had come. They had lost sight of *Victory* some time ago. He scanned all around. This place was like a cathedral built to worship size, hoping to diminish a being's spirit by showing its insignificance.

"Why haven't they tried to contact us by comm?" Riker asked.

Maddox shrugged.

"Maybe the better question is why they've refused our calls," Meta said.

"I watched the playback of your conversation with the sphere's android, sir," Riker said. "The android seemed eager to speak with you face to face. This...absence seems suspicious."

Maddox couldn't see what to do differently, so he began walking again.

Time passed as they traveled. After a while, the monotony made the hall seem timeless, their efforts useless. Nothing ever changed.

"I've read about Dyson spheres before," Meta said. "I always thought the outer layer would be rather thin. This layer strikes me as extremely thick."

"Isn't that relative?" Riker asked.

"To what?" Meta asked.

"That we're tiny compared to the sphere," the sergeant said. "I imagine an ant thinks my garden back home is enormous. We're the ants here."

Maddox slid the rifle's strap from his shoulder.

Both Meta and Riker noticed. She drew a thick-barreled gun. Riker drew two regulation-sized pistols.

The captain aimed the rifle down the hall, pressing the stock against his shoulder as he peered through the scope.

"What is it, sir?" Riker whispered.

"I see a body," Maddox said, as he continued to peer through the scope.

"Is it dead or alive?"

"I judge it dead," Maddox said, "as the pieces are spread on the floor. What's interesting is that I see wires, struts and resistors."

"A dead android," Meta whispered.

"Who destroyed it?" Riker wondered aloud.

"Exactly," the captain said. "The reason no one met us could be lying out there." With the scope, he scanned around the scattered pieces and then beyond. Abruptly, he lowered the rifle. "Let us proceed with caution, as it seems there are factions within the sphere willing to fight for their beliefs, one of which is non-communication with us."

Ten minutes later, they neared the scattered pieces. There were wires, struts, rotators, resisters and clots of dark matter on the floor.

Meta knelt by the first dark clot. With a metal pin, she shoved into the substance. "It's blood," she said.

Riker took several steps forward, toeing something. "This is hair," he said, pointing at it with a gun. "Whoever did this loves androids as much as we do."

"If this was an old kill," Meta said, "the blood would have crusted a long time ago. This happened recently."

As before, Maddox slid the rifle off his shoulder, using the scope to scan ahead. He saw nothing else unusual.

"We keep going," he said.

They left the destroyed android behind, possibly the one who had spoken to them only a short time ago.

Fifteen minutes later, a loud *clang* sounded from ahead. The floor quivered under their feet.

"That's wonderful," Riker said. Before he could say more, alien-sounding *squeals* caused the sergeant to snap his teeth together.

Meta frowned as she glanced at Maddox.

The captain gripped his rifle.

From ahead came more clangs and squeals and then a loud and long whooshing sound. The squeals became higher-pitched, filled with pain and rage.

"We should retreat back to the ship," Riker said.

"Go ahead," Maddox told him, as he began to stride toward the noise.

"Are you crazy, sir?" Riker shouted.

Maddox began to run toward the sounds as they intensified. He wanted to see what was going on around the bend.

-38-

Maddox skidded to a halt. The others raced to catch up. What the captain saw in the distance caused a cold feeling to crawl up his neck. Swiftly, he raised the Khislack and peered through the scope. The sight confirmed his worst fear.

He had seen ancient exoskeletons of Swarm creatures before. Six thousand years ago, the Swarm had attacked *Victory* in its home system. When he and the others had boarded the starship several years ago, it had been full of crusted slime and well-preserved exoskeletons of Swarm boarders.

The red-colored beasts scampering away from a metal humanoid construct struck him as creatures of the Swarm. They were around the size of a medium-sized dog and had hardened exoskeletons like beetles, but with whippy scorpion tails. They also had braches—legs after a fashion—six of them. Four helped them run. The last two could have acted like pincers.

The metal humanoid thing was huge and heavy, maybe one hundred tons in weight. It had two legs that clanged with each step. A tube sprouted from its chest. The edges of the orifice were blackened with what seemed like soot. As Maddox watched, a long tongue of liquid fire arched from the tube and licked among the fleeing Swarm creatures.

Some curled immediately and began to crisp with wisps of black smoke, giving some idea of the fire's heat. Others threw back their ugly heads and squealed in agony. Several spun around, charging the metal thing.

Individual rays from the construct's fists fried the attacking beasts. The stench of the burning creatures finally reached Maddox through his EVA suit. It reeked horribly.

Meta reached him, panting, and groaning in complaint at the noisome smell.

"Bugs," Maddox said.

"What do you mean bugs?" she panted.

"Swarm creatures."

"Oh no," she whispered, her eyes becoming wide. "They're not extinct?"

"Apparently not," Maddox said, "and they're on the Dyson sphere with us."

"At least they have an enemy," she said.

Riker finally stumbled up with phlegm rattling in his throat "What is that thing out there?"

"An excellent question," Maddox said. He'd lowered the rifle. Now, he raised it again to look through the scope.

The construct—it appeared to be twice the height of a man—finished slaughtering the red creatures.

"What's it doing?" Riker said, his voice rising. "Is it headed here?"

"Yes," Maddox said.

"Is it coming to kill us?" the sergeant asked.

"I imagine we will find out soon enough," Maddox said. He lowered the rifle.

"We have to run," an exhausted Riker said.

"Do you have a reasonable destination in mind?" Maddox asked.

Riker stared at him. "Captain, this…" The older man turned toward the construct. "That thing moves bloody fast when it wants to."

"Let us hope it knows the Ludendorff android welcomed us onto the sphere," Maddox said. "Otherwise…" The captain watched the approaching construct, feeling the floor vibrate each time one of its metal feet struck the deck.

***

Maddox stood in front of the others as he studied the approaching construct.

It was an alien humanoid design with squatty legs, a long torso and a boxlike head. The sooty flamethrower had retreated into its chest cavity. The thing lacked a neck, although the box-head could rotate back and forth. In place of a face, it had a screen. The screen now activated, and the Ludendorff android from earlier regarded them with the sun still shining behind it.

"I'm glad to see you haven't come to any harm," the android said.

"Were those Swarm creatures?" Maddox asked.

"Think of them as vermin," the android said with a wave of its hand. "It's more suitable."

"That fails to answer the question."

"Come now, Captain," the android said. "That is a surly attitude. The sweeper saved you from death. You should rejoice."

"If you hadn't dragged us into the sphere, we wouldn't have needed saving," Maddox said.

"Logically reasoned, but still rather sullen, my boy," the android said. "This is the revelation of a lifetime. I am willing to give you all the answers you want. Surely, you must recognize the importance of the event."

"You have suggested before that I will be unable to inform Star Watch about these revelations."

"Does that matter?"

"I am a Star Watch Intelligence officer," Maddox said. "It matters a great deal."

"Bah! I should leave you to the vermin. But," the android said, brightening. "I won't do that, as much as your ingratitude warrants it. You will follow the sweeper. It will bring you to a transport tube. In less than an hour...well, you shall see, my dear boy. You shall see indeed."

The construct turned around, ready to head the way it had come.

"Just a minute," Maddox said. "Did the vermin destroy the android that would have met us?"

The construct faced them again. "The vermin made a rare entrance into the substructure," the android said on the face screen. "It won't happen again, I assure you."

"And if it does?" Maddox asked.

"I have no more time for idle chitchat. You must hurry to me. I've waited far too long for this meeting. I wish to expedite it."

"Because more vermin are on their way here?" asked Maddox.

On the screen, the android leaned toward him. "Would you like to face the vermin on your own, Captain?"

Maddox had seen their numbers earlier. He doubted the three of them had enough bullets to destroy all the red creatures.

"We're ready to go," the captain said.

"Wonderful," the android said.

The construct turned deeper into the hall and took a step in that direction.

***

Car-sized incinerator vehicles were busy burning the exoskeletons by the time Maddox and the others reached the battle-site the captain had witnessed through the scope.

"Do you mind if we stop a moment?" Maddox asked.

"I do indeed mind," the Ludendorff android said from the construct's face-screen.

Maddox eyed a dead creature as he walked past. It was bigger than some of the others with greasy-looking muscles attached to the outer exoskeleton. The braincase was small. It did not seem like an intelligent creature. Were they Swarm life or merely a lower order species from the Swarm homeworld?

"Where did the Swarm originate?" Maddox asked the android.

"Not from anywhere in the Orion Arm," the android answered.

"Is that the extent of your knowledge?"

"That's all I'm going to tell you for now. I'm sure you understand the carrot and stick principle."

"Perfectly."

305

"For now, I'm employing the carrot. Would you like me to start using a stick?"

"Lead on," Maddox said.

"Right," the android said.

The three of them followed the construct, leaving the crisped corpses and incinerator vehicles behind.

"Why didn't we ask if we could ride one of those?" Riker whispered to Maddox. "My feet are killing me."

"I prefer to remain a free agent for as long as possible," Maddox whispered back. He became thoughtful. "How did the creatures enter this area?" he asked the other two. "There must be side entrances. Keep your eyes open for them."

As if he had heard their whispered conversation, and perhaps he had, the android in the face-screen said, "We're almost to the transfer tube."

"Captain," Riker said, urgently, as the sergeant grabbed Maddox's left sleeve.

Maddox saw hatches open in the far wall parallel with them. Out of the hatches poured more red creatures. They scampered fast, with their whippy tails high in the air. Behind followed bigger creatures of exoskeleton form but a different shape. They moved slower than the small ones. Their locomotion was different too. Instead of four legs, they had fifty or more centipede-like appendages. Those moved fast in a revolting manner, almost making it seem as if the bigger, taller creatures rolled along on the floor.

"Stay where you are," the android said from the face-screen. "This will take but a few moments' work."

The metal construct began to run at the charging creatures, the clangs causing the floor to vibrate more than earlier.

"What now, sir?" Riker asked. "Those look like more creatures than the robot can handle."

"Agreed," Maddox said. "We run for the other wall. Maybe a closer inspection will show us hatches we can use."

"And if the creatures are driving us there, sir?" Riker asked.

"We'll find out soon enough," Maddox said. "Start running. I'll catch up with you."

"No," Meta said.

"Do as he says," Riker told her, grabbing an arm, yanking her along. "The captain can outrun either of us any day. He means to act as a rear guard to give us time."

Meta gave Maddox a searching look. He nodded. Then, she ran with Riker for the opposite wall.

Maddox followed them by walking backward, keeping his eye on the battle. He estimated hundreds of the smaller creatures, maybe half as many of the bigger ones.

The construct's chest tube appeared. A liquid arch of flame crossed the distance, burning smaller creatures. They squealed like stuck pigs, a vicious, evil sound. None of the creatures slowed their advance, however. They all surged toward the construct.

The alien robot beamed one of the bigger ones with a fist ray. Maddox found it interesting that the creature didn't drop right away. It took several seconds of beaming before the outer exo-armor began to smoke. Finally, the creature hissed and began to thrash on the floor.

Maddox looked behind him. Riker and Meta were a third of the way to the wall. He faced forward again. The little creatures charged the construct. More died to its flames. A few charred ones reached it. The metal thing began to stomp on those, squishing them so black gunk jetted in the air.

That was interesting. They concentrated on the construct as if they could defeat it. Their means escaped the captain.

A shrill squeal sounded. It was different from anything he'd heard so far. It came from the back of the attacking horde. It seemed to come from a slower black creature. Was that the smart one directing the others?

A few of the surviving scampers ran past the construct after Maddox. The vile creatures squealed with delight.

Maddox looked back. Meta and Riker were closer to the wall. Kneeling, Maddox raised the Khislack. He used the scope, targeting a small head. He squeezed the trigger.

The stock pushed against his shoulder as the bullet cracked. The .370 grain exploded the head of a charging creature. The carcass lost motive energy, skidding across the floor. Maddox switched targets and killed the next one.

When he lowered the rifle, Maddox noticed a strange pause in the battle. The construct and the Swarm creatures had all stopped to stare at him. It was an unwelcome feeling.

"Do not go that way!" the android shouted. "Keep going up the hall. I'll stop them and guide you to the transfer point."

Before Maddox could shout a reply, the horde of creatures charged the construct anew. As the larger ones neared the metal humanoid, they spat black globs of substance. Some of those globs struck the construct. Immediately, a chemical reaction took place as the black gunk boiled away metal like acid, producing a stench like ancient rust.

"Run up the hall," the android shouted. "Don't use the side hatches."

Maddox spun around, sprinting as fast as he could go toward Meta and Riker.

"There are hatches!" the captain shouted. "Use them!"

Neither Meta nor Riker turned back toward him. They had almost reached the other side of the hall.

As Maddox sprinted like a greyhound, he noticed outline images that hadn't been visible while they traveled in the center of the corridor. Those looked like hatches. Why didn't the android want them to use the doors? Would they lead to even more Swarm creatures, or would they find something that the android didn't want them to see?

As Maddox covered the distance, Meta reached a hatch. She felt along it and finally tried something. The hatch slid up into darkness.

Maddox looked back. The construct flamed creatures as rusty-smelling smoke rose from it. Other creatures swept past the metal thing, coming for Maddox and his people.

He faced forward once more, straining to reach his comrades as they darted through a dark hatch.

-39-

Maddox reached the others in the darkness. The corridor was like a normal starship's hallway, perhaps a little bigger.

"This must be a service hall," Riker said.

Maddox soon led them, using a light on the EVA helmet. Much too soon from behind came crawling, scratchy sounds.

"Why doesn't the android gas them?" Meta panted. "Surely, it can track the creatures. Couldn't the android simply seal the area and pump out the air?"

Maddox moved at a half-trot, concentrating, afraid of running into a wall or some other object. That might tear the suit or worse.

"They're gaining on us," Riker said, shortly.

"Right," Maddox said, coming to a halt. "Get behind me."

"No," Meta said. "Keep running until they're almost on us. Then, we'll all fight together."

Maddox hadn't told them about the acid-spitting creatures, as he didn't want to demoralize them.

"Do as I say," he told Meta, sternly. "We're not a debating society but a military organization."

"Now you listen to me," Meta said.

Riker grabbed an arm.

She shook it off. "We're about to die. I'm not going to—"

"We're not about to die," Maddox said, almost sounding angry. He strode past Meta, shoving her behind him. Then, the captain bent on one knee and raised the rifle. He switched it to

309

infrared sighting. The last several hundred meters had been in a straight line. He saw the little scampers coming as red blobs.

"Keep going," he said. "I'll catch up."

"Maddox—"

"Meta," he said, with more emotion than he cared to use. "Just do as I say."

A flash from the barrel and a loud boom heralded a squeal of pain farther down the corridor. No one could see it in the darkness, but Maddox grinned fiercely.

From his firing position, he began to methodically kill the smaller, faster creatures. Several took two shots. None so far took three. Maddox used several magazines to stop them and temporarily clog the corridor with their piled bodies.

The captain rose, shouldering the Khislack. He loved the rifle. There was none better for long-ranged work.

With the helmet lamp, he hurried after the others, soon reaching them.

"Are any left?" Meta asked.

"Yes, but it won't take long for them to remove the dead."

Soon, Maddox listened to the sound of his labored breathing. They kept hurrying through the corridors, always going right when they had to make a choice. The sergeant began to limp, slowing their rate of advance. Maddox finally grabbed the man's biological arm, putting it over his shoulder. He helped the sergeant move faster.

Too soon, the captain heard the scrape of claws on metal. The surviving creatures were closing again.

Maddox removed the sergeant's arm from his shoulder, spun around, dropped to one knee and raised the rifle. He was getting low on ammo, not having expected hordes of creatures to trail them.

Tight-faced, the captain began to fire. The bigger ones took three bullets to kill, never more and never fewer.

He checked. He had three bullets left. With extreme deliberation, Maddox fired, killing another of the big ones. That left just two more. Setting the rifle on the floor, Maddox drew the suppressed pistol.

He gripped it two-handed and fired shot after shot, putting down the final two Swarm creatures.

It surprised Maddox to find that his hands shook as he holstered the pistol. He wasn't that tired. Did he feel relief? Yes, it would appear so.

He picked up the Khislack. Silently, he berated himself for having put the remaining ammo so deep in his backpack.

With a growing sense of relief, he jogged after the others. They had stopped to wait for him, which made him angry.

"You were supposed to keep going," Maddox said.

"Sir," Riker said. "Can't you see?"

Maddox shined his light around the sergeant. Ah. He did see. The two of them had found a hatch.

"We've been waiting for you," Riker said. "Are you ready?"

"Open it," Maddox said.

Riker grabbed a lever with his bionic arm. Slowly, he moved the handle. It creaked with age until something clicked in the hatch.

The captain drew his gun. Meta aimed hers.

Riker pulled. Dirt spilled into the corridor as did hurtful sunlight.

Immediately, the faceplates of their EVA helmets darkened.

"Have we reached the interior surface?" Meta asked in a hush.

Maddox stepped toward the hatch. There were stairs leading up, with dirt on most of the steps. Some of them had moss and lichen growths.

"Watch your step," the captain said. He led the way, with his suppressed pistol ready.

The steps twisted around and went steeply up. Soon, Maddox reached the top, his helmet passing it. He spied tall ferns growing around the opening with a shattered and torn-off cover lying nearby. Climbing higher still, he stepped on the surrounding soil.

Something crunched and crackled underfoot. With a boot, he kicked away dirt, revealing yellowed bones. He looked around. Ferns grew everywhere, the biggest ones twice his height. It felt like the Jurassic Age of Earth. Craning his head, he looked up at the sun, the star. They were definitely inside the Dyson sphere. It gave him a strange feeling.

"Should we mark the exit?" Meta asked.

Maddox shook his head. "I'll remember the way."

Meta cocked her head.

"He's telling the truth," Riker said. "Once the captain has gone somewhere, he can always find his way back. It's uncanny but useful. I'm surprised you didn't know that by now."

Meta knelt by the bones, fingering them. "This is interesting, don't you think?"

"They're bones," Riker said with a shrug.

"Exactly," Meta said.

Maddox turned sharply, staring at her.

"What am I missing?" Riker asked.

"They're bones," Maddox said, "not exoskeleton shells."

"Are those human bones?" Riker asked.

"Maybe," Meta said.

"Are they are the port admiral's bones?" the sergeant asked.

Meta squeezed the bone in her hand, crumpling it. "I doubt that. These seem very old and brittle."

Maddox nodded thoughtfully. Soon, he walked several steps away, shrugged off his pack and let it hit the soil. Resting on one knee, he opened the pack and extracted extra .370 ammunition. He reloaded the empty magazines.

"The air is breathable," Meta said. She held an analyzer, tapping it.

"The air could hold dangerous substances we can't recognize as yet," Riker said.

"One of us should take off his helmet," Meta said. "If he's fine after a time, we can all do likewise."

"Or take off *her* helmet," Riker said.

"No one is taking off his helmet yet," Maddox said. "It's far too early for that."

"What do you suggest, sir?" Riker asked.

"We'll eat," Maddox said, "rest for a while and take a look around. The android didn't want us to go this way. I'd like to know why. If we can't figure it out soon enough, we'll backtrack. The port admiral is missing and this place has *Victory*. We have to free them both as soon as possible."

They sipped from concentrate tubes in their helmets. Then they settled back for ten minutes. Afterward, Maddox rose to his feet.

"Do you feel better?"

"No," Riker said. "You've let me rest just long enough for my muscles to tighten up."

"Well, this is better than Loki Prime," Maddox said.

Neither Riker nor Meta replied to that.

"Right," Maddox said. "Let's go…that way." He pointed in a direction that might have been east.

"Why that way?" Riker asked.

"Today," Maddox said, "one direction is just as good as another."

***

They marched through a forest of ferns with the sun heating their EVA suits. At first they went uphill, then down for a kilometer and then even more sharply up.

"Maybe the entire Dyson sphere is filled with ferns," Riker complained.

"The Swarm creatures imply otherwise," Maddox said.

"What about that, sir?" Riker asked. "Were those really Swarm creatures?"

"I don't know for sure, but it makes the most sense from what we know."

"Do you suppose the Dyson sphere is a giant…laboratory?" Meta asked. "Did the Builders make it and turn it into a zoo?"

"That's an interesting idea," Maddox said. "What leads you to that conclusion?"

"That it's so empty," she said. "If the Builders had made it to live in for themselves, why doesn't the place abound with them?"

"That's assuming Builders made this place," Riker said.

"True," Meta said.

Maddox thought about that. It was as reasonable a hypothesis as any. He found a steeper section of slope but kept going as the ferns lessened ahead. With a burst of speed that

313

left the captain panting, he reached the very top of a large mountain.

He leaned against a lone fern, looking over a vast panorama of mountain slopes with fern forests. The mountains and ferns went on for kilometers while farther away…

Maddox slipped off the Khislack, using the scope. He lowered the rifle and fiddled with the scope's settings.

"What are you doing, sir?" Riker asked.

"Setting it for maximum magnification."

The captain raised the rifle again. The scene leaped into view. There was a distant valley that lacked ferns. Instead, strange-shaped mounds of dirt towered there. He spied red, purple, green, and…movement.

"Swarm creatures," Maddox whispered.

"What do you see, sir?"

"I've found…a nest, I suppose."

"A Swarm nest?" Meta asked.

"Yes."

"Look in the opposite direction."

Maddox lowered the rifle, glancing at Meta. He swiveled in the opposite direction and raised the Khislack. He scanned distant slopes. He swept the area back and forth.

"I don't like this," Riker said. "A Dyson sphere filled with bugs. We should have listened to Ludendorff."

"To the android," Meta corrected.

"Interesting," Maddox said.

"What did you find, sir?" Riker asked.

"It looks like a bulldozer," Maddox said. "Yes, it's knocking down ferns with a bulldozer-type of vehicle."

"Are bugs driving it?" the sergeant asked.

"I'm looking for—ah-ha," Maddox said. "I see a driver. It isn't a bug, as you say, Sergeant."

"Well," Riker said. "Don't keep us in the dark, sir. What have you found?"

"Humans," Maddox said. "I have found humans in the Dyson sphere, and I don't think they're Port Admiral Hayes' people."

"Why's that, sir?" Riker asked.

"They're the wrong color, for one thing," Maddox said. "For another, they're much too small. This is curious."

The captain lowered the Khislack. "We have a choice. Do we return to the service entrance and find the android or do we hike out there to talk to humans who possibly can't speak our language?"

Riker sat down, picking up moss and tossing it onto the ground. He looked up. "I don't like the idea of hiking anywhere with the possibility of meeting with more Swarm creatures."

"Reasonable," Maddox said.

"I'd like to meet these people," Meta said. "It strikes me that the android didn't want us to. That makes me doubly interested in talking to them."

"Yes," Maddox said. "I feel the same way. Therefore, let's get started. I want to reach these people before any of the Swarm creatures reach us."

-40-

The route proved exhausting, as there were no trails and the ferns made it difficult to scout ahead. Nor could they climb the ferns to get a better look, as the plants were too weak to hold them.

Maddox often led them around steep areas lest they tumble down the mountain. At times, they came upon sheer rock faces that not even the captain could have scaled. That took even more time detouring.

After several hours of hard going, Maddox began taking longer breaks, allowing the sergeant to rest more. Eventually, Meta and he took turns helping Riker.

"At this rate it will take days to reach the bulldozer," Meta said at one stop.

Maddox sat against a fern, having grown thoughtful. He studied Meta, asking, "Have you seen any insects? I mean small ones like grasshoppers and flies, not the Swarm bugs."

Meta frowned before shaking her head.

"Sergeant, what about you?"

Riker was sprawled on the ground in his EVA suit with his eyes closed.

"No little bugs, sir," the sergeant muttered, "just sweat in my eyes."

"Everything was new in the beginning," Maddox said, quietly. "The Dyson sphere was exciting enough for us, the very fact of its being. I've been thinking, though. There should be animal paths, something to indicate wild creatures. We've seen nothing to indicate animals or insects. That suggests the Dyson sphere is devoid of lower life-forms."

"You're right," Meta said. "There aren't any birds or birdlike creatures, either."

"How do the Swarm creatures and humans survive?" the captain said. "What do they eat?" He shrugged. "How does the eco-system maintain itself? Without insects—"

"There's something else," Meta said, interrupting.

Maddox raised his eyebrows.

"I haven't seen any sickly ferns or any rotting ones on the ground."

"There were the brittle bones," Riker said from where he lay.

"Yes," Maddox said, "which highlights Meta's point. We haven't come across anything else decomposing: no exoskeletons, no fallen ferns, animal bones, nothing."

"What would explain that?" Meta asked.

Maddox shook his head before studying ferns. "I should have seen it earlier," he said, shortly. "Notice, there are no small ferns. All of them are full grown."

Meta examined the nearest ones and then those farther out "You're right. Is this a park?"

"A groomed forest?" Maddox asked.

Meta nodded.

"It would appear so," the captain said. "The question becomes: who grooms it?"

"The humans used a bulldozer and the Swarm built dirt towers," Meta said. "I doubt either of them grooms the park."

"A reasonable assumption," Maddox said, thoughtfully.

Riker sat up. "We're making a mistake, sir. We should head back to the service hatch." He waved an arm. "This is detouring from what we came to do. We have to leave the Dyson sphere, not learn how it operates inside. How does marching out here help us free *Victory*?"

"The android didn't want us to see this," Maddox said. "That suggests we should see it so we know what is going on."

"Are the little humans running the bulldozer going to help us get off the sphere?" Riker asked.

"I suspect you're right. They're not going to aid us."

317

"While the Swarm will kill us if they catch us," Riker said. "This trek is just adding extra risk we don't need."

Maddox climbed to his feet. "You may be right, but I still want to see these humans. We should continue hiking if we're going to reach them sooner rather than later."

Riker groaned as he stood. "There's another thing to think about, sir. What if the little humans believe we're aliens, demons or something equally terrifying to them? We may be walking to our deaths."

Maddox stared into the sky. Did the sergeant have a point? He thirsted to understand the situation on the sphere, but that wasn't germane to the wider war. They had to break free of the sphere and find a way back home. That was the ultimate goal. But the sphere, the android, the Shanghai androids, the AI box with Ludendorff's engrams and the saucer-ship... It seemed reasonable the Builders had fashioned the Dyson sphere. That meant—

"What are you thinking?" Meta asked. "You look so solemn."

Maddox regarded her. Abruptly, he sat back down, brought up his knees and wrapped his arms around them. The extent of the situation—the Builder pyramid in the Mid-Atlantic on Earth, the Dana android during the journey here, the possibility more androids had replaced various people on Earth—

"What's that?" Riker asked, as he stared into the sky.

Maddox heard a humming noise. He jumped up, looking around.

"Over there," Meta said, pointing.

Maddox saw a saucer skimming a mountain, heading toward them. It came fast, the hum increasing in volume. The inner saucer was a glowing bulb with a disc spinning around it.

"What now, sir?" Riker asked. "Do we run?"

"No."

"Should we shoot it?" the sergeant asked.

Maddox silently debated the idea.

The craft had begun slowing down, although the disc continued to spin just as fast around the glowing bulb part. The craft appeared to be ten times as large as a Star Watch shuttle. Bullets weren't going to stop it.

318

"What if it's a Swarm craft?" Riker asked.

Maddox shouldered his rifle. "I doubt it is. If the Swarm ran it, why did the creatures earlier use claw and spit against the robot? They would have used weapons. No. This saucer must belong to whoever runs the sphere."

"I hope you're right, sir," Riker said.

In another few seconds, the strange, humming craft hovered fifty meters above them. A slot opened in the bottom glowing part, and a beam shot down at them.

Maddox didn't feel any pain. Riker shouted in alarm. The captain glanced over, seeing Riker's feet lift off the ground at the same moment that a feeling of weightlessness came over the captain.

As the beam continued to shine on them, Maddox, Meta and Riker began to float toward the saucer. The captain spied the sergeant. The man shouted but Maddox couldn't hear anything. The beam seemed to interfere with their short-way comm units.

They rose quicker, only slowing down at the end. Maddox, Meta and Riker entered the glowing bulb section of the ship, floating into a metal room with a bench and a screen on the opposite wall.

The opening closed and each of them gently landed on the floor.

"This—" Riker said

Motion caused them to stumble, and the sergeant to quit talking.

Maddox regained his balance and went to the bench, sitting. Meta and Riker followed his example. A second later, the screen flickered. They saw mountains and fern forests below. The scenes swept by faster as the craft picked up speed.

"Mighty big of them to let us see where we're going," Riker muttered.

"Look," Meta whispered.

Maddox noticed, all right. The ferns disappeared. In their place were the odd dirt structures he'd seen earlier. Instead of ferns, the mountains and then a plains area had millions of earth towers. Among them scurried masses of Swarm creatures.

"They're endless," Meta whispered.

They watched for ten more minutes, absorbed with the scenes before they started to become monotonous.

"Why is the...the pilot showing us all this?" Meta asked.

Maddox had no idea.

"Finally," Riker said, "something different."

The dirt towers and bustling Swarm creatures gave way to a vast dome possibly twenty kilometers in diameter and nearly as tall at the top.

"It's shimmering," Maddox said, softly.

"We're heading straight for it," Meta added.

"Maybe it's a force field," Maddox said.

The saucer didn't slow down, but zipped through the dark force field—if that's what it was—and hovered over an area of boxlike metal structures. The star no longer shined in the sky. Both had vanished. Instead, diffuse light glowed from the force field.

The saucer began to descend toward the largest structures. An area dilated open into what looked like an underground hangar. There were other parked saucers settled into huge holders. Theirs floated past the others until it hovered over a dark opening in the floor.

"I don't see anyone waiting for us," Maddox said.

The original entrance in the saucer floor opened. At the same time, the bench began to ease into the floor.

The three of them stood. Then, the floor began to shift under their feet, angling toward the opening, becoming steeper and steeper.

"Maddox!" Meta shouted.

He grabbed her hand.

Afterward, the three of them lost their footing, sliding down the floor toward the opening, falling out of the saucer toward the darkness below.

-41-

Maddox tried to hold on to Meta's hand as they kept falling but something pulled them apart. They kept staring at each other for as long as they could.

The force pulling Maddox yanked him in one direction, and Meta and Riker, he saw were pulled in another. He continued to fall but his rate of descent slowed. A new force tugged at his EVA suit. In a moment, it tore off him along with the helmet, backpack, Khislack, belt, pistol and knife. He retained his Star Watch uniform and his boots.

At that point, Maddox, holding his breath since the helmet removal, slowed even more. He tried breathing, and began coughing and wheezing at a harsh metallic stench.

Mists wafted against him. Cold air blew and then hot. Meta and Riker had disappeared some time ago.

At last, Maddox floated down toward light. He saw a cubicle waiting for him, one that lacked a top. Gently, he floated into the cubicle, watching a glass top slide into place. The chamber was twenty by twenty and contained a cot, a sink and a toilet.

Was this a prison?

A green gas billowed up from the floor. Maddox held his breath as long as he could. He inhaled finally, smelling the awful gas. He swayed and realized he was about to fall, so he stumbled to the cot, toppling onto it as he passed out.

***

Maddox opened his eyes. He lay face down on a cot. He felt fine and heard nothing. Slowly, he sat up. The sight startled him.

He was in a long row of glass cubicles. Behind them were more rows, hundreds, maybe a thousand. Many of the cubicles contained a single being. Many of those occupants were Swarm creatures of varying shapes and sizes. A few were little people as he'd observed running the bulldozer.

"Hello, Captain."

Maddox whirled around. Professor Ludendorff sat on the cot in the cubicle next door. The professor had longer hair than he recalled, and the man wasn't as tanned as when he'd been aboard *Victory*. His clothes looked disheveled and worn.

"Are you another android?" Maddox said.

Ludendorff frowned, shaking his head. "I have no idea what that's supposed to mean. You look well enough. Did you hit your head coming in?"

Maddox ingested the professor's words. He stood. Whatever the gas had done to him, it hadn't left any aftereffects. He approached the glass separating them.

"Is there a speaker?" the captain asked.

Ludendorff pointed to the left.

Maddox found a clear-colored speaker grille that barely differed from the glass.

The captain retreated to his cot and sat down. His legs felt a little shaky. Maybe the gas had affected him after all. He glanced at Ludendorff.

"What is this place?"

Ludendorff shrugged in a disinterested manner.

"Are you an android?" Maddox repeated.

The professor scowled. "Your questions imply you've met androids before that looked and acted just like me."

"More than just androids," Maddox said, "but also a hologram with your engrams running it."

Ludendorff looked away as if pained.

"Are you pretending to be the real Ludendorff?" Maddox asked.

"No."

"Oh?"

"I am the real Ludendorff. There is no pretense to it."

"I see," Maddox said. "Well, if that's true, why did you rush out to the asteroid in the Xerxes System? I never did understand that."

"Clearly, it was a mistake," Ludendorff muttered.

"No, not really," Maddox said. "The rest of us made it out of the Xerxes System. The android posing as you brought a Swarm-Builder device out of the asteroid that helped us defeat the Destroyer."

"I'm glad I could be of assistance," the professor mumbled. "It sounds as if you finally found out the android was an imposter."

"We did." Maddox looked around again. "Who runs the prison?"

"You're mistaken," Ludendorff said, still staring elsewhere. "This isn't a prison."

Maddox mulled that over. "Is it a zoo?"

Ludendorff finally faced him with a hint of excitement. "You always were a quick study, my boy. It's not exactly a zoo, but a laboratory."

"Who runs it?"

"That should be obvious. A Builder."

"The mysterious Builders," Maddox said. He smiled faintly.

Ludendorff noticed. He rose quickly, walked around his cot several times and finally ran his fingers through his hair.

"I've been here a long time," the professor said. "It's been discouraging, to say the least. The Builder was quite curious—"

"Are you saying you've been in this glass cage for all these months?"

Ludendorff nodded.

"Then all the androids I've seen of you—"

"The Builder used them."

"Why?" Maddox asked.

The professor snorted. "Isn't it obvious, my boy?"

Maddox shook his head.

"You've piqued its interest."

"Just me?" Maddox asked.

"You and Starship *Victory*. The AI is much more powerful than you realize."

"Dana uncovered extra computing power."

"Ah," Ludendorff said, sitting again. "Maybe you do realize how powerful Galyan is. How is Dana?"

"I don't know."

Ludendorff seemed crestfallen. "She didn't join the expedition?"

"An android of her certainly did," Maddox said.

Concern crossed the professor's face. He brushed that away with his hand. Afterward, he tapped his chin, finally nodding.

"Tell me what happened since the Xerxes System. Then, I'll answer what questions I can."

"I'd prefer you to answer my questions first," Maddox said.

Ludendorff straightened, and some of his old personality seemed to assert itself. "I am the oldster here, my boy. I have far more secrets than you do. Thus, we shall show deference to age. I've wasted away in confinement far longer than I've ever had to endure. It's taken you ages to get here. My curiosity is burning out of control. Our time could endure for years or it might be over in a moment. You're—well, never mind about that now. Tell me about the Xerxes System, my android double and the alien Destroyer. I've wondered about the Destroyer until my head felt like it was going to implode."

Maddox eyed the man, trying to decide if this time he looked like the real Professor Ludendorff. He gazed at the other cubicles, at the Swarm creatures. Some spit at the glass. The black gunk didn't acid-burn the glass, or whatever it was, but slid down onto the transparent floor, soon draining away.

That reminded Maddox of the alien Destroyer's spongy floor.

With a shrug, Maddox began to tell the professor of the battle against the alien Destroyer. He included what others had told him, adding Strand's part in the cloaked star cruiser.

Ludendorff sat on his cot most of the time. He raised a knee, holding it with his hands as he leaned back. The professor grinned at times, scowled at others, and laughed at his favorite moments. He was fascinated with his android replica in the meeting with the Lord High Admiral in Geneva.

"Yes, yes," the professor said. "I think I'm beginning to understand."

"Could you enlighten me then?" Maddox asked, having grown weary of talking.

"Excuse me a moment," Ludendorff said. He went to his sink, turning on a tap, putting his mouth over it, drinking from it like a young boy. He rinsed his hands afterward, crouched by the sink and opened a panel. He took out a wafer and ate it. Afterward, he dusted crumbs from his shirt.

"Thank you, my boy," the professor said. The older man had put his hands behind his back, beginning to pace back and forth beside the separating glass. "I'm beginning to understand what happened."

Maddox waited. If this was the real Ludendorff, and he had been here since shortly after their time in the Xerxes System—it was amazing the man hadn't become stir-crazy. Maybe he had.

"There used to be more of us," Ludendorff said. "I mean Strand, me and the other Methuselah Men. We're old, much older than anyone suspects. The Builder modified us long ago, well before the Space Age."

"Six thousand years ago?" Maddox asked.

Ludendorff stopped pacing to stare at him. "Good heavens, my boy, not nearly that old. I'm close to nine hundred years old. Six thousand—" Ludendorff shuddered.

"Strand is just as old as you?"

"Give or take a few years," Ludendorff said.

"The Builders modified you, you say?"

Ludendorff sighed. "A single Builder did so. He was the last one. Once…" The professor shrugged. "The Dyson sphere is ancient, much older than the Adok starship. I believe the mass of Builders left long before that time."

"When?"

"Around the time of the Swarm invasion of our region of space," Ludendorff said.

The professor marched to his cot, sitting down. "The Builders are ancient as far as races go. I have no idea as to their origin. In some previous millennia, they fought a timeless war against the makers of the Destroyer. Those aliens came from somewhere other than our galaxy. I know little about them or the timeless war, but it drained the Builders, not physically but spiritually, I think. They turned the Destroyers back in the end, although they captured the one vessel and modified it."

"Why?"

"I have no idea. I just know that after the timeless war the Builders changed in a fashion I haven't been able to perceive. Most of them left. A few dabbled with their hobbies. I think that's the best way to view it. The one here traveled around the Orion Arm. He was the last Builder in our region of space, a lonely individual with his own program of entertainment."

"What was your task?"

"Eh?" Ludendorff asked.

"Why did the Builder modify you and Strand? What instructions did he give you?"

"We were conduits for data, giving reports at various intervals. I gave my last report around five hundred years ago. At first, we didn't think much about it. The Builder often let us go our own way for years at a time. Then, it started to become suspicious. Strand and I decided the Builder must have died. But we've been cautious all these years just in case. The Builder had left us certain restrictions, you understand. One of them was to leave Builder artifacts alone. I no longer believe it died, and I do not believe it is happy with either of us."

"So…for five hundred years the Builder has been doing what?" Maddox asked.

"Hibernating, I believe."

"In the Dyson sphere?"

"That makes the most sense, yes." Ludendorff exhaled in a drawn out fashion. "You have to understand, the Builder always used robots, androids and other cybernetic tools to advance its program. In this way, the one Builder could keep a stellar empire running for as long as its spirit lasted. In retrospect, I think the last Builder has grown weary. Many of the robots, androids and cybernetic toys may have shut down, only coming back online again with the Builder's recent revival."

Maddox tried to envision that. What he'd seen before with the silver drones in the Xerxes System when *Victory* had been chasing the Destroyer, and the strange thing trying to control the alien world-killer from the inside…

The captain looked up. "The Dyson sphere is like a haunted house?"

"Not exactly," Ludendorff said. "The interior surface has its zoo exhibits."

Maddox shook his head. "I don't think it's a zoo. When the saucer caught us, we saw endless kilometers of Swarm towers, dirt structures."

"Really?" the professor said. "Tell me about it."

"No," a soft voice said in the air. "That is all for now."

Maddox raised his eyebrows, studying the professor. The man looked surprised too. Ludendorff asked Maddox something. The professor's mouth moved, but no words came through the speaker.

Maddox approached the glass. He shouted.

Ludendorff shook his head, indicating he couldn't hear the words.

Maddox pounded on the glass.

The professor watched him for a moment. Then, the older man shrugged, went to his cot and lay down.

Maddox didn't feel such resignation. "Who are you?" he asked into the air. "Are you the Builder? Why did you want me to come here? Why have you trapped me? What happened to my people?"

There was no answer.

A moment later, Ludendorff jumped up. He signaled Maddox frantically.

The captain nodded.

Ludendorff pointed along the edge of his cubicle.

Maddox walked to the edge of his, peering down a narrow hall between the next row of glass cages. A large Swarm creature approached in the narrow hall. It wore a harness with items hooked to the frame. The blue-colored creature stalked in a jerky manner like a giant praying mantis. It had mandibles and strange, outsized orbs like a mantis, and it was the size of a large cow.

The creature stopped before Maddox's cubicle. With a stalk and pincer, it removed a device from its harness, clicking a button. The nearest glass wall slid into the floor. The Swarm creature re-hooked the device to its harness as it stepped into Maddox's cage.

-42-

A number of thoughts tumbled through Maddox's mind. Was everything he had been learning a lie? Did the Swarm really control the Dyson sphere? That was a horrifying idea. But why would Swarm creatures attempt to trick him? There didn't seem to be any useful reason. The only conclusion Maddox could see was that Swarm creatures had secretly learned to move through many areas of the sphere. In other words, this was a stealth attack.

The captain set himself in a close-combat stance. There was nothing in the cubicle to aid him. He didn't see how he could breach the creature's exoskeleton. The praying mantis-like pincers looked deadly. Somehow, he had to keep the creature from cutting him in half or from holding him and nibbling off his face. Maybe his best bet would be a flying kick, breaking a leg joint. If he could cripple the monster, he might be able to squeeze past and run for it.

Maddox wiped an arm across his mouth. Maybe even better would be unhooking a few of those items from the harness. Maybe one of them was a weapon. But if that were true, wouldn't the creature use a weapon against him?

Maddox made a face. The creature stank. Its exoskeleton glistened. Was that grease it had rubbed on or a natural secretion?

The thing shifted a little more into the cubicle.

Maddox flexed his fingers. Maybe he was foolish, waiting for it to attack. He needed to take the fight to it. His inner revulsion against the creature troubled the captain. Until now, once he knew to do a thing, he could—he would—do it. Yet he found himself reluctant to attack a monster he had little probability of defeating.

I need a weapon.

The creature brought a weapon to its mandibles, clicking it.

"Why do you caper and leer at me? Do you not possess a modicum of sanity?"

The robotic-sounding words shocked Maddox. He couldn't comprehend their meaning for a moment. He flinched at the words, believing the attack had come through sound. Bit by bit, though, his mind grabbed onto the words and replayed them.

"Is…?" Maddox had to concentrate. It was hard ripping himself out of combat mode. He licked his lips, trying again. "Is that a communicator?"

The creature clicked the "weapon" again. "You have correctly analyzed the situation. You possess sanity. I congratulate you."

Slowly, Maddox straightened. He forced his mind to work, to analyze as the creature said. Small discs were attached to its thorax. Tiny filament wires went from them to a box with rapidly moving lights. Did the creature "hear" his response through those?

"Who are you?" Maddox asked.

The thing moved up and down on its legs, hissing.

Maddox backed away until he bumped against glass.

The creature clicked the communicator. "You are not a controller to demand information from me. I resist your control attempt."

"You tried to…control me," Maddox said. "You asked about my mental state."

"You are non-Swarm."

"What does that mean? That I'm contemptible?"

"No, you are not contemptible because you do not rise to Swarm status. You lack Swarm status. Yet, you compete against the Swarm for precious resources. You are an enemy, an enemy—I shall eliminate."

Maddox's lips peeled back and his eyes flashed. His original assessment had been right.

The creature scuttled toward him.

With a shout, Maddox shoved off the glass. He charged the creature. It flicked a pincer at him. Maddox hurdled the slashing member, with his booted foot landing on the other side. Propelling himself faster, Maddox also reached out. He grabbed an item on the harness and ripped it free. He leaped as the big creature spun around on its spot in the cubicle. The thing slashed again, but Maddox wasn't there. He rolled several summersaults, going past the spot where the glass wall had slid out of sight. He pressed the device on a likely spot.

The glass wall shot up into position, sealing the creature in the cubicle.

Maddox stood panting, staring at the angry creature. It struck the wall to no appreciable damage. It dawned on Maddox that his mind had known which device to grab. He had seen the creature open the cubicle and remembered in a hind-part of his mind which device it had used. Some might have called this lucky, but Maddox knew better.

Moving in front of the professor's cubicle, Maddox asked what he should do.

The professor pointed at his ears, shaking his head.

Maddox pointed in either direction, shrugging exaggeratedly afterward.

Ludendorff shook his head, no doubt indicating he didn't know the right way to go.

The captain glanced at the bug. It watched him avidly. He sauntered in front of it, finally waving.

The thing struck the glass so quickly that Maddox jumped back before he could reason that the glass protected him.

The captain gestured at the bug, giving it the finger. Then, he decided to go in the direction the bug had come, as that implied an exit.

Maddox walked down the narrow corridor of glass cages. Other creatures turned toward him, watching. Most of them were other forms of bugs. A few were the small humans. He waved at several. None of them ever waved back. Most of them looked upon him with amazement. He had no idea why.

Soon, the sameness of the endless cells caused Maddox to stop. Just how far did these cubicles go? He couldn't see a limit.

He glanced at the device again. Had he really picked the right one? That seemed too coincidental. He aimed the device at an empty cage and pressed the switch.

Nothing happened.

He searched for a setting but couldn't find one.

"Is this a game?" he said into the air. "Are you testing me?"

Nothing happened.

"I'm right," Maddox said. "This is a test. My asking the question means I've solved another one."

"Yes," a soft voice said near his ear.

Maddox spun around, but no one was there.

"Are you testing my friends, too?" the captain asked.

"No."

"No," Maddox said. "I didn't think so."

"Why not?"

"Originally, you wanted me to come alone. That means you wanted to see me specifically. Well. How about it? Let's see each other."

"Why did you attempt to open another cell?"

"To check if this device really closed mine earlier," Maddox said.

"Why would you doubt it?"

"How was I able to choose the right device in a moment of high stress?"

"I have been asking myself that for some time. It was most remarkable. I should point out that Commander Thrax Ti Ix is even more upset over your superlative escape than you are."

"I'm not upset."

"A poor choice of word perhaps," the soft voice said.

"You admit to making mistakes?" Maddox asked.

"All life-forms are capable of error. Or do you believe that you are immune from the rule?"

"I'm not immune."

"Only the mythical being known as the Creator is immune from error."

Maddox cocked his head. He wasn't sure, but it sounded as if the soft voice held a hint of rancor just now. He filed that away for later.

"Tell me more about Commander Thrax Ti Ix," the captain said.

"How is that germane to your present situation?"

"He's not a true Swarm creature, is he?"

"What causes you to think he is Swarm at all?"

"He told me he's a Swarm creature."

"Yes?"

"And he looks like one," Maddox added.

"And you feel that looks can be deceiving?"

"I've had enough androids turn on me already that I no longer trust looks at all," the captain said.

"When you were aboard your starship outside the sphere, you did not believe the android speaking to you was Ludendorff, did you?"

"No," Maddox said.

"What about the one in the cell?"

"He was real."

"Are you sure?" the soft voice asked.

"One hundred percent," Maddox said.

The voice did not speak.

"I've just passed yet another test," Maddox said. "You're beginning to become impressed with me in spite of everything."

Again, the voice did not respond.

"You're welcome," Maddox said.

"I did not say 'thank you.'"

"You didn't need to. It was implied."

"You are an arrogant creature."

"Human, I'm human," Maddox said. "That makes me the height of creation."

"You believe in the Creator?"

Maddox had been right. The Builder—he was fairly sure he spoke to the lone Builder—had an issue with the Creator. Was this the right time to play that card? The captain couldn't think of a better time.

"The Creator is self-evident," Maddox said.

"Explain such a preposterous belief."

Maddox nodded, deciding to goad the Builder further. If a being were old and bored, anything to alleviate the boredom would be welcome. That would be his operational logic for this.

"It's a simple formula, really," Maddox said, in an off-handed manner. "When I look at my rifle, I realize someone made it to perform a specific task. If I were to suggest that chance had fashioned my rifle, people would think I'm crazy. Now, take my eye, as an example. It is much more complicated than my rifle and also performs a specific task. It is more logical to believe my eye came about through design than believing random chance assembled me over time."

"Therefore, what?" the voice asked.

"Therefore, humans, animals, plants work to a design, which implies a designer, one I choose to call the Creator."

"Ah, you are so confident," the voice said. "You have the advantage of ignorance. I, however, must wrestle with exceedingly great knowledge. My data and reasoning has expanded throughout the millennia. I know…so much, so very much."

"Are you like my starship's AI?"

"Insults will not aid you here, Captain."

"I meant no insult," Maddox said. "Instead, I seek data so I can make the most rational decision regarding you."

The voice was silent.

"Does that trouble you?" Maddox said.

"Your actions are transparent, hybrid."

Maddox stiffened.

"Well, well, well," the soft voice said. "It is true. The term 'hybrid' visibly displeases you. Perhaps that is part of your uniqueness. Yes. You have passed the tests, hybrid. I will bring you to me. Or should I say," the voice murmured, sounding pleased with itself, "that Commander Thrax Ti Ix will escort you to the transfer tube."

Maddox whirled around, seeing the praying mantis creature scuttling rapidly down the narrow hall toward him.

-43-

"I could have bested you," Commander Thrax Ti Ix said through its communicator. "It would have saved us time and trouble. Now…go in the direction I show you."

Maddox resisted turning his back on the creature.

"Go," said the soft voice in the air. "Or do you think I am trying to ambush you?"

"Why do you hate me, Commander?" Maddox asked the giant bug.

The creature began to quiver.

"Do not excite the commander," the soft voice said. "Do not seek to interrogate it. The creature reacts badly to that for reasons of Swarm psychology."

Maddox relented, heading in the direction the bug pointed. The trek took twenty minutes of solid walking. During it, the captain kept looking back. He could sense the bug's hatred. That seemed like the right word for it. It was strange, but Maddox had never thought of an ant having emotions before this. Could Swarm creatures have emotions? If the commander was an example, he could easily envision it.

At last, Maddox went through a garage-door-sized exit. He found himself in a huge hall. The commander pointed toward a platform. Maddox soon climbed up it, and so did the bug. A podium rose from the center of the platform. The commander tapped controls on the podium.

The platform continued to rise as they floated through the giant hallway.

Soon enough, it landed beside a dome of shimmering light the size of a convenience store on Earth.

"If I ever see you again," Thrax Ti Ix said, "I will tear you apart and squirt on your carcass."

Maddox regarded the creature, which immediately began to quiver. He debated some parting words, but decided that until he had his gun, he would act in a cordial manner.

Jumping from the platform, Maddox neared the shimmering dome. The hairs on his arms stood up, and he heard a faint hum. Steeling himself, he plunged through the light and found himself falling down a huge hole.

The captain barely suppressed a shout of surprise. Then, he composed himself. He would ride this out.

He fixated on Meta in his thoughts, wondering how she was doing. He shut his eyes and crossed his arms. The fall continued unabated. How far could he drop? He must have reached terminal velocity by now.

Maddox practiced a calming technique, counting the length of each inhale and exhale, and trying to lengthen them during subsequent breaths. He wasn't going to let the Builder rattle him. This could possibly be the most important interview he'd ever had. According to Ludendorff, this was the last of its kind in the Orion Arm. Maybe others lived elsewhere. This Builder appeared to have an army of robots, androids and cybernetic organisms at its disposal. The professor believed the thing had gone to sleep the last five hundred years. Was it good or bad that it had woken up again?

I guess that will depend on its goals.

Maddox noticed he was slowing down. He opened his eyes and wished he had kept them shut. It felt as if he floated through stellar space. Stars surrounded him, but in patterns and constellations that he'd never seen before. This must be a gigantic chamber kept in weightlessness.

"Captain," a soft voice said.

Maddox twisted around. He realized that he'd stopped falling and now floated weightless. With a shock, he saw that some of the star patterns were blocked out. A black outlined shape was in the way. Where the head might have been, a series of lights winked. If this was the Builder, he couldn't get an accurate idea of what he saw. It was more an absence of sight, which didn't make much sense.

"You are confused," the soft voice said.

When the words sounded, the winking series of lights brightened the tiniest bit.

"Are you the Builder?" Maddox asked.

"Yes."

"Why can't I see you?"

"Because it is my prerogative as the oldest living thing in the Orion Arm to cloak myself in darkness," the Builder said.

Maddox studied the darkness. He couldn't tell if the Builder had a humanoid shape or not. Did the thing wear a cloak? Edges of something rippled as if in a breeze, even though this chamber had none. If that wasn't a cape, could it be wings?

A feeling of disquiet filled Maddox. Was there another reason why the Builder didn't want to show itself? Was its shape hideous to a human, devilish?

"You really are like monkeys," the Builder said. "It is amazing."

"Why did you bring me here?"

"Captain Maddox, it is unseemly that you immediately attempt to interrogate me. I have gone to considerable effort to bring you here at the end. We will enjoy certain decorum. This is a stately affair. I am a Builder, *The* Builder as far as you're concerned. Without me, humanity would have been snuffed out ages ago. Without me, a derivative of you would be swinging through the trees, scolding the great cats for daring to dominate the ground."

"Are you claiming divine status?"

The Builder chuckled softly. "How you prod and poke, hoping to engage a reaction. I have instructed you, though, to act with decorum. Otherwise, I will teach you a hard lesson. It won't be of any benefit to you or your crew, but it will amuse the commander. Such boorishness might even persuade me in Thrax Ti Ix's favor. I doubt you would appreciate that."

Maddox closed his mouth lest he say more. He looked around at the stars. It finally dawned on him what the Builder

337

had said. It or he had gone to considerable effort to bring him—Maddox—here at the end.

The end of what? Maddox wondered. He didn't like the sound of that.

"Your silence is much better than your chimping," the Builder said.

Maddox folded his hands in front of his stomach. He breathed deeply, striving to calm himself.

"It is awe-inspiring, is it not?" the Builder said.

"If you mean the stars," Maddox said, "I quite agree."

"I do mean the stars."

Maddox held his tongue, unsure about the correct thing to say. He didn't want Thrax Ti Ix winning anything.

"The fact that you and I can be awed by the stars is a sign," the Builder said. "They show the insignificance of our being. Galaxy upon galaxy awaits intelligent life. We Builders have constructed mighty artifacts throughout the Milky Way Galaxy. That is your term, by the way, not mine."

"What is your term, Excellency?" Maddox asked in a slow-speaking manner.

"You would not understand it, but I will say the word nonetheless."

The Builder spoke, and the words were like a roaring waterfall against Maddox's ears.

"That was my real voice. For your comfort, I use this one."

"I appreciate your consideration, Excellency," Maddox said, his ears ringing.

"Very good, Captain, you are a quick study. You have judged the situation and now react correctly. I am glad I took the time to induce you here."

Maddox waited, finally asking, "You sent the Shanghai androids and the Ludendorff hologram to me?"

"Yes."

"You believed I wouldn't come unless you acted as the professor?"

"You do not need to ask me that, as you already know the answer. Please, Captain, don't make these moments tedious. They are among my last, and I prefer to enjoy them."

338

"Would you..." Maddox hesitated. It was time to think as never before. This wasn't about action, but about thought. It was Intelligence work. He was uniquely gifted among the operatives of Star Watch Intelligence to use this opportunity.

Yes, it was time to revert to form. He was an Intelligence officer primarily. Drawing a gun to blast his way out of an error had become his usual method lately. Today he must think and choose his path with care.

"Excellency, when did you first come to Earth?"

"It was during the Swarm explosion."

"Approximately six thousand years ago?"

"Seven to eight thousand Earth years ago," the Builder said. "Yes, I built Atlantis for my use, and I allowed others to copy the pyramid. That was my original error. I interfered with your species' development. I deeply regret that."

"You didn't fashion any Methuselah People at that time?"

"I did, but they died out. I hadn't yet discovered certain important processes. Extended life produces problems. Every so-called improvement causes problems to appear. It took me a long time to realize it was more than simply accounting for entropy."

"During the Swarm Explosion is when you went to the Adok System?"

"It is so," the Builder said with a sigh.

"Do you regret that action as well, Excellency?"

"Deeply," the Builder said.

"The Adoks would have perished without you."

"They perished *with* my help. In the end, it made no difference."

"Your help also destroyed a Swarm invasion."

"If you only knew," the Builder said softly.

"Humanity needs the ancient starship now, without—"

"No," the Builder said, the word hardening in the air. "I have done enough damage. Before I leave, I will rectify some of my worst errors of the past."

"Do you refer to the Adok starship?"

"Of course," the Builder said. "That was my other reason for bringing you here. I want Starship *Victory* back."

Maddox frowned. "Will you destroy the starship?"

339

"No, no," the Builder said. "You know nothing about my crimes. Doesn't my name imply construction?"

"Yes," Maddox said.

"Yet, I have destroyed in a monstrous fashion. I have become the very thing my people loathed and fought against for what seemed forever."

"Do you refer to the timeless war against the makers of the Destroyer?"

The Builder groaned as if in deep agony. It seemed to grow then, to blot out more stars. The sound also grew louder.

Maddox clapped his hands over his ears.

Slowly, the keening dwindled and so did the extent of the star blockage. Maddox experimentally removed his hands from his ears.

"Have you no pity, Captain Maddox? Do you hate me that much for having to clear my slate before the Creator?"

"I don't hate you at all," Maddox said.

"You will."

Maddox didn't like hearing that. "Will you kill Meta and the others?"

"Yes."

And me?"

"Yes," the Builder said.

"Do you bear me malice?"

"None," the Builder said.

"You're right. I do not understand. I would consider it a blessing if you told me."

"You are quick with your barbs, Captain. I can well understand why the New Men hate you. They will win the war, you realize. They are the future of humanity. There is no stopping it now."

"I hope to prove you wrong."

"I know," the Builder said. "I can forgive you that. You do not see the big picture. You look out only for your own well-being."

"Yes," Maddox said. "I suppose that's another way that I'm just like you."

The Builder did not respond.

Maddox practiced his breathing. He felt as if the great contest was about to begin. He had to change the Builder's mind. Maddox needed *Victory*, and he had to return to Human Space. Whatever this ancient being had done… Maddox wasn't going to let the Builder get in the way.

"A long time ago," the Builder said in a heavy voice, "we fought the Nameless Ones. They constructed the Destroyers. Those were mighty engines of annihilation. I realize you are among the few to understand that. The Nameless Ones sought out life, snuffing it out for reasons we could never fathom. That was a terrible thing, to fight others awesomely powerful like ourselves. Yet, we could not communicate with them other than by dealing them death or dying in turn. That long time of battle demoralized us as a people. We rose up to stop the horror here. I do not know what happened in other galaxies."

"The Nameless Ones came from outside our galaxy?" Maddox asked.

"It is almost inconceivable, I realize. The distances involved and for no positive reason—they were all too sane, you understand. But they worshiped annihilation. To them, life was evil and they stamped it out."

The Builder sighed. "You destroyed the Destroyer, Captain. I am awed at your exploit. Many have desired to do what you did, but among the weaker races, only you achieved the impossible. That is why I brought you here, Captain. Before the end, I wanted to meet the one who had done the unmanageable. Whatever you are or are not, you did wonderfully that day."

Maddox said nothing.

"That ancient war against the Nameless Ones was so far in the past. We turned them back. We saved life in our galaxy. We should have quit then and gone our way, having done our duty to the Creator. But we could not. We grew vainglorious at our deed. We built in grandeur everywhere. We brought knowledge to planet after planet. We coaxed species after species to advance to new heights. Oh, we believed we were the gift to the universe. We believed that, up until the time we picked up the tools of genocide and tarnished our souls with black annihilation upon those who were not Builder."

341

Maddox waited, listening, using every mnemonic device he could so he would remember everything he learned today.

"Builders acted as judge and jury. We killed by the trillions. That stained our souls so fast, so very fast. I do not know why I was immune the longest. Perhaps I was the boldest, always considered the best warrior and strategist among us. I remained here while everyone else departed in despair and shame."

Still, Maddox waited.

"I used to believe it was the curse of the Nameless Ones upon us. Now, I see that the sin was in our hubris. We believed we could decide which species was good and which was bad. Can you conceive of such gross arrogance?"

"Easily," Maddox said.

"We had ranged through the stars—" The Builder fell abruptly silent. "What did you say?"

"I can easily imagine such arrogance because it sounds quite logical," Maddox said, "even practical to me. I would gladly decide what species is good and bad in relation to my own."

"But...but that is monstrous."

"Perhaps if you gave me a concrete example I could understand better and see the error of my thinking."

"I'm unsure if you're exalted enough to understand."

"Ah," Maddox said. "You are wise and I am a dullard, is that it?"

"You are a clever talker," the Builder said. "You seek to turn my own words against me. Perhaps I shall tell you. Maybe you've earned it. Your brilliance helped destroy a thing we Builders had been unable to destroy. It wasn't for a lack of ability but desire. It all seems to come down to desire, doesn't it?"

Maddox waited, unsure what lid he'd torn off.

"We used the tool left behind by the Nameless Ones. I designed the control unit that would allow us to wield the genocidal machine. It happened six thousand years ago after the sacrificial Adok defense. We watched the Swarm annihilate a race. It was horrible. Some of us spoke boldly, saying we should have interfered directly. Why had we held back from

342

war? We had stopped the Nameless Ones. Why couldn't we use our might to stop the scourge of the Swarm?"

"You wielded the Destroyer against them?" Maddox asked.

"In star system after star system," the Builder said, sadly. "We brought the Destroyer to bear, annihilating nest after nest. We burned the Swarm from a thousand worlds, creating a dead zone between what you now call Human Space and the Beyond versus regions closer to your galaxy's center. We gave your species ample room. If we had not, the Swarm would have reached Earth in time. Your species would have died under the Swarm occupation."

"Thank you," Maddox said.

"Your words are teeth, biting with sarcasm."

"You are in error, Builder. I mean 'thank you' with all my heart. If you had not acted, I would never have been born."

"Yes, yes, I realize that. But who were we, Captain, to play Creator like that?"

"Are you asking me to feel bad about existing?"

"No…no, that would be illogical. You fail to grasp—"

A loud, waterfall sound washed against Maddox. Once more, he clapped his hands over his ears.

"Captain," the Builder said.

Maddox slowly removed his hands.

"I did not mean to let you hear that. My pain and guilt is deep. You have no idea. How could you? You are young and short-lived. You strive during the entirety of your meaningless existence."

"You will excuse me if I disagree with you about its meaninglessness," Maddox said.

"We annihilated trillions of Swarm creatures, pushing their boundaries back a thousand light-years. We wanted to give others a chance to flourish. We—"

"Builder," Maddox said.

"Why do you interrupt me? I am baring my soul to you."

"You said you drove the Swarm boundaries back—a thousand light-years?"

"That is correct."

"You mean there is a giant Swarm Empire out there somewhere?"

343

"Oh, yes. It encompasses nearly a tenth of our galaxy."

A cold feeling settled on Maddox. This was grim news. Then he realized something else. "If the Swarm is so prevalent, why are you so sad about slaying a few in the past?"

"Because I slaughtered *life*," the Builder said. "Don't you understand by now? I thought you were quick-witted. Successful life is what matters, not merely life that has a similar image as us."

"What do you mean by successful life?"

"Yes, that is the crux of the matter," the Builder said. "It is the equation I've finally solved. Five hundred years ago, I could bear no more. But I hesitated taking the final step. So I tried another way, hoping that time might heal my wounds. I shut down the majority of my systems. I hibernated, letting my experiment mature. Moving the Destroyer from what you call the Xerxes System sounded an alarm so I awoke. What I found on the Dyson sphere—see, I know your term for it."

Maddox nodded.

"I discovered a nearly complete Swarm conquest of the entire sphere," the Builder said. "I had placed a small Swarm colony here before heading for slumber. I also put humans on the sphere. They are nearly dead, a small colony of scientists and soldiers using ancient Adok technology to hold the onrushing Swarms at bay. I give the humans two more years at most. Then, they will succumb to the Swarm hordes. Then, the Swarm will have conquered the Dyson sphere."

"And you conclude what from that?" Maddox asked.

"It is an obvious conclusion. You should see it clearly. But I understand, you are too species-conscious to understand the stark reality. The Swarm is more worthy to survive than humanity. It is that simple. They have passed the test."

"What does that have to do with *Victory* and me?"

"I have collected thousands of starships in the past. I brought them through the sphere so they are drifting in the inner side of space at a Venus-like orbit from the star. Thrax Ti Ix will lead a new and improved Swarm upon the galaxy, to go to his brethren and give them what you call Laumer Drive technology."

"Why would you do that?"

344

"As an offering for the trillions of deaths we Builders brought about in the past. It is the least I can do to help expedite my sins before the Creator."

"The Swarm will annihilate humanity," Maddox said.

"Why should that bother you? Humans are the inferior species. Life is what counts. The Swarm produces life in the greatest quantity. What other measure is there?"

"Bugs aren't superior to humans."

"Which would survive under the harshest conditions? You and I both know the so-called bugs would."

Maddox floated in the stellar room stunned. The idea flummoxed him. The captain shook his head, forcing himself to think, to talk and to try to persuade the Builder to a different course of action.

"Is Thrax Ti Ix a normal Swarm creature?"

"Define normal," the Builder said.

"Have you modified Thrax Ti Ix?"

"Of course," the Builder said. "It is another one of my parting gifts. We Builders stymied their evolution once. I have now accelerated it."

Maddox turned away, beginning to wonder if the Builder was sane.

Steeling himself, Maddox faced the darkness. He couldn't let the dimensions of the problem stifle his thinking. He had to outwit the Builder. Yet, was such a thing even possible? Yes! He had to find its weaknesses, its vulnerabilities. It would seem that guilt before the Creator was the sore spot. He would attack it there until the thing grew weary of him and killed him or he succeeded. Maddox had to win not just his life, but also the life of all humanity. It was a goal worth every effort.

-44-

"This is very interesting," Maddox said. "I admit that my thinking is limited. Floating in this chamber, however, and speaking with an exalted intelligence such as you has begun to broaden my scope."

"I find that doubtful, although it is reasonable my presence should stimulate you."

"Your words have washed over me like waves. I am drenched with new possibilities and new ways of seeing reality. Can you forgive me for my former outbursts against you?"

The Builder was silent for a time. Finally, it said, "I am seeking the Creator's forgiveness. It would be surly of me to withhold forgiveness to one so far beneath me at the same time."

"That part troubles me, your exalted nature, I mean."

"How so?" the Builder asked.

"Your concepts outstrip my own."

"That is true. Yet, I don't see how it could it be otherwise."

"No doubt, no doubt," Maddox said. "For instance, I'm having a hard time understanding your modification of Thrax Ti Ix."

"I thought you might, as the commander is a Swarm Captain Maddox."

"What?"

"It is like you, a hybrid."

"Oh."

"The word 'hybrid' does not trouble you now?"

346

Maddox shook his head. "If the commander is like me, it's no wonder we clashed."

"No," the Builder said. "That would have happened in any case. Swarm creatures stamp out all life that is non-Swarm. That Thrax did not do so immediately is a testament to his hybrid nature."

"Interesting," Maddox said. "By the way, isn't it wrong to simply stamp out life?"

"Not for Swarm creatures," the Builder said.

"It's wrong for a Builder to stamp out life, but not for a Swarm creature?"

"That is correct," the Builder said. "And that is so because the Swarm is the most successful life-form in our galaxy."

"Oh," Maddox said, as if deep in thought. "I think I understand. We know they're the most successful because they kill everyone else."

"That is one way to say it."

"Interesting," Maddox said. "I guess that would make the Nameless Ones the most successful life-form in the universe."

"No! They were pure killers."

"Just like the Swarm," Maddox said.

"No, No," the Builder said. "You do not understand. The Swarm kills, but they also construct world-sized hives. The Nameless Ones only destroyed, never built."

"They built the Destroyers," Maddox said.

"Yes, but that was the only thing they built. The Swarm makes hives on a thousand worlds. That is the essence of life, to build, to grow, to expand with life."

"That would make you Builders the highest life form," Maddox said.

"No. We lost our spirit. The Swarm does not have the same type of spirit. Thus, it lacks our weakness."

Maddox closed his eyes. His head had begun to throb from all these conflicting concepts. He pushed the pain aside, though, concentrating on the moment.

"Did you put cybernetic interfaces in Thrax Ti Ix?" Maddox asked.

"Of course."

"The commander is not fully Swarm then."

"Incorrect, the commander is a superior Swarm, a hybrid creature."

"The commander is superior because it is more like a Builder now?" Maddox asked.

The Builder did not respond.

"I am beginning to suspect that your vast age has clouded your thinking," Maddox said.

"You may be right. I am unsure. Speaking with you has been a mistake. I yearn for certainty. It is the chief reason I desire an ending. Thrax Ti Ix begged me to forgo this conversation. The commander suggested…well, it doesn't matter."

"Did Thrax suggest the test in the glass cell?"

"It did indeed," the Builder said.

Maddox clapped his hands.

The darkness recoiled from him. "Do not do that again. I detest the noise. What was that supposed to signify?"

"I believe the Creator just spoke to me," Maddox said, thinking quickly.

"Why would the Creator speak to a hybrid like you when I am right here?"

"Why wouldn't the Creator speak to me? In fact, I may be the obvious choice. Humanity yearns to live. Thus, in me, it asks you, 'Why do you wish to annihilate us?'"

"I do not wish such a thing," the Builder said.

"You are releasing the Swarm upon humanity, giving them warships they never made."

"We destroyed many more warships of theirs six thousand years ago."

"That was your error, not ours. You are causing us grief for your guilt."

"I am making restitution for our savagery in the past," the Builder said.

Maddox laughed scornfully. "That's some restitution you have going. You murdered one group six thousand years ago and now are ensuring the mass murder of another by giving these Swarm an unfair advantage against us. Your sense of right and wrong is very odd indeed."

"I must do this in order to pay for my wrongs," the Builder said.

"Don't you know that you can't pay for them?"

"You cannot know such a thing."

"You didn't let me finish," Maddox said. "You can't pay for your wrongs as a mass murderer by making sure another mass murder takes place. And to think that you're doing this for life. It's a joke on a vast scale, but a joke just the same."

"I have grown weary of your bombastic statements. It is time—"

"Let us fight," Maddox said.

"You desire to fight me?" the Builder asked in wonder.

"No," Maddox said. "I desire to fight for survival. You want a test. I'll give you a test. Release my crew, release the professor, the port admiral and his people, and the humans in the sphere, and let us duke it out with the Swarm in their new warships."

"They will destroy you."

"I accept that if they can do it. I'm here to tell you, though, that I'll destroy them. In that way, I'll prove myself a better champion for life than them."

"By killing?" the Builder asked.

"I'm using the same measure you are, one that will doom humanity to extinction. The least you could do is not be a hypocrite about all this."

"It would take time for Thrax Ti Ix to gather the Swarms to their warships."

Maddox had wondered about that, hoping it was so. He said, "Survival of the fittest. Isn't that your credo?"

"Hearing it from you makes the concept seem sordid."

"I can tell you why that is if you want me to," Maddox said.

"Please tell me," the Builder said.

"I still have spirit. You've lost yours, which is why you wish to end your life. In fact—"

"Give me silence," the Builder said in an ominous tone.

Maddox fell silent.

The two of them floated in the stellar chamber. The darkness drifted away from Maddox, with the blinking lights

349

slowly moving along the Builder's head area. After a span, the darkness moved closer again.

"I have decided," the Builder said in a soft voice. "You have the right to life. You did not ask for help, but for the chance to fight for survival. I suspect the battle between you two will destroy the sphere. I will thus remain here and die in my guilt. It is a fitting end, the two champions of life battling over the remains of the Builders."

"I do have one request," Maddox said.

"You disappoint me. What is it?"

"I would like a hyper-spatial tube in order to return home to Human Space."

"Let me ponder the request."

Once more, the Builder drifted away. It returned sooner this time.

"I will agree. But I will also give Thrax Ti Ix a tube. I will give the commander the chance to bring its fleet and jump technology to the Swarm Empire in a single bound across space. Do you agree to this condition?"

"Yes," Maddox said.

"It would have been better for you to deliberate such a thing. But you have made your choice. So be it. Now go, Captain. I have become weary of your presence. You have stolen what little peace I had attained. Now, I wish the end to come as soon as possible."

Maddox might have said more, but he winked out of the Builder's presence. He vanished from the stellar chamber, finding himself in a room with Ludendorff, Meta, Riker, Admiral Hayes and three small people wearing elaborate suits.

It was time to get ready for the final Builder test.

-45-

Admiral Fletcher woke up by degrees. A harsh chemical stench was the first thing he noticed. He wanted to turn his head, to get away from the smell, but he found that impossible to do.

"Where am I?" was his first silent question. It was quickly followed by, *"What happened to me?"*

He remembered Pa Kur's interrogation. The New Man had gone berserk. He'd moved so fast, like a fly one tried to catch but couldn't. Pa Kur had shot the Marines, shot the one-way glass and attacked.

Yes. Now Fletcher recalled. He'd had a force blade, clicking it on and shoving the raw energy into the New Man. That should have been the end of it.

I thought I died.

Fletcher opened his eyes. He saw blurry shapes over him. Were they operating? It seemed likely. Maybe it wasn't time to wake up. Maybe he should close his eyes.

He did, opening them later in the dark. He tried to talk, but no one heard him. That was just as well. He was already tired and wanted to go back to sleep.

The third time he opened his eyes, a nurse smiled at him.

"Hello," he whispered.

"Hello, Admiral," she said.

"Is it bad?" he whispered.

Her smile became the sweetest thing he'd ever seen. "Not anymore, sir. We've all been waiting for you to wake up."

351

"Is the fleet—?"

She put a warm hand on his arm. He loved her touch. He hoped she never let go.

"The doctor is coming. He can explain the situation better than I can, sir. Until then, just relax."

Fletcher must have fallen asleep again, because the fourth time he woke up, the captain of *Antietam* stood by his bed.

She frowned down at him as he opened his eyes.

"Oh," she said, stepping back. "I should go."

"Hold it," Fletcher said. He spoke a little louder than a whisper. This time, he had more clarity of mind. He realized that he had been out for a while. Doctors had operated on him. It had taken him time to recuperate.

The captain moved up to the bed.

Fletcher turned his head on the pillow. It took time. He turned back toward the captain, his eyes searching.

"Is there anything I can do for you, sir?" she asked.

"Yes, raise the bed so I'm not lying here like an invalid."

The captain picked up a clicker, pressing it. The bed raised the admiral's head and torso.

"That's good," Fletcher said. He was breathing harder, and his head began to hurt.

"I should call the doctor," the captain said.

"No," Fletcher said breathlessly. "I want a situation report, and I want it now."

"We're several jumps from the Thebes System," the captain said, appearing nervous.

"What else?" Fletcher said. "What are you hiding?"

"Third Admiral Bishop is in nominal command of the Grand Fleet."

"What?" Fletcher said in a hoarse voice. "I'm out a few days and that blue-nosed bastard grabs the reins. You never should have let that happen. That scoundrel, that dog of a Windsor League—"

"Here, now," the tall Earl Bishop said, stepping forward. "I might begin to resent those words."

Fletcher was breathing hard, with a rattle in his throat.

A doctor hurried into the chamber, glancing at Fletcher, Bishop and then Fletcher again. "Everyone out," he said.

352

"Belay that order," Fletcher wheezed. "I want to get to the bottom of this."

"Sir," the doctor said.

"Stand down, I said," Fletcher wheezed. "I'm perfectly fine."

"I would oblige you, Doctor," Bishop said, "but this is too important."

"What in blazes are you babbling about?" Fletcher demanded.

"Admiral," the doctor said. "You're delirious."

"I certainly am not," Fletcher said. "I'm dead tired. I sound awful, but I am quite lucid. What is the matter? Why is Bishop here, to murder me in my sleep and solidify his hold on command?"

The Windsor League earl looked away, turning a crimson color.

"Sir," *Antietam's* captain said. "You have it all wrong, sir. It isn't like that at all."

Fletcher felt his heart flutter and his face grow cold.

"This is too much," the doctor said.

"Give me a stimulant," Fletcher said.

The doctor shook his head.

"Do it," Bishop said.

Fletcher squinted at the tall earl. Was he being foolish? Would he kill himself if he accepted a stimulant? Maybe he should—

A hypo hissed as it injected a stimulant into him.

Fletcher stared at the offensive medical instrument and then at the doctor. The man wouldn't meet his eyes.

Bishop faced him again, putting his longer fingers on the cot's rail. The earl didn't wear his monocle. He looked better without it, more human.

"I'm afraid I've been something of an ass, Admiral," Bishop said. "I'm here to admit it to you, and, well, to tell you I'm sorry."

"What?" Fletcher said. Was he hearing right?

Bishop nodded. "I'm not often in the wrong, and when I am, I can maneuver my way out of trouble. You've been right all down the line, Admiral. I'm not too small of a noble to see

353

that. The truth, sir, is that the fleet needs you and I need you. The men and women don't trust me like they trust you. I've kept everyone in place, and doing it as you said for some time. How you knew to attack those star cruisers in the Hades System I will never know. That and losing more hammerships showed me you know what you're talking about when it comes to facing the New Men. They're a cunning bunch, but you're better than they are, Admiral."

"Am I delirious?" Fletcher asked the doctor.

The doctor had a hard time keeping a smile off his face. "You heard correctly, Admiral."

Fletcher eyed the tall, Windsor League noble. "Are we in trouble?"

"Possibly," Bishop admitted.

"You need me to talk to the crews?"

"I do."

"That's it, is it?" Fletcher asked. "That's why you're here saying you're sorry."

"Now see here, old chum. I mean what I've been saying."

"Stow it, Bishop," Fletcher wheezed. "I'm not interested. We're in a war and the New Men are near. Is that right?"

"I believe so," Bishop said.

"Doctor," the admiral said, "how long do I have to think clearly?"

The doctor checked his watch. "A half hour, perhaps, no more than forty-five minutes more. You're still very fragile, sir."

Fletcher pondered that. "Tell me the situation," he told Bishop.

The earl cleared his throat. "As the captain said, we're several jumps from the Thebes System."

"Which means we've been advancing fast," Fletcher said.

"We have," Bishop said.

"You've been taking risks to get us here fast, too, haven't you?"

"I don't deny it."

"How many ships have you lost so far?"

"Three battleships, fifteen cruisers and twenty-nine destroyers," Bishop said.

"What the bloody Hell have you been doing with my fleet?" Fletcher shouted hoarsely.

The earl stiffened and his features turned crimson again.

"He did damage nine star cruisers," *Antietam's* captain said. "The New Men were tricky, though. They managed to—"

"Damaged?" Fletcher shouted. "He *damaged* a few enemy vessels, did he?"

"You must calm yourself, Admiral," the doctor said. "If you keep this up, you'll have a relapse."

"How many star cruisers did you *destroy*?" Fletcher asked, panting as he did.

Bishop shook his head.

Fletcher gasped as he went limp, staring up at the ceiling. He could feel strength and energy leaving him. He couldn't let himself get so angry. Bishop had lost forty-seven combat vessels. That was—

"I have found critical intelligence," Bishop said. "I dare say this intelligence was worth the…the lost vessels."

Fletcher stared at him. Could this be true? They needed something for all those losses.

"A Patrol frigate reached the Thebes System," Bishop said. "The captain was a cagy fellow, managing to slip out, barely making it back to the Grand Fleet. I lost the three battleships and most of those destroyers making sure he reached us. It's clear the New Men didn't want the frigate bringing us its news. I gambled on the vessel, I admit it. Fortunately, the Patrol officer's report was quite illuminating."

"What did he see?" Fletcher whispered. "Tell me while I'm still awake."

"The orbital space around Thebes III is crammed with haulers of every description," Bishop said. "Every missing vessel of 'C' Quadrant must be there. Shuttles are bringing them cargos hourly. More haulers are entering orbit, while the full ones blast off for an inner system Laumer-Point that takes them out of 'C' Quadrant. In other words, they're heading into the Beyond."

"The haulers might be high-tailing it to the Throne World," Fletcher whispered.

"I deem that very possible," Bishop said. "Or they could be heading to Parthia or Odin."

Fletcher recalled those systems, independent planets, the first to feel the New Men's wrath.

"The Patrol frigate also recorded mass readings from Thebes III's surface," Bishop said. "This is wonderful news, Admiral. The readings can only be one thing: the missing peoples of 'C' Quadrant."

Fletcher stared at the third admiral. "Yes," he said, finally. "That is good news. Wonderful news, as you say."

"There's one more item," Bishop said. "The enemy's main fleet is concentrated there. The frigate captain counted fifty-seven star cruisers."

Fletcher felt himself go cold.

"We still badly outnumber them," Bishop said.

Fletcher grunted.

"I know you're weak," the third admiral said. "I wouldn't ask this unless it was critical. Firstly, let me say that I understand better your caution concerning the New Men. It is well founded. You also may be the only one among us who can pierce some of their traps. The Grand Fleet needs your cunning, old chum. And it needs your words. If you are able, we need you to talk to the commanders as you did the day you faced down the enemy's decoy forces. The officers—the men, too—trust you, Admiral. I lack their trust. I've lost too many ships for that. Morale is dropping. This is the moment to maneuver our way into the Thebes System and stop whatever the New Men are doing. This is the time to annihilate their invasion armada."

"Fifty-seven star cruisers are not so easy to annihilate," Fletcher said.

"Nine of them have sustained damage," Bishop said, "some of that heavy damage."

"That will help," Fletcher admitted.

"What do you say, sir?"

Fletcher raised an arm. It took some doing. He rubbed his gritty eyes. He could feel his body's weakness striving to pull him back under.

"I am weak," the admiral said. "I can't give that talk yet, not in any meaningful way."

"It would probably kill you to do something like that now," the doctor said.

"Here's what we can do," Fletcher told the third admiral. "I want situational reports. I'll look for their traps when I'm awake. But for the day-to-day running of the Grand Fleet, you will continue to issue the commands."

Bishop appeared troubled.

"You think that makes you too much of a figurehead?"

The tall earl shook his head. "I have miscalculated. The New Men are better than I expected. I don't want to lose our side any more fighting ships. I may have disgraced my family house."

Fletcher became thoughtful. He had lost his nerve after facing the New Men. The Lord High Admiral had seen something in him and had pushed him back into the arena. Maybe he had been too hard on Bishop. Maybe he had just seen the earl's grasping ways, unable to see the good in the man.

"We're going to work together," Fletcher whispered.

Bishop stared at him.

"You're going to win glory for your house by rolling up your sleeves and facing the toughest opponents in the universe. I'll work on recovering faster and thinking deeply on the enemy's dispositions. But I need you, Third Admiral, to hold this fleet together by using all your political cunning and maneuvering of people."

Slowly, Bishop nodded.

"I'll save my speech to the men for later," Fletcher whispered. He could feel himself slipping under. He had already stared slurring his words. "Is that a deal?" he mumbled.

"It is, old chum," Bishop said.

"Then get started," Fletcher said.

"Yes, sir," the earl said, saluting smartly before heading for the exit.

-46-

The next six days proved hectic beyond anything Maddox had known. Without Ludendorff's vast knowledge and cunning, the process would have taken considerably longer.

The three smaller people—two men and one woman—were from the Kai-Kaus, the last surviving humans on the Dyson sphere. The three were the elders of approximately ten thousand humans left. During this time, Maddox had learned they were a technologically perceptive people, using Adok equipment. That meant they knew how to build and operate neutron and disruptor cannons and Adok shields. Their advanced weapons were all that stood in the way between them and annihilation from the endless Swarm hordes.

Port Admiral Hayes told Maddox what had happened to the flotilla in the Xerxes System. It was close to what the captain had expected. After many days of careful scouting, the flotilla had approached the Nexus. Just as had happened with *Victory*, a hyper-spatial tube had sucked them into the Dyson sphere system. There, the saucer-craft had indeed incapacitated the ships' computer systems. Soon thereafter, gas canisters had attached to each Star Watch vessel, rendering the crews unconscious. After that, the port admiral couldn't say what had happened. For weeks now, each of them had been in a separate glass cell.

The new lease on life caused everyone to work overtime with zeal.

358

During the first two days, the Kai-Kaus fought three major engagements against masses of Swarm soldiers on the sphere's inner surface. The Swarm attacks never stopped. The last thousand Kai-Kaus died at their posts so the rest could escape into the substructure and the waiting spacecraft outside.

It was a bitter race loading people and high tech cargos onto *Victory* and the port admiral's ships.

Nine thousand Kai-Kaus among the various spaceships meant *Victory* was near capacity for the first time under Star Watch's control.

"It looks like Star Watch scientists won't have to study you anymore," Maddox told a revived Galyan on the bridge. "With the Kai-Kaus and their imports, we can start arming new starships with Adok technology as soon as we get back to Earth."

"You are optimistic about defeating Commander Thrax Ti Ix here," Galyan said.

"I'm hoping the bug's lack of familiarity with its new ships will give us a winning edge."

"The Swarm creature may have been studying the craft for some time."

"I hope you're wrong," Maddox said.

"I am monitoring the sphere while we speak," Galyan said. "I know the port admiral also has his people watching it. The problem is that the sphere's mass is simply too much. Thrax Ti Ix could come out on the other side. He might already be out, advancing to do battle with hundreds of starships under his control."

"I have a plan," Maddox said.

"The disruptor cannon can destroy some of the Dyson sphere," Galyan said. "That will not be enough to demolish the entire structure quickly enough to destroy the Swarm's new space navy."

"I never thought it would."

"You cannot mean a stand-up battle against them?" Galyan said. "We lack the numbers to defeat them."

"True," Maddox said.

"I admit to bafflement, Captain," the AI said. "What is your plan?"

"You and I are going to defeat them," Maddox said, "along with some stolen Builder tech to help us."

"You should have already informed me of my part of the task."

Maddox raised his right arm. A wristband blinked on it. He tapped the band. "Have you found it, Professor?"

A tiny screen showed a sweaty Ludendorff. "It's in my possession, but this is…" The older man shook his head.

"I want you on *Victory* on the double, Professor," Maddox said. "I don't know how much longer we have. Can you be here in an hour?"

"Make it two," Ludendorff said.

"No, make it a half-hour." The captain had noticed Valerie waving to him. She pointed at a screen. He nodded, seeing strange spaceships easing out of a vast opening in the sphere's outer skin.

"Is the Swarm coming through?" Ludendorff asked from the wristband.

"Yes, Professor," the captain said. "Our time has just run out. Get here as fast as you can."

-47-

The Kai-Kaus were crammed aboard the two *Bismarck*-class battleships, the three Star Watch strike cruisers, five destroyers, two escorts, three supply vessels and Starship *Victory*. None of Kai-Kaus' advanced technology had been fitted to the ships, although a chief technician was on each bridge to help the commanders. Together with the Kai-Kaus' baggage, it made for an incredibly tight fit aboard each vessel.

The *Leipzig* and *Vienna* led the way toward the latest sphere opening. They were old battlewagons, heavy on the hull armor with heavy-mount lasers. They did not boast the latest wave harmonics shielding, one of the reasons the Lord High Admiral had sent them to the Xerxes System rather than "C" Quadrant to face the New Men.

Behind the two bruisers came the strike cruisers. The rest of the flotilla stayed at a Luna-like distance from the sphere. They had spread out, watching the sphere for other openings. It seemed likely to everyone, especially the Kai-Kaus technicians, that the first Swarm move was a deception. The first gambit usually was, they said.

"Come on," Maddox said. The ancient Adok vessel was midway between Hayes' battlewagons and the others.

The captain hadn't expected Thrax Ti Ix to move so quickly. He'd hoped the logistics problem would give the Swarm commander nightmares. He'd also hoped the hybrid bug didn't have many space commanders yet. It looked as if Maddox had been wrong on both counts.

"There, sir," Valerie said. She tapped her board.

On the main screen, Maddox saw another hatch open on the sphere. A shuttle blasted out of there. That was Ludendorff with Keith piloting. They were the last humans on the Dyson sphere, not counting any final Kai-Kaus volunteers who had survived on the inner surface.

As the shuttle raced for *Victory*, Swarm craft continued to slide out of the huge opening, the place the battleships maneuvered to.

"I see seven enemy ships so far," Valerie said. "They're big, too."

Maddox nodded. The seven craft were saucer-shaped with a massive ball in the center. Each had a little more mass than a Star Watch cruiser. That meant the Swarm already had an equal tonnage of spaceships outside the sphere as Star Watch did.

Heavy beams lanced from the *Leipzig* and the *Vienna*.

Maddox sat forward on the command chair, with his right hand bunched into a fist. He waited, waited—

A cheer erupted from the lieutenant and the Kai-Kaus technician on the bridge. She was a slight woman wearing an elaborate uniform with outrageous collars that almost hid her elfin chin. Her name was Lady Shana, and she had a Mohawk like the Native American tribe of that name. She wore gloves with tiny tools in the fingertips and had proven herself a technical wizardess so far.

Valerie and Lady Shana cheered because the lasers struck Swarm hulls. Either the saucers didn't have shields or Swarm soldiers didn't know how to turn them on yet.

Leipzig and *Vienna* pounded the first saucer, burning away hull armor so giant globules wobbled away into space.

The Swarm craft fired back with particle beams. They combined on the *Leipzig*, brightening the shield to a cherry color. The Kai-Kaus techs had helped in one endeavor there, able to quicken the energy bleed-off from the shield. That allowed the *Leipzig* to absorb a greater amount of energy before the shield faded to brown and approached failure.

362

At that point, the first targeted saucer blew apart in a mass of metal, water, squirming Swarm creatures and expanding air. Heat and gamma rays also radiated outward.

The other Swarm craft stopped firing.

The two battlewagons picked a new target, starting on the next saucer.

That's when the enemy craft showed their true power. The ball parts glowed radiantly and the ships began to move with incredible velocity. The six saucers charged the two battlewagons. In doing so, they made room for more Swarm craft to burst out of the sphere opening.

Maddox shook his head. He didn't like this.

Port Admiral Hayes must have disapproved as well. One of the strike cruisers eased forward, launching a salvo of antimatter missiles.

The minutes ticked away as the battleships destroyed another two saucers. The first wave survivors began firing the particle beams again. That's when the antimatter missiles ended the fight, blowing the rest of the saucers in chain-reaction annihilations.

By that time, though, another seven saucers had renewed the process.

"The Swarm commander is baiting us," Lady Shana said. She had a translator to help her communicate with them.

"Why do you say that?" Maddox asked.

"This is a ruse," she said. "The real attack is gathering elsewhere."

"I suspect you're right," Maddox said. "What do you suggest we do?"

Lady Shana grew tight-faced. "We must kill the creatures while we can. Once we can't, we die. That is the only philosophy in battle."

Maddox nodded.

After the fifth saucer assault of seven perished to heavy lasers and antimatter missiles, Keith brought the professor onto *Victory*.

Maddox hurried to Galyan's AI core chamber. As he did, Valerie appeared on his wristband comm.

"Yes?" the captain asked.

"I'm patching the Port Admiral though to you, sir."

The tiny screen wavered for a second. Then, Port Admiral Hayes appeared, an older man with sunken eyes.

"I'm running low on antimatter missiles," Hayes said, promptly. "The *Leipzig* has already blown a laser coil. We can't keep this up for long."

"What else do you suggest, sir?" Maddox asked.

"How far are you with your plan?"

"I hope to start testing it soon, sir."

"What does that even mean?"

"Fight until you can't, sir."

"Yes?"

"If the enemy is still around after that, we die."

The port admiral stared at him. "Yes, Captain, that we will. Good luck, son."

"Yes, sir, to you too," Maddox said.

The screen wavered once more, going blank.

Maddox broke into a sprint. This was going to be tight, and he had no doubt the saucer ships were a Swarm feint as Lady Shana had suggested. That was okay, though, because they still had some time. As long as they had wriggle room, and *Victory*, he might be able to save the human race from this unsuspected menace. He wasn't as sanguine about saving the Kai-Kaus and *Victory*. They had to do this right the first time, because he didn't think Thrax Ti Ix was going to give them another.

***

Professor Ludendorff, Lady Shana and Maddox working as a go-for attempted to install a Builder AI box into Galyan's computing core.

"I still do not see how this will aid us," Galyan said, watching from the hatch. For whatever reason, the Adoks had decided long ago that a holoimage could not enter its own AI core.

"It's easy, Galyan, at least in theory," Maddox said.

Ludendorff and Lady Shana carefully made adjustments with tools Maddox had no idea how they operated. The captain was trusting Ludendorff, which might have future repercussions. He hoped the professor had too much on his mind to worry about subterfuge for later.

Once or twice, the professor eyed the captain speculatively. Maddox hoped it was his imagination. He hoped Ludendorff wasn't putting a new backdoor into Galyan. Did the professor think this was as wild a longshot as Galyan did?

"Do you remember what you did in Greenland?" Maddox asked the AI.

"Do you mean in my taking over the system's computers?" Galyan asked.

"Exactly," Maddox said.

"Go on."

"I'm hoping with this box installed you'll have more understanding concerning Builder tech. Maybe just as important, you'll be able to appear on the Dyson sphere as a holoimage."

"I suspect you're right," Galyan said. "How will that help us?"

"I'm going to piggyback on you," Maddox said.

"That is impossible. You are flesh and blood."

"The professor is rigging it so my engrams can go over as a program."

"You are going to make a copy of yourself?"

"No," Maddox said. The very idea made him queasy. "The professor will put a brain amplifier on my head. That will energize a temporary engram program that can piggyback with you onto the Dyson sphere."

"For what reason?" Galyan asked.

"I'm going to seek out the Builder one more time and keep him occupied."

"That is a dubious proposal," Galyan said. "By your account, he or it is unstable."

"Commander Thrax Ti Ix is going to win, Galyan."

"Then why are we fighting?" the AI asked.

"Thrax is going to win unless we can figure out a way to destroy the Dyson sphere in one giant orgy of destruction," Maddox said. "While I'm distracting the Builder, you're going to figure out how to blow the whole sphere."

"That is not rational, Captain. We lack sufficient firepower to destroy a sphere of a star system's worth of mass."

"You're not listening," Maddox said. "You're going to use the sphere's systems, blowing up every circuit and engine in one instant of time."

"That will work?" Galyan asked.

"I don't know. Will it?"

"I am analyzing," Galyan said. The holoimage froze with his eyelids fluttering. The eyes snapped open an instant later. "That is an ingenious plan, Captain. If it works, it could cause a vast explosion, destroying everything on the sphere."

"We need more than that," Maddox said. "We have to destroy the sphere in such a way that all the debris, the system mass of it, blows inward at Thrax Ti Ix's fleet."

"Captain," Galyan said. "That is pure genius, if of an evil sort."

"No, Galyan. That shows my fitness for survival."

"I do not understand."

"Quiet, you two," Ludendorff snarled. "This is incredibly difficult. Nothing is going to happen if I can't link this blasted device to the core."

Maddox nodded. It was time to let the experts do their part.

***

Two hours later, Maddox was back on the bridge. The endless supply of Swarm saucers had finally taken its toll on the flotilla.

Battleship *Vienna* limped away as coils of energy burst through broken hull armor. The battleship had destroyed forty-three saucers, seven of the kills taking place while *Vienna's* shield was down. The antimatter missiles were gone. It was just conventional missiles now with laser turrets and destroyer guns to slow down the enemy.

"How many spaceships are inside the sphere?" Valerie asked.

"It's not the number of ships they have," Maddox said, "but if we have enough time to stop them before they're through."

"How did you figure we could win?" the lieutenant asked.

"It seemed like a good idea at the time."

She shot him a glance.

"The alternative was a quick death," Maddox said.

Valerie was about to reply when a bright light flared on the main screen.

Battleship *Vienna* blew up. One moment, the battleship's damage control teams tried to bring the fires and spurting coils under control. The next, something went critical over there. Hull plates blew away and flames roared in gigantic funnels from various places on the battleship. The dying battlewagon began to tumble end over end. A few escape pods raced away. X-rays reached out, killing everyone who made it into a pod. No one survived the *Vienna's* death, not even the countless Kai-Kaus who had hoped to leave the sphere.

"So it begins," Lady Shana whispered. She had come to the bridge for a kit she'd stashed here. "Hail to He Who is Nameless, the One who begins and the One who ends life."

"More saucers are coming through the hangar hatch," Valerie said. "Oh-oh, they're not just bringing out seven this time. I count fourteen. They've brought out fourteen saucers in a group."

"The port admiral must see that too," Maddox said. "He's bringing up his destroyers."

"For what it's worth, sir, I'd rather fight to the end than simply die in bed, or in a cage doing nothing."

"Truth!" the Lady Shana said.

Maddox sat back. It had seemed so simple while in the stellar chamber. The Builder—

A red light blinked on his armrest. Maddox pressed a button. "Yes?"

"It's ready," Ludendorff said, his voice ringing with success but tired nonetheless.

"Will it work?" Maddox asked.

Ludendorff brayed a harsh sound. "My boy, I have no idea. It's a longshot, and I would never think to try it against a Builder. I think the Builder must have coded something in me to worship it. But that doesn't matter now. This is worth a try."

"I'm on my way," Maddox said. "Lieutenant!" he said.

Valerie whipped around, her eyes wide.

"You have the bridge," Maddox said. "It's time."

"Good luck, sir," she said.

"Tell me to win," he said.

"Sir," she said.

"Yes?"

"Beat the Builder and this Thrax Ti Ix bastard," Valerie said.

Maddox nodded as he hurried for the exit. That's exactly what he was going to try to do.

-48-

Maddox sat back in a chair as Lady Shana settled a silver band over his forehead.

"Are you ready, Captain?" Galyan asked from the open hatch.

"I am," Maddox said. "Are you?"

"Let us begin the adventure," the holoimage said.

Lady Shana went to a bank of controls. A Builder AI box nearby glowed with various colors. "You shouldn't feel anything," she said.

Maddox waited.

"Maybe you'll feel a little something," Ludendorff said, quietly. The professor tapped controls. Lady Shana typed upon hers.

Maddox grew sleepy. Then, it felt as if a river of fire burned on his skull. He arched back and tried to roar. Nothing came out of his mouth, though. The fire burned as if the metal would sink through his forehead. The agony grew.

Maddox lost the use of his vision then. The stench of the chamber disappeared. He no longer heard. The sense of touch departed.

"Hello, Captain."

Maddox turned around, although he didn't know where here was.

"Who's there?" Maddox said, although he didn't hear the words exactly.

"Wait a moment. There. You should be able to see now."

Maddox did. It was a blue world of circuitry and glowing connections. Nearby was a shape of zeroes and ones.

"Is that you, Galyan?"

"Yes, Captain. You appear much different than before."

"I'm in your world now."

"No," Galyan said. "You merely sense in my world. Are you ready?"

"Let's do this," Maddox said, wondering why he didn't feel pain anymore. He was still in the chair with the band around his head. But his "senses" were now with the "self" or personality of the AI.

In a flash of computed time, the "self" of Galyan leapt across the stellar distance from *Victory* to the Dyson sphere.

Maddox was stunned as the images impinged upon his senses. They came so fast, from so many directions. It was disorienting.

"Do you know what to do?" Maddox asked.

"Oh, yes. I can link the countless systems. But even at computer speed, this is going to take time. Captain, the Builder is coming. I must—"

"You are an industrious mite," the Builder said, softly. "Come, we will finish the interview."

A new pain filled Maddox. Something remorseless ripped him from Galyan. The captain didn't know it, but his body in the computer core chamber on *Victory* began to buck and thrash. His life-signs began to deteriorate immediately.

"You are dying, Captain," the soft-voiced Builder said.

Maddox felt himself to be back in the stellar chamber. The darkness that was the Builder had become more pronounced while the stars were harder to see than last time.

"You have separated yourself from your body," the Builder said. "You have done so mechanically. Yet, the results are the same as if you had achieved a psychic separation. Without the integration of the Adok computer, your body cannot sustain itself for long."

"It is of small matter," Maddox said.

"You wish to achieve nonbeing?"

"Not particularly." Maddox said. "But I'm curious concerning the Creator. This will bring me the knowledge more quickly than otherwise."

"Practicing self-death is wrong," the Builder said.

"You're doing it."

"I have been shutting down sustaining systems. When they stop, my organic processes will be unable to sustain me. I will die of natural causes."

"Yet, you're willing yourself to die. You're self-dying. That is wrong. Perhaps the Creator will punish you for it."

"I hope not."

"What is your verdict between Commander Thrax and me?" Maddox asked.

"Your side will lose the struggle soon after your body ceases to be. Commander Thrax Ti Ix is about to burst through the sphere. I will give Thrax a hyper-spatial tube to expedite the commander's conquest of Human Space. Instead of working outward in, the commander will begin in the center at Earth and conquer his way outward. I am curious as to how the New Men will defend against the Swarm. Alas, but I will be gone by then."

"Did you know I could not win?"

"I gave you less than a one percent chance."

"Well, you gave me the chance. I appreciate that."

"I find your gratefulness surprising. It is not like your former persona. Something is different. I perceive..."

Maddox tried to shield his thoughts, having no idea if the Builder could read them, since they would likely be thoughts in zeroes and ones right now.

"Captain Maddox," the Builder said. "You have attempted a ploy against me. I cannot say I approve."

"Isn't the only verdict success or not?"

"Not altogether," the Builder said. "I thought I made this clear."

"You seem to have a bias toward the Swarm. Is it possible Commander Thrax has beguiled you in some fashion?"

"No," the Builder said. "That is impossible."

"Maybe if you study the last few years with him—"

"No!" the Builder said.

371

"Why wouldn't you check?"

"I have just checked, you gnat. I cannot believe this. You are correct. The commander has corrupted me with a Swarm virus. This is inconceivable. How did it happen? Yes, it must have happened during my slumber. This is a disaster. I no longer know if this self-death is really my thought or something put there by the commander."

"Let me fight Thrax my way," Maddox said.

"No. It is too late."

"Am I dead?" Maddox asked.

"No, you have seconds left."

"Then send Galyan and me back," Maddox said. "Allow me to destroy Commander Thrax. It is wrong that humanity should perish because of your error."

"That is cruelly stated," the Builder said.

"I have very little time left," Maddox said. "Thus, I find it hard to act in a decorous manner."

"Captain—ah, it doesn't matter. Nothing matters."

"If that's true," Maddox said, "send me back. Let me fight to the end."

"Go," the Builder said. "Your insistence has wearied me. It is time to end this farce. I have failed miserably. But I will make sure you can never interfere like this again."

Maddox attempted to ask the Builder what it meant. At that moment, vertigo struck. Maddox felt his "self" sucked away from the Builder's presence. In an instant, he rejoined Galyan.

"Captain, it is too soon," Galyan said. "I wasn't able to reach all the connections."

Maddox couldn't respond. His "self" flashed across the void of space and back into the computer core chamber aboard *Victory*.

Maddox roared with pain, opening his eyes but seeing nothing. His forehead burned with agony. His hands reached up and tore off the silver band.

Sight flooded back into his brain. He smelled burned circuits. Zapping noises assaulted his hearing. He tasted bile and sweat trickled down his back, which thrashed against the chair's fabric.

"No!" Maddox shouted, lurching out of the chair. He stumbled, crashing against a wall and sprawling onto the floor. From there, he watched the Builder AI cube explode, sending electric bolts writhing through the air.

Ludendorff, Lady Shana and a scrambling Maddox barely made it out of the room in time. Then more blasts erupted from the chamber, and an explosion hurled the captain from his feet.

A body landed beside him, a black charred corpse with grinning teeth. Maddox fixated on that, wondering if Ludendorff or the Lady Shana was dead.

People burst into the room, shouting. Maddox felt hands grabbing him, dragging him across the floor. He realized one of the people was Meta.

Am I going to live? Is Galyan still functional?

Whooshing sounds filled his hearing until cold foam surrounded him. Someone lifted him—

Maddox groaned.

"He's alive," Riker shouted.

"What happened?" Meta asked. "Did it work?"

Maddox groaned again. He felt shell-shocked, uncoordinated.

"Take him to the infirmary."

"No," Riker said. "The captain would want us to defeat the Swarm. Give him a stimulant. We have to blow the sphere."

"He's right," Meta said a moment later. "He'd want that."

Why did the others talk about him in the past tense? What did he look like? Who had thudded down as a corpse a few seconds ago?

Maddox felt movement, a sting in his side and more movement. His thoughts began to jell. He opened his eyes. Meta and Riker carried him into a room, setting him in a chair.

Maddox tried to look at himself.

"Not yet, sir," Riker said.

"Is something the matter, Sergeant?"

"A trifle, sir," Riker said, trying to sound cheerful.

"Look up," Meta said. "Take a look at the screen."

Maddox focused on the screen. It showed a portion of the Dyson sphere. Saucer after saucer poured from various openings. They were like a mass of bees in flight.

373

A ping in his skull caused Maddox to shudder.

"He's going into shock," Riker said.

"No," Maddox whispered. "Watch. It's about to happen."

"What is, sir?"

"The destruction of the Dyson sphere," Maddox whispered, feeling desperately tired.

"He's delirious," someone said.

The destruction began on the sphere's North Pole. A gigantic explosion blew metal off. The destruction grew, more explosions adding to the mayhem.

"I hope we're leaving," Maddox whispered.

"Keith is piloting *Victory*," Meta said.

Maddox smiled, which hurt his face. What was wrong with him? He tried to examine his arms. Meta held his head, keeping him from doing that.

"Wow," Riker said.

Maddox looked up at the screen again. More of the sphere began exploding. The sheer mass of the sphere was bewildering. Things could explode at the speed of light, and it would still take time for it to travel across the face of the gigantic sphere.

"What's that?" Meta whispered.

Maddox noticed a weird alteration. It appeared as if a ghostly tube thrust out of the sphere. The tube was long, reaching…reaching…reaching farther than Maddox's eyes could see. What did the ghostly tube signify?

At that point, the explosions on the Dyson sphere reached a critical mass. Debris in incalculable amounts blew outward. Clouds of debris reached the escaping saucers. The mass obliterated one saucer after another in an orgy of destruction.

It didn't stop there, but continued to annihilate the ancient structure.

Maddox realized the ping of awareness must have been some last connection with the Builder. It had destroyed the ancient sphere, a work of wonder, a palace of technological prizes, a storehouse of knowledge such as no human must have ever had access to before.

"Galyan," Maddox whispered. "I need to speak to Galyan."

No one said a word.

It finally dawned on Maddox what had happened. The AI core chamber had exploded, electrocuting one of them, maybe badly burning him.

Victory and some of Port Admiral Hayes' flotilla had won free of the sphere and escaped Commander Thrax Ti Ix. But they may have lost the ancient AI and any means of reaching Human Space in the next several years, if ever.

-49-

Maddox woke up in the infirmary, his skin covered with a healing salve, while bandages covered the majority of his body. He itched horribly.

"Hello?" the captain said.

A man snorted and stood, appearing in the captain's view. With his hand, the man brushed his own hair before grinning in a lopsided manner.

"What has you so amused, Sergeant?" Maddox asked.

"You're alive, sir, and doing well according to the medical machines. Ludendorff is worse off, but he'll make it."

"The Lady Shana?" Maddox asked.

Riker's smile fell. "I'm afraid she wasn't as lucky, sir. Meta says the lady took the brunt of the first discharge. It seems she did it for you, shielding you from the worst of it."

"What?" Maddox said.

"The Kai-Kaus believe they're indebted to you. One of the elders told Meta it was Lady Shana's privilege to die so you could live."

Maddox found that he couldn't swallow. He turned away.

"It's all right, sir," Riker said, patting his arm.

Maddox stiffened in pain.

"Oh, sorry about that," Riker said. "Your skin is still tender."

"What's the military situation? How long have I been under?"

"About ten hours," Riker said. "We're doing fine, heading toward a weird beacon."

"Does anyone know what the beacon is?"

"I do," Galyan said.

Maddox stared in silence at the dim holoimage. It didn't have the same clarity as before, but the little Adok was there.

"You survived," Maddox exclaimed.

"That seems obvious," Galyan said. "I am here, thus, I am existent. How could it be otherwise?"

"Right," Maddox said. "Why are you dimmer than before?"

"My backup system does not have the same connection with the extra computing chamber Dana discovered. It will take time to reconnect them."

"You never told us about a backup system."

"Correct," Galyan said. "I did not even know I possessed one. I have been looking forward to your recovery, Captain. I have questions concerning the end on the sphere. An irresistible force yanked me from my task. Do you know what that was?"

"The Builder," Maddox said.

"Did it destroy the Builder AI box on purpose do you think?"

Maddox thought back to the final conversation. "Yes, I believe so."

"Interesting," Galyan said. "There is so much I would have liked to catalog. I had begun the process on the sphere. Given time, I could have recorded the Builder's knowledge."

Maddox considered that, and he realized humanity had almost leaped...maybe millennia in technology all across the board. Maybe Galyan could have recorded further back than ancient human history. The AI might have recovered records of the timeless war against the Nameless Ones.

"In the final analysis I recorded nothing," Galyan said. "The Builder caused me to lose everything. The loss is incalculable."

"I've been wondering about something," Riker said. "What was that ghostly tube we saw at the end? No one knows. Valerie tried analyzing it, but she couldn't pick up any readings that made sense. Did you see it, Galyan?"

"Of course," the AI said. "My analyzer gives it an eighty-six percent probability of being a hyper-spatial tube."

"Eighty-six percent?" Maddox asked.

"Eighty-six point three two eight percent to be precise," Galyan said.

"Yes, one must strive for precision," Maddox said.

"Are you ribbing me, sir?"

"He is," Riker said, "although the captain would never admit it."

"If that was a hyper-spatial tube," Maddox said, "would that imply Commander Thrax employed it?"

"I believe so," Galyan said. "It was impossible to tell, but my sensors combined with logic imply the starting point was from inside the sphere. That means an unknown number of Swarm-run vessels escaped. Do you have any idea where the tube went?"

Fear boiled up in Maddox. "Thrax Ti Ix went to Earth."

"The tube was pointed in the wrong direction to reach Earth," Galyan said.

"What direction did it go?"

"Toward the center of the galaxy," Galyan said.

"Ah," the captain said. "Yes, the commander went one thousand light-years or more. The Builder told me earlier it was going to give Thrax passage back to the Swarm Empire."

"That sounds ominous," Galyan said.

"For the future, it does," Maddox said. "We have no idea how far the Swarm Empire is from us at present."

"My records indicate the Swarm never discovered wormholes. Will Commander Thrax bring them this technology?"

"I'd say that's a near certainty," Maddox said.

"This is grave news," Galyan said. "My long vigil in my star system may have been in vain."

"Hardly that, Galyan," Maddox said. "Because of you we have advanced warning of a coming peril."

"Thank you for your kind words, Captain."

Several beeps sounded from a nearby board.

"Oh-oh," Riker said. "That's going to bring Meta. She's going to give you another injection, sir. Your body is working

378

overtime, building new skin tissue. You're going back to sleep for a while."

Maddox nodded. "You never did tell me. What are we traveling toward?"

"I did say," Riker told him. "It's a beacon, a large one shaped like a silver pyramid."

"Where is it?"

"At the end of this star system," Riker said. "It was cloaked before. Valerie found it soon after the Dyson sphere's destruction. Galyan figures something on the sphere kept the cloak in place. Once the Builder died, the cloak stopped working on the pyramid."

"A silver pyramid," Maddox said. "Does that mean we might be able to find a hyper-spatial tube after all?"

"We're all hoping, sir."

The hatch slid open and Meta walked in. "Everyone out," she said. "I have a patient that needs tending. The rest of you are just going to be in the way."

Galyan disappeared, while Riker winked at the captain. Then, the sergeant sauntered out, whistling an old tune between his teeth.

***

Because of his increased metabolism, Maddox healed faster than the professor did. The captain was up in time for Lady Shana's funeral. It was a moving affair, and it helped cement the Kai-Kaus to Maddox even more than before.

The next two days flashed by in hard work as the Kai-Kaus repaired the damage to *Victory* and tried to settle into a normal routine aboard the starship. The Adok vessel matched velocities with the port admiral's slowest ship, which was slow indeed.

Maddox decided there was one positive to the destruction of Galyan's AI core chamber. If Ludendorff had practiced any deviousness there, the annihilation of the core chamber had trumped it.

After a journey of many days across the system, the flotilla of Star Watch vessels began to brake.

Maddox was on the bridge in his chair. It was the first time since the core explosion that he could wear clothes without discomfort. Galyan had zoomed in on the silver pyramid, putting it onto the main screen at maximum magnification.

"Is there any noticeable difference to this Nexus compared to the one in the Xerxes System?" the captain asked.

"None that I have been able to decipher," Galyan said.

Maddox tapped his chin before glancing at the others. "Any suggestions?" he asked.

"What's the mechanism for turning on a hyper-spatial tube?" Valerie asked.

"Exactly," Maddox said. "I have no idea."

"We're back to Meta's memory of her time with Kane," Valerie said. "They went inside the Xerxes Nexus, but they didn't use a hyper-spatial tube. It could take a long time to figure this out."

Maddox nodded.

"And the longer we take," Valerie said, "the more damage the Builder's android doubles could be doing back on Earth."

"Yes," Maddox said.

"What does the professor suggest we do?"

Maddox shook his head. He'd spoken a little to Ludendorff about hyper-spatial tubes. The professor had finally begun to recover from his injuries. Unfortunately, the Methuselah Man was still too tired to talk for long. Maddox wondered if the professor could be faking his tiredness. He didn't like the possibility. After everything they had been through, he wanted to be able to trust the man. With an inward sigh, the captain realized he'd have to continue keeping an eye on Ludendorff.

"Until recently, the professor hasn't known about the Dyson sphere or hyper-spatial tubes," Maddox said. "He told me we're back to being primates before a black monolith, baffled by technological mysteries beyond our understanding."

"Sir?" Valerie asked.

"I didn't understand the reference, either," Maddox admitted. "We're going to need the best Kai-Kaus minds, the professor's insights—"

"Captain," Galyan said. "I am detecting a silver whirlpool. It is similar to what we detected by the Xerxes System Nexus.

Do you suppose the Builder programmed the pyramid to activate a hyper-spatial tube at our approach?"

"That strikes me as the most sensible explanation."

The vast sense of relief at seeing the silver whirlpool surprised Maddox. The reality of being stranded one thousand light-years from the Xerxes System had tightened in him for so long that he had no longer been consciously aware of it. With its release—

Valerie laughed with glee.

Keith shouted, pumping a fist in the air.

"We're going home," Maddox declared.

"Yes, sir, mate, Captain, sir," Keith said as he laughed.

"I have a question," Galyan said.

"What?" Maddox said with a smile.

"How do we know that this hyper-spatial tube will actually take us to Earth?" the AI asked.

Maddox blinked at the holoimage as some of the good feeling evaporated. "Is it pointed in Earth's direction?"

"Affirmative," Galyan said.

Maddox nodded decisively. "Well. We'll use the Laumer Drive and enter the tube, hoping for the best—unless you have a better idea."

"I am sorry to say I do not."

"Right," Maddox said. "It's time to tell the others and get ready for the voyage home."

-50-

Dr. Dana Rich's eyes flew open. She shivered a second later, realizing she was cold. She also happened to be quite nude.

With agonizing slowness, she brought up her hands and pressed them against a clear substance. That did not immediately compute in her thoughts. She felt around, pressing her palms and fingertips against chilly glass. Glass...she looked around, absorbing what she saw.

I'm inside a glass tube.

How had she come to be here? How—

Dana's eyes widened. She realized that not only was she standing up in a tube but that hundreds of others stood in their own glass tubes. There were rows of tubes, each of them with a naked occupant.

She recognized people from the Atlantis Project. And was that Brigadier O'Hara? How had the Iron Lady managed to find herself in a tube?

Dana groaned. The big old man in the end tube in the third row appeared to be the Lord High Admiral of Star Watch. If he was in a tube...who ran the war effort against the New Men? Who ran Star Watch? What had happened to the Earth?

A hatch opened and a woman in a strange uniform stepped into the chamber. The woman wore a military-style hat and frowned as she studied them.

At that moment, Dana's tube began to rise. It did not take the doctor with the glass, but freed her from confinement.

"You must stay where you are," the uniformed woman said. "There has been a malfunction. We are going to fix it in the next hour or two."

"Who are you?" Dana called out. "What happened to us?"

"Those questions are immaterial during the emergency," the uniformed woman said. She forced a smile. "You are under treatment for your own good. Remain in place, I implore you, and everything will be fine."

Dana took several steps out of a small circle, doing the exact opposite of what the woman suggested.

The uniformed woman drew a stunner from a holster. "Dr. Rich, you must obey me. As I have said, this is for your own good. We do not wish for you to be damaged in any way."

Dana was confused. The last thing she remembered…was exiting a submersible that had brought her to an incredible find at the bottom of the ocean. Yes, a deep, underwater pyramid—

Wait. *Damaged?* The woman had said they did not wish for her to become damaged. Who talked like that?

"Why am I a prisoner?" Dana said, loudly.

At that moment, other tubes began to rise.

"Stay where you are," the uniformed woman said. "The equipment will come back online in moments. This is an emergency. We ask you to bear with us and stay in your circles."

"Who do you mean by *us*?" Dana called. "Who are you?"

"Never mind, Doctor," the woman said. "This is your last warning."

Dana hadn't forgotten the skills she'd learned during her prison sentence on Loki Prime. Before that, the Brahman Secret Service had given her field training. She didn't have Meta's strength, but she was formidable just the same.

Dana began to back up, putting distance between the stunner and her.

"What are you doing, Doctor?" the uniformed woman called.

"Maybe I can find an emergency outlet," Dana said. "I'd like to help."

"No. You are sick. We are treating you, all of you. This is for the best."

383

"Thank you most profoundly," Dana said. "I feel so much better already."

"Stay where you are," the woman said. "This is your final warning."

"Charge her!" the Lord High Admiral said. "She can't shoot all of us." So saying, the naked old man began to run at the armed woman, his fleet slapping against cold tiles.

"I don't want to do this," the woman said, raising her stunner. "Don't force me to fire. You are an old man and cannot sustain stun damage."

"I'll be damned if I'm going to be a tame prisoner," Cook shouted in a deep voice. "Come on, people! You may be naked, but that doesn't mean you can't fight. Charge with me. Charge!"

A few others rallied to the old man's poignant cry, among them the gray-haired Iron Lady.

The uniformed woman pressed the stunner button. A blot of force ejected, striking the Lord High Admiral on the chest, knocking him unconscious onto the floor. She re-targeted, knocking another down.

Dana sprinted to the back of the chamber. She might have felt foolish running naked, but she was too determined. She saw a pile of clothing back here. Maybe someone had forgotten them.

The stunner kept discharging, dropping people, and the others wavered. Only a few had charged. Then, the Iron Lady went down too.

"I will show no mercy," the uniformed woman shouted. "I will hurt you unless you submit."

The people in front came to a stop. Those behind bumped up against them, and then they all stopped. Soon, everyone waited sheepishly, staring at the uniformed woman with the stunner.

At that point, another uniformed person entered the large chamber. He was a lean man with angular features, and he, too, drew a stunner.

"You must go back to your circled spots," the man said.

Dana knelt by the articles of clothing. She looked up sharply, recognizing the voice and face of Captain Maddox.

What was he doing down here in the Atlantis Project? Why would he help those who stunned the Lord High Admiral and Brigadier O'Hara?

Obviously, one of the others wondered the same thing. "I recognize you, Captain Maddox," he spoke up. "Why are you keeping us prisoner?"

Maddox appeared to think about that. Finally, he nodded. "Do you believe you're Major Stokes?"

"I am Major Stokes," the naked man said.

"No. You're an android."

"What?" Stokes said.

Maddox regarded the naked throng. "Listen. This is a terrible joke, a prank, call it what you will. The Builder is responsible for it. He activated this pyramid under the sea some time ago. It was constructed in the distant past. Why it came on now, I don't know. What it did, however, was begin a duplication process. The real people you were modeled after were captured and duplicated. Fortunately, Star Watch Intelligence with Spacer help broke the conspiracy. You are all androids who think you are real people. We're trying to decide what to do with you. Unfortunately, we can't just let you go free or you would create chaos."

"Why do I feel as if I'm the real Major Stokes?"

"Because Builder technology is the best," Maddox said. "You are proof of that. The Builder desired androids that truly believed they were alive."

Dana rummaged through the clothing. Her heart beat quicker as she saw a black-matted gun. She picked it up. It was a revolver. Opening the cylinder, she saw that it had all six bullets.

"I see you crouching back there Dana," Maddox shouted. "Come, join the others."

Dana stood, canting to the side. She let her arms hang, holding the revolver against her thigh. She moved toward the throng, making sure her body blocked the weapon from the captain's sight.

"Will the Lord High Admiral be well?" Dana shouted.

Maddox glanced at the downed Cook.

Dana walked faster. She had to get closer. She wasn't a crack shot like the captain. He was uncanny in fighting skills, almost as good as a full-blooded New Man.

"Why do we feel shame at being naked if we're androids?" Stokes asked.

That was a good question, Dana realized.

"I have already answered your question," Maddox said. "You have all the attributes of a real person."

"Wouldn't that make us real then?" Stokes asked.

"That is a theological question," Maddox said. "I am not skilled on the topic."

Dana's heart flared with certainty then. The real Captain Maddox would not have admitted to such a humble attitude. That thing was an android pretending the real people were the androids.

"You're not skilled in theology?" Dana asked.

"I have said as much," Maddox told her.

"What else are you unskilled in?" she asked.

Stokes looked at her sharply. She gave him the barest of nods.

"What are you hoping to achieve, Doctor?" Maddox asked.

"You don't seem like Captain Maddox," Dana said.

The captain laughed. "That is because of faulty wiring in you. The others here do not perceive any fault in me."

"I do," Stokes said.

"I am Captain Maddox. I am real. I live, I breathe, I eat, I think—"

"Enough," the uniformed woman beside him said. "You will not convince them in that manner."

Maddox looked at her. "I am real," he said.

"You appear to be malfunctioning," she said. "You will take yourself to the replicator for repair."

The people glanced at one another.

"No!" Maddox said. "Your words—they indicate I am an android."

"Does it matter?" the uniformed woman said.

"Yes! I am real. I breathe, I eat, I—"

386

A single shot rang out. The high velocity bullet cracked against Captain Maddox's skull, knocking the android against the bulkhead.

"Grab the stunners!" Dana shouted. "Go! Get them!"

The people looked back at her.

Dana stood in a shooter's stance, with her right foot forward, the revolver held with both hands.

The uniformed woman stared at the knocked down Maddox and then at Dana. She brought up her stunner.

Another shot rang out, hitting the uniformed woman in the head. Like the first shot, this one hurled the targeted android against the wall.

With a roar of desperation, the crowd of people surged forward, with Major Stokes in the lead. Behind them, Dana ran to catch up. If she had to, she was going to put a bullet through each android's eye, finishing the wardens who had kept them on ice for who knew how long.

***

Despite the circuits, coils and showering sparks, Dana felt soiled by exterminating the two androids. She had shot each again because they had refused to stop struggling.

Now, their group had two stunners and Dana had two bullets left.

"Ready?" Dana asked. She wore the female android's panties, various articles of clothing going to different people.

"Let's do this," Stokes said, one of the men helping a disoriented Lord High Admiral onto his feet.

Dana eased open the hatch to chaos. Several androids—she assumed they were androids—ran through a vast chamber, clutching multicolored boxes against their bodies.

The boxes must be important, but why—

Dana wrinkled her nose. That was an electrical fire, she smelled. Yes, she could hear crackling flames. In the distance, something exploded.

Someone in the group screamed.

A man in back roared, "We have to get out of here."

Dana shut the hatch and whirled around. "We have to keep our heads. Remember, people, we're on the ocean floor. If you panic down here, we're dead."

A woman began to sob.

"That's it," Dana told her. "Get it out of your system. I want you to help me. Are you ready to help me?"

The crying woman looked at Dana with confusion as tears streamed down her face. Her sobbing grew more intense.

Dana stepped to her, hugging the woman and then shaking her. "I need your help," she said directly into her face. "You have to pull it together now. There's no more time."

The woman stopped wailing, sniffling instead as she began to hiccup. "I'm okay," she whispered. "I can do this. Thanks."

Dana looked at the others. "Something happened down here. Maybe the pyramid's computers have a virus. Maybe the place is simply too old. We have to commandeer a submersible and get to the surface."

"What if the androids attack us?" a man said.

"We destroy any android getting in our way," Dana said. "Is that clear?"

"But if—"

"For Heaven's sake," Stokes said. "What's wrong with you people? This lady is a lifesaver. I plan to listen to her. I think the rest of you should too if you want to live." The major turned on the sniffling woman. "Do you want to live?"

She nodded emphatically as she wiped her nose.

"Right," Stokes said. "Then we follow Dr. Rich's command. Whoever doesn't—" Stokes jerked a thumb at the Lord High Admiral— "will have to answer to him during a court martial later."

Dana took a deep breath. She wasn't used to leading during a fight. She could lead during a scientific study or—

The doctor shook her head. She'd have to think like Captain Maddox. He knew how to lead a group. She couldn't believe she had killed the captain's android. She had half wondered if it would feel good after all the slights she'd endured in the past. It had not felt good, though. The real Maddox had been too good to her for too long to feel any resentment against him anymore.

"We're heading for the dock," she said. "Grab what you can on the way there. Put down whoever you have to so we can survive. We all have to stick together, though. And we're not waiting for anyone."

She glanced at a few people. They nodded back.

"Get mad," Dana added. "Androids have been living your lives. They might have screwed up everything for you and for Earth. If that doesn't make you angry, I don't what will."

"We're ready," Stokes told her.

Dana nodded, realizing she was hesitating to do this. This could get them all killed. She didn't want to die. She didn't want—

With a shout, Dana hurled open the hatch and walked into the vast chamber. She kept going, looking around.

The fires had increased. There was harsh smelling smoke gathering on the ceiling. She couldn't see any running androids now.

In a throng, with Dana in the lead with her two-bullet revolver, the group surged across the chamber.

Some of the people coughed explosively. Others hacked, spitting on the floor.

"Which way are the docks?" a man wailed.

"Shut up," Dana called back. "Keep your composure. Maybe we can do this without having to fight and kill."

Or be killed, she thought to herself.

It struck Dana that she led a VIP throng to the submersibles, if there were any left at the docks. The Iron Lady, the Lord High Admiral, Commonwealth senators, bank presidents, high-level bureaucrats—

What was Earth like? Dana assumed the androids had taken their places and wondered what they had done. It was an awful feeling.

She turned a corner and came upon three androids dragging a heavy sled full of strange equipment. The androids stopped to stare at them.

"Hands up," Dana said, aiming the revolver at the three.

"Don't be absurd," the lead android said. "This is our—"

A shot rang out and the android toppled onto the floor. He began to thrash as sparks showered out of his blasted eye.

"What about you two?" Dana asked. "Want to cease existing?"

The two androids threw their hands into the air.

"Back up," she said.

They let go of the cables they'd been using to drag the sled and took three steps back.

"That's good enough," Dana said, as people thronged behind her.

She kept the gun aimed at these two. At the same time, she knelt by the slowly thrashing android, taking an automatic from a holster.

The two with their hands up didn't appear to be armed.

"What is this?" Dana asked, pointing at the sled of equipment.

Neither android said a word.

"I can still kill you," Dana said.

"This is an emergency repair unit," one android said. "The leader hopes to repair the damage created by a random pulse signal."

"What signal?" Dana asked.

"The one from the Dyson sphere," the android said.

"That doesn't make sense."

"That is because you are a wet body with limited knowledge," the android said.

"The…computers in the pyramid received a new signal?" Dana asked. "Is that what you're saying?"

"Correct."

"When did this happen?" Dana asked.

"Less than an hour ago," the android said. "The pulse came with the arrival of Starship *Victory*."

"I'll be damned," Dana said. "So this has something to do with Captain Maddox, does it?"

"That is our working assumption."

Dana smiled wryly. She should have known.

"How long are we going to jabber here?" Stokes asked.

"You're going to lead us to the docks," Dana told the androids.

"We cannot," the speaker said. "We must bring the repair unit to the leader. We must attempt to repair the damage. You must release us."

Dana hesitated.

The android that hadn't spoken until now turned to the speaker. "Let us kill the woman and those with her. Then, we can take the repair unit to the leader."

Dana used her last bullet, dropping the one who had made the suggestion.

The last android raised its arms even higher than before.

"Do you want to cease to exist as well?" Dana asked, all too aware the revolver was out of bullets.

The thing shook its head.

Then, Dana realized the three of them had struggled to move the sled. With just one android left…

"Okay," Dana said. "Go ahead. Drag the equipment to your leader. I don't care anymore."

She backed away, handed the empty gun to a woman behind her and jacked a bullet into the semiautomatic's chamber. Afterward, she started for the docks again.

A glance back showed the lone android slipping and sliding on the floor as it tried to drag the sled by itself. It wasn't going anywhere, but that didn't seem to deter the thing. It was like an ant trying to drag a bug too big for it.

The rest of the journey proved uneventful compared to what had already transpired. With the semiautomatic in hand, Dana reached the docks. She handed the gun to the same woman who had taken the empty revolver and went to the controls.

The doctor's fingers flew over a board. Five minutes later, Dana led the throng through a tube into a waiting submersible. It looked like they might escape to the surface after all.

"What's it like up there?" Stokes said, walking beside her.

"I have no idea," Dana said.

Stokes appeared thoughtful. "What have our counterparts done?" He sighed. "I hope they haven't soiled our names."

Dana didn't want to think about it, but she had a bad feeling she was going to have to very soon indeed.

-51-

Dana sat in the submersible's control room. Major Stokes piloted the vessel. A groggy, Brigadier O'Hara leaned her forearms on the weapons board.

The Lord High Admiral was in sickbay, having developed an ugly cough, his skin stark white. The android had warned him about his inability to take a stunner shot. It appeared she, or it, had been correct.

"Just a minute," Dana said.

Stokes glanced at her. He piloted the vessel away from the underwater dome. So far, no other submersibles appeared to be after them.

"We can't leave them there," Dana said.

"What do you have in mind?" Stokes asked. "You want to save the androids too?"

"You misjudge my idea," Dana said. "We can't leave the androids down there trying to fix the situation. Some of the most important people on Earth and in Star Watch are in our submarine. That means the androids kidnapped us at great detriment to our society."

"True enough," Stokes said.

Dana chewed on her lower lip. "The pyramid appears to have been a trap."

"No doubt about that," Stokes agreed.

"We have to destroy it."

The major raised his eyebrows. "Do you understand what you're saying? The pyramid is priceless. It has Builder tech, or tech beyond ours. These androids are incredible. Maybe we can use them."

"Use them how?" Dana asked.

Stokes shrugged. "I can imagine Star Watch wanting to make shock troopers out of them, using the androids against the New Men perhaps."

"That's a wretched idea."

"I don't see why. It will save humans from having to risk their lives in infantry combat."

"You saw what just happened. We were captives. If you allow robots or androids to fight for you, soon, they will rule. No, men and women must do their own fighting. Besides, why wouldn't the androids become a worse menace than the New Men?"

"It was just a suggestion," Stokes said.

"Then you agree with me?" Dana said.

Stokes appeared thoughtful, finally shaking his head. "I'm afraid I don't, Doctor. There could be more people trapped down there. The devices we might uncover—"

The submersible shuddered.

Dana and Stokes looked up at the main screen. Two torpedoes zoomed out of the tubes. The torpedoes began a tight turn toward the dome and the pyramid underneath.

Both Dana and Stokes turned to Brigadier O'Hara. The Iron Lady wore an android's uniform. Her fingers still rested on the firing buttons. Slowly, she turned to regard them.

"This is war," O'Hara said in a ragged voice.

"Ma'am," Stokes said.

"Better get us out of here," O'Hara said. "The coming concussion could damage our submersible."

Stokes whirled around, tapping his board.

Dana swayed back against her seat as thrust shoved the submersible ahead. The Iron Lady had made the decision for them.

Turning to her board, Dana activated it. A screen flickered into focus just in time for her to see the results.

The torpedoes slammed against the dome, igniting. Bubbles explosively surged upward from the first impact site as some of the underwater building's hull plating blew apart. The second torpedo did likewise, sending bubbles geysering toward the distant surface.

Moments later, the submersible rocked from the underwater concussion. The bulkheads groaned ominously all around them.

"Don't do that again," Stokes shouted.

Like a crabby little girl doing the opposite of what she was told, O'Hara pressed the firing buttons again. A second later, two more torpedoes zoomed into view.

Stokes swiveled around. "Ma'am, I beg you to desist. You'll destroy us, too."

Brigadier O'Hara looked up with a haggard expression. "Androids, Major, androids held us captive. It was a nightmare. We can only presume android doubles have taken our places. I can hardly conceive of a worse horror."

"I can think of several," Stokes muttered.

O'Hara shook her head. "I loathe them. The very idea makes me tremble with revulsion. I want to squish them flat like wasps."

Stokes eyed the brigadier.

Dana heard the hysteria in the Iron Lady's voice. O'Hara seemed to be on the very edge.

"Have you been underwater before?" Dana asked her.

Slowly, O'Hara turned to Dana. "What?" the brigadier said.

Dana repeated the question.

"No," O'Hara said.

"It's a…a pressurized feeling," Dana explained. "It takes getting used to."

O'Hara frowned, soon nodding.

More explosions told of the second pair of torpedoes slamming against the dome. Time passed, and the concussion rocked the submersible again, although with less force than last time.

"You'll begin to feel better once we approach the surface," Dana told the brigadier.

"I hope you're right," O'Hara said. "I feel…distressed."

"This is a distressing situation," Dana said.

O'Hara nodded. "How do you maintain your composure? It's quite impressive, down here."

Dana gave the brigadier a wintry smile. "I've been traveling with Captain Maddox for some time. This kind of situation is actually rather commonplace with him."

O'Hara reached up, putting a stray strand of hair into place.

"One of the androids told us something interesting," Dana said. "Starship *Victory* has returned. With the vessel came a pulse that apparently began a chain-reaction down there. I wonder what Maddox has achieved this time."

"When he left," O'Hara said, "he was headed to the Xerxes System."

"Bingo," Dana said. "The Nexus must have something in common with the ancient pyramid down here. He's figured out something critical again."

O'Hara regarded Stokes. "Can you make this thing go any faster?"

"We're near its operational limit now, Ma'am."

"What are you thinking?" Dana asked the brigadier.

"Yes," O'Hara said. "That's what we must do. We have an advantage. At least, I suspect we do. We must think of a way to use our present advantage against the impersonating androids still functioning in our places."

"Right," Dana said. "We've escaped our captivity. Maybe the androids impersonating us don't know that yet. Maybe destroying the dome—"

"I doubt I got them all," O'Hara said.

"Maybe you crippled their headquarters, though."

The haggard expression hardened. "Despite my dislike of the underwater psychic pressure," O'Hara said, "I believe we should go back down and complete the dome's destruction."

"I do not think that is a good idea," Stokes said. "We've managed to get unbelievably lucky so far. That luck will not hold if we push it too far."

"Luck had nothing to do with it," O'Hara said. "The doctor's decisive action is what saved our lives."

"The Lord High Admiral helped when he charged," Stokes said.

"Yes," O'Hara said. "The man is courage exemplified, but it was Dr. Rich who incapacitated the enemy."

ıe of that matters now," Dana said, interrupting. "We
ı plan, a way to thwart the androids who are
ırading as us."

ı plan," O'Hara said. "Yes, I believe you're right. Come,
ır, let us put our heads together. You and I shall devise
ıngency plans so we'll know what to do once we surface."

* * *

They bypassed the dome's surface air-pad in the Mid-
tlantic, deciding androids likely controlled it. For hours,
ıtokes piloted the submersible, keeping away from any other
submarines they spotted via sonar.

After a time, Dana and the brigadier went to see the Lord
High Admiral.

The old man sat up in bed, his skin still far too pale. His
eyes looked rheumy and bloodshot and his breath came in
labored gasps.

"What were you thinking charging an android with a
stunner, Admiral?" O'Hara chided.

Cook gave her a ghastly grin, as if he had enjoyed his
lonesome charge.

"Have to set...an example," Cook said in a hoarse voice.
"Couldn't wait for anyone...else," he said. "Besides...I've
sent...too many fine people into combat lately. It was good to
have a turn again." He stared off into space. "Yes, very good,"
he said, softly.

Dana couldn't help but admire the Lord High Admiral. She
liked and trusted him. What was his android double doing right
now?

"We should try to figure out when the androids captured
each of us," Dana said. "I recall my last thought." She told
them about coming down to the dome.

"Oh," O'Hara said. "Yes, that's a good idea. Let me see. I
recall...eating at Hop Sing's Eastern Delight. They have a
wonderful noddle and the best orange chicken. I ordered my
meal..." O'Hara frowned, soon shaking her head. "That's it. I
was waiting for my plate. Then, I found myself in the tube,
shivering."

It turned out there was a two-month difference between their kidnappings.

"Sir," O'Hara said. "Do you recall what happened to you?"

Cook was staring intently at the brigadier. "I most certainly do," the old man said. "You called me to a rendezvous in the forest outside the city. You said it was urgent. I landed in my private air-car, and you and Major Stokes approached. Brigadier, I distinctly remember you spraying a canister of knockout gas in my face."

"Not me, sir," O'Hara said, "but my android double."

"Yes, yes, of course," Cook said. "I'm still feeling groggy. Damned android shot me directly over my heart. I think it did that on purpose."

"Well," Dana said. "We've learned the androids are crafty and seem to have some idea that they're not real."

"We know that how?" O'Hara asked.

"Yours and the major's android doubles clearly worked together to kidnap the Lord High Admiral. In order to do whatever they're trying to achieve, they would have to know the goal. We have to unmask the androids."

"Hopefully, without creating a worldwide panic," O'Hara said.

"That's secondary," Dana said. "We have to stop them from doing...anything irreparable. My intuition tells me the androids are probably going to do something to Starship *Victory*. If I know the captain, he's already unmasked the problem in some fashion. The trouble is, no one on Earth will believe him, particularly if *you* don't believe him, Brigadier."

"You mean my android double not believing him," O'Hara said.

"Of course," Dana said. "What else could I mean?"

The brigadier looked away, becoming solemn.

Dana had a feeling she'd touched a nerve. What had the brigadier done to upset the captain?

The Iron Lady snapped her fingers impatiently. "I wish this tub could go faster. We have to get to Geneva and the controls of power as soon as we can."

397

-52-

Captain Maddox sat transfixed in his command chair, watching the building fleet with something approaching despair. He hadn't believed the Lord High Admiral would keep a grudge under these conditions. Maybe as distressing had been the refusal of the Iron Lady to take any of his calls.

Victory and Battleship *Leipzig* had interposed themselves between Luna Base and the rest of Port Admiral Hayes' flotilla.

They had come out of the hyper-spatial tube three-quarters of the way to Earth from Mars. That was incredibly accurate considering the distance they had traveled from the Dyson sphere.

The flotilla had accelerated and braked shortly, following the directions of Luna Command. Now, the Lord High Admiral had informed Maddox that he was under arrest as a traitor to Star Watch.

"You are hereby relieved of command," the Lord High Admiral said on the main screen.

Seven *Gettysburg*-class battleships led the way. Together with a dozen carriers and as many heavy cruisers, they had taken up station near Luna Base. More warships from the Home Fleet were on their way here.

Maddox's mouth was dry and his eyes had begun to hurt with a gritty feeling.

"You have not yet acknowledged my command," the Lord High Admiral said.

"I am too stunned to reply," Maddox managed to say.

"Who is on the bridge with you?"

Maddox stirred, glancing at the others. Valerie stared at him openmouthed. Keith had swiveled all the way around. The Kai-Kaus chief tech slowly shook his head in dismay.

Only Galyan seemed unconcerned. The little Adok holoimage studied the Lord Admiral with interest.

"Lord High Admiral," Maddox said.

"I have finished speaking with you," Cook said. "You are relieved of command. You will report to the brig on the double."

The words drained out of Maddox as he leaned back against his chair.

"This is not right," Galyan said.

Maddox turned to the AI. "I don't want to start a fight with the Home Fleet."

"I haven't heard a reply," Cook said, sternly. "I expect even a hybrid like you to listen to orders."

Valerie sucked in her breath. "I can't believe this," she whispered.

"You left Earth and the Solar System against my orders," Cook said. "You cannot expect any leniency now, Captain."

For once, Maddox did not have any words. He hadn't expected this, certainly not from the Lord High Admiral.

"He can't do that to you," Valerie said.

Maddox didn't even glance at her. A feeling of disgust had begun to fill him.

"If you remain on the bridge," Cook added, "I will order the battleships to open fire."

Maddox's head snapped up. A fire burned in his eyes.

Valerie launched out of her seat, stumbling before the main screen. "Respectfully, sir," she told Cook, "this is a monstrously bad idea."

"Who are you?" Cook said.

Valerie blinked with astonishment. "Who am I? You know me, sir."

Cook had a thunderous scowl. Suddenly, he nodded. "Yes, yes, of course I know you. You are Lieutenant Valerie Noonan."

"How can you say it like that?" she asked. "Is something wrong with you, sir?"

Cook raised a fist and brought it down on his desk. "That is enough from you, young lady. You will return to your station or I will relieve you of duty as well."

"But—"

"That is an order!" the Lord High Admiral shouted, pounding the desk once more.

Crestfallen, with her head hanging, Valerie shuffled back to her station.

Maddox had become more alert throughout the exchange. He glanced at Galyan.

"The man is an android, of course," Galyan said. "I did not detect it immediately, but I can see it now. I have been playing back previous files of him juxtaposed against what I have witnessed here. The most reasonable explanation is that he is not himself."

"Right," Maddox said, quietly. He should have realized it from the beginning. The shock of the command— "I've reacted emotionally," he whispered to himself, surprised.

Galyan heard that and nodded. "It would have been difficult not to have reacted in such a manner. You are human after all."

"Lord High Admiral," Maddox said, "I will, of course, comply with your lawful order. It would be wrong of me not to do so."

Cook scowled but nodded curtly.

"Before I do so, though," Maddox said, "I had thought you would want me to report to you on your secret order."

Cook opened his mouth, hesitating before closing it.

"You gave me personal orders, sir, and said that I must report to you in person. You spoke of a conspiracy, one that had infiltrated everywhere—"

"Captain Maddox," Cook said, sternly. "Why are you speaking like this?"

"I understand, sir," Maddox said "I wasn't supposed to breathe a word of this to anyone. But your order just now—"

"Captain," Cook said. "You will immediately take a shuttle and come at once to Luna Base."

400

"I—"

Maddox quit talking as one of the most unusual events occurred since he'd joined Star Watch Intelligence. Guards burst into the Lord High Admiral's office.

The big old man turned around in surprise. "What is the meaning of this?" he shouted.

Guns went off, propelling the admiral off his chair onto the floor. An exact replica of Cook strode forward, a haggard image of the man. He held a big smoking gun, aimed it at the Cook on the floor and emptied the weapon at it.

Sparks showered and electrical discharges erupted from the shattered android who had impersonated the Lord High Admiral Cook.

The big man with the smoking gun turned toward Maddox. His features were slack and his eyes extremely tired.

"It is finished," the Lord High Admiral said in a tired voice. He smiled wearily, put the gun onto the desk and slumped into his chair. In a bone weary manner, he lifted his arms and laid them on the synthi-wood top.

"Captain Maddox," the Lord High Admiral said, "once more we all owe you our lives. I realize many of you seeing this transmission must be stunned. I have just killed an android. I, along with many others including Brigadier O'Hara and Dr. Dana Rich have escaped from an undersea base in the Mid-Atlantic Ocean."

"Yes!" Keith said, slapping his board.

"A pulse signal reached the underwater pyramid with the arrival of Starship *Victory*," the Lord High Admiral said. "It started the revival process of many of us who had been kidnapped. I don't know what you did, Captain, but I dearly want to hear about it."

"I take it I'm not relieved of duty," Maddox said.

"Is that what that thing said?"

Maddox nodded.

The Lord High Admiral leaned forward, staring into the screen. "Captain Maddox is not relieved of duty. He is a hero to the planet and to Star Watch. I personally congratulate you, sir, for your heroic service in the Beyond. I am eager to hear of your exploits and those of your famous crew."

401

"Professor Ludendorff is with us," Maddox said.

"The real Ludendorff?" asked Cook.

"Yes, sir."

"Excellent. Bring him to Geneva with you."

"I have others, too, sir," Maddox said. "They have—"

"Report at once to Geneva, Captain. I'm tired and need to rest. We'll speak soon."

"Yes, sir," Maddox said. "That was quite an exploit, sir. You held your gun rock steady."

"Never mind about that," Cook said, although he smiled as he said it. "I imagine we have a lot to discuss."

"Yes, sir," Maddox said. "We most certainly do."

-53-

Fifty-two hours after Maddox had met with the Lord High Admiral, giving the old man and the Iron Lady a detailed explanation of his time on the Dyson sphere, the captain prowled in a bad quarter of Paris.

He had come for a very specific purpose. Galyan had discovered the situation. It had happened after Dana boarded the starship and reconnected the extra computing chamber with the AI's backup.

Galyan had immediately spoken with Maddox about the possibility. Normally, the captain would have gone to the Iron Lady with the information. His time with the Builder and his new importance as the spokesman for the Kai-Kaus had shifted Maddox's outlook.

He would take care of this himself.

Normally, on this kind of foray, the captain would have brought Sergeant Riker with him. Instead, he wore his wristband with a tight-beam connection to the starship in Earth orbit. He had also brought Meta. She was deadlier than the sergeant was and she wasn't as beholden to Star Watch Intelligence as Riker would be.

The Kai-Kaus were going to bring big changes with their Adok technology. Soon, the first Star Watch battleships with Adok shields and disruptor cannons would heavily shift the balance of power in the Commonwealth's favor. Depending on what happened out in "C" Quadrant, the invasion of the Throne

World seemed more feasible than ever. There was one catch, however.

How close was the Swarm Empire to Human Space? Could humanity still afford the luxury of a deadly war between the New Men and the old-style peoples?

There was no way to contact Fletcher other than by sending a courier ship to him. That could take weeks, even months. Except…maybe there was a way to contact someone far distant in "C" Quadrant almost instantly.

Galyan had informed the captain that Ludendorff had been on the starship several times since *Victory* had come into near orbit. The AI had carefully watched the professor. The Methuselah Man also happened to be under careful surveillance by O'Hara's best people. None of that seemed to matter to the professor.

Tonight, Ludendorff was in Paris. He said he hadn't been in the famous city for over four hundred years. Since it was just a short hop from Geneva, the professor had convinced O'Hara to let him take a break from what was going to be a weeks-long debriefing.

"He's in the cellar of this building," Galyan said through an earpiece.

Maddox glanced across the street. Meta noticed it as she looked upward at the stars. The crossing of her right hand over her left arm meant she understood his signal.

The captain didn't sense that anyone was tailing him. The starship upstairs in orbit hadn't seen anything either. But one couldn't be too careful. Maddox crossed to a side street, walked down stairs and entered through a basement door.

It was dim in the hallways, a rundown place for the poor. Maddox passed a woman who watched him a little too carefully. It made him extra alert. He turned a corner and noticed something on the floor. He pretended to tie his footwear. He wore boots but that didn't matter for this. As he knelt, the captain picked up an extremely unique piece of fur. He recognized it as slarn fur from Wolf Prime.

"Galyan," Maddox said, softly, using sub-vocalization from the microphone on his throat. "Do you remember the slarn hunter Villars?"

"Cesar Villars?" Galyan said. "Yes, I do."

Maddox stood thoughtfully, sliding the piece of fur into a pocket.

The captain had reason to remember the creature and the man. Slarns were vicious hunting beasts from Wolf Prime, famous for their violent temper, dangerous teeth, claws, speed and cunning. Slarn fur was prized throughout the Commonwealth. Rugged men trapped slarns on Wolf Prime. If they survived several years of it, the trappers could become quite wealthy.

Maddox had originally found Ludendorff on that winter world, studying Swarm ruins. The professor had kept bodyguards, one of them being Cesar Villars, a young Methuselah Man of murderous intent.

The white-haired slarn hunter had been a blocky man with a thick neck and an ugly scar running across his right eye and down his cheek. It had come from a slarn's claw. The eye-socket had contained a smooth ball bearing, which had really been a tech tool giving the man radar vision.

Villars had been tough, had learned to hate Maddox and desired to kill Meta. The captain had finally incapacitated the dangerous hunter, handing him over to Star Watch Intelligence on Earth during the time of the Destroyer Incident.

Maddox wondered about Cesar Villars, android doubles and Methuselah Men. Maybe one of the android doubles had quietly released Villars from confinement when it had had the chance. Ludendorff would undoubtedly want his bodyguard because the professor implicitly trusted the man. Ludendorff had modified Villars' thinking, making him completely loyal to him. For all Ludendorff's help in the Dyson sphere and star system, the professor still had his secret agenda.

The piece of slarn fur meant something.

"Scan the area to see if Villars is in the building," Maddox told Galyan.

"Scanning," Galyan said, "scanning. Oh. This is interesting. Villars is here. How did you know, Captain?"

"An educated guess," Maddox said. "Is Villars with the professor?"

"That is an affirmative."

Maddox allowed his lips to stretch into a grimace. Villars should have been kept under lock and key for the rest of his life—or sent to Loki Prime. If ever there were a candidate for a prison planet, it would be Villars.

What was the professor up to so quickly? Maddox thought the Methuselah Man should have some gratitude for once. Maybe living hundreds of years changed one's perspective. Maddox liked to think it wouldn't have changed his, but he had no idea if that was true or not. First, he'd have to live hundreds of years.

The captain's head twitched. He needed to concentrate. Villars was one of the most dangerous men he'd ever faced. If the professor had brought him here…

Maddox eased down a flight of stairs. Ludendorff must know he—the captain—was coming. That's why he'd summoned Villars. What else made sense?

"Galyan?" the captain sub-vocalized. "Could you narrow down a beam and strike someone from orbit?"

"Negative, Captain. I lack anything of such precision. If you leave, I could destroy the building, though."

"I'll keep that in mind."

"Captain," Galyan said into his earpiece. "Villars has circled. He is approaching you from behind. The professor is ten doors down from your present location."

Maddox reacted at once, drawing his suppressed pistol. In three strides, he was around a corner. He took two more steps back, crouched, raised the pistol and waited for Villars to appear.

"Villars has stopped," Galyan said. "Logic dictates you are under surveillance."

Maddox continued to wait, wait, wait…

He heard quiet stitching sounds and a thud. Then, silence. Maddox scowled. Before he could decide his next action, Galyan spoke in his ear:

"Villars is down, sir. He has stopped breathing. Meta shot him from behind."

"Say that again," Maddox sub-vocalized.

"Meta and I agreed it would be for the best, sir," Galyan said. "I detected Villars before you were aware of him. After informing Meta about the slarn hunter—"

"Galyan, I am in charge of the mission."

"I understand that, sir."

"You will never do something like that again."

"Your odds against Villars were not good, sir," Galyan said.

"I've defeated him before."

"He had high-tech devices to aid him and a severe grudge against you, sir. He was highly motivated to kill you. Meta is skilled at assassination. Given Villars hatred—"

"Forget it," Maddox said, standing. "I thought you said we were under surveillance."

"You are."

"How did Meta sneak up on Villars then?"

"I…adjusted their surveillance cameras," Galyan said. "It is good to have my entire arsenal of functions restored. Wouldn't you agree with that, sir?"

"What's Ludendorff doing now?" Maddox asked.

"He has put up a private screen, sir. I can no longer tell. Perhaps he is aware of Villars' death."

"Adjust his surveillance cameras again," Maddox said. "Show me hurrying to Meta."

"Done."

With his gun in hand, Maddox sprinted soundlessly toward Ludendorff's door. He tried to twist the handle and snatched his hand away, biting his lower lip so he wouldn't yell at the shock of pain.

Without hesitation, Maddox aimed at the lock and shot it out, causing wood to splinter. He shoved the door with his shoulder, bounding in like a leopard. The professor had earphones over his ears. The older man snatched up a laser pistol—

Maddox fired, obliterating the weapon, causing Ludendorff to thrust a portion of his hand into his mouth.

The Methuselah Man's eyes burned with anger. "You're making a terrible mistake, young man," Ludendorff said around his hand. "If I say the word, you're dead."

Maddox said nothing to that, waiting.

"This is bigger than you," Ludendorff added.

Maddox spied the table. On it was a complex machine composed of strange bulbous sections. It had a tiny screen, odd controls and—was that a microphone? It reminded him of machines he'd seen on the Dyson sphere.

The professor removed the hand from his mouth. A spot of blood welled on the fleshy part between his thumb and forefinger.

"This is your final warning," the professor said

"Villars is dead."

Ludendorff smiled. "Then what is that shadow behind you?"

"Me," Meta said, stepping forward.

The professor frowned. "Your assassin killed poor Villars?"

"Poor Villars must have intended to kill the two of us," Maddox said. "He got exactly what he deserved."

Ludendorff looked away. He sighed. "You've complicated my life ever since I've met you. I can't stay on Earth. You must realize that. I cannot remain in the open with others controlling my comings and goings."

"You're not a slug who lives under a rock," Maddox said. "You're a person."

"Captain, there are many factors in play with me. There are too many dangerous people who would rather have me dead."

"Maybe if—"

"I do not desire to hear your moralizing, young man. I see the big picture better than anyone else does. I must proceed with my plans the best I know how in order to save the human race."

Maddox stepped farther into the room. It had metal bulkheads and hatches, and contained advanced equipment everywhere.

"Is this a secret bolt hole?" Maddox asked.

Ludendorff watched him.

Maddox glanced back at the door. The wall was thicker than normal. He had shot the lock to open the outer, fake door. For whatever reason, the professor had not sealed the real hatch that would have secured this place like a bank vault. Could Ludendorff have wanted him to enter here? Then why let Villars loose like that? Did the professor believe he and Meta would have killed the slarn hunter? That would imply Ludendorff had sacrificed Villars.

What was Ludendorff's game? The Methuselah Man played much deeper than Maddox understood. Maybe he should just stick to the present issue.

"Why did O'Hara let you out of Star Watch Headquarters?" Maddox asked. "She knows how dangerous you are."

Ludendorff smiled sadly. "After all this time, don't you realize that I have contingency plans within contingency plans? O'Hara was persuaded that it would be in everyone interests to let me reconnect with Old Earth. No one saw the harm in letting me wander around the planet, revisiting my old haunts."

"You have agents or helpers planted in Star Watch Intelligence itself?" Maddox asked.

"Leave, Captain," Ludendorff said in a suddenly harsh voice. "I don't want to hurt you. I owe you for rescuing me from the Dyson sphere, from the Builder. I try to pay my debts. My programming for survival is too powerful, though, to resist eliminating anyone trying to hinder me for long."

Maddox's head swayed. This was a surprise. "Are you the best of the Builder's androids?" the captain asked.

Ludendorff shook his head. "I am flesh and blood, young man. But the Builder did something to our minds long ago. It's why Strand and I have survived where the others perished. I have an imperative I cannot ignore. Even with the Builder gone..."

"Don't you want to be free of its conditioning?" Maddox asked.

"I am who I am, Captain. It's too late to change that."

Maddox glanced back at Meta. She held a spring-driven gun. It had caused the stitching sounds earlier. She aimed the weapon at the professor's head.

Approaching Ludendorff, Maddox sat in a chair across the table from him. The captain laid his suppressed pistol on the table.

Ludendorff raised his eyebrows.

"So that's it," Maddox said, indicating the machine with its bulbous sections. "Why couldn't Riker and I find it before?"

"I don't know what you're talking about," the professor said.

"That must be your long-distance communication device," Maddox said. "Riker and I searched for it after you were captured in the silver drone base. You must have already dismantled it."

Ludendorff stared at him.

"You should have brought all the pieces down at once," Maddox said. "It was the multiple trips to *Victory* that caused me to remember it."

Ludendorff shrugged. "There was no way around that, I'm afraid."

"Hmm," Maddox said. "Who are you intending to call?"

"Given your intelligence, you should have already figured that one out."

"A New Man," Maddox said.

"Correct."

"You're going to tell him…" Maddox frowned. "Ah, you're going to tell him about the Swarm and Commander Thrax Ti Ix, I presume."

Ludendorff nodded.

"Do you believe the Swarm Empire is near Human Space?" Maddox asked.

"I don't know about the empire, but certainly Swarm warships must be near. At least, it's a definite possibility, especially given Thrax's wormhole technology injection into the empire."

"Why will you tell the New Men?"

"The most obvious reason is because they're the only one with a receiver that can pick up my transmission. The second reason… I've explained it before, Captain, but maybe you've forgotten. The New Men aren't a monolithic group. There are factions among them. Besides, if Swarm bugs are in the universe in force…we finally know the Swarm still exists. I've suspected that for quite some time. So has Strand. He believes we must unite humanity into one powerful imperium to face the Swarm. But the Builder informed you that the Swarm

410

Empire holds one tenth of our galaxy. How does one fight an empire with that kind of resources when we hold less than a tiny fraction of that?"

"We may not have to face the Swarm for centuries."

"Or we may have to face them in two years' time," Ludendorff said.

"Two years isn't long enough to form humanity into a fighting imperium."

"Which is exactly why I'm sitting here ready to call," Ludendorff said.

Maddox considered that. "The Commonwealth has Adok technology now. That should help us against the Swarm."

"For a time, certainly," Ludendorff said.

"That still doesn't answer my question. Why call the New Men, any of them? What are you planning to tell them?"

"The truth, Captain. That we've found the Swarm. That it's too late to try to conquer Human Space. We have to rethink our grand strategy."

"We?" Maddox asked. "Are you aligning yourself with the New Men?"

"Definitely not," the professor said. "I misspoke. That's all."

"Or you made a Freudian slip," Maddox said.

"Think what you like."

"Are you suggesting that you're going to try to convince the New Men not to fight Admiral Fletcher's Grand Fleet?"

"If I can," Ludendorff said, "if I'm not too late."

"If the Grand Fleet survives its encounter with the New Men, humanity will have that many more warships to rearm with our Adok technology. If the New Men knew that, it might cause them to try to annihilate the Grand Fleet at all costs. Maybe it will cause them to attempt to attack Earth before we're rearmed."

"I'm aware of the various ramifications," Ludendorff said. "I'm going to call in order to stop the fighting if I can. I'm not going to tell the New Men—my few allies among them— anything that will encourage them to keep attacking Admiral Fletcher or make a sneak attack on Earth. In light of the Swarm Empire—however far it might be from us—all humans, brilliant or stupid, strong or weak must unite in order to survive the bugs."

Maddox could see the professor's logic. The question was: could others switch their focus so easily? Once people were filled with outrage against aggressors, they often did not stop until the others were smashed. Besides, how wise would it be for regular humanity to let the New Men off the hook?

Still, Ludendorff wasn't trying to stop Fletcher from fighting. He was trying to stop the New Men. What was the right decision? What was happening in "C" Quadrant? Was the Grand Fleet on the verge of success or annihilation?

Maddox picked up his pistol and shoved it in its holster. "Make the call," he said.

"If you would leave then, please," Ludendorff said.

"No. I'm going to listen to what you have to say."

"I'm afraid I must insist on privacy."

Maddox smiled wanly, waiting.

Finally, Ludendorff scowled, picking up the microphone. He leaned forward and began touching select spots on the ancient communicator.

-54-

The Grand Fleet entered the Thebes System. The fleet had maneuvered through the last star systems, with a mixture of daring with the lesser vessels and ultra-caution with the capital ships.

Admiral Fletcher had lost six destroyers and fifteen escort vessels since awakening, but not another capital ship. The journey had also taken longer than Bishop believed reasonable. Now, though, they had arrived in the same system as the New Men's invasion armada.

Fletcher sat in his chair on Battleship *Antietam's* bridge. The fleet had come through a Laumer-Point at the outer edge of the system. Now, the fleet began a slow acceleration for Thebes III in the inner system.

The Grand Fleet moved in four separate formations. The outer, thinnest formation stretched before the three blocks of capital ships. The forward vessels were destroyers and missile boats acting as a screen.

The three blocks were each a mixture of Star Watch battleships, Windsor League hammerships, and carriers and cruisers of all varieties. Fletcher had configured each block, so they had a near parity of numbers and hitting strength.

Altogether, the Grand Fleet possessed 149 capital ships and 182 lesser vessels, making for a total of 331 warships with accompanying supply vessels. It was still an impressive fleet. But would it be a match for the New Men?

Fletcher absorbed the incoming data. The Grand Fleet worked at peak efficiency, sending hard-accelerating probes at the enemy as well as scanning with sensors and watching through advanced teleoptics. It took time to gather the data. But ten hours after arriving in the system, Fletcher had a solid picture of the enemy.

The New Men possessed an incredible *eighty* star cruisers. That was far more than he had counted on—eighty of those bastard vessels with their red fusion beams and unbelievable shields.

If one figured each star cruiser was worth four Star Watch vessels of all kinds, that gave the enemy an equivalent value of 320 warships. That meant the two fleets were nearly equal in fighting power.

Fletcher pondered that. He had three carriers with jump fighters and the new antimatter missiles. He had new wave harmonics shields on his best ships and a good number of hammerships, which were worth two Star Watch battleships. That would up his number some, possibly giving him an equivalent of 350 to 360 warships.

Of course, the New Men would undoubtedly have a few new wrinkles too.

No matter how Fletcher looked at it, this was going to be a bloodbath. Yet, that was fine with him. He'd come out here to hit the enemy, to drive him out of "C" Quadrant. Unfortunately, so far, Fletcher hadn't freed any captive people. That bothered him.

The best that he could envision was to smash the invasion armada forever. Eighty star cruisers implied the New Men had brought all their reinforcements from the Throne World. This could well be the full extent of the enemy's ship power.

The data kept pouring in. There were tens of millions of people on Thebes III. There were also masses of space haulers, tramp vessels and cargo hulls in orbit around the Earthlike world. There were fewer ships than the Patrol vessel had seen almost two weeks ago. That would imply many of the ships had already started for the enemy's Throne World. Did the haulers carry equipment or Commonwealth people?

The admiral stood unsteadily. A faint feeling washed through him. He hadn't yet fully recovered from his injuries.

"Sir," an aide said.

Fletcher waved the nurse aside. He sat back in his chair with a suppressed groan. It wouldn't do for the bridge crew to report seeing weakness in the admiral.

"Are you feeling well, sir," *Antietam's* captain asked him quietly.

Fletcher wasn't going to say that he felt faint. He motioned the battleship's captain closer.

She bent low.

"Let Bishop keep giving the overall orders for now," he whispered. "You can relay that via a shuttle, can't you?"

"Of course, Admiral," the captain said. She straightened, hesitated and then asked, "When are you going to let everyone know that you're back in charge, sir?"

They had decided a week ago to let the fleet know he was recovering but that Bishop held overall command until then. It would be a last minute surprise telling the fleet that Fletcher had returned to command. It would hopefully bolster confidence, having him retake the helm at the most critical juncture.

In truth, Fletcher still didn't know if he was ready to run a battle, the most important of his career and possibly for humanity. In his study, he could ponder and come up with plans. They had been doing it like that for almost two weeks, letting Bishop make the day-to-day fleet decisions. It wasn't the best way to do it, but it had gotten the Grand Fleet this far.

Using his right sleeve, the admiral blotted his forehead. It was sweaty and his breathing had become ragged, but still he waited. He didn't want to stagger off the bridge.

"Sir," the nurse said again.

Fletcher angrily waved the man back. Then, he gripped the armrests of his chair, wondering what his enemy counterparts were thinking in the inner system.

-55-

Strand was furious but he kept a calm, serene face before the assembled commanders of the armada.

The Methuselah Man hadn't seen so many free-minded New Men for quite some time. Those of his cloaked star cruiser had all gone under the knife. Strand only trusted those he utterly controlled. Attending this meeting was a calculated risk, one he hadn't taken for quite some time.

It was a strange feeling, an angering sensation, really. Still, he knew that it was important for his survival to take risks now and again. If one tried to remain safe every second, he lost his edge. It was only a matter of time. Survival literally demanded a few risks to keep ennui at bay. Pushing the edge also helped keep his mind sharp.

Strand had safeguards in place, of course, but it was wise not to fool himself into thinking these assembled commanders were completely harmless to him. They were eighty of the deadliest beings alive, the commanders of eighty star cruisers. Combined with his own cloaked star cruiser and the hidden mines strewn through the system—they would crush the arrogant humans in their oversized fleet. It had taken time, bringing eighty star cruisers to one system. This represented the entire power of the Throne World, here, today, in this place.

"I suggest we make a reversal," Golden Ural said.

Everyone attending the meeting stood, even old Strand. Each New Man and the Methuselah Man stood behind a

416

podium in a vast circle, facing each other. In the center of the chamber was a holoimage of the Thebes System, showing the advancing Grand Fleet among other things.

What a vain and grandiose title the humans give their Grand Fleet, Strand thought.

"A reversal in what manner?" a New Man named Ba Lars asked.

Golden Ural fixed his intense gaze on Strand. Ural was the tallest New Man in the room. He radiated strength and determination. He was the Emperor's man and the commander of the armada, fresh from the Throne World.

"The Swarm exists," Golden Ural said.

Strand became more alert than usual. The phrasing of the thought implied...

"That is an interesting assertion," Strand said. "Perhaps you can explain it in greater detail."

"The Swarm has an empire of vast extent," Golden Ural said.

"How vast?" asked Strand.

"One tenth of our galaxy," Golden Ural said.

"Nonsense," Strand said. "You cannot possibly know such a thing."

"If I did know," Golden Ural said, "then what?"

Strand realized that the only one who might know such a thing would be the Builder. It had disappeared a long time ago. Could Ludendorff have spoken with the Builder recently? If so, that would imply Golden Ural had been in contact with that sissy meddler. That was a dangerous change indeed.

"You say the Swarm exists," Strand said. "Tell us. How near is their closest star system?"

"That is unknown," Golden Ural admitted.

"I believe it is most likely that the Swarm is thousands of light-years from us," Strand said.

"I would agree that is one possibility, perhaps the most likely."

Strand shrugged. "Such a distance means that struggling against the Swarm is for our descendants far in the future."

"Even though I think an event is unlikely," Golden Ural said, "it can still be. Thus, the Swarm could be near. The truth is we do not know their distance from us."

"I submit that you also do not know that the Swarm exists," Strand said. "That was a spurious statement just now and I give it no weight. Which of you here will act on a rumor generated through sheer fright due to the thought of facing the sub-men?"

As one, the New Men turned to Golden Ural, no doubt to see his reaction.

The tallest of them appeared unconcerned with Strand's outrageous slander. It was one of his keys to power, his ability to shrug off what would send others into a killing frenzy.

"The turtle daring to peek out of its shell would speak to us of courage," Golden Ural said in a lofty tone. "Mighty Strand, who is ready to flee our meeting in an instant lest one of us dares to test his immortality, knows much about *fright*."

A few of the New Men nodded as Strand grew hyper-alert. Golden Ural had just obliquely threatened him.

"See how he watches us, brothers," Golden Ural said. "He fears us because we are his superior."

In that moment, Strand seethed with hatred against Golden Ural. But he cloaked it, saying, "I invite you aboard my star cruiser, Commander. Show me your courage by accepting my invitation."

"Sweet Strand," Golden Ural said, "who dares to open a New Man's skull in order to put his filthiness in the brain. No, I will decline your offer, you who used to call yourself our master."

"You tread on dangerous ground," Strand warned.

Golden Ural showed his teeth. "The lone wolf snarls, trying to frighten the pack by its fierceness. You are not one of us, Methuselah Man. You are alone in this universe, alone with your intricate schemes."

"Whatever I am," Strand said, "you are evading the issue. How do you know anything about the Swarm?"

"The professor told me."

So, it was true. That meddler Ludendorff had a long-range communication device. It would appear that Golden Ural did as well. It amazed Strand that Ural would freely admit to this.

418

"Observe," Golden Ural said. He picked up a clicker.

The holoimage in the center of the chamber changed, showing a Dyson sphere. Out of it flew saucers against attacking Star Watch vessels. A close-up showed a destroyed saucer. The squirming creatures in space were undoubtedly bugs in spacesuits. A ghostly column appeared, departing from an exploding Dyson sphere.

"The surviving Swarm creatures go to their empire," Golden Ural said. "There, one of them will give the bug empire Laumer Drive technology."

"This is an interesting fabrication you've created," Strand said. "I congratulate you on your deception. I imagine some here will even be fooled by it."

"You still do not understand," Golden Ural said. "The Swarm is real. The bugs are not extinct as we believed. We must prepare for them. We have what we came for, women in abundance and workers to help us open up a hundred new worlds. Why risk our armada in battle when we may need these ships tomorrow or a vast host of them ten years from now?"

Strand ingested the idea, mulling it over. Could Golden Ural be right? Could Ludendorff finally have reached the Builder's system? This was thunderous news if true.

"The Grand Fleet won't give up without a fight," Strand said. "The subhumans surely believe themselves capable of destroying us."

"I have a way out of the impasse," Golden Ural said.

"You have begun to teach them how to fight," Strand added. "They have evaded several critical traps. They have become more cunning."

"I have studied the battle files," Golden Ural said. "Admiral Fletcher evaded the various traps. It appears your assassin killed him. You must have recognized Fletcher's danger and decided to eliminate him."

"I did eliminate him," Strand said. "He had become one of those rare great captains the subhumans vomit up from time to time. Since Fletcher's death, Third Admiral Bishop has blundered his way to the Thebes System."

"Therefore," Golden Ural said. "Since Fletcher is dead, the risk is less to us in letting the subhumans live. After we leave

Human Space, we will send scouts deep into the Beyond. If the Swarm is still far off, we can regroup and smash the sub-men several years from now. They will grow careless in time as they always do, squabbling among themselves like children."

This would not be Strand's first choice. "How do you propose convincing the subhumans they should not attack our star cruisers?"

Golden Ural told him his idea.

Afterward, Strand nodded. The Emperor's commander was cunning and ruthless. Strand would rather smash the Grand Fleet now and continue the conquest of Human Space. Still, Golden Ural had a point. The New Men had what they had originally come for. Maybe this time around, Strand could keep better control of the situation. He would bargain with the Emperor, getting new seed corn so he could go far away in the Beyond and start again, making sure he kept complete control forever of his creations.

-56-

Fletcher listened in as a tall and arrogant New Man named Golden Ural proposed a bargain to Third Admiral Bishop.

The Grand Fleet was halfway across the Thebes System. The eighty star cruisers had formed their famous cone of battle, but had only slightly accelerated. In the meantime, giant haulers headed out of their Thebes III orbit toward an inner Laumer-Point.

"This is the bargain, Third Admiral," Golden Ural said. "We will give you the people on the planet. You will allow the rest of the spaceships to depart unharmed. We, then, shall leave you in peace, returning to the Beyond from whence we came."

"What's in the haulers?" Bishop asked.

"Equipment," Golden Ural said.

Fletcher almost pressed a switch to interrupt and ask what else they held. He didn't have to, though, because Bishop asked just that.

"You are rude," Golden Ural told Bishop, "but you are inferior so one must make allowances. The ships also contain women, many women, and strong backs to help us open new planets for colonization."

"Why so many women?" Bishop asked. "Do you hate your own so much?"

Golden Ural stared out of the screen. He seemed to have stiffened. Slowly, he turned his head one way and then the other.

"Sub-man," Golden Ural said. "You...you should not speak to me like that."

"I have no idea why not," Bishop said. "Have you seen the size of our Grand Fleet?"

Golden Ural seemed to have frozen. Finally, his lips moved, but his eyes remained cold. "We are superior to you, sub-man, except for one particular. Our genes do not produce girl-children, only boys. Our chief scientists labor at the dilemma. Until it is...corrected, we must find breeding partners where we can. This time, we chose the women of 'C' Quadrant. They will bear us many fine New Men."

"You're kidnapping Commonwealth women?" Bishop asked in amazement.

"Our survival demands we act."

"You've ensured war for a million years," Bishop said.

Golden Ural shrugged. "If you desire battle, we shall destroy your Grand Fleet. Before we do, however, we shall drop hell-burners on Thebes III."

"You mean murder everyone there?"

"The people on Thebes III will surely die, yes. We have used the planet as an assembly area. Naturally, we have already chosen the best specimens. They are already en route deep into the Beyond. The bulk of the people from 'C' Quadrant are still quite alive, however."

"You have a teleportation system, don't you?" Bishop asked.

"As I said," Golden Ural told Bishop as if he hadn't heard the question, "Thebes III has been the assembly area. You can save the vast majority of 'C' Quadrant's people. Or you can watch them all die before battle. The choice is yours. If you agree to our terms, we will leave Human Space for good and go our way. You can tell your people that we fled in fright from you. In that way, you will enjoy the privileges of victors. Or you can watch millions die needlessly and then die in battle yourselves. Which will it be, Third Admiral? You have several hours at most to decide."

***

422

A hasty meeting began in *Antietam's* conference chamber. Kim Sung, Sub-commander Sos, Earl Bishop, Admiral Fletcher and others including Commodore Harold were in attendance.

"Well?" Fletcher began. "What do you think?"

"Eighty star cruisers means we have an even fight on our hands," the Respectable Kim said. "We could lose our fleet and the remaining people of 'C' Quadrant."

"So we accept their offer?" Fletcher asked.

"Maybe so," Kim said. "Something is better than nothing."

"Do you think the New Men will keep their word?" Fletcher asked.

"This I do not know," Kim said. "But these people on Thebes III—they are alive. We came to save them, yes?"

"What about the people leaving in the haulers?" Bishop asked.

"Some perish, many live," Kim said with a fatalistic shrug.

"I agree with the Respectable's thinking," Sub-commander Sos said. "We thought all the people of 'C' Quadrant were dead. Now we have millions and the New Men are leaving."

Fletcher glanced at a brooding Bishop. Then, the admiral faced the others. "We came here to crush the New Men. Yes, they have more star cruisers than we expected. But I can't believe they have more than this. If we cripple this armada, we have severely crippled the New Men. I say, let's hurt them badly."

"And millions of people will die," Harold said.

"Yes, and millions will die," Fletcher said, as he stared at a bulkhead.

"I don't call that good arithmetic," Harold said.

Fletcher looked at the others. "The New Men began this war. Now, we have to defend ourselves. If they bomb the planet, I will dedicate my life to finding theirs and nuking it to kingdom come."

"So we tell them to go to Hell with their offer?" Harold asked.

"No," Fletcher said. "We tell them to leave the haulers and tramp vessels behind. They're Commonwealth ships, after all. The New Men have already kidnapped who knows how many

423

people. I'm not going to be party to watching more leave when I can do something about it."

"It strikes one here," Bishop said, touching his stomach. "This stealing of our women is like a kick in the gut. I loathe it."

"They're also taking men," Fletcher said. "Don't forget that. Good men to live like slaves opening planets for them."

"New Men only breed boys," Bishop said in a hollow voice.

"Right," Fletcher said. "That's the other reason we don't let them take any more of our people. Eventually, the women they already have will grow old. The New Men will die out then, and I say good riddance to them."

"That's a savage attitude, Admiral," Harold said.

"They attacked us and bombed our planets," Fletcher said. "I'm giving them nothing but battle. They don't get to take anyone more from us without a fight."

"But the millions on Thebes III, Admiral," Harold said.

Fletcher's features turned stony. "When it comes down to it, I don't think the New Men will do it."

"Are you kidding me?" Harold said. "These are New Men. What won't they do?"

"We're accelerating at them hard," Fletcher said. "If they want to get away, they can't stick around much longer. No. They have to run to survive. Unless they do, I'm attacking them." He faced Bishop. "You'd better tell Golden Ural that."

"Why don't you tell him, Admiral?" Bishop asked.

Fletcher shook his head. "The next time I speak to a New Man, I'm going to kill him. I'm tired of bargaining with them. We came here to destroy their ability to harm humans. Well, let's do just that."

***

"The sub-men called your bluff," Strand told Golden Ural in another large meeting.

"I did not think Third Admiral Bishop had it in him," the armada commander said. "If I didn't know better, I would think these words came from Admiral Fletcher."

"Fletcher is dead," Strand said.

424

Golden Ural studied the other commanders. "I say we leave the system."

"And give the subhumans those in the haulers?" Strand asked.

"We have already taken many others," Golden Ural said.

"We need *all* of them if we're going to open up more worlds," Strand said.

"Sometimes, a bird in hand is worth more than two in the bush," Golden Ural said.

Strand remained silent.

"As I said," Golden Ural told the others. "We have already transported millions of breeding partners. Greed is senseless. It is particularly so when a terrible menace looms in the Beyond against us."

"The fact of the Swarm mandates we grow quicker rather than more slowly," Strand said.

"We can come back for more women later," Golden Ural said. "Even if the subhumans were to try, it would take them ages to find the Throne World."

"Unless Professor Ludendorff tells them the coordinates," Strand said.

Golden Ural shook his head. "That is the final point to this. The professor agreed to keep the Throne World's coordinates secret if we retreated from the Grand Fleet."

Strand became alert and then thoughtful. "The professor would not agree to that unless he had found something powerful to aid the sub-men. I have changed my mind. We should smash the Grand Fleet since we're already here in mass."

"We already have enough so we can leave intact without feeling any personal loss," Golden Ural told the others. "Our colonization drive can accelerate on schedule. We have millions of new women, enough for two or three for each New Man. What do you say, brothers? Should we fight a needless battle or should we use a calculated strategy and hit the subhumans in the future once we're stronger?"

Strand tried another ploy, but it was too late. The New Men made their wishes known. The greater majority wished to leave while they could and continue the great colonization project with the women they'd already shipped home.

"So be it," Golden Ural said. "We shall take our winnings and exit the battlefield. Let the sub-men prance while they are able. Soon, we shall be back in overwhelming force to conquer them."

-57-

On Earth, Captain Maddox hesitated as he approached the brigadier's office. He wore his wristband connecting him to Galyan while keeping a tiny earpiece inserted so the AI could whisper to him.

Maddox knew this was breaking Star Watch's regulations. An officer wasn't supposed to wear any kind of surveillance equipment in headquarters. As a matter of course, Maddox knew that Galyan had already fiddled with the scanners searching him as he'd entered.

Doing this troubled Maddox. Yet, it also troubled him that the brigadier had on occasion distrusted him. Stokes having shot to kill him in Greenland still rankled. Being locked away in the first place at the brigadier's orders—

Maddox strode for the Iron Lady's office. Because of those events, he would wear the wristband and allow Galyan to watchdog him.

Soon, Maddox sat before Mary O'Hara, crossing his legs as he acknowledged her greeting.

She folded her hands on her synthi-wood desk, smiling bravely. "Captain, these have been trying times, to say the least."

"Yes," he said.

"I…" O'Hara looked away. "I'm sorry, Captain. I never should have put you in the Greenland complex. I…I thought I was doing the right thing at the time. I thought…"

427

"We all have to make hard decisions sometimes, Ma'am." Maddox uncrossed his legs. "Dana told me what you did down in the Mid-Atlantic. You made tough decisions quickly, and you saved them a wrestling match with their consciences by firing those torpedoes into the dome."

"Do I hear disapproval in your voice?" she asked.

"Good people might have still been trapped in the underwater dome."

O'Hara studied her folded hands. "If it's any consolation, Captain, I've already sent Intelligence teams to the dome. We...we discovered humans. Blasts badly mutilated some of them. We used their dental records, uncovering more androids on Earth."

O'Hara squeezed her fingers together. "I'm getting old, Captain," she said, quietly. "I'm finding my job more difficult by the week. Sometimes, I make the wrong choice. At other times, I make the right choice for the wrong reason. This time, I believe that's what happened. We had to destroy the dome. To be more precise, we had to destroy the amok android base while we had the chance. Just like a combat mission, good people lose their lives sometimes. I'm not proud of that."

O'Hara pulled her hands apart, looking up with haunted eyes. "I do what I must so the human race survives. That means I take matters into my own hands at times. You wouldn't be here if I didn't."

"Ma'am?"

O'Hara opened a drawer, extracting a slim file. She slapped that onto the table, pushing it across to the captain.

"That's the real history of your mother and your earliest days. I hid you, Captain. Others would have...swept you off the board before you were given a chance to prove yourself."

With the slightest of tremors in his hand, Maddox took the file. He weighed it silently.

"Thank you, Ma'am. I appreciate this. I...I have spoken hastily. Forgive me, please."

"You've only spoken the truth, Captain."

He tucked the file under his arm. "Sometimes, one can forget who his true friends are."

The brigadier nodded gently, her features softening.

Maddox cleared his throat. "Ma'am, the New Men retreated from the Thebes System. Admiral Fletcher also found the missing people."

A courier vessel had reached Earth with news several weeks old concerning the Grand Fleet. Fletcher had reported about the empty cities on the various colony worlds.

"How can you know these things?" O'Hara asked.

"There's no way I can know," he said.

"But you do."

Maddox nodded. "There's another thing. The New Men's sperm is damaged. They cannot impregnate a woman with a girl, only a boy. Part of their invasion goal was to gather millions of women for breeding. Another reason was to gather men to help them open up new worlds for colonization."

"Ludendorff," O'Hara said. "You once spoke about a hidden communicator on *Victory*." The brigadier studied him. Suddenly, she pressed a comm switch on her desk. "Find the professor at once. Tell me when you have him in custody."

Maddox crossed his legs, waiting.

"We won't find the professor, will we?" the brigadier asked.

"It's doubtful."

"Did you help him escape?"

"I owed the man a debt for what he did in the Builder System."

"What about your debt to him for sabotaging *Victory* during the Destroyer Incident?"

Maddox looked away.

"Hmm," O'Hara said. "I wonder if you were still angry with me because of Greenland."

Maddox shrugged.

O'Hara put her hands on the desk. She sighed heavily. Finally, she stood and came around the desk.

"Stand up," she told him.

Maddox stood.

The brigadier stared up at him. "How tall you are, Captain." Before he could reply, she swept her arms around him, hugging him tightly.

429

Maddox turned his head, enduring the emotional display. It meant nothing. It was—*comforting*, he decided. Finally, he patted her on the back.

The Iron Lady released him, walking around the table, sitting and regarding him.

Maddox sat hastily.

"Welcome back, Captain Maddox," she said.

"Thank you, Ma'am."

"We'll manage without the professor," she said. "Is Fletcher on his way home?"

"I don't know that, Ma'am. I should think not, though. He will be securing Thebes III and its precious prize, the remaining people of 'C' Quadrant."

"Do you suppose we're not ready to know all that Ludendorff has stored in his mind?"

"I'm not sure if that's it, Ma'am, or if Dr. Rich and the professor can figure out how to use a Nexus better on their own than in our company. We're going to need to know how to use the silver pyramids."

"Hmm," the Iron Lady said. "What about you, Captain? What do you think the man who outwitted the last Builder should do next?"

"First, Ma'am, I want to relax for a few days. Then…I'm not sure. Maybe we should search for the Throne World and keep the New Men honest. Maybe we should build a more powerful Grand Fleet with disruptor cannons and go to the Throne World, demanding our people back."

"And if the Swarm shows up while we're…bickering with the New Men?"

"We should find out how near the bugs are to us as quickly as possible," Maddox said.

"I imagine *Victory* would make the ultimate Patrol vessel."

"I'm sure Galyan would agree with you."

"Why don't you ask him right now and find out?" the brigadier asked.

Maddox might have blushed if he was capable of such a thing. Instead, he stood up. He should have known he hadn't fooled the brigadier. "I have a date, Ma'am. If you would excuse me?" he asked.

"Go, Captain, find a few hours of relaxation. You deserve it. The Commonwealth may have survived the New Men's first invasion attempt, but we've found that our universe is much more dangerous than we imagined. We will all have plenty of work to do in the coming days."

"Yes, Ma'am," Maddox said, "until later, then."

She made a shooing motion with her hand.

With the file tucked under his right arm, Maddox turned and headed for the door. It was good to have straightened things out with the brigadier. Yes, very good indeed.

-Epilog-

Soon after the captain's meeting with the brigadier, Sergeant Riker returned to his cottage in Switzerland. He did not phone ahead as was his usual custom. Thus, he surprised Mrs. Tell as she ate a meal in his house.

Riker ladled himself a bowl of soup and sat down with her. It was tasty onion soup, which he almost ruined by breaking thirty crackers over it, turning the bowl into a cracker-onion mush. As the sergeant ate, he asked about the latest village gossip.

Mrs. Tell told him about Mr. Talleyrand's Great Dane. The giant beast had broken its leash again, digging in Mrs. Petain's garden. The dog had destroyed countless tulips, a row of radishes and chased the cats out of the yard.

Small Mrs. Petain had been furious, scolding the dog, shaking a finger in its face. The big beast had wagged its tail throughout, finally ending the lecture by licking her nose before trotting home.

Riker smiled at the story, absently adding several more crackers to his onion mush.

He would have to see this Great Dane for himself. Maybe he could help restore peace by buying a dozen tulips and digging Mrs. Petain new holes for them.

Mrs. Tell told him a few more choice tales before cleaning up and leaving.

Riker sat on his couch, watched some soccer on TV and dozed until the stars came out. He was home. Tomorrow, he would go buy the tulips. Maybe in a day or so he would go to the nearby pub for a few beers. Right now, it was good just to relax.

He put his hands behind his head, wondering how long he'd get to stay home before the next assignment.

***

Professor Ludendorff piloted what appeared to be a pleasure yacht for the Spokane Corporation. It was a large vessel with a captain, mate and three crewmembers. Except for one of the crew, the hired help slept during a night cycle.

Ludendorff braked as the space yacht approached Saturn with its glorious rings. He hadn't left the Solar System, although his whereabouts were unknown to Star Watch Intelligence.

It had been a simple matter, evading his minders. He had set up for many eventualities. Ludendorff gave himself a vacation every twenty years or so. His imprisonment in the glass cage on the Dyson sphere had been taxing. Once he was free of Earth and the constant surveillance, he had relaxed.

"There you are," Dana said, entering the small bridge.

Ludendorff turned around and smiled at the sight.

Dana wore a shimmering gown, high heels, makeup and an exotic hat and scarf. She noticed Saturn then, her gaze fixated upon it.

Ludendorff slicked his hair back. It had been some time since he'd enjoyed the doctor's company. He had taught her some unusual techniques many years ago. Perhaps it was time to indulge again.

The professor came to her, taking her hands, holding her at arms' length and admiring what he saw.

"Is this a mistake?" she whispered.

"All life is a mistake," he said.

"Do you really believe that?"

He closed in, feeling the press of her body against his. He kissed her. Good memories rushed to his forebrain.

"Dana, Dana," he whispered.

"Say you won't leave me this time."

433

"You know I never will," he said, knowing that wasn't true. But couldn't the two of them enjoy some time together?

"What will you do next?" she whispered.

Ludendorff leered at her before he took her right hand, guiding her off the bridge toward his cabin. It was good to be in the Solar System again.

***

Valerie thought about taking a tour through Detroit, seeing if anything had changed. Keith had talked about returning to Glasgow, to the bar.

Maddox did not believe either of those ideas would benefit his people, his family.

So, he took them on a vacation to China. First, they visited the Great Wall. They walked on the parapets and felt the cold winds blowing out of Mongolia.

"China back then was like the Commonwealth today," Valerie said. "It stood alone against barbarism."

"Keith," Maddox said. "Fly us to Beijing as fast as you can go. There's too much thinking going on here."

The Scotsman did just that, racing the flitter in an exhibition of speed and daring.

It rained the entire time they were in Beijing, though.

"Next stop, Shanghai," Maddox said.

"What do I know about gambling?" Valerie asked.

It turned out, very little, as she lost her back pay because she drank too many Long Island Iced Teas and tried her hand at the Roulette Wheel.

"It was a cheap lesson," Meta told her later.

"There was nothing cheap about it," Valerie said, sulking.

Finally, the captain had Keith fly them to Tibet. On the captain's dime, he bought backpacks, climbing gear and supplies. For the next week, they hiked from one ancient temple to another.

The brisk winds, freezing cold and exercise kept them occupied. The quiet temples put them in contemplative moods. But it wasn't until Meta started a snowball fight that lasted a half hour that they finally seemed to let their guards down. First Valerie, then Keith and finally Meta burst out laughing.

Each of them fell backward into the snow, each making a snow angel as their laughter turned into giggles.

Maddox had smiled, and he hadn't dodged the various snowballs as he easily could have. Because of that, he had large red welts on his face where the others had pelted him.

"Laugh, Captain," Valerie said. "Unwind for once."

"Yes," Keith said. "You work so hard. You need to let yourself go once in a while, sir."

Maddox nodded. Maybe they were right.

"You poor dear," Meta said from the snow. "You…" She became quiet.

"What's wrong, Meta?" Valerie asked.

"I don't want to think about it," Meta said. "I just want to enjoy the moment."

"What do you say to that, sir?" Keith asked.

Maddox inhaled the cold mountain air. Then, he shouted, startling each of them. He lunged at Meta, grabbed her left hand and hauled her to her feet. He ran through the snow, pulling her after him. He ran and ran until they were out of sight of Valerie and Keith.

Maddox whirled around, catching Meta, hugging her. He picked her up and dropped her in the snow, taking a handful of it and mashing it playfully in her face.

"Why you," she said, grabbing him, pulling him down. They rolled in the snow many times. Finally, breathing heavily, they stared into each other's eyes.

"It isn't over, is it?" she whispered.

"If you mean that the human race is still kicking, the answer is yes."

"Are we part of them?"

Maddox thought about the brigadier, about what he'd read in his file about his mother and his babyhood. Mary O'Hara had kept him alive when others had wanted him dead.

"Yes," the captain said. "We're definitely part of humanity and the Commonwealth. Come. Let's go back to the others. Let's enjoy our time together. The enemy will soon be at the gate. Then we'll go back to work."

"I love you, Maddox," Meta said, as she leaned against him.

He held her chin, kissed her luscious lips, and said, "And I love you, Meta."

They walked hand in hand through the Tibetan snow, happy to be together and happy to be alive.

***

In orbit, Starship *Victory* cruised high over Tibet. The holoimage of Driving Force Galyan stood on the otherwise empty bridge, studying the main screen. It showed a close-up of Meta and Maddox.

The "leathery" face was creased in an Adok smile. The owl-like eyes shined.

Galyan watched over the others as they relaxed. Because he never got tired, he could do this for them. They were his family, and as long as he had them, he would never be alone.

It was a wonderful thing to know, but even a better one to feel. Thus Galyan remained at his post, content with his place in the universe.

The End

Made in the USA
San Bernardino, CA
21 March 2019